Magic's Design

Magic's Design

CAT ADAMS

TOR®
paranormal romance

A TOM DOHERTY ASSOCIATES BOOK
NEW YORK

MAGIC'S DESIGN

Copyright © 2009 by C. T. Adams and Cathy Clamp

All rights reserved.

A Tor Book
Published by Tom Doherty Associates, LLC
175 Fifth Avenue
New York, NY 10010

www.tor-forge.com

Tor® is a registered trademark of Tom Doherty Associates, LLC.

ISBN-13: 978-0-7653-5963-6
ISBN-10: 0-7653-5963-4

First Edition: February 2009

Printed in the United States of America

0 9 8 7 6 5 4 3 2 1

Dedication
and Acknowledgments

As with all of our books, we would like to dedicate this work first to Don Clamp and James Adams, along with the rest of our family and friends who have offered patience, kindness, and unwavering support.

We also want to take the time to specifically thank our wonderful agent, Merrilee Heifetz, plus Claire Reilly-Shapiro and Kari Torson at Writers House, who have helped us so much and so often. Thanks also to our terrific editor, Heather Osborn, at Tor; former editor, Anna Genoese; plus all the staff of sales, marketing, publicity, and ad/promo who make our books possible!

Finally, we would also like to take this opportunity to thank Kate Bradshaw David of Katyegg Design, www.KatyEgg.com, for her help learning the intricate art of pysanky, as well as wonderful AbsoluteWrite.com members ideagirl, Izunya, Puma, Christine Blevins, Lisa Spangenberg, Patti Wigington, and December Quinn for their help with Ukrainian history, magic systems, art, and folklore. You guys are the best!

Magic's Design

CHAPTER I

𝒟arkness and fear clawed at the back of Mila's mind, so desperate and needy that she could barely think. It pressed in on her from some distant place, as it had so often in the past. Intense feelings made it worse—whether anger, fear, or pain. Today it was worry. Her best friend Candy was sitting across the table from her, unknowingly deciding whether Mila was going to cut coupons and pay the mortgage this month, or whether she was going to be eating, but under a bridge.

With a satisfied sigh, Candy removed the triplet jeweler's loup from her eye. "Exquisite. Really, Mila. Every line is perfectly straight, the colors the exact jewel tones the client wants. This is museum quality. If the others are as good . . . and I know they will be, I'll take them all."

All Mila could do was nod as Candy turned the second pysanka, with a simple "call of spring" design, over in her hands. She wanted to feel happy that her friend was impressed with the intricately dyed "Easter eggs." After all, she'd spent most of her life studying the craft that had been passed down in her family all the way back to pre-Christian pagan times. But even through her pride, the darkness closed in tightly, worse today than in years. Every blink of her eyes made another world appear. Blink—the warm, varnished table became icy stone with sharp edges that she could swear were cutting into her palm. Blink—the bright sunlight outside the restaurant was transformed into darkness, eased only by tiny blue dots of light in the distance. Blink—the scent of fresh-baked garlic bread and rich marinara sauce turned damp and musty. The back and forth between the sensations was making her queasy.

"Okay, so how about two hundred? Will that work for you?" Slowly, Mila's mind pulled out of the dark cavern— yes, it definitely felt like the caves she and Baba Nadia used to explore. With effort, she focused back on where she was . . . turned away from the evil hiding somewhere in the darkness.

But her heart fell as Candy's words sunk home and the darkness came calling again, forcing her to dig her fingernails into her palms to keep it at bay. Only two hundred? Damn. She needed at least three to pay the bank. She'd hoped . . . after all, there were *five* eggs, and duck eggs to boot. No. She had to stand firm. Surely her best friend would understand. It would mean more scrambling tomorrow, but the eggs were worth twice that. She felt her mouth grimace and worked not to show her disappointment too strongly. "Oh. Um . . . y'know, Candy, I'm not really sure I can let them go for that. I mean, the marriage fertility egg alone took me six hours to design and dye."

Candy's face got an odd expression. Then realization struck her and she threw back her head and laughed. Her perfect blonde mane of hair flowed and gleamed under the lamp.

Mila felt a pang of envy. Candy was her best friend in the world, truly. But sometimes she couldn't help but be a little bit jealous of the other woman's stunning looks and size-six figure. Mila had always wanted to look like that. Instead, she was petite and curvy, with a tendency to gain weight. Her dark hair fell in unruly curls. The one feature she really did like was her eyes. They were wide and green, with naturally long black lashes.

Candy shook her head. "Ohmygod, you silly goose! Of course they're worth more than that. I mean two hundred *each*. And naturally, I have the cash with me, 'cause I figured they'd be perfect. You always make perfect eggs."

It was all Mila could do to breathe. Two hundred *each*? A *thousand dollars*? She could not only pay the mortgage, but she wouldn't have to worry about badgering Sela for rent until after she came back from spending the holidays with her family. She could even pick up enough groceries and cat food to last until payday. Woo!

Another snort from across the table brought heat to her cheeks. "Geez, give me some credit. You thought I meant two hundred for *all* of them? I know how hard you work on them, Mila. I tried to get you three hundred each, but the client topped out at two. And they're well worth it. He'll be pleased." With a flourish, Candy pulled a wallet embroidered with stylized dollar signs from her tooled leather purse and counted out the money from a stack of hundred-dollar bills. "I suppose you're going to do something horribly practical like pay bills with it. Or are you going to do what I think you *should* do and blow it all on yourself at the after-Christmas sales? You never seem to get around to buying anything nice for yourself."

Mila folded the cash and tucked it in the zippered compartment of her purse with a grin. "Trust me, Candy. Paying the mortgage to have a roof over my head, a warm furnace, and a fridge full of food will be nice enough."

Candy blew out a little breath onto her nails, as though they were wet. "You don't have a *mortgage*. It's not like you'll lose the house or anything if you miss a payment. Live a little . . . you get paid on the first."

She sighed. Candy never could understand the concept. "It *is* a mortgage—or it will be as soon as I have the deed. But since the loan paid for fixing the roof, upgrading the electrical, and putting in a bathtub, I'll keep calling it a mortgage." But she couldn't deny Candy had a point. She did tend to skimp on herself and her family where the house or car were concerned. "But if there's enough left over, I might be able to spring for a few late gifts for Mom and Sarah. And I only sent Baba a card this year. It would be nice to give her something pretty. She likes warm fluffy scarve—"

A flash of pain lanced through her forehead, tearing a gasp from her throat. Then, like an icy breeze through a doorway, she felt a chill settle over her, strong enough to make her shudder. But it was when the pins-and-needles sensation overtook her toes that she began to panic. *Oh God, please not now! Not in the middle of a restaurant.*

She fought to stay calm. Panic would only make it happen faster. Moving her head slowly toward her friend she let the barest whisper ease gently from her throat. "Candy, my toes are going numb. We need to get out of here."

Candy's hand flew to her open mouth to prevent an alarmed screech. She had practically been a family member, growing up next door to Mila. She'd seen a number of Mila's *episodes.*

"Crap! Okay, yeah. We need to get out of . . . but they haven't even brought the food yet." She blew out a frustrated breath and looked around the restaurant frantically, searching for their waiter as Mila slowly began to gather her purse and put on her coat. "Well, hell. Okay, I'll just leave a fifty on the table. That should cover it. Maybe I can come back and get it and . . . no, that won't work either. Oh, crap."

"Shhh," Mila warned as another spasm pounded her temples. "Not so loud." Like the barest beginnings of a migraine, she could feel the symptoms unfurling in her mind. The slightest trigger would send her thrashing to the floor, screaming and uttering names and words that had no meaning. Anything could do it: a loud noise, a bright light, even touching something that was hot or cold. Going from a warm restaurant to the winter air outside was going to be tough.

A few years ago Mila's sister Sarah had filmed an episode on her cell phone after their mother dropped a soda and it exploded. She'd wanted Mila to see *why* everyone had treated her with kid gloves her whole life. Her mother likened the episodes to epileptic seizures, but the doctors and neurologists had never been able to find a physical cause.

Mila fought back tears. She hadn't had an episode in so very long. Maybe if she could ease through this, not make a scene, she might actually be able to keep her—*Shit. The car.* She looked toward the window as she pushed back her chair and stood. "I drove." She could see her pride and joy out on the snowy street through the glass. The little silver Corolla was used, with high miles and a flaky heater, but it was hers. And, with another storm threatening, she couldn't afford to be late to work every day again by taking the bus.

Candy reached out to touch her hand as tears threatened. She'd worked so very hard, waited so long. "Oh, sweetie . . . your license. And you just finally qualified. No, we won't risk that. They don't have to know. C'mon. We'll hurry. I'll drive you home and you can pick the car up tomorrow when you're feeling bet—"

But as the door to the restaurant opened, the bell she'd considered charming rang, seeming too loud to her ears. The sound ripped along sensitive nerves, and the icy air hit her like a club to the head. She felt herself falling . . . felt Candy drop everything to reach for her.

The world went black, darkness crushing her mind like an empty eggshell. Another mind, with thoughts not her own, became her reality.

$\mathcal{M}$agic breathed through the air, so subtle that Talos had to close his eyes to see the flickering rune from behind darkened lids. Fire magic tickled along the birthmark on his wrist—the mark that branded him a mage. He held every muscle motionless behind the massive stalagmite, watching the escape unfold. He could tell his best friend Alexy struggled not to leap forward by the way he twitched under his cloak. But it would only be a few more minutes until Sela was in position, and then they could close in and make the capture.

The obsidian wall of Rohm Prison rose to the highest reaches of the cavern, dwarfing the group of four crimi- nals, huddled under the shimmering black silk capes that made them nearly invisible to the casual eye. The cool moist air began to smell of molten glass as they laid enchantments to cut through the thick volcanic stone. First fire enough to make the surface glow red, then icy water to crack it. The tree alone knew how long they'd been visiting this same spot, but it must have been some time, judging by how large a passage they'd carved.

"Should we step in, Tal?" Alexy's whisper was so faint that even next to his ear, Tal could barely hear. He frowned slightly. Sela should have contacted him by flaring his mark, but she hadn't. Thus far, the Guilders hadn't actually done anything *wrong*. If they stopped them now, the men could simply claim they were gathering glow moss or mushrooms to sell at market. The moss hung in thick strands from the craggy overhangs, where the obsidian stopped and the regular rhyolite began. Everybody knew the shelves near the waterfall in the distance held the best jack-o'-lantern mushrooms for miles.

Tal stared at the twinkling blue lights that faintly illuminated the darkness while he thought. Imported Australian cave worms seemed to thrive here. They'd infested a lone piñon tree jutting from the stone and decorated it with sticky phosphorescent saliva. How ironic that the king's latest method to conserve magical energy was the source of light for a prison break.

He shook his head and heard a frustrated half-snort from his friend, so he twisted his lips and spoke softly. "We have to catch them *entering*. They need to actually breach the wall or the commander will have our skins for a coverlet."

Alexy shuddered. He knew as well as Tal did that Commander Sommersby was fully capable of doing just that. Muttering a curse, he whispered, "Well, for what it's worth, I'm glad you followed your instinct, guv. We never would have spotted them if we'd been guarding Gate Six like we were ordered."

"Bloody hell! It's about time." The almost imperceptible whisper from the darkness caught their attention. Tal didn't recognize the voice, but it didn't matter. These three

Guilders had done what all the supposed *experts* claimed was impossible—they'd broken into the highest-security prison under the earth.

Why doesn't anyone listen when we tell them there are problems? He tightened the leather strap on his battle glove, causing Alexy to follow suit. Whether or not Sela was ready, they had to act. The horrors the human world had been subjected to by the residents of Rohm in the past would *not* be repeated. Not while there was breath left in Tal's body.

"*Halt*—Overworld Police Agency. You're surrounded. Remove your focuses and keep your hands where we can see them." In a rush of movement, he stood and held his palm toward the trio, emerald focus stone at the ready. Alexy was moving into the darkness to flank the law-breakers. The men turned to face him. They likewise raised battle gloves and Talos felt his eyes widen and heart pound as the faint light refracted into a thousand pieces on one man's palm. A *diamond* nearly covered the man's glove. Nobody he knew had ever managed to tame such a complex stone. But he couldn't get a better look at the man or the glove before he raced into the breach in the prison wall.

Tal only managed to fire one blast of magic before he was forced to dive face first to the cave's floor. White light, bright enough to blind him, hit the spot where he'd stood. The heat from his opponent's stone melted the stalagmite he and Alexy had been hiding behind. Boiling black sludge rolled toward him. The edge of his cape caught on fire before he could see enough to put it out. The scent of molten rock, normally a comfort, was now his enemy.

He heard a battle cry to his left and three heads turned as one to the sound. As usual, Alexy was diving into battle with all the caution of a rabid skunk. Thankfully, his skill matched his recklessness. One criminal was already unconscious on the ground.

Tal kept his body glued to the floor as his lieutenant's hand raised. The entire prison rumbled as formidable earth magic erupted from Alexy's ruby focus to throw the other Guilders off balance.

"Damn, damn, damn," he muttered as bouncing bits of black glass and stalactites rained down on his head from Alexy's attack. Not even his best shielding could keep all of the rocks from bouncing off his skull and scratching his arms. Well, if that didn't bring the guards inside out to help them, nothing would.

As the cursing fugitives erected hasty air charms and raced for cover, Tal whispered, *"Trivoa svet."* He clenched his fist and concentrated. In bare seconds, he felt precious energy from the lights inside the prison dim just before it burned through his veins on the way to the maze of silica crystals overhead.

Red-gold light filled the cavern, and he finally saw Sela, floating high above him with arms extended in a threatening gesture toward her opponent. "No trickery, illusionist . . . or I swear by the Sacred Tree I'll throw you from the sky."

Tal likewise aimed his focus at the man, seeing that Alexy had the water witch under control near the broken prison wall. "As she demands, lawbreaker . . . drop down your glove and descend slowly, or I'll let her do just that." He kept his eyes moving between the two criminals, since they could finally be called that. "Mind that third man, Alexy. Keep him and anyone he's attempted to release pinned inside and do what you can to repair the breach. We should have seen guards by now. That worries me. Sela, draw whatever power you need to from the lights to contact the commander."

Tension filled the air as the illusionist, his pockmarked face filled with hate and rage, dropped his focus glove into Tal's waiting hand and slowly rode the air currents down to the ground. Tal raised the glove for a closer look while keeping one eye firmly fixed on the descending illusionist. The stone was a good sized dark blue lapis stone in a worn but exquisitely crafted pig leather glove. Lapis stones this fine weren't easily found around Rohm and the tooling of the leather reminded him of another he'd seen. "Not from around here, are you, lawbreaker? This glove looks like the work of Grand Master Thetus of Vril. Vrillian, are you? Who are you trying to break out?" While he waited for an answer, he started sorting through the charms he knew that would immobilize an air Guilder. There weren't many. Usually air magic trumped that of other Guilders. But there were a few very old spells these youngsters had probably never heard of that should be effective.

The Vrillian kept his lips pressed tight together, almost as if charmed. Tal knew better, of course. The man had been speaking just minutes before and no magic had filled the air. Still, sometimes, it was better to let the criminal think they had the upper hand. Often they made a mistake that made all the difference in prosecution.

The lights flickered and dimmed overhead as Sela's body tensed to make a psychic link. A quick eye flick revealed that Alexy had already made the ground rise up to encase the witch's lower body and wrists and a silencing spell glowed around his head. He was ready to transport. Glittering pebbles and dirt began to swirl around in a cyclone of magic before depositing themselves in the rift in the wall to waist high. It was only a temporary measure. Alexy had the skill to repair the wall fully, but not the energy. Not with one of the area's rolling brownouts about to occur. Likely the brownout was what the criminals had been waiting for. Then they could simply stroll out with their comrades, the guards none the wiser until the power was restored.

"Good plan overall, Vrillian. But nobody has ever broken out of Rohm. As you can see, it's too well guarded."

His lips parted and a snarl cut the air. The waterfall in the distance was almost loud enough to cover up the man's mutter as his slippered feet touched the ground. But not quite. *It shouldn't have* been *guarded.*

That raised Tal's brows. "It shouldn't? And why is that?" But the illusionist wasn't talking now. His lips had sealed again. Only his clenched fists and flashing dark eyes revealed his anger that was being slowly replaced by a growing fear. Tal decided to prod him along a little to see if he'd break. He smiled broadly just before casting out the immobilization charm he'd been building up the energy for in his focus with a quick flash of his hand. "No answer? Well, that's all right. I'm sure your fellows will be glad to discuss the matter at length, once I tell them you've told me all about your plan. The witch has seen us talking. I wonder if he could hear what's been said." He enjoyed seeing the frantic look in the man's eyes at the words, just before the charm froze him completely.

"Tal! Look out!" Sela's panicked voice from above made instinct take over. He dropped to the cavern floor and rolled, scanning the area frantically, just as the brownout dimmed the lights. A blast of blue-white light from behind the hastily constructed pile of rubble in the wall gap seared his pupils and blinded him. The next thing he heard was Alexy's pained grunt and the clatter of rocks being blasted out of the opening.

Darkness descended abruptly on the cavern, so deep that not even the cave worms could be seen. Powerful magic rode the air, choking the breath from his lungs. The magic was accompanied by a bone-chilling cold that whistled through like an Arctic blast. This was no brownout. It was much, much worse. Tal gasped for enough air to shout. "Sela, get down! Find a safe position. Stay silent." He said the words even as he scrambled through the unending black, seeking cover with blind fingertips that quickly grew bloodied on the sharp volcanic glass.

If he was right, the three of them were no match for what had just been released from prison. The infamous fire mage Vegre was the only Guilder who was known to be able to control the Creeping Darkness; a spell that removed heat and light so completely as to achieve total darkness over an area. Their only hope was to survive long enough to either seal the gates to the outer world or report back to the king.

"Blackguard! *Befou*—" Sela's voice, filled with rage and

contempt, was cut off as a flash of light engulfed her. Surely she hadn't—? Why in the name of the Blessed Tree would she ever *consider* casting a death curse? He watched Sela fly backward through the air toward the waterfall. The thick, wet collision of flesh and bone against stone was followed by a whimper and then silence. A man's scream cut the air and then a blast of power shot out. Clenching his fists, he bit his tongue until he could taste coppery blood. He would *not* be baited. As much as it pained him, he wouldn't give away his position by speaking or racing to her side to help her. Instead, he searched for enough magic to fuel a spell. His stone was completely empty and the Creeping Darkness was doing its job. The shadows were beginning to pull on his life force reserves and, through him, others in the O.P.A. The spell would bleed their power to the caster . . . to Vegre. Tal would die, strangled with his own power.

Tal reached outward with his senses, seeking other fire mages, his sister, the citizens of Rohm, the Sacred Tree of Life. Anyone he could connect to outside of the agency. He could sense death in a growing circle around him—the prison guards, some of the prisoners, and even a few travelers on the road to town. But strangely, not Alexy or Sela. They lived, if just barely. He stretched himself further, hoping against hope that Vegre hadn't managed to cover the entire kingdom with his spell.

"I can hear you breathing, mage." The amused, gravely voice seemed to come from every direction. It was all Tal could do to remain motionless and try to find the mage among the magic, to strike. He might not have spells or blasting energy, but he was skilled in hand-to-hand combat. Vegre had been in prison for a very long time. "Yes, definitely a mage. Your fire tastes sweet on my tongue. What shall we do with you after you're drained and helpless? Suffocate you in earth? Boil you in steam? We must reward you, after all, for attempting to foil my escape."

There. A telltale footfall in the scattered rubble as the dark mage chuckled. He turned his head slowly, trying desperately not to make a sound. The distance was difficult to gauge, but he had to try.

As carefully as he could, Tal slipped his charmed handcuffs from the case on his belt. The spell Vegre had used wouldn't affect them, since there was no power to steal until they snapped closed. All he had to do was attach the cuff to an ankle or arm and the charm would activate—drawing magical power from him to create a bright light. They were perfect for criminal Guilders, even if the magicwielder escaped from custody. They were easy to track, and quickly lost life force. Even better, the cuffs had no effect on humans, other than as traditional, sturdy handcuffs. That made them perfect for carrying topside, without any danger of them falling into the wrong hands.

Tal couldn't depend on the charm draining Vegre's energy, because of the Creeping Darkness spell. Still, at least there would be light.

Gathering his feet under him silently, he tried to time his movements to the sounds around him. While he knew he had no power to cast, the others might not know that. So, he hoped for the best and leapt forward with a bold battle cry that should paralyze his opponents. *"Pryval!"*

Pain erupted when his neck snapped back. He'd collided with a body and both of them went to the ground. Tal held tight to the cuffs and reached out to grapple with the person under him, searching through the cloak for a limb—any limb small enough for the charmed metal band to lock around. His opponent didn't speak, but he was well muscled and vicious—leading Tal to believe he was dealing with one of the original trio. The prison didn't feed or exercise their criminals well enough for them to be muscled.

"Bloody hell!" Tal winced as fingernails raked across his face. The opponent then found purchase in his hair and his skull was slammed against the stone floor hard enough for him to see stars. Blood from the scratches stung his eyes. Unfortunately, he couldn't use the same techniques, since his job was to bring the prisoners back to their cells generally unharmed. Still, he could certainly defend himself, and he doubted his superiors would object to a some-what *vigorous* defense, considering the heinous crimes the prisoners were convicted of.

He punched and kicked blindly, giving as good as he got. The battle was more difficult than it normally would be, since not only was it pitch black, but he had to keep one hand free to attach the cuff when he found an opening. Un-fortunately, the man's arms were well covered with thick leather all the way down to his fingers, and the cuff had to touch bare skin. He swung his free arm backward and connected with what felt like the man's stomach with his elbow. He put enough force behind the blow to make the man exhale air in a whoosh. But then a sharp blow to Tal's mouth from what felt like a knee made him taste blood. The scent of rank sweat and his opponent's foul breath made him want to heave, but at last, he found an ankle that was barren of cloth. He slapped the cuff against the ankle and knew it had locked when a quiet humming reached his ears.

"Bastard!" The man howled in pain and annoyance just before shoving Tal completely off and shaking his leg, try-ing to stop the charm's stinging.

Tal watched carefully, waiting for the slow, pale blue light that would begin to chew away at the darkness. Seconds later, charm met spell and although the mage tried to cover the cuff with clothing and hide in corners, the whole purpose of the charm was to prevent that. Thankfully, the cavern was somewhat secluded and there was only one exit.

Tal's eyes grabbed onto what light the cuff provided to look around. The first thing he saw was the lifeless body of the illusionist on the ground. His skin had blackened and was oozing yellowish pus. But that made no sense. Sela hadn't *finished* the curse. If she had, she'd be just as dead as this criminal. The Befouler curse was a last-ditch death curse that pulled the life energy from the caster to kill another. But it killed both. Tal couldn't imagine why his comrade would have lost her control enough to con-sider it. This was certainly critical, but not worth her life.

Movement to his left pulled his eyes away. A tall man with arms crossed over his chest stared down at him with an amused expression. Recognition blazed and Tal felt an immediate hatred for the man. He'd been only a child when last he saw this face—twisted with anger and hate as he was hauled by thick chains through the smoking wasteland that had been the village of Blackshear. Tal's parents were buried there, along with half of the populace of the village. Unfortunately, Vegre's arrogance hadn't changed a bit, despite centuries in prison. As Tal suspected, there was no cuff glowing on his ankle.

With frightening speed that the old mage shouldn't have been capable of, he spit the word, *"Pryval."* Tal felt his body freeze in place, every muscle becoming rigid except his throat and mouth. That was odd and spoke of a very carefully laid spell.

Vegre regarded him for a long moment, before grabbing his wrist. He pulled up the sleeve and twisted it sharply, making Tal hiss in pain. The mage's eyes lit up at the sound and then he smiled, revealing darkened stumps of teeth in several places. "As I suspected . . . a mage, but not a craftmaster. Still, it's gratifying to know the academy is teaching young constables to think on their feet. But surely you didn't believe I would sully myself with fisticuffs?"

Tal couldn't keep the sarcasm from his voice when he responded. "Of course not. Why would I expect that you'd do something yourself when you can risk a mindless lackey's life instead?"

Vegre's face lost its humor just before he delivered a stinging backhand to the side of Tal's face. From the immediate sensation of swelling, he was pretty sure he'd have a black eye from it tomorrow, if there was a tomorrow. He then watched as Vegre ripped off one of his sleeves and stuffed it in his mouth to prevent him from speaking. That was confusing, since a silencing charm took very little power.

The man's voice still carried a hint of accent from his native Brittania, but apparently he'd adapted in prison enough to use more modern speech patterns. "You should mind your tongue considering your circumstances, Constable. But we'll see how loose your tongue is when your heart, and the hearts in those around you, grind to a halt to feed my escape." He smiled slowly and hissed a word, eyes gleaming with malevolence in the pale light as his servant finally dared to come close. *"Venticulari."*

Tal had never heard that particular curse and had no idea what it might do. But from the evil light in Vegre's eyes, he was sure it wasn't good. Even his last hope—that Vegre would remain trapped in Rohm without access to the overworld, was short lived.

"Come, Hubert. I believe you mentioned Gate Six is just a few yards from here, and is fire keyed." He turned right at the edge of where Tal could see and gave a jaunty wave. "Fare thee well on your journey into death, Constable. I would stay to watch, but I can't rely on the abilities of my . . . how did you describe them?" He tapped his finger on his jaw for a moment. "Ah, yes. *Mindless lackeys.*" Vegre looked at the man by his side with disapproval. "I sadly can't argue with your assessment."

Tal suddenly felt an odd sensation in his chest. A brief stuttering ended with a sharp stab that pulled a muffled cry from his throat. Vegre heard the sound, even as Tal tried not to panic and fought to work the gag out with his tongue. He smiled again. "Still, I'm free and healthy, while you're about to be distinctly . . . dead, so I suppose I have no complaints with the ultimate result." He held out his arm almost casually and Tal realized the diamond focus was his. "Melt." It was a simple spell, designed for glass making, but with the power of the spell and focus behind the word, the thick stone column binding the water witch dissolved into molten glass that steamed and hissed as water magic instantly cooled it.

"Thank you, Grandmaster Vegre!" He looked down at Alexy's still form. "And as for you—" The witch kicked Alexy so hard in the dim blue light that he lifted from the ground. "Something to occupy your dreams before you die, Alchemist."

Tal was so preoccupied watching the event that when the cavern lit up, he turned surprised eyes back to Vegre, who shrugged. "I see no reason why you can't watch the others die alongside you . . . the O.P.A. apparently still adhering to their ridiculous notion of comradery." The thought of Tal watching the others die seemed to amuse Vegre greatly, for he gave a genuine smile and chuckled as he walked into the distance, followed closely by his two servants, callously abandoning his unconscious lackey to capture or death.

Another flutter in his chest, followed by a stab, deeper than the first. He would have doubled over from the force of it if he could have. The pain seemed to flow through him until it wasn't just his heart that was failing. Every vein, every organ felt as though daggers were being shoved in repeatedly. It was no wonder sane Guilders didn't use this curse. Even people who chose to kill seldom stomached torture.

It took long minutes before he could work his tongue and jaws enough to spit out the gag. Unfortunately, that didn't remove the paralysis spell. He still couldn't move except to scream . . . and he refused to give Vegre the satisfaction. No, he had to break the immobilization first, before he could do anything else. But, at least with the Creeping Darkness spell gone, he could pull on magic in the cavern and beyond.

That made him pause and wonder. It was almost as though Vegre *intended* for him to do this. Otherwise, why remove a beneficial spell that was providing him energy? Or, maybe he was overthinking Vegre's motive. It might be that he simply couldn't maintain all three spells simultaneously, but didn't want Tal to discover that weakness. Either way, he needed to take advantage of it.

He closed his eyes and turned his attention inward. He searched for the runes that were corrupting his life force. They were invisible to the naked eye, but in his mind he could see the traces of colored energy that affected him. He could unwind them, but it would take a steady flow of energy. He reached out with his senses, eyes still closed, searching. He could feel Alexy, Sela, and the captive. Oddly, they were barely affected by the Venticulari spell. At least they weren't going to die as quickly as he was. To time a spell like that . . . to layer the effect from person to person—that took a level of skill that Tal had only known a very few Grand Masters to achieve. But at least his companions were alive.

After a few minutes of searching, Tal realized that they were nearly the only things that *were* alive in the area. Either the guards and prisoners had been relocated or they were dead. Moss, worms, mushrooms . . . all dead. As far as he could reach out, there was nothing but cold, lifeless stone.

And then he realized the trap. Alexy and Sela were unconscious, unable to free or save themselves. Tal would have to save them, but the only way to do that would be to free himself before the spell took him down. Unfortunately, the only energy to pull on was the life force of the others. If he did that, the spell would work that much faster. They would indeed die together, and it would be Tal's fault.

He couldn't do that, but to do nothing would also ensure their deaths, since he was confident that whatever Vegre did to knock them out would last until long after he was dead and they would be too weak to fight the spell—if they could even figure out what spell was on them.

"Vegre, you bloody bastard! I'm on to you. And I'll find a way to beat you!" He screamed the words into the cavern and thought he heard echoes of faint laughter return.

Again he closed his eyes, shutting out the distraction of his injured teammates. He had to search inside himself, reach for the doorway to the spirit of the Sacred Tree that had never failed him in times of crisis. His foster mother had always called him blessed for his connection to the Tree's life magic. While he couldn't imagine why he had been singled out to be able to touch the Tree's essence, he wasn't above using it to save himself and his friends and prevent the scourge on humanity that Vegre represented.

He imagined a doorway, and carefully created the runes in his mind that would invoke the protection of the Tree.

At first, he could only catch flashes of light and warmth. But slowly, he heard laughter and female voices . . . smelled the spices of home and cooking, felt happiness flow in and through him—and he knew he had tapped into the essence of the Tree.

Pain lanced through his mind as another spasm gripped his heart. A chill settled over him as the power of the Tree raced through veins and tried to correct the damage from the spell. The wintery blast was both frightening and cheering. "Not me," he whispered to the light. "If I guide you, will you help the others?"

He'd never addressed the Tree's spirit directly, but then he'd never been faced with this situation before. His eyes shot open in surprise and alarm when a decidedly feminine voice responded to his plea. "Where am I? Who are you? Who are *the others,* and how am I supposed to help?"

The honest confusion in the voice stopped him cold. How could the spirit of the Sacred Tree not know how to help? It was life, hope, the heart of the whole of Agathia. It was the source of all magic in the world. Couldn't the spirit do *anything?*

Still, it was *people* who manipulated the energy. It was the guilds that originally learned to harness the magic and bend it to their will. So, perhaps the raw energy source *didn't* have the knowledge to do what he asked. "You need merely open yourself to me and I'll do the rest."

There was no answer, so he presumed the spirit agreed. He concentrated on the pure thread of magic that was bright enough to imprint on the back of his retinas. Time and again, he pressed the magic to his will, dissolving the runes that held him motionless. The sudden release dropped him to his knees and made him acutely aware of the cavern around him. The cool damp air filled his chest and it felt brand new—as though he'd never been to the waterfall before. The glowing strands of saliva seemed to twinkle like stars. Even the stark black obsidian of the prison walls was intoxicating. He wanted to reach out to touch the stone, feel the cold slickness under his fingers.

But there was no time. Even as he marveled at things he'd known all his life, he felt the power fading. It would be enough to save them, but just. He raced first to Alexy's side, ignoring the flash of pain in his chest that the abrupt movement cost him. The runes surrounding him were weaker, but still formidable. Even without speaking directly, the spirit seemed intrigued by the symbols . . . as though it recognized the runes, but in an esoteric way, not for what they actually *did*. "Here . . . and here." He guided the magic to dismantle the runes around Alexy and felt an instinctive sort of understanding follow, as though the spirit was relearning a skill that had been forgotten. The energy stream was decidedly weaker when he finished, but he couldn't help but smile when Alexy's eyelids fluttered open.

"What in the king's bloody balls happened to me?" Alexy's voice was hoarse, as though he'd been screaming, even in his sleep. "I feel like I've been run through a clothing wringer backward."

Tal shook his head. "I'll have to explain later. I don't know how much time I have left to save Sela."

Sela. That name seemed to ring in his head like a bell, but the confusing images that followed in his mind made no sense to him. Richly waxed furniture, a fluffy gray cat, and the thick, cloying scent of flowers—none of them were things he could attribute to the stark, no-nonsense police agent he'd worked with for the past two years.

He ran toward the waterfall to the last place he'd seen her crumpled form. But she was gone. Only a small dark stain of blood remained on the damp stone. "Sela?" He looked up and around, turning in a full circle, in case she'd woken up and crawled or flown to a safe place. He called again, louder. "Sela! Where are you?" Only the rumbling hiss of the waterfall replied.

"Are you certain she was here?" Alexy was still woozy

and was slurring his words more than a little. But as soon as Tal released Sela from the spell, she could use the small amount of healing magic she knew to fix that.

"She was here when I went to help you. She *can't* have gone far. Sela!" Alexy began calling for Sela as well, picking up on Tal's increasing concern. She had been unconscious, just like Alexy, while he was working with the Sacred Tree. How could she just disappear?

He realized he was worried about her—far more than he should be. She'd been missing before . . . had been *captured* before. Yet, concern filled him to the point that he raced into the darkness, searching.

"Tal! What are you doing?" Alexy's voice grew fainter as he ran through the cave, looking in every cranny, high and low, for some sign of her. A bit of cloth, a few strands of golden hair. But there was no evidence she had been this way.

Another spasm ripped through him, and this time he couldn't fight back the scream of pain. He found himself on the ground, with Alexy standing over him, but he couldn't remember falling. There was only pressure—strangling his heart, pressing against his eyes, making his limbs feel leaden and sluggish. As the pressure increased, so did the stabbing, stinging, burning that made him want to tear off his own skin.

"C'mon, guv. Stay with me." He could hear the words, but he couldn't seem to make his mouth move. The realization that he couldn't tell Alexy what the spell afflicting him was, nor that Vegre had been the caster, terrified him. He began to thrash on the ground, clutching at his throat, trying to make his lips form the words. But every movement intensified the pressure until he couldn't even think:

Make it stop! The plea, scream, demand came from inside his head, but it wasn't his voice. It was the powerful female cry of the Tree spirit, who was trapped inside the spell with him.

I can't make it stop. It's a spell. I'm going to die soon. The simple statement was met with abject panic from the spirit.

No! You can't. I'll die with you.

Tal went still. He couldn't imagine that the Sacred Tree could *die*. That wasn't possible. It was all-powerful, never-ending. It had existed from before he was alive, hundreds of years. It was the Tree that had drawn the ragged survivors of the Blackshear massacre from the overworld to their underground sanctuary.

But if the spirit could die, then it was too late. He couldn't think through the pain to form a counterspell . . . even if he had the magic. He couldn't move his lips enough to speak. His heartbeat was slowing and he knew somewhere in the darkness, Vegre was laughing at him.

Tal looked up and saw Alexy mouthing words. The veins in his neck were standing out so far that he must be screaming, but Tal couldn't hear whatever he was saying. A cotton-fluff haze seemed to muffle everything, from sound to sensation and even the room was growing dim.

I'm not willing to die with you. This isn't my fight. The voice in his head was panicked, but there was a thread of cold iron in the declaration. Sadness filled him with the knowledge that the Tree spirit was going to allow him to die in solitude. Yet, didn't he vow to sacrifice himself, separate himself from the Agency, when it came time to die? Wasn't that part of . . . part of . . . what, exactly? He remembered a vow, and how important it had been at the time, but he couldn't seem to remember the words.

His eyes flicked open again. When had he shut them? Alexy's eyes seemed to be leaking, dripping moisture onto his face. That seemed odd, but he couldn't remember why.

Enough of this! The shout in his head was sure and strong, and was accompanied by a sound. No, more than a sound, it was a hundred sounds, a thousand. Tumbling, flowing, grating against one another . . . one moment an angels' chorus, the next an out-of-tune orchestra. The cacophony of noises made his chest vibrate and his lungs struggle for air.

And then everything went black.

CHAPTER 2

"*Sela!*" Mila's eyes shot open and she sat up in a rush. The darkness that had claimed her mind made her disoriented and sick to her stomach. Bile rose in her throat from a panic that she couldn't seem to shake, forcing her to swallow repeatedly to keep it down. If only the room would stop spinning as easily.

The door opened and Candy rushed in. She sat down on the bed and put a comforting hand on her shoulder. "Hey, girl. Sela's not here, remember? She's at her folks's for the holidays." Mila blinked repeatedly as she tried to focus on the here and now. The dark cavern and the blond man who had been crying and mouthing words she couldn't hear were fading into the recesses of her mind. At least the pain was gone, as was the tingling in her toes. But she could still remember the face of the man who had tortured her in the dream. "Vegre. His name was Vegre." It seemed terribly important that she remember that and say it out loud.

"Who's name is Vegre? You still with me, Mila? You're home now. It's Candy. Remember?"

Mila finally *looked* at her friend. The darkness dimmed enough that she could recognize her own bedroom. The century-old burled oak bed posters flickered like a tigereye stone under the thin shaft of sunlight that managed to get through closed curtains. She sighed and snuggled deeper into the thick down mattress and sighed in relief. "I'm home. How in the world did you get me home?" That thought was followed by another moment of panic. "Oh *crap,* I have to call work."

Candy rolled her eyes and let out a snort of air. "Please, do you think I'm an idiot? I called your work, told them you got waylaid by that cold going around and wouldn't be back this afternoon." She lifted one foot to display it to her friend. "And I should take back half of the money I paid you. Just *look* at these boots."

The suede boots, normally the color of a pureblood palomino horse, were soaking wet and stained with both mud and salt. Mila knew they were her pride and joy . . . handcrafted for her on a rare trip to Italy. The fact that she allowed them to get in that condition was incredibly touching. "Ohmygod, Candy! I can't believe you aren't in tears. Did you *carry* me all the way home?" She couldn't help but glance down at her size-fourteen body, and then at Candy's delicate size six.

Her friend laughed and patted her comforter-covered leg. "God, no! I'm lucky if I can lift my purse most days. You were actually able to walk with some help. I told them in the restaurant that you had a bad cold, too, and the medicine had made you a little loopy, so one of the waiters helped us to my Jeep." She let out a small chuckle as she stood and walked to the window, where she opened the drapes to let in more light through the sheers. "It was pretty easy to keep up that white lie, since you kept sneezing and calling him Alexy." She turned and wiggled her eyebrows. "Found out his name is Robert . . . while he was asking me for a date." One hand went to her hip flirtatiously. "That's the only reason you're off the hook for the boots, by the way."

One word stuck in Mila's mind from the story. *Alexy.* Why did that name sound so familiar? It tickled in her mind, struggling to find a link, but whatever the name meant was gone. She shrugged and then ran fingers through her crunchy, tangled hair. "Just another one of those rambling moments, I guess. You know how the episodes are. Congrats on the date, I suppose. That wouldn't have seemed to be a dating opportunity to me. So, how'd you get me up the front steps into the house?"

Her friend snorted expressively. "Hell, girl. Your problem is that nothing *ever* seems like a dating opportunity. Probably why I get more dates. But I got lucky when we got here, too. Your neighbors, Bryan and Jeff, were home taking down their Christmas decorations. They helped me get you upstairs." She paused and looked at Mila sternly before tapping one manicured nail on her hip. "I'm really ticked off that they knew nothing about your condition, by the way. You *promised* me that you were going to tell them, so they could look in on you if something like . . . today happened." She raised eyebrows in only slightly mock frustration. "Hmm?"

Mila had no excuse and she knew it. All she could do was let out a frustrated breath. "I know I promised you . . . and Mom. It's just that . . . they think I'm *normal* around here. You remember how they talked about me behind my back when I lived in Aurora. I felt like some sort of circus freak. Everybody watched me with greedy eyes, like they were waiting for the next show." She threw back the comforter and sheet and shivered from the sudden rush of chilled air in the drafty bedroom. "You don't know what it's like, Candy. People have actually told me that they were afraid to invite me to parties, because they don't know when I'll *go off*."

Her friend looked suddenly uncomfortable, shifting weight from foot to foot and staring at the floor. "I never really thought about it from your side. It's just that we worry—"

On impulse, Mila dashed across the room and threw her arms around Candy's shoulders, not caring when a splinter from the old unvarnished floor embedded in her heel. Slender arms gave her a hug tight enough that her words were muffled. "I know. And I love you guys for it. I really do know how hard my condition is for you and the family. But please . . . give me a little space, and try to have faith in me." She pushed backward and held Candy at arm's length. "Please?"

There was a knock on the front door just as Candy opened her mouth to reply and they both turned to the sound. Mila stepped back and looked at her mess of clothing, grimacing at the deep wrinkles in the woolen skirt. "Any chance you can get that for me while I change? I can't even imagine who it would be in the middle of the day."

Candy twisted her arm and lifted the edge of the fluffy red sweater covering her watch. She shook her head and uttered a small nervous laugh. "Um, I'm betting it's your grandmother."

Mila's jaw dropped and heat rose to burn her cheeks. "You called Baba Nadia? What were you thinking?"

Her friend was unapologetic as a crescendo ringing echoed up the stairs from the ancient bellpull. "Would you rather I'd called your *mother?* You were unconscious for the better part of an hour, Mila. I didn't dare call for an ambulance. You'd lose your driver's license. And your baba used to do that . . . *thing* to bring you out of an episode when we were kids. Remember?"

"Thing?" Mila asked as the knocking started again. She vaguely remembered how Baba would roll eggs on her stomach when she was sick—ancient Ukrainian folk medicine that was amazingly effective when done by the right person. And Baba was one of those people.

"You remember how she used to wander the neighborhood when we were kids, knocking on doors to treat sick people?" Candy shivered as another ring persistently sounded downstairs. "I always hated sitting in strange people's living rooms, when half the time I didn't understand what they were saying. And God! Those foul-smelling plasters on our chests and hot-wax readings."

Mila furrowed her brow. Really, she didn't recall spending all that much time with Baba as a girl, but she must have if Candy remembered it. She sighed. "Well, we might as well get it over with. Stall her if you can, while I change into something *suitable,* huh?"

Her friend looked slightly panicked. "Don't take too long. That woman terrifies me, and there aren't many people who can still do that."

They were in agreement about that. The Penkin matriarch was a force of nature who could casually walk by a junkyard and have the guard dogs whimper and crawl away with tails between their legs. *Dog Whisperer* had nothing on her grandmother. As Candy left and closed the bedroom door, Mila went to the closet and flipped through hangers before finding a pressed pair of black slacks and a white shirt. The embroidery on the collar was in similar jewel tones and design as the eggs she'd sold to Candy. Baba loved bright colors and the fact that Mila had done the stitching would win points on a crucial day like this.

She'd just pulled the splinter from her foot and was buttoning her shirt when Candy's unusually tentative voice came through the closed door. "Um, Mila? It wasn't your grandmother at the door. It's two guys for Sela. I told them she wasn't here, but they insisted on talking to you." She lowered her voice to a whisper. "They're all stern and distant. I think they're cops, but they wouldn't show me a badge. Doesn't Sela work for the Feds?"

Someone for *Sela?* Nobody ever came to see her roommate, and she couldn't imagine her being in any trouble. Fresh to Denver from an Amish farm in Pennsylvania where her family eschewed all technology, Sela had gone whole hog into materialism. Working for the U.S. Geological Survey in Boulder gave her plenty of money for all the high-tech toys that she'd never had as a child. Mila could barely walk through her room without tripping on video cables from game systems, computers, and music players. "Sela's not the type for federal trouble. They're probably family. I've heard they're really disapproving of technology and the living room is loaded with it."

Candy sounded unconvinced. "Yeah, maybe. But you haven't met them. You'll see what I mean in a minute."

Mila looked again at the clothing in the full-length oval mirror in the corner, suddenly relieved the shirt had a homemade feel. If the visitors were Sela's relatives here to check her out, she just might pass the test. "I'll be right down. Could you ask if they want something to drink? I've got some juice and bottled water in the fridge."

"Will do." As soon as she heard the familiar thumping of Candy's heels down the stairs, she dashed to the bathroom at the end of the hall. One look in the mirror over the sink made her grimace and drag fingers through stubborn tangles gluey with hair spray. Maybe if she flipped her hair over her head and brushed vigorously for a minute, it would help. As she counted out stroke twenty under her breath while simultaneously scrubbing her teeth with cinnamon paste, she heard something crash to the floor down the hall.

Mila paused to listen. The rustling was definitely louder than Candy's muted alto and two males—one tenor and one baritone—down in the living room. She stood carefully and smoothed her thick waves into place, then spit toothpaste into the sink as quietly as she could.

Could Baba already be here? But no, Candy would have mentioned it, and Baba never did anything quietly. She grabbed the big metal flashlight from the floor near the door. It was both a necessity in a neighborhood that was usually the first in the city to lose power, and a powerful club for protection. After taking a deep breath, she carefully slipped out into the hallway.

She was right. The noise was definitely coming from Sela's room. The door had been closed since she left nearly a week ago, but now it was slightly ajar.

Through the crack, she could see Sela, racing between her dresser and an open suitcase, stuffing clothing inside haphazardly and muttering to herself. Her face was covered with bruises and there was a dark spot on the back of her head that looked very much like dried blood. *"Sela?"* She whispered the word, not wanting the people downstairs to hear—especially since Candy had already told them that Sela wasn't here.

Her roommate turned so quickly she nearly fell, her face a mask of terror. She raised a hand straight-armed from her shoulder, causing Mila to take a step backward. It took a few moments for recognition to come to Sela's eyes, but when it did, the arm dropped.

Mila rushed forward, keeping her voice down, despite her excitement. "Sela, when did you get home? There are some people downstairs looking for you. Have you talked to them yet?"

Her roommate looked at the open door to the room in abject horror before tiptoeing over to close it. "I haven't been downstairs yet, because nobody knows I'm here. There are men following me, Mila. You have to tell them that I don't live here anymore."

The disapproval must have been clear in her expression, because Sela's face fell. She continued whispering, more because she wanted to find out what was going on before there were interruptions. "You *know* I won't do that, Sela. How many times have I refused to lie for my boss, even when annoying clients come to the office? What's going on? How did you get up here without coming through the door downstairs? Are you in some sort of trouble? Should I call the police? I can certainly stall whoever's downstairs until they get here if you're in danger."

Sela ran fingers through her short blond hair in frustration and only then noticed the blood that came away on her fingers. She looked down in shock, apparently just realizing how she must appear. "Look, Mila. I know this must seem strange, but you have to believe me—it's imperative that the men downstairs don't see me here."

Mila folded her arms over her chest and raised brows, stern with disapproval, in what her brother always referred to as her *Baba face.* "Go on. How did you get up here, and why don't you want those men to see you?"

Few people could stand up under the Baba face, and Sela was no exception. She looked again at the suitcase and then at her watch before replying. "All I can tell you is that there are things going on that you don't understand and will have a hard time believing. I *like* you, so I tried my best to keep you out of this, but it's too late now. But trust your gut, Mila. You're more unique than you can ever imagine. There are people who would . . . who *have* killed—" She looked toward the door at the sounds of movement outside. "Oh *hell,* there's no *time.* Just, keep an open mind and *be careful.*"

With that, she turned away and started throwing things frantically into her bag.

Mila felt like an idiot standing there, just staring at the woman who she'd lived with for nearly two years now—but apparently didn't know at all. Rational thought said that Sela was delusional from the blow to her head, but instinct . . . her *gut,* told her differently.

Before Mila could frame her first question to get more details, she felt a strange, prickling sensation flow through her feet. It was pins and needles, but of a different sort than before an episode. This was deeper and heavier . . . more like claws that grabbed and held, filling her skin with heat and pain. She felt her head snap around at the precise moment that Sela's did—toward a spot near the window that was shimmering. With an abruptness that made Mila gasp, a greenish haze replaced the sparkles and a tall man stepped into the room as though the window was a door.

Mila froze as she recognized the man who'd tortured her in the dream. Clothed in black silk, he reeked of death and decay. Mila expected to run from the room, from the man who'd stolen the life from her body, planned to scream and cower. But instead, she stepped toward him aggressively, surprising herself. She forgot to lower her voice, but it didn't really matter anymore. "You're not welcome here, Vegre. Get out and leave us alone."

While his eyes had been only for Sela, the mention of his name drew both his and Sela's eyes toward her. He stared at her for a long moment but then shook his head. "I don't know you, human, but that you own my name means your death." He raised his hand and uttered a single word. *"Moratay."*

"Avatay." The word slipped out of Mila's mouth, completely unbidden. It was such a surprise to hear him to utter that old word—part of a game she and her sister Sarah had played as kids. It was similar to *Marco Polo* that her friends played, but the second word had to be uttered before the first word finished, otherwise you lost a point. She felt heat hover in the air around her face and then it blew

around her and Sela. The energy hit the wall hard enough to blow apart the old plaster over the brick. The resulting blast of noise didn't seem possible from the light breeze that had passed around her.

A flurry of footsteps bounded up the stairs just before a hard shove sent her sprawling to the floor. The words came seconds later. "Get down, Mila!" She felt another rush of heated energy singe her hair, like walking past a bonfire when the wind changes. Out of her peripheral vision, she saw Vegre grab Sela's arm and start to drag her toward the roiling, bubbling gash in reality.

Even as her mind screamed, *Leave this alone! Run! Hide!* she reached out and grabbed Sela's ankle with both hands and pulled, struggled to keep Sela from being abducted. It was as though her sudden help spurred Sela on, because she began to fight in earnest—kicked and scratched and screamed nonsensical words at her attacker.

The door burst open, slamming against the wall so hard that the old patterned knob embedded in the plaster. Mila caught her breath as two men raced in with Candy and Baba Nadia at their heels. The blond man . . . he was the same one who had been in her dream.

"Alexy! Help her!" Mila's eyes locked on those of the dark-haired man who'd shouted. She didn't recognize him . . . not at all, but she felt like she *should.* His movements, his energy, felt so familiar that it was almost like he was a lover she'd forgotten she had. But then, when the blond moved forward to help, the name the man had called him finally struck home in her mind. *Yes. He is Alexy.* Time seemed to still as Mila took in the implications. Even a woman's scream nearby seemed distant within the buzzing in her head as she stared at the blond and felt a surge of deep friendship . . . comradery that had no romantic ties, but was equally as strong.

"Oh, my God! Is that Sela? What's happening to her?" Candy's words from the doorway drew Mila's gaze away from the men. Vegre had disappeared through the passage, and only Sela's lower torso remained in the room, stretched painfully—her pant leg taut over a twitching leg. She was halfway between here and . . . wherever, held only by Mila's fierce grip on her booted ankle. The next scream made her realize that holding her like this was hurting her. Even Alexy hesitated and looked to the other man for guidance.

"Think it'll come off if I help pull?" It took a second for Mila to realize that *it* was Sela's leg.

The dark-haired man looked stricken at the thought and seemed to struggle within himself for an answer. He opened his mouth finally, but it was her baba's calm, gentle voice that broke the silence.

"Yes. Too much of her is on the other side. Mila. You must let go."

She felt her eyes welling as she stared at the crackling green hole of energy. "But I can't. He'll kill her. She said so, and I've seen what he's capable of."

"He? Who took her?" The dark-haired man moved across the room and knelt down beside her. His dark eyes were intense, flickering with an internal fire that seemed to warm her toes. "Did you hear a name?"

"Vegre. His name is Vegre." The name made three of the four others in the room flinch and her grandmother reached instantly for the cross under her shirt. She kissed it and closed her eyes. "Then she is doomed. But please, Mila . . . don't help him by prolonging her torture. Let go." Another scream punctuated the air, lending credence to her baba's words.

"Wait!" cried the dark-haired man suddenly. "Not yet." He ripped off a leather driving glove with a large chunk of green glass over his palm. He held it for a second and then with a look of determination, made a throwing motion into the flickering void. He turned his head and nodded. "You can let go now. We'll find her."

Something made her comply. But she'd been holding on so tight that it was hard to open her fingers. The man had to help her pry them open against the constant tug from the other side of the sparkling goo. At last she felt Sela's leg slip away. The moment the last bit of spiked heel disappeared, so did the sparkling.

It was suddenly still in the room until Alexy let out a frustrated sound. "Tal, what in bloody hell were you thinking? He'll spot your glove in a second and we'll wind up dead from a soul-sucking spell before we can make it back to base."

The dark-haired man, Tal, looked at him calmly and then smiled. "Cloaked it first and put on an attachment spell."

The frustration slipped away from Alexy's face, to be replaced by a brilliant smile that was obviously his normal expression by the many laugh lines around his eyes. "That's bloody brilliant. I'd never have thought of turning a focus into a tracker."

Mila felt apart from herself, numb and fuzzy after the frantic activity that resulted in failure. It was Candy's voice that turned their laughter serious again. "Would someone *please* explain what's going on? Spells? Trackers? Weird green—" she fumbled for her next words, "goopy things that people disappear into?"

Baba patted her on the shoulder. "All in time, Candace. First, though, we must refresh and do a reading. Before I reveal more, to you or—" she motioned to the men with a stern look, "—them, we must have calm energy."

Tal rose from his squat and flipped one side of a long cape back over his shoulder in a practiced gesture. He offered Mila a hand up and she realized she was still sprawled facedown on the floor. Rising to her knees she took the hand, marveling in the gentle strength that seemed almost . . . chivalrous. "Um, thanks."

The sensation of his touch wasn't what she'd expected. His hand was overly warm, heating her skin until her toes tingled. Her body ached from that one touch, but there was also a familiarity there, a sensation that she'd been touched by him before . . . intimately. It was a struggle not to gasp or throw herself at him and she noticed that as soon as she was on her feet, he let go, as though burned.

Tal turned toward Baba, his voice gruff, yet breathy. "Apologies, Grandmother, but we've got a criminal to track. Sela's strong, but his followers are many. If we don't find him soon—" He paused, and anger filled his face. "Well, we won't consider that. We *will* find him."

Baba's wide body filled the doorway and she gave another of her patented looks over crossed arms. "You are weak and will only endanger the witch further if you proceed without ritual. Come. You will eat herbs and drink tea and be healed. Otherwise—" She paused and stared at the men with the most dangerous expression Mila had ever seen. "I will put you down where you stand."

CHAPTER 3

*T*al stared at the old woman in the doorway in disbelief. Surely he must have heard wrong. "Madam—"

But she raised her hand to stop him. "There is nothing to your words, unless over tea. You may not leave this home until then, or you will surely regret it. Candace, Ludmila— come. You will assist. We will leave the Guilders to discuss their options." A burst of raw power punctuated the words, enough to tighten Tal's chest.

The same horrified surprise that was painted on Alexy's face was probably spread across Tal's at the old woman's words. He had never seen her before and yet he thought he knew *every* Guilder that voluntarily lived topside. He'd also never felt magical energy such as hers. It was warm and cold simultaneously and tasted on his tongue like ripe fruit. But . . . she'd called them Guilders and had recognized Vegre's name. *What in the name of the Tree is going on?*

Apparently, the other two knew better than to argue with the stern matron, and followed her almost meekly. But he heard the blonde named Candace whisper to the other when they reached the hallway. "What's a *Guilder,* Mila?"

The other woman shrugged before disappearing around the corner.

Mila. It was a pretty name, and she was certainly a lovely woman. There was something strange about her though, something he couldn't seem to erase from his mind. His fingers still tingled from where they'd touched her hand, and he couldn't seem to shake the feeling that he shouldn't have let her go . . . should have pulled her close and held her tight. It was disconcerting enough that he couldn't tear his eyes from the doorway, even after she was long gone.

He was still staring after them when Alexy stepped closer and lowered his voice. "This is getting very strange, Tal. Who is that old woman? She's a Guilder, no doubt about it. I touched her magic, but it kicked me back when I tried to explore the measure of it—like I was a new apprentice who had made the mistake of pressing the guildmaster. Do you think she's in forces with Vegre?"

Alexy was right. There were far larger things going on here. He shook his head as frustration began to set in. "I wish I knew. The odd thing is that I almost feel like I should *know* these women from somewhere. The old one reminds me of someone from long ago." He paused, trying to remember but eventually shook his head. "Maybe it'll come to me. But we need to decide what to do— where to go from here. We need to find Sela, but it would be foolish to just leap into the void without examining *why* she was taken, and from here." He looked around the room. "So, what do we know for certain so far?"

Alexy nodded sharply, his training kicking in. "Vegre and other unknowns have broken out of Rohm Prison."

Tal turned and started flipping through the open travel case on the bed while nodding. "We know the guards at the prison are dead or spellbound. Or, I suppose they could be deserters or in cahoots with the breakout. Time will tell on that. We know Vegre found a gate to this world and it somehow exits into this room . . . which isn't an approved location. Or," he mused, "has someone managed to create a spell to make portable gates in and out of Agathia?"

Alexy thought for a moment and then shook his head. "I'd say no. Guilders have been trying to do that for centuries, but gate spells are under such tight restrictions that the king's guards would have known immediately if someone had tried to cast one—especially around the prison complex. No matter how close the kingdoms are to war, they'd never allow that. Someone would have captured them long before they got to this stage. I presume Kris would have told you if they'd broken up a gatemaking ring. Yes?"

He nodded, trying to think of any reason his sister would keep such vital information from him and the O.P.A. "At least she'd tell me if she wasn't instructed *not* to—and I can't imagine why anyone would give that order, short of treason by an advisor or guard that they wouldn't want the Agency to be involved in." He ran a finger along the edge of a large television mounted on the wall. His finger came away dusty. "We know Sela was with us when the battle started and then she disappeared when we both got hurt."

Alexy pressed his palm to the window glass that Tal had noticed looked down onto quiet, snow-covered homes, many still decorated with holiday trimmings. He pulled it away abruptly, as though burned. Tal watched him look at his hand and shake it with an odd expression before speaking. "Ow. We know her magic signature was still strong enough to lead us back to this house, and apparently there's some sort of shielding spell on this room that stings like crazy. It's not earth or water magic, but I don't know enough shield spells in other trades to judge what they might be. Oh, and what did you think about the old woman knowing Sela was a witcher?"

Tal wouldn't be able to sense shields for a little longer yet, considering how far down his reserves were, so he'd have to rely on Alexy's skills. "Yes, I wondered about that. Very few people know Sela originally trained in the witch guild. She's an illusionist now because her water working skills weren't as strong. But that tells me the old woman either is very powerful and sensitive or has inside knowledge of our agents, since Sela didn't switch until *after* she joined the O.P.A. I haven't decided which option is worse."

He started pulling open drawers and began feeling under the clothing, searching for . . . something. Anything that would provide answers instead of the never-ending stream of questions. "We know that Sela somehow kept the information that she *lived* here secret from us for quite a while. She's had these possessions some time considering the dust and wear, and none of it is Agathian."

Alexy was still feeling along the edges of the windows, trying to get a measure of the spell, hissing and swearing as his fingers reddened. "Craters, this spell has some punch to it! This room is completely blocked . . . windows, doors, even the wall edges. Must have taken some time to do. A single spell wouldn't manage it. This room would be invisible to outside scrutiny by anyone except perhaps a guildmaster or royalty." He sighed. "I don't know about you, but that screams illegal activity to me. Of course that leads to another question. Where'd she get topsider currency? Technical items like these computers and video players aren't just handed out like festival sweets."

A queasy feeling was forming in Tal's gut. He never liked to think ill of a fellow agent, but there was too much evidence in this room to ignore or believe mere coincidence. "Do you think she went bad?"

Alexy let out a slow breath and then shrugged. "She risked her life to try a befouler spell on Vegre. I can't imagine that someone in cahoots with him would try that. It would mean her death—to pull enough energy from her own life force to destroy someone as strong as him. The only reason she didn't finish the curse was because he knocked her out."

Tal nodded. He'd had the same thought. So, there must be another reason. "Right, then. Let's take an energy sample in this room back to the commander for testing. We can at least find out what magicwielders have been in and out of here in the last week. That'll tell us something."

Alexy nodded and pulled on his battle glove. "It'll take

a few minutes to track the energy back that far in time using just a focus stone—especially with the disruption the gate caused. I'm pretty weak right now." He glanced toward the door with a look of longing. "Really could use some tea. They might even have some food down there. It feels like days since we ate."

Tal shook his head and rolled his eyes. "You always think with your stomach. Business first, Lieutenant. Then we'll decide how to get out of here without raising any alarms on either side. We can eat when we get back home."

The resulting sigh was enough to make him shake his head again. But at least Alexy had assumed the proper position on the floor and was already meditating to begin the energy search. Meanwhile, he began searching the room. This seemed to be where Sela lived while topside, and he immediately wondered why she had come *here* after disappearing in the cavern, instead of reporting back to him.

He looked around the space slowly. The furniture was nice and appeared to be about the same age as the house. It was only the accessories that were new. The clothing in the travel case had been tossed in haphazardly, but had been chosen with care and were obviously well made. The colors and textures didn't match items he'd seen Sela wear before, but they were too small for the other women in the house . . . unless there were more residents than had shown up so far. "Alexy?"

His friend opened one eye and raised a brow while remaining cross-legged on the floor near where the portal had been. "Yes?"

"Finish up and then meet me downstairs. I think it's time we had a chat with these ladies."

Alexy closed his eyes and rubbed his free hand on his belly with a smile. "Bless you, guv. Save me a scone."

With a nod that he knew Alexy wouldn't see, he left the bedroom and headed down the hallway. The house was elegantly appointed, with heavy dark furniture that was obviously well cared for and slightly threadbare but clean Persian carpet runners that had been loom woven long ago. It reminded Tal very much of his foster mother's home before the magic started to be rationed. That was one nice thing about the topside world. Wood products weren't rare. Most at home had to be magically created, and were temporary—for entertaining. The ones here could remain unchanged for centuries.

He heard a tentative sound as he passed one room and backed up to investigate it. The open door revealed a cat staring at him from amongst rumpled bedcovers. It was a fluffy mass of the deepest charcoal with a pug nose and whiskers so thick and long they drooped at the tips. It mewed again in invitation and then cocked its head questioningly. Tal had always had an affinity with cats. They seemed drawn to his fire magic and he often found them following him around, seeking a warm lap to curl up in, when he was on topside patrol. He inclined his head and squeezed his eyelids together in what he'd learned was a friendly greeting to the species. Once again, the cat seemed familiar, but he couldn't remember why.

The cat likewise closed eyes and squeezed and started to stand, probably to come for a pet, but he raised a hand. "Not right now," he said quietly. "I'll try to come back later, but I've no time at the moment." He broke eye contact to affirm it and was pleased to see in his peripheral vision that the cat settled back into the deep piles of bedding.

He reached the living room again, where Candace had tried to convince them that Sela wasn't in the house— even though she clearly was. But he remained convinced she hadn't been lying when she said it. That told him that Sela had somehow gotten into the house without the others knowing. Perhaps through that twice-damned gate.

Muted voices from behind a slatted door off the dining room told him where the kitchen was. He paused to listen before walking in, and was glad he did.

"Tell me of this Sela. How does she come to live here?" The old woman's voice was stern and disapproving and it affected the tone of the answer.

"You make it sound like some sort of back-alley drug

deal, Baba. Sela was just my roommate. She's lived here about two years and this is the *first* weird thing that's happened. It's not like I'm stupid. How could I have foreseen something like this?"

Candy's tentative voice came from slightly farther away, as though she was on the other side of the room. "That's not quite true, Mila. Don't you remember how Sela rented the place? That was a little creepy, wasn't it?"

"I do not know this word, *creepy*," said the older woman. "Tell me of this."

There was a long pause where the only sound was bubbling fluid that smelled of sweet herbs and flowers. It was similar to the tea his mother made, but a bit sharper. Finally, Mila spoke. "Yeah, I suppose that was a little strange. She just showed up one day and said that she was answering my ad in the paper for a roommate."

Candy broke in. "Except that Mila hadn't put *in* an ad. We'd talked about it, but she hadn't decided for sure that she wanted someone living here."

"At least until the probate finished. But here it is, two years later and they're still fighting it. Thank heavens I work for a law firm, or I'd be bankrupt trying to keep this house."

The old woman's voice lost the anger and filled with a comforting warmth that told Tal while she might be stern, she cared very much for Mila. "Miss Armstrong was a good woman, Mila. She gave you this house in kindness. It will not be taken from you by greedy *skusas* who don't respect their elders."

"I hope so, 'cause it's been going on too long as is. If I didn't know how important it had been to Lillian that her nephews never got their hands on this house, I probably would have given up long before now. But yeah, Candy's right. It was strange how Sela just showed up like that. She checked out, though. Good credit history, no criminal record, paid the rent on time, and didn't mess up the bathroom. She's been a good roomie overall. In fact, more than once she bailed me out between paychecks."

"But where did she get the money?" Conversation in the

other room stopped, and Tal realized he'd spoken aloud. The slatted door opened, and Mila gave him an annoyed glare.

"Well, you might as well come in if you're going to eavesdrop." The door closed again, leaving him to blush in peace. But after a moment, when the silence continued to drag on, he was forced to take a deep breath and push open the door.

The same scent of flowers and fresh herbs, but far stronger, struck him the moment he entered the tidy kitchen, filled with bright colors and dark wood. Most of the floral scent originated from Mila. It was sweet, but not cloying—more the fresh subtlety of a cool orchard than a garden. Cherries and orange blossoms, with apple overtones. He realized he was just standing there, sampling the air while staring at her. And she was staring back, her nostrils flared and eyes wide.

It was Candy who cleared her throat with an impish smile that made both of them start. Mila's face immediately dropped from the slight smile to a more disapproving expression that matched her earlier words.

"So, how much did you hear?" Mila tried to sound stern, but her light blush gave her away, and when he smiled, her eyes dropped to examine her oddly translucent teacup on the table.

"Introductions first, Mila. Where are your manners?" Again the younger woman reddened, all the way to her ear tips. The old woman dipped her head and waved a hand at an empty seat. Her thick accent made all of the vowels round and expressive. It was obvious English wasn't her first language. "I am Nadia Penkin." He sat down dutifully and dipped his head as she continued. "This is my granddaughter, Ludmila Penkin and her friend, Candace Hawkins."

"Most people call me Mila." She shrugged and caught his gaze again with those dark eyes, so that he barely heard her friend in the corner.

"And I'm Candy."

Manners forced his gaze away from Mila once more. Bowing his head slightly, he decided that trying to pretend he was a simple human was useless considering Mrs. Penkin's abilities . . . and her threats upstairs. "I am Craftman Talos Onan, a midlevel commander in the Overworld Police Agency. My friend upstairs is Alexy Duvrot. We are—"

"You are a mage. Your friend is an alchemist—a dirt-dog," said Nadia. "Fellow Guilders."

"Baba, what is a *Guilder?*" Mila blurted the words out, her frustration apparent. "You keep saying that like I should know."

Tal opened his mouth to reply, but again Nadia spoke up, in outraged surprise.

"How you not know, Mila? I tell you many stories when you are little about the Guilders. The caves . . . we go visiting when you are young." She gestured to Candy. "I take *both* of you, so I can show you our ways. How you not know?"

Mila and Candy exchanged confused looks and shrugs. But moments later, Candy's face registered understanding. "Wait! Do you mean the *geeders?* The tiny Ukrainian magic folk who live underground like fairies? *Those* stories?"

This time, Nadia's face looked confused as she mouthed the words, but then she laughed. "Ah. I see. My English, it was not so good when I came here to America. I not say all the letters like I do now. Yes. Yes, these men are *geeders*. But proper is Guilders, and not so tiny. You see?" She patted a hand gently on Tal's arm, then turned his wrist over to show the birthmark on his forearm. She fingered it a moment and furrowed her brow, making him squirm in embarrassment. His mark was faint and twisted—a mark that should belong to an apprentice instead of a crafter. "This is Guilder. He is mage . . . fire guild. You see his mark? Like the one on your middle toe. His friend is alchemist, earth guild, like your baby toe. Sela, she was water witch guild, like your second toe."

"What do you mean, *like my toes?* What do those designs you painted there have to do with any of this?"

The old woman looked taken aback by Mila's words.

She reared back in her chair and watched the young woman carefully for a long moment before asking a question that seemed as steeped in careful wording as a criminal interrogation. "You remember . . . Viktor's *gardens?* Yes?"

Only Candy's eyes widened in excitement. "*Ohmygod!* I *loved* the gardens! The spinning flowers, the wishing pond, and oh—remember all the Christmas trees?" She stared at her friend's blank face in astonishment. "C'mon, Mila. How could you forget those purple whatzits? The sparkling flowers you begged your mother to buy for *months*."

The grandmother's voice was cold when she spoke, her eyes flashing from an anger that was so deep it could produce any result. Tal felt his hand tighten on where his focus should be and realized it might have been foolish to throw it through the gate.

"She's forgotten because she was *made* to forget." Then started a string of words that were more muttering than conversation. Nadia touched the golden necklace she wore and then threw her hands wide as though to embrace the Tree. "She promised . . . swore on her *mark* she would not do this thing. Who knows what might be altered, or *lost* inside the mind? No, it must not stand. But first I must know more from your mother, Mila. It was done to you a very bad thing."

Mila's face grew alarmed, as it should. If she was right . . . *craters,* a memory alteration spell. That must be what Nadia was alleging happened. It was illegal in all the known realms, so she was right to be angry with whoever had done it! To remove the training of a Guilder forcibly was dangerous in the extreme. It could cause wild manifestations of magic because of the loss of knowledge of how to control the power.

Tal cleared his throat to catch their attention. "That could have legal repercussions if true. Please tell me . . . I've never felt magic such as yours. What guild do you craft under? Who should I contact to report this violation of your granddaughter?"

Mrs. Penkin growled, a deep snarl that could easily have come from an angry animal. "To tell that tale, you must first be refreshed. Mila, you will tell me what refreshment he requires, please." At Mila's startled expression she rolled her hand. "Quickly, quickly. You must think . . . what is that expression . . . on your toes now. We must learn what damage has been done."

"But how—" Her confusion was obvious as she raised her hands in frustration. "If this is something I used to do, I don't remember it. I just don't remember, Baba. How can I?"

Her grandmother sighed. "Is like egg rolling, yes? You use your *other* eyes to see his pain and weaknesses. Close the eyes that see this world to see the next. Try hard to remember how we played the healing games. You will have to fight to find your past, Mila, to find the truth of my words. At each of us you look, tell us what we need." She clapped her hands sharply, making all of them jump.

Mila looked to Candy for guidance, but she just waved her hands before raising herself to sit on the dark granite countertop. "Not my thing, remember? I never could *see* sickness like you guys could. Can't focus what's not there, sweetie. But c'mon. You used to do it all the time. I'll bet if you try you can."

Tal stood up to go back and join Alexy in investigating. There was nothing to be learned here that wasn't simple curiosity. He wanted no part of an apprentice's attempt to rediscover her magic. He didn't have the time or energy to waste fending off miscast spells.

But it was as though the old woman had read his mind. "No fretting, young mage. Mila was very skilled for one so young. She will remember if she tries. Sit, please, yes? This will help you and your friend greatly. My mark's vow."

That stopped him. A Guilder didn't call upon their birthmark to make an oath lightly, and her eyes bore out the promise when he turned to meet them. Under the circumstances, he shouldn't trust her—shouldn't trust any of them. And yet he did. He'd learned to trust his instincts, in the same way he'd trusted them to leave his post and check the prison perimeter. He tried to put aside his concerns and open himself to the experience. Perhaps there were things here that could benefit him. And he really had no idea where to start searching for the gate until Alexy was done. "Very well. But I must insist that no magic leave the premises, nor change any aspect of the evidence. And, if either of us is attacked, we'll defend ourselves by the full measure of the Saxon Accords."

Mila and Candy had wide eyes from his warning. He had seen the look before, and it mollified him slightly, because it was born of both fear and lack of understanding, rather than any sort of deviousness. But Mrs. Penkin merely nodded. "Is fine. I would expect such a response, but we will not attack, yes?" She held up a hand and pointed it to the stove in the far corner of the large room. "Mila, you will stand there so you can see us without turning." When she didn't immediately jump to her feet, the grandmother clapped her hands again. "Come, come. We have little time and much to do. The mage will not harm us so long as we do not harm him or hide things from him. Those are the elements of the Accord." She turned her head and raised her brows. "Yes?"

A quick nod was all he could manage before Mila was on her feet and stepping lightly to the corner of the room. His eyes followed her automatically, even when he tried to pull them away.

"I'll do my best, Baba. It's been a long time, but hopefully it's like riding a bike, and I'll remember as I go."

Once in the corner backed by the stove, she took a solid stance and cupped her hands lightly at her sides. The muscle memory of the act seemed to surprise her and she let out a slow breath then looked relieved.

She closed her eyes and a shudder overtook her. Without warning, a cloud of energy settled around his shoulders. It was fluffy, frothy, like being covered in cotton, fresh from the fields. He closed his eyes and could see the net of magic that she'd thrown around the room. No mere spell, this. She *was* the energy, and he could feel it press at him, raise the hairs on his skin until he shivered with anticipation. His own power, what little was left, rose to greet this tentative touch, and it leapt up like pouring fuel on a flame.

He was enveloped, consumed, and the force of it made him place palms on the table to keep from falling out of his chair. With a gasp, he opened his eyes and could see the magic in the air . . . ghostly tendrils that dipped and danced, but with purpose.

Candy was awestruck, her eyes following the threads around almost hypnotically. Nadia Penkin merely smiled and nodded, as if to say, *You see? She has been trained.*

The magic began to swirl around him now, in tighter circles. He caught his breath and closed his eyes once more as the cottony sensation turned to an urgent stroking that did more to his body than simply raise hairs.

Every nerve was alive and raw as strokes became pinpoint prickles that both hurt and felt wondrous. The scent of flowers became pine needles, then fresh dew on a cool morning. Trickles of water rolled down his face, or maybe it was just his imagination. But he certainly wasn't imagining how his body was hardening, in a skin-tightening rush that began to heave his chest. It was only through sheer willpower that he didn't snarl and rush across the room to grab Mila and kiss her. He wanted to run hands along her sweat-soaked bare skin, bury his face in that long hair and have her until his flesh was satisfied. Even gritting his teeth couldn't keep back the involuntary moan as he struggled, and that's when he saw Nadia's brow furrow with the beginnings of concern.

When he finally turned his gaze to Mila, she was wide-eyed, her hair blowing in the wind of energy she was creating. She was beautiful, wild, and as hungry as he.

He watched without moving has she moistened pink lips nervously. Her nipples hardened to tiny pebbles under her shirt as he stared, as the magic began to affect her, and she squirmed in her stance, trembling with need.

She shook her head frantically as if to fight off the sensations, but she was losing. It only made it that much more difficult not to bolt from his seat. He closed his eyes again and concentrated on the patterns of colors. But even they were erotic in his current state, flowing and dancing . . . sometimes fluid and other moments twitchy and desperate. His hands ached to touch something and nothing he did could end it, not with the taste of magic in the room.

Finally he could stand no more—he didn't care who would see, or what they would think. He opened his eyes and stared at her, looking for some sign. Her lips opened and she reached out one hand. When he stood, she moved forward in anticipation and even Nadia's frantic hand pulling at his cloak wasn't enough to stop him.

But then the telephone jangled, harsh and jarring. Just that tiny sound was enough to break the spell and Tal was able to stop himself before he reached her.

"Hello?" When he heard Candy answer he looked up and realized it was her mobile phone that had rung, rather than the house unit. Mila was looking rather sheepish, leaning against the oven door with head hung, contemplating her shoes. Tal couldn't help but admit that he felt the same. *Tree help me, the things I was thinking.* His own mother would have backhanded him if she'd known and he was a little surprised that Mrs. Penkin, while watchful, wasn't berating him.

"A tonsillectomy? Why didn't you tell me before?" Candy jumped down from the counter, landing on the tiled floor with a bang that turned all eyes to her. "Of course. I'll meet you there in an hour. Which hospital?"

The woman didn't act panicked, so it apparently wasn't an emergency. But it took Tal a moment to realize that he felt *capable* of taking on an emergency, when moments ago he would have had to struggle to sprint out to the roadway.

He was energized, refreshed in a way that seemed to lift years from his shoulders. The sensation was familiar from long ago and it told him which guild these crafters hailed from, even though it wasn't possible. He feared even uttering the name out loud, for the guild house of the Parask, the soul-conjurers, lay deserted, burned to the ground by fearful topsiders. And for good reason, if whispered tales were true.

Few would speak of what happened during that turbulent time, but there had been rumors, as there always are. Some of the oldest masters whispered that the Parask had gone dark—had joined Vegre in creating the plague that had not only destroyed most of the world's magicwielders, but half of the human population, as well. Others claimed that the Parask had simply grown too close to the humans by interbreeding and had caused a magical illness to become a medical one. Either way, the kings refused them entry into Agathia when magicwielders fled the topside world. They were shunned, outcast. Children with Parask potential were . . . *encouraged* to pursue other forms of magic. Those who didn't were executed.

"I'm sorry. I know there's a lot going on now, but I've got to go to the hospital." Candy gave her friend an apologetic look before turning to Nadia. "My favorite niece is scheduled for a tonsillectomy at St. Catherine's this afternoon and she wants to see me before they put her under the anesthetic. "If you want, I can drop you off at your car on the way."

"You will *drop* us on the way back," Nadia corrected firmly before taking a long drink of tea from her cup. She continued, "I, too, have reason to go to St. Catherine's. A friend has requested I do an egg rolling for her daughter. Mila, you will accompany me." Tal didn't miss the stern look she gave the younger woman. "You need the practice."

"No, Baba." Mila spoke firmly enough to draw the eyes of everyone in the room. "The car can wait. I'm not leaving this house until I know what is going on. Someone broke into my home and kidnaped my friend. Who's to say they won't be back? And while these 'Guilders' claim to be police, we have only their word for it. I'm not even completely positive I believe you about having my memories altered. Why would Mom, or anyone else, do that to me?"

The old woman gave her granddaughter a look that would have made a lesser woman quake in her boots, but Mila stood firm, feet planted solidly, her jaw thrust forward in a stubborn line.

"Bah!" The old woman spat the word out. "You have *healed* this man. You have the measure of him, as a mage and a man. Can you say with honesty you do not trust him? Can you say you do not trust *me?*"

A dark flush crept up the younger woman's cheeks, but she stood her ground.

Nadia's eyes narrowed. "Candace, Constable, give us a moment if you please."

It wasn't a request, despite the wording. Tal winced, but complied. He had no desire to witness a craftmaster dressing down her apprentice.

CHAPTER 4

The spell to activate the tracking of his glove was a simple one. Just as well, because Tal wanted to save his energy. If . . . no, *when* he found Vegre, he'd need every ounce of his strength and cunning to capture him.

He crossed the living room to stand in front of the fireplace that took up most of one wall. Turning the lever, he opened the flue. With a muttered word and a hand gesture, he called fire to the logs that had been laid in the grate.

Vague images flickered in the orange and gold flames; he could see wide white halls, and bustling figures in loose-fitting cotton clothing. He fed more power into the spell, and the fire bent to his will, focusing more clearly. "Where . . . show me where." He whispered. In answer he heard the hollow, echoing sound of voices in the far distance.

"That is just amazing." Candy's awed voice came from

behind his left shoulder. "I swear I can actually smell the disinfectant."

He started, and the flames responded, flaring upward alarmingly before he shut them down completely.

"You know this place? The one revealed?"

"It looks like either one of the big clinics or the admissions area of a hospital. I don't know which one though."

"It doesn't matter," he assured her. "I've activated the spell. I can follow it now. I will speak with Alexy. Your friend made a valid point. Gates are not so easily made nor common that they will willingly discard this one. They may well come back. It is worth leaving him to stand guard while I follow the trail."

"Assuming Mila has no objections," Candy said firmly. "It *is* her house after all."

He sighed. Whether she objected or no, the gate needed guarding. Still, it would be better, and easier, to play along and be polite for as long as possible. "Fine." He agreed. "We will tell your friend."

"*Ask.* You will *ask.* Don't just presume she'll go along."

Tal didn't answer, just crossed the room to push open the slatted door, stepping right into the middle of the argument he should have known was occurring.

"*E*nough, Mila. We are Parask. We do not refuse to heal just because the way is difficult, yes?"

Tal stiffened at Baba's words and his words came out in a dangerous rumble. "So, you *are* soul-conjurers. Can you give me one good reason why I shouldn't strike you down right here? Stop you from causing harm to a young human?"

Mila and Candy turned to him with dropped jaws, but Baba just waved her hand in dismissal. "Pah! Pay him no mind. I see nothing has changed bottomside. Their minds are still as the tiny mouse hole in the wall. If he believes the lies they tell, he is of no use to us." Baba began to gather her things. "Stay or go, young mage. But do not make the mistake of thinking you are crafter enough to stand in my way."

Tal wouldn't be put off. He raised one eyebrow and crossed his arms, his thick woolen cape fluttering into the air. "What part of it is lies, lifer? That your guild betrayed us, or that you doomed millions of humans to death?"

That stopped Baba, but only long enough to stare at him, as though memorizing every pore of his skin. "You were not there, so you do not know who betrayed *whom*. It is as I have always said. All lies do is confuse those who come after. It was the kings who betrayed *us*—who made my daughter-in-law so full of fear after they killed Mila's father that she risked the life of her child to make her forget your kind. It is a pity. I would have thought a constable of the O.P.A. would have more brains than to believe the pigslop the palace claims is cake."

Tal's eyelids narrowed, but he was more thoughtful than angry. "Guilders are remarkably long lived by human standards. Why would you think I wasn't there to see your betrayal of our people?"

Baba stepped over to the table, getting so close to his chest that even by Ukrainian standards, she was violating his space. Mila could feel energy rising in the room, stinging her skin enough to make her rub palms against her pants to ease it. Baba's words were a whisper, but they seemed to scream into the room, over her and Candy's tense breathing and the bubbling of herbs on the stove. "Because I would know you, mage, and I do not. As you say, we are remarkably long lived. If you *were* at Blackshear, you were too young to understand the politics being played. So I will give you the, what is it called?" She paused for a brief moment and then raised one finger. "Ah, yes. The benefit of the doubt. I will not hold against you the foolishness of your elders. But neither will I allow you to slander my family or my people."

He nodded once, just a tiny dip of his chin, but his eyes kept a healthy amount of suspicion. "You seem very convinced of your clan's innocence, and I've seen no evidence you mean anyone harm. And," he said with a small, bitter laugh, "I've had more than one occasion to sample the *cake* from the kings. I will offer to withhold judgment for the time being." Baba nodded just before he glanced behind him and listened for a moment. "But I'd caution you not to invoke your guild name around my partner. He's a little too fond of cake and has little self-control to guide his talent."

A faint fluttering, crackling sound made her turn away from Tal, quickly enough to bump his arm. It pulled a small hiss from him that brought a tiny smile to Baba's face. "I learned long ago to hold my tongue, but you see that I can defend myself if necessary."

She didn't wait for an answer, but walked across the room to examine the green leafy vine hanging from a basket suspended from the ceiling. It was looking rather ill. Mila joined her at the window and picked up one of a dozen wilted leaves that littered the formerly clean floor. "Oh, man! This was fine yesterday. I hope I haven't been giving it too much water."

Baba sniffed one of the leaves, then wrinkled her nose. She reached out, quick as a snake, and grabbed Mila's chin. She turned her face this way and that, staring at her with eyes slowly growing concerned. "You look too well. Where did you pull the power?"

Mila tried to pull back out of her grasp, but it was as if she was held in a vise. "I don't know what you mean, Baba."

She let go of her face, and rolled her hand expansively. "The power, Mila. You healed the mage. Even I can see it. But where did the energy come from? We soon go to a hospital with many sick people. Killing a vine is a tiny mistake, but if you cannot control your abilities, more than mere leaves will be dropping to the floor. You must concentrate now. What life did you end to save his?"

An uneasy feeling formed in the pit of her stomach and she looked again at the yellow, sickly leaf draped across her palm. She couldn't resist a quick sniff, and realized why Baba had wrinkled her nose. It smelled decayed, like a compost pile that needed turning. Had she really caused this? "You think *I* killed the vine . . . when all that magic was floating around the room?"

Baba shrugged, raising her hands into the air helplessly, while Candy paled. "Who else? There is only so much life on the planet, Mila. You must take from Saint Peter's pocket to repay the debt to Saint Paul, yes? The mage was weak and needed life. You can choose to draw from your own life or take the life from another when you heal. It is as I used to tell you when you were little, when you tried to save the life of your pet rabbit. What will you give? Who will you sacrifice and is it worth it?"

The memory of the talk came back in a rush—the first memory she'd had of her childhood in years. They'd been out in the backyard next to the bunny cage. Her 4-H project had gotten pneumonia and was dying. Her own carelessness had caused it. She'd forgotten to give the medicine when it was just a cold and her mother couldn't afford a big vet bill right then. In tears and panicked, almost anything was worth the price. "I gave up a day of my life to save that bunny. I remember now."

Baba nodded and leaned back against the counter. Tal seemed extremely interested in the discussion. He was staring at her, hanging on her every movement. "You offered the value of a day for a mere pet?"

She blushed, and couldn't figure out why. "He was pretty . . . white with a black nose. And it was my fault he was so sick."

"Not the mark of a callous betrayer, eh, mage?" Baba's smile was lightly mocking but understanding in that odd way she had about her. Then she turned back and motioned to the slowly falling leaves. "But today, you chose different. You sacrificed the plant for the man. It was not a bad choice, but you must *know* it was a decision before we visit the hospital. You can not pull life freely from the air when so many there will have so little, yes?"

The situation came home to Mila with frightening clarity. Baba was telling her that if she helped save one person, something else would have to give. If Baba's friend was really sick, then healing her would cost someone . . . somewhere. If a bunny cost a day, what was a human? A week? A year of her life? She just couldn't remember and it would make her look like an idiot to ask. Obviously, she couldn't risk anyone else. When she'd started to look at Talos, she couldn't focus enough to do anything more than just heal him. She apparently picked a target by instinct and moved the energy from one place to the next. She didn't even remember targeting the plant, but must have.

"I wish I could have trained you longer, Mila. But your mama, she wouldn't allow once Mikel was gone. I think it hurt her to watch you craft—reminded her too much of him. But I never thought her anger with the kings would go so far. She blamed them, yes, and now it has cost us all. We will have to train hard now that you know you can do this, yes? You must be ready to battle."

Train? Battle? *What the hell—?* "Um . . . we're still talking about healing, right?"

"Of course," said Baba calmly. "Today we heal. Later we train, bring you back to your potential. The worlds, they are colliding, yes? *You* are responsible to protect the humans now. My time will likely end before this is done. Vegre will not be easy to bring to justice and I am old."

This conversation was going downhill quickly. But when she opened her mouth to reply, an odd voice echoed into the room. It was unearthly and echoing, with a singsong quality. It reminded Mila of the horror movie when the little girl was talking through the television.

"Al . . . os. An . . . you . . . hear me?" Tal raised his right arm and bared the birthmark that Baba had showed her. It was vivid red, glowing lightly. He winced as it flashed like a strip-club neon sign. "I can hear you, Kris. But why are you flashing my mark? What's wrong?"

The woman's voice seemed to steady somewhat, even though it still echoed slightly. "Only way to . . . reach you without them knowing. What in . . . raters is going on . . . ere, Tal?"

Tal furrowed his brow and stared at his arm. Mila kept wondering if a face was going to pop out of his arm as hard as he was watching the mark. "You should already have the report. There was a breakout from Rohm. We tried to stop it, but failed. Sela went missing and we tracked her topside. But she's been taken, and we think it was by the black mage Vegre. There was an unauthorized gate here, and Alexy is doing a magic signature track right now. We'll be back down there soon and I'll tell you more."

"No! Not here. Stay topside. Afraid . . . you'd say that," said the voice he called Kris. "Problem is . . . *you're* accused of the breakout. All-points bulletin for your capture or death and Rohm in lockdown. It's why I . . . contact . . . you like this."

He stared at his arm like it had sprouted wings. "*What?* Sela made her report during the breakout, describing the three Guilders and Alexy contacted Commander Sommersby to tell him we were going to track the escapee and search for Sela. We have full permission and are *supposed* to have backup arriving soon."

There was a pause, long enough that Talos spoke again. "Kris? Are you still there?"

"Still . . . here. But more than one problem now, big brother. Commander S . . . says never heard from you, and report that you and Duvrot staged breakout was submitted . . . by Sela."

CHAPTER 5

*I*t was difficult enough for Tal to keep his feet, much less refrain from screaming his indignation at Kris. The best he could do was pause for a long moment and stare at his boots while his face grew hot and sweaty. He swallowed to return the hot acid to where it belonged in his stomach. He knew the others were listening, and he still had no guarantee that they weren't criminals themselves. But he couldn't simply walk out of the room to continue the conversation.

It might imply some sort of guilt. "Obviously, there's been some sort of mistake. You don't believe I'd be involved in something like that, do you?"

The answer was at least slightly reassuring. "Certainly . . . not. But you realize . . . the problem, yes?"

Tal nodded and let out a slow breath. "Even if Commander Sommersby is somehow involved, nobody would dare stand up and accuse him. And a trace of magic energy at the scene of the breakout will find my, Alexy's, and Sela's signatures. Couple that with Sela's report, and our word won't mean much, eh?"

"Pre . . . cisely. I'm sorry . . . Tal. The best I can . . . offer you is to fight for you down here. Try to find . . . evidence of someone lying."

He shook his head. "I don't want you involved, Kris. If you start digging, you could wind up behind the bars, instead of guarding them."

The abrupt burst of noise could have been a laugh. "Give me some . . . credit, brother. I've already prepared . . . memory potion. Even I won't remember this talk. But I've taken notes that I'll leave for myself at . . . home. And nobody would ever think to . . . look for evidence where I'm speaking to you from."

He tried to imagine where in Rohm nobody would look for Kris. She was a fixture of the best shops and knew every restaurant owner in the city. "Where are you?"

Another burst of laughter. "Dressing room of . . . bridal fitter. Surprisingly good shielding in these places."

Why on earth would a wedding seamstress need shields on the dressing rooms? But he had to admit that nobody would *ever* expect to find his sister there. She'd had both boyfriends and girlfriends in the past, but she was married to her job and considered personal liaisons a form of cheating. It was actually brilliant.

He was surprised to hear a comment from inside the room, reminding him that he was being overheard. It was Candy who spoke, to Mila. "That makes perfect sense. I suppose in a magic society you'd want to prevent jilted exes from cursing a dress or a woman making herself irresistible. Pretty smart, really."

"Do I hear voices . . . Tal? Is someone lis . . . tening in?"

He sighed and shot an annoyed look at the women, who bit lips and blushed apologetically. "I'm at a house topside where Sela lived with a hu . . . another Guilder." It was only fair to identify them properly. It might be an outcast guild, but there was no question they were magicwielders, and quite possibly crafters.

"Didn't know . . . Sela had a . . . home in the overworld. Glad you have some . . . help. Is there anything you . . . need from me before I go back?"

Tal thought back to the questions he and Alexy had raised upstairs. "Yes, actually. Find out if Sela's family has had a change in their standard of living in the past two years that can't be easily explained. Anything outside of inheritances or job changes. You know the right questions. Then, find out if there have been any gatemaking rings broken up by any of the palaces. The gate into Sela's room had to be cast by someone down below. Finally, see if you can get me a list of any guildercents in the Denver area. Maybe Vegre managed to enhance someone."

He heard Mila whisper an aside to her grandmother, "Guildercent?"

The answer was also whispered, again telling Tal that Nadia had once lived among his people. "A human with varying percentages of magic parentage. We once lived side by side after all, and passion infects us all equally."

He was surprised when Mila looked to him for verification. He dipped his head once, not really sure why it was important to him that she understand more about his people. But it was. "Oh, and run a search for my battle glove down there. I'll be interested to see if there's been any sign of it *after* Alexy and I left Rohm."

"Was it taken from you in battle?"

"I threw it through the gate in this world after cloaking

it. If it shows up at all there, we'll get some idea of where they went when they left here." He itched the skin near his mark. The continued discussion this way was making it burn. He could see wisps of smoke as the heat singed his arm hairs. If he didn't stop soon, the skin would blacken and it would be a week or more before he could communicate this way again. But he didn't dare touch it directly. The spell was delicate enough, especially with Kris doing it under cover of shielding. Any disruption could break the connection. But Great Holy Tree, it was getting harder to concentrate.

"That wasn't very . . . smart, brother. Not only will it tie you closer to the criminals if found by . . . wrong people, but being without a focus with a mage of Vegre's abilities on the loose . . . could kill you."

He shrugged, even though she couldn't see it. "All I could think of on short notice. I'll find a rock shop in town to get a temporary crystal."

Kris snorted, making his skin vibrate. "Hardly a substitute for a battle-proven stone. The only decent flawless stones are ones . . . humans wear as decoration. You'll either have to steal one or luck into it without a pile of overworld currency."

Mila's face grew animated and he turned to stare. She cupped a hand to her grandmother's ear and excitedly whispered something. It was too quiet to make it out, but her grandmother smiled and patted her hand, causing Mila to leave the room rather suddenly. He wasn't sure he liked that, but he didn't follow or stop her. It made no sense that he trusted these people, but he couldn't seem to help himself.

"I'll manage. But we're going to have to stop talking soon. A memory potion won't do much to erase scorch marks on your skin."

"True enough. Be very careful, brother. You won't hear from me again until I sift through . . . my notes enough to realize I must have talked to you. I'll try to find out the information and reach you . . . somehow unless . . . blows over before that."

In Kris's usual style, as soon as she was done speaking, she ended the conversation. No closing, no notice. His arm simply stopped burning and the red glow diminished. But with the thousand questions that kept swirling around in his mind, it wasn't until one of the women cleared her throat that he remembered that he was standing motionless, staring at his forearm.

Apparently, they were waiting for him to do or say something. But there was nothing *to* say—at least not until he had a long discussion with Alexy.

Candy stared at him. Giving a delicate cough she nodded in Mila's direction. She'd apparently returned while he was distracted.

Until that moment he had honestly forgotten why they'd come back to the kitchen. Too much was happening, too fast. Kris's news, in particular, had shaken him to the core. Still, there was nothing for it but to soldier on. "My pardon, Mila." He swallowed, hard. "While I must follow the trail of my glove, I believe it is prudent for my partner to stay here, and guard the gate." Candy's eyes, narrowed, so he hastily added, "With your permission, of course."

Nadia Penkin started to wrap a vivid red cloak around herself, embroidered with white and yellow runes. "You know my feelings on this, Mila." She gave a delicate sniff before turning away from the younger woman as she picked up a large carpetbag.

Mila sighed and shook her head as if she were weary of arguing. "Fine. He can stay. There's not much in the fridge, but he can help himself to what's there. Do you have any leads on Sela and Vegre?"

"I've activated the tracking spell. It should be easy enough to follow. The images were quite clear, so they haven't gone far."

"You should've seen it." Candy spoke admiringly. "I could actually watch the whole scene in the flames, and I could hear the voices. It looked like one of the clinics, or maybe a hospital."

Nadia turned, giving Tal a look that showed renewed respect. "Well done, Mage. *Very* well done."

Tal met her eyes without squirming. In truth, he'd been surprised himself that he'd been able to capture sound. He'd never been able to before. Then again, this was his battle glove he was tracking. Perhaps that was it. Then again . . . he shook his head. No. It was his imagination. There was nothing about this place, or these people, that would make his magic stronger.

The old woman's expression grew thoughtful, with just a hint of amusement. "Interesting. It might be that Mila has finally come into her power. It happens at different times for all of us. But it also may be that your magic strengthens each other's. Lifecraft is often drawn to firecraft, like a moth to a flame." She looked at him from underneath a thick woolen cap. "Tell me, Mage—did you feel overheated during the healing? As though you would burst into flame?"

He shook his head. The grandmother was a worldly woman, but he didn't want to admit what he had been feeling at the time. It was even worse when Mila pushed open the door and their eyes met. Once again he could feel her magic push against him, slide through his clothing as though it wasn't there. "I can say that I felt heated, to be sure."

Mila smiled almost shyly. Stepping to within a foot of him she held out her hand. It took some effort to pull his gaze from her heart-shaped face and deep green eyes to look into her open palm. But when he did, he couldn't resist reaching out his hand to touch the object she held. The domed slab of blue-white stone was set in a frame of pure gold and covered most of her small palm. But what intrigued him were the swirls of colors that swept across the face of the gem—cobalt blue, rich crimson, and orange the color of an autumn sunrise. He could feel the energy of the stone. The activation spell still worked and it called to his magic, began to glow like a rainbow as it filled itself with residual energy. He could smell the colors, like individual petals of a flower. "Where under the world did you find a fire opal that size? It's absolutely perfect, and looks like it was intended to be set in a focus glove."

"I don't know anything about focus gloves, but you mentioned needing a loose gemstone, and I had this one upstairs in my jewelry box. I don't remember where I got it, but I've had it for years."

"It was her mother's focus, and her grandfather's before." Nadia's voice reflected a pride that Tal couldn't help but mirror when he heard the next words. "Sylvia has both Parask and Mage blood in her veins. The Bakus line were well respected firecrafters during my time."

He felt his brows raise and he couldn't keep his voice from cracking just a bit from the sudden dryness of his throat. "Was Vladimir Bakus one of your ancestors? The hero of the Ural wars?" He directed the question to Mila, but she just shrugged. It was her grandmother who answered.

"Sadly, Mila would not know. What little she knew of her Guilder ancestry was probably removed in the spell. But yes—her maternal grandfather, five removed, was indeed Craftmaster Bakus of the mage's guild. This was *his* focus stone."

Alexy took that moment to walk in the room, and let out a low whistle at the stone, still glowing nearly a handsbreadth tall in Mila's palm. "Bloody hell, Tal. Where'd that focus come from? It's as big as the commander's."

"Belongs to the ladies, it seems." He motioned to Mila. "She comes down from the Bakus mage line. This was the very focus he wore." Alexy whistled low with raised brows and dipped his head to Mila almost reverently. He might be a dirtdog, but every schoolchild in Agathia had read the old bard tales of the Ural battles between the two mage houses—the Sima, where Bakus crafted, and the Terel, where Vegre's forefathers wove their evil. It was long before the guilds were established and one of the primary reasons *why* they were formed. Hearing that would go a long way to convincing Alexy that the women had more to offer than if they were merely soul-conjurers. But Tal still was reluctant to mention it, at least not until his friend had seen something positive about their craft.

Alexy furrowed his brow. "Um . . . could I talk to you for a moment first?"

He nodded and touched Mila's hand. "It's a lovely stone. Thank you for showing me." He'd turned to follow Alexy out to the next room when she grabbed his arm.

"Wait. You don't understand. This is for you . . . to replace the stone you lost. Your sister said you should have one and, well, it's just been sitting in a drawer in my room. It's a gift."

Both he and Alexy froze, crowded together under the door header, and turned their heads in near unison. If the look of shock on his own face was anything like Alexy's, they looked like fools indeed. "You can't be serious. That's a powerful heirloom stone. I could never—"

Nadia nodded her head sharply. "Mila asked my permission. We have no more mage crafters in our line. But I understand your reluctance, and would feel the same. If you would prefer, consider using the stone temporarily, until you recover yours."

Alexy nudged him in the ribs. "That's a hell of an offer. This would crack that diamond of his right in half with that iron will of yours behind the blast. Imagine . . . the opal that took down the whole Terel clan. Vegre would shake in his boots."

Mila pressed it forward until it nearly touched his cloak. "Please. I know you're going to try to get Sela back. If this can help, it would make me feel better for you to have it. It won't do her any good sitting on my dresser upstairs."

Tal wasn't even sure he could handle a stone this powerful. Although he was old by Agathian standards, he wasn't as powerful a mage as many others. *But imagine the good I can do if I can tame it—*

He nodded and accepted the stone, again feeling the gentle tug as the stone filled its reserves. "A loan then. Not a gift. I promise to return it as soon as Vegre is returned to prison, yes?" Without waiting for a reply, he pushed by Alexy in to the main room. It was too much really, and he was already nervous about being responsible for this important of a stone.

"Hell of a stone, Tal. Really. You'll do it proud."

Tal took a deep breath. "Before you tell me what you found let's sit down for a minute. There's something you need to hear, and you're not going to like it one bit."

CHAPTER 6

$\mathcal{M}$ila took a deep breath as she walked through the hospital's main doors. There was something that had always disturbed her about visiting people in a hospital. It wasn't just the antiseptic smell, or even the faint but lingering scent of bodily functions that bothered her. It was that even the muted colors, sleek architecture, and soft voices couldn't hide that there was so *much* sickness, so much pain.

Things she'd always felt were starting to make sense. She'd felt her bunny's pain, like she'd felt when her sister was sick. Small flashes of memory had been popping back into her head since what happened with Tal in the kitchen. Flowers that covered her hands with glitter, dipping her painted toes in a pond, and feeling very important to be *asked* to. Even though part of her didn't want to believe, she couldn't escape the images that came to her mind unbidden. She couldn't pretend the connection she'd shared with Tal hadn't happened. Worst of all, she couldn't forget what she'd wanted him to . . . *do* to her. Yikes!

And now, the part of her that was remembering, that *needed* to heal, was becoming overwhelmed. Her head began to pound from the pressure and her bones ached enough that she needed to sit down before she fell down.

"You feel it too, yes?" Baba whispered the words softly

as Candy went to the registration desk to ask after Suzanne. "The suffering, the silent cries that tear at your soul? They beg for relief. But remember, you cannot help them all or risk replacing them."

She nodded, feeling slightly out of breath from the press of the dozens . . . no, *hundreds* of patients who unknowingly grabbed at her, tried to snatch some comfort from her healing energy.

"You're shaking and quite pale. Are you in distress?" Tal's voice was warm and concerned.

He was still with them. The trail of his glove had led right here, to this hospital. The knowledge that a dangerous escaped criminal might be hiding among all these helpless people was a sobering one. Taking a deep breath, Mila stiffened her spine. "I'll be okay. It's just a little too much all at once." She turned to smile at him but caught sight of her reflection in the glass of a vending machine before their eyes met. She really was pale. Her skin was almost translucent and her eyes seemed far too bright to be real. She had to blink before she realized it wasn't just reflection off the lights . . . her eyes were glowing a pale, unearthly green. He reached out and touched her arm and her heart caught in her throat. His fingertips felt like a flame-filled hearth on a cold winter day. Even through her down jacket and sweater she could feel the deep soaking warmth. A deep longing filled her and she had to fight not to press herself against him to ease the chill she didn't even know she had.

Candy returned quickly. "The pediatrics unit is in the south wing on this floor." She turned to Baba, "The receptionist said your friend is in room 208." She pointed in the direction of the elevators. "Apparently it's the fourth door down the hall to the right when you get off the elevators."

Baba gave a curt nod and turned to leave, but stopped at the sight of Candy's brother hurrying across the lobby toward them.

"Candy, you're here! And you brought the Penkins with you."

The relief in his voice was palpable, and it brought Mila up short. She'd known him almost all her life, but she'd never seen him look like this. It was normal for a parent to worry about their child prior to surgery, but the big blond man seemed almost frantic. His clothes were rumpled, his hair mussed, as if he'd been tearing at it with his hands, and his deep blue eyes had dark circles under them. The girl was only here for a tonsillectomy after all—a routine thing.

"Tim, what's wrong? Is she all right?"

He shook his head, his expression growing frustrated. "I don't know. They *say* it's fine. I suppose I should believe them. They're the doctors. But it *feels* wrong, like something's *sucking* at her; and nobody believes me. They just keep passing it off as parental hysterics." He turned to Baba. "Can you do an egg-rolling on her? Please? My wife thinks I'm crazy, but I don't care. I know it works. I remember how much good you did in the neighborhood. I might not have the healing gift you and Mila do, but I could always sense things. And there's something wrong with my baby."

Baba's expression grew grave. "I believe you." She patted his arm with her hand. "But I am old, and not as strong as I once was. Mila has come into her power. She is stronger than I and will do the rolling for your daughter." She opened the carpetbag to pull out a yellow styrofoam box of eggs. Flipping it open, she removed two, sliding one in each of the two pockets of her cape. Then, closing the lid she pressed the box into Mila's hand.

"You can do this, child. I know it. Just concentrate hard to remember what I taught." She turned to Candy. "You will know where I am if you need me."

At that she turned and bustled off, leaving Mila feeling confused and more than a little nervous. Tim was looking at her with such desperate expectation that it was honestly frightening. What if she failed? What if what she did didn't help the child, but actually made things worse? What if she drained herself too far and couldn't stop? She abruptly remembered *that* part of the past far too clearly—the danger of dying.

"Please, Mila." Candy whispered the plea, and when Mila turned to face her friend she saw tears brimming in those beautiful blue eyes.

Candy didn't say another word, and she didn't need to. She had no children of her own, and doted on her ten-year-old niece.

Taking a deep breath to steady herself, Mila tried to project a level of confidence that couldn't be further from her true feelings. "Of course." She gave Candy an encouraging smile. "No problem."

Candy's return look carried such a weight of trust and hope that Mila was afraid she'd be crushed beneath it. But she had no choice. Not really. She was Parask, and as Baba had said, the Parask did not refuse to heal just because the way was difficult.

"Thank you so much. This means more to me than you know." Tim reached over to give Mila's shoulders a squeeze before hurriedly leading the women down the hall to the south wing. It wasn't until they were nearly there that she realized that sometime during the conversation in the lobby Talos had disappeared. And while she knew he had his own business to attend to, she was surprised at how keenly she felt his absence.

*T*al regretted having to leave without so much as a word to his companions, but at least he had his eyes on one of the *true* criminals, so that was something. Mila had good instincts, among her other . . . *attributes* which, even now, he was struggling not to concentrate too much on. Those glowing eyes, so filled with magic that he wanted to wrap himself inside. And she didn't *remember* their kind? It made him nearly sick to his stomach that someone would do that to her.

No, better to return to the task at hand. Mila's gaze had

kept moving toward a particular man in the lobby, as if she noticed something odd about him. The action had drawn Tal's attention to the man despite magical concealments. It was the witcher, the one who'd kicked Alexy, and he was searching the hospital for something . . . or *someone*.

While the others were distracted, Tal pulled on the power of the stone Mila had given him to create his own magical cloaking and followed the Guilder out a side door of the building and into a darkened corner near the parking garage where a second man was waiting. It was dark enough that he didn't have to worry about been seen, so he allowed the cloaking spell to slip off his skin. The familiar lightheaded sensation followed as the frayed edges fluttered into the breeze. Casting, for him, was much like attaching small lead weights to his clothing. At first you hardly noticed them. But the further you traveled, the quicker you tired. It wasn't difficult, but the concentration required to maintain distance and speed was taxing.

"Did you get them? He's grown tired of waiting." Tal's attention was drawn to the nearby conversation. Edging closer until his back was pressed against the cool concrete, while the smell of auto exhaust stole his breath, he listened intently to the whispers from the shadowy figures.

A small rustle was followed by a trembling tenor. "No. She hasn't called me yet, Cardon. I don't know what the problem is. All I'm getting is her voice mail."

The resulting growl from the witcher, Cardon, made the first man flinch. "I told you before, Bowers—don't *ever* call me by my name. Names have power where I come from."

Indeed they did, and Tal couldn't help but smile. There couldn't be many men in the witch guild with such a name. Five years ago, it would have been short work to bespell the man at a distance, without knowing a thing about him, to make him reveal all he knew. But such techniques were very magic-intensive, and were now only used in the most dire cases. Still, there were enough lesser spells that could be cast with a name that the same purpose could be achieved. Cardon . . . it didn't sound like a given name, but he knew most of the surnames of the older witch families, and didn't recognize it. *I'll have Alexy check it out when we meet back up at the house.*

Whether she liked it or no, Mila's house would be their temporary base until they could make other arrangements. There were layers of protective spells already in place. Too, he wanted to keep an eye on the Penkin women—and not just because the younger was so distractingly pretty.

By now Alexy should have contacted several guildercent friends in the city to try to find another place for them to lay low when it was time to move on. They needed time to figure out what was happening below. He'd been right— Alexy hadn't liked the news from Kris at all. But after he'd finished a vigorous, and rather creative round of swearing, he'd calmed down and helped to plan their next move. They'd agreed there must be a reason *why* Sela had chosen to live with Mila Penkin, yet not ever discuss Agathia or her role in the O.P.A.

Bower's voice snapped him out of his musings. "I'm sorry, Car . . . I mean, *sir.* She was supposed to get them at a lunch meeting and call me, but something must have happened. Tell Vegre I'll keep trying, no matter how long it takes. Where can I reach you after you leave here?"

Cardon let out a muffled noise that could have been a swear, a curse, or just a note of frustration. "There's no way to reach me once I leave. Even satellite signals can't get through to Vril."

Tal fought the impulse to laugh out loud. Short of returning to the foot of the prison, Vril was the one spot in all of Agathia where Vegre couldn't hide from him. Tal had both family and friends in Vril. Someone would have noticed Vegre and the others. It was a tight-knit community where strangers didn't often tread. *If only there was some way to go there myself . . . talk to people directly.* News traveled slowly to the region, set deep under the mountain range the topsiders called the Appalachians. Unfortunately, neither he nor Alexy had enough local currency to hire transit that far. Unless perhaps the women—

"We'll find you. Just get the package, locate the source, and stay put until we come for you."

"Oh . . . um, about that." Bowers's voice raised a few notes and he edged away from Cardon. "See, after the old guy dumped his stock and killed himself rather than sell to me, I decided to be more cautious."

Cardon froze and raised one hand. It didn't seem to frighten Bowers, but Tal tensed and struggled not to leap out to stop the possible murder. "You're making me nervous, Bowers. Tell me everything now, or I'll have my master ask you instead."

Bowers raised his hands and waved them quickly. "No, no. It's not a bad thing. It's just that I hired a third party to do the buying this time. It's her job—she acts as a middleman when a buyer doesn't want his name known. So, I don't know the name of the crafter who's actually *making* the eggs. You hadn't said that locating the artist was *required*." The tone of his voice made it clear that he didn't relish that part of the job, and was trying to find some way around what was being required of him—which made Tal suspicious about what would happen to the artists he *located*.

Cardon lowered his hand and instead grabbed the front of Bowers's shirt, pulling him close. "Listen to me. The instructions were very clear and didn't include *third parties*. You find psyanky crafters in the city, you buy their stock of eggs, deliver them to me with the location of the crafter, and dispose of them in a way that doesn't make the authorities ask questions. Nothing more." He shoved him away so hard that Bowers hit the building wall with a thud and then slid down to the ground, groaning. "Now, you get your ass back to work. You find this so-called *third party,* make her tell you the name of the crafter, and do the job you're being paid for. Otherwise, your services will no longer be required. You know what happens then."

Bowers leaned forward with a small sob, clutching at the other man's flowing cloak. "No! No, please, Cardon. You promised to use your magic to save my wife. You visited her room, right? She's going to be okay?"

Cardon's voice lowered to an ominous chuckle. "That's not why I was here, as you well know. I was looking for the woman. But yes, I did look in on your mate and did the first part to cast away the sickness. Still, what can be cast can be removed, Bowers. She's safe . . . for now. But by the Blessed Tree, if you don't . . . no, wait. I'll amend our bargain. If you're too *squeamish* to do what you agreed, then deliver the name and location of the crafter when you turn over the eggs. We'll handle the rest."

Bowers looked up so that his silhouette was that of a beggar praying for relief. "And you'll still heal Maria? You swear?"

"You wife will be healed from her cancer. My word." There was a sickly sweet edge to the voice that made Tal not trust the words, but Bowers apparently didn't hear it, because he collapsed, burying his face in his hands in relieved tears. One of Cardon's boots raised up and he kicked Bowers away from him. "Now get out of my sight until you have those eggs." With a flourish of cloth, Cardon swirled and stalked into the darkness.

There was no need to follow Cardon. Tal knew where he was going. It was Bowers he needed to keep track of. Luckily, he was fairly certain the man was either full human or a very low guildercent who wouldn't notice a tracking spell. By the time he met with Cardon again, it would have done its purpose. Then it would just be a matter of finding out what it was Vegre was trying to gather. It must have something to do with increasing his power over either the human or magic world. Nothing less would be worthwhile to Vegre. Tal had read his profile during his stint of guarding at Rohm. He was what the humans called a "classic megalomaniac." To crush, to destroy, or to rule as despot. It was all he lived for, and no mere prison sentence—regardless of the number of centuries, would change that.

Tal closed his eyes and concentrated. Hearing Cardon and Bowers talk about eggs reminded him forcibly of Mila. Using the focus that had been in her family for generations gave him a ready link to her. With next to no effort his magic linked to hers, and he felt the power of her working. There was a darkness underneath the spell that made him wonder what in blazes was happening.

Bowers was getting up, but Tal felt irresistibly compelled to check on Mila, and he couldn't be two places at once. *Wait. Bowers said his wife is here.* And, if she has a serious disease, she won't be leaving soon—especially after a "miraculous" cure. Human doctors distrusted the unexplained until there was no other choice. She would be here for several days to come, going through tests to verify what healing magic might achieve. Yet, Cardon didn't seem the type to be a healer. Perhaps even that was a lie. *But either way, Maria Bowers isn't going anywhere soon.* It was time to head back inside and find out why he felt so uneasy.

"Carole, be a doll and get me some coffee from the cafeteria?" Tim put a wheedling note into his voice. His wife gave him a long look through narrowed eyes, but rose from her seat next to the child's bed. Mila got the distinct impression that, had the others not been present, Carole would have snapped at her husband, telling him to get his own damned coffee.

Still, she went, which was the main thing, with Candy and Tim following her out into the hall to guard the door so that Mila could work undisturbed.

The child hadn't even stirred. In fact, she was so still and pale—her skin nearly as white as the starched sheets on the bed—it was alarming. Mila didn't even need to open her senses to know that something was seriously wrong with this child that had nothing to do with inflamed tonsils.

Stepping next to the bed she gently stroked her hand across the child's smooth cheek. *I'll do what I can, Suzanne,* she promised. *Hang in there.*

First, I need to see where the damage is. She closed her eyes and let her mind drift, forcing aside her sorrow to look at the sickness as a *thing*. More flashes of memory swept back. Darkened bedrooms in strange houses where old people speaking strange languages moaned and wept. And Baba gently encouraging her to open herself. Then more memories of Baba walking through the gardens with her, encouraging her to let the energy of the flowers fill her to refresh her after a healing. She remembered Viktor in that moment. He always reminded her of Friar Tuck from the Robin Hood stories, with a ring of white hair and a chubby tummy under a plain cotton tunic.

The recollection sharpened and it cleared her mind. She closed her eyes and opened herself. The moment her inner eye focused, she saw a pattern of colors. But then violent revulsion swept through her and her whole body recoiled so hard that her knees hit the sidewall of the adjoining bed.

Squirming, pulsing tendrils of blackish-purple energy covered Suzanne's torso. They chewed away at the rainbow of other colors she'd come to expect from the girl. Mila had never seen anything like it in her life, and didn't have a clue where to start to remove it. She leaned forward slightly and tried to sort out where it had originated and where it was going next.

There. It had started on the neck. There was a black spot, almost like a burn, just under Suzanne's jaw. It was the darkest point on her small body, and all the runners were below it. Mila opened her eyes to see if there was any other sort of mark on her skin. She felt a surge of satisfaction when she spotted it. The faint bruise, in the final stages of yellow and pale green, was the contact point for the sickness. But now it was a question of what caused the bruise. She presumed that the doctors here would have checked for poison and drugs, considering she was getting ready for surgery. So she discounted them, as well as any sort of known childhood illness. Another flash. This *wasn't* something she recognized—and she realized she knew what chicken pox, measles, mumps, and even meningitis *looked like.* Even a few rare cases from the old country . . . smallpox and radiation sickness, that had made her grandmother call in specialists. This was something totally new to her. She'd never seen this pattern, nor encountered so dark and pervasive a color shift.

Perhaps *liak*? Could this be a fear sickness? Should she do a wax reading to find out what sort of fear?

The part of her brain that was still trying to comprehend all these strange *new* ideas was appalled at the thought of using folk medicine over the obvious benefits of a hospital, yet her brain kept twirling on until the skeptic in her was silenced.

"There wouldn't be a bruise with fear sickness," she mulled under her breath while tapping one finger on her leg. "And it must have happened days ago by the condition. It's just taken this long to manifest. No, something attacked you . . . whether intentionally or by mistake. What was it, sweetie? *Who* was it?" She whispered the words, knowing that Suzanne couldn't answer.

There was no time to lose. She'd originally thought it was overkill to bring along a whole ten eggs, but Baba had been right—*better to be prepared than be forced to return later.*

She reached into the carton and removed the first egg. Her fingers checked it for damage by sheer muscle memory. A quiet rustling in her mind reminded her that the slightest crack would make it ineffective.

But no, it was perfect . . . snowy white and now warm to the touch between her sheltering palms. Words flashed like lightning the moment she stroked the smooth shell and she couldn't help but speak them. *"Misiatsiu novyi, sriblo-zlotyi, dorohyi,"* she whispered in Ukrainian, and would follow in English. Yes, that was right. Baba had taught her the incantations, but decided her accent of the old tongue was so poor that the extra words would guarantee the healing spirits would understand what was being asked of them. "New moon, golden-silver moon, dear." With a flourish, she held the cupped egg to the window. Darkness was falling outside and she could see the faint edges of the moon through thick clouds. "*Pomahai, ochyshchui vse.* Help, cleanse all. *Zmyvai, obchyst', obmyi, osviaty.* Wash, cleanse, wash, bless. *Shchob buva zdorovyi, iasnyi, chystyi, iak, ty.* So she will be as healthy, as bright, as pure as you."

Mila felt the warmth in the egg increase, felt healing energy fill it until it seemed to glow with an inner light and vibrated against her skin. Rolling the egg on Suzanne would be like placing a baking soda poultice on a bug bite. It would both suck out the sickness into the egg and pour healing energy in its place. A shiver flowed over her skin and a buzzing filled her ears as she stepped toward the bed. As always, the scent of fruit blossoms filled her nose, covering over the faint but lingering scents of cleansers. "*Schhob ii bile tilo, zhovti kosti, chervona krov, syni zhyly.* That her white body, yellow bones, red blood, blue veins—" She placed the egg down on Suzanne's neck with closed eyes. Panic surged through her for a moment. The girl's back arched and her mouth opened wide, as though screaming. The egg fought violently against her pressing palms, struggling against whatever this was. "*Tsila ii budova, duly zdorovymy vid vsiakoi boli!* Her entire body would be healthy from all pain!"

With a reverberating screech, the egg exploded and her eyes shot open. Black goo covered the white sheets, thick as tar and smelling of sulphurous rotten egg. "Dear Heavens, what *is* this sickness?" There was no time to think about the fallout of a staff member walking in and seeing . . . and worse, *smelling* this mess. She reached for another egg and repeated the incantation, more quickly this time. The second egg also exploded, and the black tendrils she could see behind her eyelids had only shrunk the tiniest bit. It would take a *case* of eggs to remove this and it could easily take hours. The only thing she could do at this point was to patch things up as best she could and have a talk with Baba about how to proceed.

But . . . could she do the same thing for Suzanne that she'd done for Talos? Could she attach to the girl, use waves of her own life force to heal, instead of relying on the tiny bits of energy that the eggs would hold?

It was certainly worth a try, because what she'd done in the kitchen had only taken a few moments. There should be plenty of time. The risk was that if she opened her senses fully, the very thing that Baba had warned against might happen. She could accidentally seize onto the life force of someone who couldn't afford to lose it. *Or worse, every patient here might be able to attach to me—drain me completely.* Hadn't Baba once talked of healers who had been killed in the course of a healing? Mila couldn't imagine any worse way to die.

But Candy would never forgive her if she didn't at least *try,* and there was a good chance she wouldn't be able to come back if Carole had her say.

She looked again at Suzanne's pale face, once again relaxed against the pillow. She was better, but it wasn't enough. Mila knew she really had no choice. She needed to do this now, before she lost her nerve. Rising to her full height she steadied her stance and fixed her inner eye on the dark tentacles blossoming from Suzanne's chest. There was no word for this, no rhyme or spell to be spoken. Instead, she had to open the door.

The moment she thought about it, another memory assaulted her. Baba had once explained that there was a locked vault door to all the magic in the world in her head. She'd actually taken Mila and Candy to a bank where she convinced the manager to show the two of them how the vault was constructed. "You see," she'd explained, "the bars . . . how they slide into the wall in all the ways? That makes it strong—hard for those who seek to get in to break it. You must make such a door, Mila. Soon . . . soon it will be important that you lock yourself away, for it is not you that is locking the magic *in,* but the magic that you are locking *out.* Too much magic can contaminate, give sickness until you are stronger."

And so she made a door, added layers and locks over the years—not even recalling she was doing it until today.

But when she walked in the door earlier and had felt the needy reaching out to her, she'd strengthened the locks, spun the dial so they couldn't get in. Even the incantation earlier was a form of lock. Like opening a single safe-deposit box in a vast room, each egg could only hold so much life force. Now she needed to open them *all*.

Except for the minor detail that I've never done it before. It had just *happened* in the kitchen. No planning, no intent. She hadn't remembered it was there. And now she was so conscious of it, she was afraid it would stick closed.

Ever cautious of the sheer force of what could come through, she carefully began to unseal the locks in her head. She was still stinging from earlier, and wished she had a few hours to do this properly. Releasing a breath she didn't even know she was holding, she cracked open the door, preparing herself for the neon bright rainbow of colors that made up healing magic.

Where is it? The ever-present rainbow was gone. It was still and dark in the vault, without so much as a whisper of sound or energy. Cool, dim, silent, and utterly without the ebb and flow of life around her. Had she used more than she'd planned with the eggs, or with Talos? Had she burned herself out by attempting such drastic healing twice in a day? Another vivid memory—of her grandmother, lying on the bed exhausted after a day of wandering the streets, healing the sick. Baba had never done more than one or two wax readings and five eggs in a day. "To do more is risking much," she would always say.

But this sickness could infect the rest of the hospital in a short time, so Mila turned her eye inward.

There was a wall there, just past the door. She could see it now. It was tall and dark and imposing. Had it always been there? She couldn't remember, but it didn't seem right. Could this be the memory block, the thing that was keeping her from her past?

Why would her mother do something like that? What would possess her to hide an entire childhood away from her own daughter? Was there something behind the wall that was terrifying, that she *shouldn't* try to resurrect? That was the problem with memories. If you didn't remember the what, you didn't remember the *why*.

The whisper sounded loud in the quiet room. "But I can't let myself be bowed by fear of the unknown. That's not fair to Suzanne."

She stepped forward in her mind toward the wall. Already there were chinks from where bright lights flowed. She pushed against the wall and realized that instead of hard and brittle, it was squishy and sticky, like taffy chewed too long. Revealing the past could take *years* if she had to pull them out one at a time.

Or she could burn it away in one blast with magic.

The moment the thought struck her, something behind the wall screamed for her to do it. Was the eagerness she suddenly felt a good thing, or a bad one?

Suzanne moaned in pain, bringing her back to the problem at hand. She had no choice. The child would die if she didn't remember whatever it was that was eluding her.

Mila opened herself and took a deep breath. She called on the power she'd felt flow through her. It connected with people in the hospital and beyond . . . one by one. With a force of will she didn't realize she was capable of, she threw a ball of energy the size of a small sun against the sticky wall in her mind. There was a shudder as new magic met old and then fire seared her mind. Wave upon wave of memories, good and bad, flowed like a tsunami—her life flashing before her eyes. Pain erupted in her head like a migraine from hell itself, and she wondered how she was even still standing.

And then she realized she wasn't—

CHAPTER 7

"*W*ha . . . hap'n?" Mila's eyes opened. She was in the back seat of Candy's SUV, with her friend giving her a worried look from the driver's position.

She couldn't seem to fumble words around in her head and her tongue felt two sizes too big for her mouth. Her head was pounding enough that even her eyes seemed to be throbbing.

"That's what I'd like to know." Tal's voice was harsh as he spoke through the open door. He climbed into the SUV, slamming the door behind him with enough force to make the vehicle rock. Candy flinched, but it was all Mila could do to keep the contents of her stomach *in* her stomach where they belonged. She let out a little whimper of distress, but there was no sympathy in his eyes.

"It's family business—and none of yours," Candy snapped. "Don't you have criminals to catch?"

Mila blinked at her friend, her jaw slack from utter shock. It was a deliberately rude thing to say and Candy was *never* rude.

"Well, it *isn't* any of his business." Candy answered Mila's look.

Talos's eyes narrowed and Mila felt heat filling the car in a rush that didn't help her nausea. "You're hiding something. I felt the magic. And anyone could have *smelled* the result of the working. Where did you take the girl? Your niece's doctor is in an uproar, berating the nurses for letting a patient leave without permission. Your sister-by-marriage is practically hysterical because her child is missing. She keeps babbling about her husband and *witchcraft*." Apparently, that was a bad, bad thing in his world, because his voice dropped by several notes and took on a threatening tone. "I ask you again—*what happened?*"

He was staring at Mila now, his eyes practically boring holes into her skull. It was a very aggressive expression, and it made him look dangerous as hell. Mila could actually feel him gathering his will, and wondered if there was a spell he could cast to force someone to reveal what they knew.

Candy slapped her hand on the top of the seat to get his attention. "Stop it! She doesn't know. She was unconscious, and my brother waited to leave until after we'd brought her out to the car."

He turned his head ever so slowly, away from Mila and toward Candy, who squirmed under the intensity of his glare. But her lips were pressed shut, her expression mutinous.

"What . . . *happened?*" It wasn't a spell, but there was a force of will behind his words that was almost as compelling.

"Candy—" Mila's voice was stern. Talos might not be part of the human authorities, but he was a cop—a magical cop—and magic was at the root of this. Whatever was happening was dangerous. She knew it without question. The snippets of memories had become full-length feature films in her head and a thrill of fear sang through her at the mere thought of the vicious illness that had been consuming Suzanne. He might be able to help, but only if they trusted him.

Candy looked helplessly from one to the other. If she was looking for a sign of weakness, she didn't find one. The two were absolutely united in their demand for the truth.

In the end, she caved. "Fine. But I don't know much." She turned to Mila. "We heard a crash and came through the door to find you collapsed on the floor. Tim ran to get Baba. When she got to the room she told me that you'd be fine, but we needed to get you away from the hospital, that all the sickness there would just drain you more. So Tim brought you out to the car. She also told us that they needed to take Suzanne to a specialist, someone who would know all about her illness, and who could keep her isolated so that it wouldn't spread. Tim agreed, so they left to take her to Viktor's house for treatment."

"So that *what* wouldn't spread? What did she say was wrong?" Mila was almost frantic to find out. "I've never seen anything like it." She turned her head to face Talos. "I blacked out because I was able to break through whatever mental block had been put on me, but the power overwhelmed me. I didn't mean to scare anyone—especially the doctors. I just wanted to help her."

"It wasn't anything I've ever heard of, Mila. It has a weird name, it almost sounded . . . I dunno, maybe like *his* kind of thing. She called it Teen something-or-other." Candy gestured toward the man in the passenger seat.

Talos's expression turned grim and his hands clenched into fists almost involuntarily. A fine trembling began in his muscles and the color dropped out of his cheeks. Mila suddenly realized he wasn't angry anymore. He was *terrified*.

"Was it *Tin Czerwona?*" He said it so it sounded like *teen chairvona* and she immediately recognized it as a Ukrainian term, but she didn't understand what it meant.

Candy blinked with surprise and nodded. "That's it. Is that bad?"

The eerie calm of his voice stilled her friend's breath at the same moment Mila's heart dropped into her stomach. "If you consider Armageddon bad, then yes."

CHAPTER 8

"You don't have to keep following right at my back, you know." Mila shrugged back her shoulder as she inserted the key in the door. She expected to bump into Tal . . . and did. It wasn't just the fact that he was being so pushy physically, either. His annoyance, born of fear, had created a rippling wave of heat that was quite literally melting the snow around them both. It was nice at first—took the place of the faulty heater in the car, but now she was sweating.

"Like hell I don't." The words were uttered in a near whisper through gritted teeth, as he held his ground despite her nudge. "It's bad enough that your grandmother snuck out right under my nose, but if Candy hadn't broken under questioning, I never would have known about a potential plague to both our people." He shook his head and let out a small growl as she turned the knob. "*Tin Czerwona* . . . and she didn't say a *word!*"

Mila stepped through the door, shrugging off her jacket before she even made it past the entry rug. "She didn't *break under questioning.* You make it sound like there were bright lights and rubber hoses involved. Candy's a good, honest woman . . . as is Baba. I'm sure there's a perfectly good reason why she took Suzanne to Viktor instead of telling your OPU, or whatever the letters are." She draped her jacket over the armrest of the nearest mahogany spoon-back chair and put her purse on the seat. Then she took a moment to settle her nerves by running her fingertips along the clean lines of the dark wood. The chairs had always been her favorites—and her love of them, along with everything else in the house, was apparently what made Lillian leave it to her.

Footsteps sounded upstairs and they turned their faces expectantly toward the stairs. Alexy rounded the corner and started down toward them, still dressed in his heavy woolen cloak. Either he'd just been out or was ready to leave.

"O.P.A.—Overworld Police Agency. And there's *no* reason good enough to take that sort of risk." He strode forward, intentionally bumping her shoulder even though she wasn't in his way. But he had a point, so she didn't rise to the bait of him being pushy. "Alexy, we've got trouble. You're not going to *believe* what happened out there. How did you do contacting your guildercent friends? We're going to need every pair of hands we can find."

Alexy didn't meet his eyes. He clopped to the bottom of the stairs and walked right by them, stopping only when he was close to the front door. "Didn't try." That pulled Tal up short and he raised questioning brows. After a long moment, Alexy finally let out a harsh breath and looked at him, one hand on the doorknob. "I'm going back, Tal. I didn't think it would be fair to leave before you got back, but I've got to go back and face the music—try to salvage some small part of my career."

"What are you talking about?" Tal's face was a study in astonishment. "You can't go *back*. I told you . . . there's corruption in the highest levels. You'll be put in prison and your career really *will* be over. And that's if you survive to see a hearing before the king."

The other man let out a snort that was equal parts derision and anger. "Yes, *you* told me. I have *your word* . . . nothing else. Tal, you're like a brother to me, but you always do this. You believe every negative thing you hear about the system, and pass it on as gospel. How many times have we finished up a case, risked everything to follow your hunches, only to discover that your predictions of doom simply didn't happen?" There was a long moment of intense staring between the two men. Tal looked away first. "You have good instincts . . . I've always said so. But nobody's showed up here, out for blood, while you've been gone. No queue of troops to arrest us. No notices in the human media about a killer at large to panic us and make us run right into an O.P.A. net. Who's to say Kris wasn't playing a practical joke on you? Wouldn't be the first time."

Tal paused, his blue eyes moving from flashing anger to unease. "I . . . she wouldn't do—"

Alexy shook his head sadly. "Wouldn't do that? Bloody hell, Tal, we're talking about *Kris* here—the woman who glued the toe of one of your boots to the backside of Captain Sommersby's trousers during training! Netted you a week of scrubbing stone floors with your own toothbrush, if I remember correctly." He fastened the neck hook of the cloak and let out a slow breath. "Look, the longer we're gone, without word, the worse it'll be for us. We're in a brownout now, or I'd contact someone using my mark. But the magic scan took all of my focus power, so I'll have to go back on foot. I'm going to leave you my focus and the scan, just in case you're right and I'm walking into a trap." He apparently surprised Tal with that admission, especially when he smiled and winked. "Like I say, I do trust your instincts. But I've got my master's trials next week. I can't risk not being there for them. I've spent years getting ready to become a master craftsman. I'll be the first in three generations of my family. Even prison's better than going back to the third ring as a failure. I won't go back there, Tal." The intensity in his eyes, the determination, was something Mila had seen before—often in a mirror. He wasn't budging, no matter what the consequence, and she realized she respected him for it.

Talos nodded seriously, his shoulders now slumped in defeat. "I know you won't, old friend . . . and you shouldn't have to. It never occurred to me that it might be one of Kris's elaborate jokes, but you're right that she's done worse. You go if you must and say whatever you have to about me to keep your position and your place in the trials. I know you'll do well." He smiled with a warmth Mila hadn't thought him capable of just moments before.

Alexy gave a tolerant, slightly amused shake of his head. "You know better than that, Tal. I'd never implicate you. I'll just tell the truth. Nothing beats the truth. Say it loud and often enough and the right people will hear it. I'll tell them what we know about Vegre and what we saw here, and that's it. I don't have to mention this house or the gate if you don't want me to. That way, you can keep searching without interference. I can come up with some excuse why you're still here, or say I simply don't know where you are."

"In a few minutes, that'll be true. I got a lead at the hospital. I was going to tell you about it, but at this point, it's probably better if you don't know."

It seemed odd to her that he was giving up so easily,

considering how concerned he was that Suzanne not reach his home world. But if he was hiding something . . . some other reason to let his friend leave, he was really good at it. Regardless, Alexy nodded agreement with a grateful look. "Well, I should be going. It's a long walk back to Castle Rock and it's not getting any warmer outside."

That made Mila reach for her purse. "Geez—I didn't realize you were planning on *walking*. Castle Rock's like fifteen *miles* from here." She pulled out the wad of bills Candy had given her earlier and peeled off a hundred, then walked over and handed it to Alexy. "At least take a cab to wherever you're going, and get some dinner while you're at it. Consider it thanks for wasting your afternoon here while we went to the hospital."

That brought a wide grin. It dissolved away the worry that had been etched on his face and made her realize that a smile was his normal state. "Food . . . and warm travel? I'd normally decline on pride issues, but my stomach just overruled my integrity." He hooked a finger her way and tipped his head toward Tal. "Hang onto this one if you're going to be up here much longer. A woman of means is worth keeping nearby."

A laugh bubbled up before she could stop it. "Hardly a *woman of means*. You're just benefitting from my selling a few eggs."

A searing hot hand on her shoulder made her flinch. She turned to see Tal's face in suddenly intense lines. "Eggs? What sort of eggs?"

She shrugged and then pointed toward the fireplace. "Pysanky. I design and sell eggs as a hobby . . . like that one on the mantel there."

While it wasn't one of her most elaborate designs, the black-on-white design was striking. Even though displayed very plainly on a block of lacquered wood, the hen's egg commanded attention. Tal was drawn toward it, but before he took more than a single step, he apparently remembered that Alexy was ready to leave. Pulling his attention back to his friend, he held out his hand. "Luck to you, then, old friend. I pray I'm wrong about the situation. You'll let me know for certain when you can?"

Alexy gave his friend a warm smile. "You know us dirt-dogs, mate. If you're not floating in the air somewhere, I can get a message to you." On seeming impulse, he reached down and grabbed a handful of soil from the potted jade tree on the small table next to the door and dropped it in the top of one boot. "This'll keep me in touch better than anything. I can communicate through the soil here. Just talk to the tree to reach me. I can't imagine they'll take my boots even if they toss me in irons. Too cold this time of year." Alexy then reached out his hand. But instead of the simple handshake Mila was accustomed to, they clasped each other's forearms tight and held for a long moment. The sense of brotherhood; comradery between them was obvious. "Stay safe, Tal. Know that I'll be working back home to bring Vegre to justice and to bring you home a hero for your efforts at the prison."

Tal let out a small chuckle. "I failed, Alexy. He got away without a scratch. They don't hand out badges of heroism for that." But then his jaw set and she could see a fierce determination fill his eyes. "But I *will* bring him back, and with the Tree as my witness, I will make him pay for the pain he's caused."

"I know you will. And that's why they'll be unfurling the banners on your return."

Even after the door closed behind him, Tal stood for a long moment silently, apparently lost in his own thoughts. Mila wasn't quite sure what to say or do. The scent of cinnamon and herbs was still strong in the air, and she wondered whether Alexy had been drinking tea while they were gone to infuse the fragrance in the air so far from the kitchen. The seconds ticked by on the old grandfather clock in the corner. The tiny whir of movement that always accompanied the minute hand just before the hour struck broke the frozen moment. While she didn't mind if he continued to gather his thoughts, there wasn't much time to grab the things she needed before driving to the cave. At least she remembered where it was now. That was something. She turned and moved past Tal. He didn't budge, didn't even seem to notice her movement. Moments ago, that would have thrilled her because he'd been so annoyingly in her face and angry. But now . . . there was something different about this stillness that worried her.

It wasn't until she was finishing putting on heavier socks that she finally heard him moving around downstairs. The sound felt almost comforting, in a weird way. Maybe it was because she was so accustomed to the absolute silence in this big old house. Sela was so seldom home, after all, and now she was—*Sela. I hope you're safe, wherever you are.*

"Mila, what manner of witchery is this that you've crafted?" Tal's voice floated up the staircase. He wasn't yelling, but something about the words caused her to hurry and finish putting on the heavy leather boots she'd pulled out from the back of the closet.

By the time she reached the top of the stairs, she could hear a strange chirping. No, more a humming—like a recording of sopranos being played too fast. She tipped her head past the bannister when she reached the bottom of the stairs and found Tal staring in awe at the little pysanka on the mantel. But it was no longer a simple black-and-white egg. It was glowing with the strength of a hundred-watt bulb and vibrating in the indentation that kept it upright on the block of wood. It wasn't the vibration that was making the noise, though. That seemed to come from within the egg, as though something was alive inside . . . and struggling to get out.

She walked up to it and stared alongside him. "What did you do to my egg? Why is it glowing and humming like that?"

He turned his head and raised his brows. "I was going to ask you the same thing. Is something wrong with it?"

She found herself shrugging and shaking her head. "I don't know what could be *wrong*. It's just an egg. It's not like it's a bomb or anything. Or, at least, it didn't *used* to be. Could it have something to do with this whole mess? The weird portal thingy or Sela?"

That gave him a thoughtful expression and he reached into the pocket of his slacks. She suddenly realized he'd removed the cloak he'd worn since he'd arrived. The charcoal-gray shirt he wore matched the cloak perfectly, but seemed made of pure silk. It flowed and stretched over his muscles like a living creature that was even more entrancing than the egg. That seemed just *wrong,* though, so she focused her attention back on the thing that could very well turn her house into a smoking pile—with her underneath.

Tal removed the fire opal and held it out toward the egg. *"Lapaty."* The word startled her, because it was not only Ukrainian, but one of the words Baba had used over and over when she was a child. It meant "catch" and she could still remember trying to wrap her tongue around the language—so strange sounding to her little American brain. Even when Baba had changed the letters from Cyrillic to the ones she recognized, they weren't pronounced the same. The 'a's were too hard, the 'y's were actually soft 'i's and the 'i's carried the sound of 'ch.' Even Candy had picked up on it quicker than Mila. But she still recognized the words when she heard them, even if she had to concentrate to re-create the word later.

The egg immediately reacted to the word. The humming stopped and moments later, so did the glowing. It was just a pretty pysanka again, with interlaced suns and trees covering the snowy whiteness. "What did you just do to it? Was that word some sort of spell, and where did you learn the Ukrainian language? You and Alexy both sound British—well, him more than you, but still." She was babbling, and she knew it, but it just seemed a day for it.

He pursed his lips and stared at the gold-bound stone. "There are any number of words, in many languages, that serve to focus power. The word itself has no power. It's just a vehicle for the will. And I have no idea what I just did. All I cast was a simple test to see if the glow from the egg was magical energy. It is, and it's of such a pure quality that it nearly stings my tongue."

"Your *tongue?*" *Could he somehow taste magic? What would it taste like?* Now that the egg wasn't glowing anymore, she reached out to pick it up—barely resisting the urge to stick out her tongue to catch whatever taste it held. Tal's hand shot out to stop her, but it was already in her hand. It felt warmer than the room, as though it was a healing egg after it had absorbed the sickness.

"Be very careful, Mila. We don't know enough about it yet for so close an inspection."

He had a point. But in returning it to the pedestal, she heard a small rattle. She shook it lightly and watched Tal wince at the sound. "That's odd."

"What is?"

She shook it again. "Hear that? That's what's left of the yolk and albumen. I prefer to dye raw eggs and leave them to dry naturally. The process takes months or years, and you have to be really careful with the eggs for fear they'll break. You can wind up with a stink bomb that will clear a building. But this egg is only a few weeks old. It can't have dried out by now. But it rattles and it's too light to still have the yolk intact."

Tal looked around the room as she continued to trace her fingers around the familiar designs. The egg was cooling now. She raised it to her nose and detected none of the faint musty scent that normally accompanied a drying egg. "Are there any other eggs about? Perhaps ones more hidden, that might not have been tampered with?"

That made her think. "Only a few in my workshop that aren't done yet. Unless . . . I wonder if Candy put the ones she bought from me in the fridge. She's more nervous about leaving them out than I am." She couldn't help but chuckle. "But then again, she has moments where she's not entirely *graceful.* She broke one Baba made when we were practicing for cheerleading squad in school. She tried to catch it and wound up wearing it. Her mom had to buy her a new uniform. Never could get the smell of rotten egg out of the fabric."

Tal apparently had smelled a rotten egg before because he grimaced. "I would probably do the same. It's not a pleasant odor."

She shrugged. "Eh. You get used to it. The scent of the dye is pretty hideous too after a few months. I know some artists who throw away their dye after every session. I can't afford that, and the dye isn't affected by a little egg slime."

"Be that as it may—" He started back toward the kitchen. "Let's see if she was kind enough to oblige us."

Mila led the way, after gently returning the pysanka to the stand. "I hope they're here. That one in there isn't a really good representation of the art. You probably noticed the scorch mark on the bottom. I held it too close to the candle when I was melting the wax and ruined it. You don't really notice it while it's sitting on the pedestal, but the others are much better . . . some of my best work."

"I'm sure they're lovely, but I'm more interested in discovering whether they glow and sing. One of the men I followed at the hospital mentioned eggs and that Vegre was gathering them up. Maybe this is the reason. He was always mad for power, wherever he could find it."

"So, who is this Vegre guy, and why was he in prison?" Sure enough, Candy had dutifully left the eggs in the padded wooden crate. She pulled out the box and handed it to him. "I mean, is he going to react . . . *violently* when we run into him?"

He gently placed the box on the counter and looked at her while opening the lid. "*You're* not going to run into Vegre, so it hardly matters. As soon as you take me to wherever your grandmother has taken the girl, you're done. You'll go back to your life and forget any of this ever happened."

Mila drew back and one hand dropped to her hip. "*Excuse me?* A criminal breaks into my house—" Tal opened his mouth, but she raised a hand to stop him. "No. He *broke* in. I don't care if it's a kicked-in door, a shattered window, or a weird green magic portal. The point is, I didn't invite him in. He kidnaped my roommate and quite possibly burglarized the house. I haven't checked to see if anything is missing because, hey—if he got in once, who's to say he wasn't in here yesterday, too?"

Tal let out a slow breath and rolled his eyes. Well, if he thought this was some sort of childish tantrum, he was dead wrong. She let him say what he had to say, but made it clear by crossing her arms and tapping one foot that she wasn't buying it. "Vegre only broke out of prison this morning. He *can't* have been here any earlier than that."

She brushed some imaginary dust off the nearest egg, her favorite. The deep brown turned out just the right shade and the outline of the two stags in rich yellow-gold raised it from just pretty to *elegant.* "So, you're an expert on magic portals for this OPI group, Officer Onan? You're willing to swear this particular portal was created by, and used *only* by Vegre, just today?" She was baiting him, and couldn't even say why. But it ticked her off that he was dismissing her so lightly and ignoring the threat this magician posed to her future. *There's just something about his attitude that's tweaking me . . . making me more aggressive than normal.* "Then how did Sela get in? She wasn't here ten minutes before you and your friend arrived. Can you guarantee that the gate won't reappear when I'm sleeping tonight and someone will kidnap me, too?"

Talos had picked up one of the eggs, a mosiac pattern of cobalt-blue, red, and black, and was inspecting it closely. None of the eggs in the container were glowing like the one in the other room and she had no clue why that one particular egg had been special. There was a moment of silence as she stared at him, let him digest what she'd said. Because she wasn't leaving this room without an answer. Of course, it didn't hurt that he was worth staring at. He had a strong jaw that was starting to sprout a five o'clock shadow. His slender nose might have been broken once upon a time, and those eyes—wow. They were nearly the same blue as the egg he was carefully placing back among the garish plastic "hay." She found that the bright yellow-and-pink plastic Easter basket hay was best to highlight the rich colors of the varnished eggs and, frankly, if she didn't pad them, top and bottom, they often didn't make it out of Candy's less-than-tender care. She hated to call anyone *clumsy* but . . . well, she was.

He offered a small nod. "You're right, of course. I *don't* know Vegre cast the gate. I don't know how Sela got into the house and I don't have a clue whether anyone has invaded your home before today, or if they'll come back." He turned his face and met her eyes.

She realized he was angry—furious, in fact. She didn't know what in particular had angered him this time, and didn't really care. She'd seen furious before and wasn't willing to back down on this. Still, staying aggressive was only going to ramp up the tension higher, so she let out a sigh and leaned back against the counter edge. "Look, I'm sorry your partner pissed you off and walked out, but that's not my fault. And, I know I'm not a cop like you. But I've got a brain, and since we can't call the cops up here—who would throw us both in the nearest nuthouse, and we apparently can't call your cops, I'm all you've got to help figure this out. Because I'm not willing to walk away from it. So you can either take me along, or I'll follow behind . . . sloppily, I might add, since I have no training."

While his voice remained stone cold, something she said must have amused him. The muscles in his jaw relaxed and his eyes lost their angry intensity. "There's always the option that I could just walk out and do it myself. Trust me when I say you can't follow what you can't see."

She met the challenge with raised brows. "Good luck on finding Baba then. You don't know where the cave is and you don't look the type to torture me to get the information."

He was nodding with a small smile and tapping a finger on the edge of the box. "Then it seems we're at a standoff. We both want answers and we only have a few days to get them. Not only will the illness the girl has fully manifest by then and be horribly contagious, but any possible trail to Vegre will be stone cold."

A few *days?* Reality slammed home in her mind with the weight of lead. It was all fun and exciting to think about racing around to solve this puzzle, but today was only Wednesday. There was a mortgage to pay, the company New Year's party to finish planning, and piles of folders on her desk at work. Then panic set in as the image of her desk blinked into her mind. "Geez! The Johnson brief! Oh, man!" She prayed to the Heavens Nancy had finished typing it after she didn't show back up at the office. The filing deadline was tomorrow and their regular courier was next to impossible to schedule this time of year. If she had to use Yellow Cab again, accounting would have a fit.

"The *Johnson brief?*" Tal raised his brows questioningly.

She slapped her palm against her forehead repeatedly, until her teeth rattled. "God, I've been such an idiot . . . yelling at you for not including me in this, when I don't have time to help anyway. I've got a job that I have to be back at tomorrow. I can be so *stupid!*" She raised her voice to a near scream and slammed shut the lid of the box with such force that she gasped and reopened it rapidly to make sure she hadn't damaged the eggs. She gingerly lifted and inspected each one while her heart beat like a triphammer. "Wouldn't *that* have been a perfect ending to the day? Where are my so-called brains today?" She let out a frustrated noise and was surprised when she felt a warm hand touch her shoulder. She looked up to see Tal staring down at her with a sad expression.

"We're both under a great deal of stress today. I keep forgetting that. You've apparently known Sela for nearly as long as I have, so of course you'd be worried. And now your grandmother is missing and your *real* life is still out there, waiting. I'm sorry. If your Johnson brief is anything close to what I'm facing when I return to Rohm, you have my utter sympathy."

She reached out and touched his hand and offered a tired smile. Her heart jumped a beat when he returned the smile and turned his hand to squeeze hers lightly before removing it. "Well, at least I can get you to the cave tonight and help you find Baba. Time moves so fast down there that I can still get back and have a good night's sleep."

Confusion replaced the sadness on his face. "I don't understand. Guilders have no power over time. It moves at the same speed in Agathia as here."

She shook her head while putting the box of eggs back in the refrigerator. "I don't know about Agathia, but where we're going, it doesn't. I distinctly remember that we could visit Baba's friend Viktor for the whole afternoon, and only an hour would have passed up here. It's how we kept the secret about Baba training me from Mom for so long."

"But this Viktor lives underground? Do you know the city name?"

She shrugged and walked back toward the living room, crooking her finger over her shoulder for him to join her. "Viktor didn't live in a city. His gardens are huge, and I don't remember any neighbors. We would explore for hours, Candy and I. If someone else lived nearby, we would have seen them. But I think I remember walking in the house once while they were talking and hearing Viktor say he was going to Virile tomorrow and asked if Baba needed anything."

That stopped Tal dead in his tracks. "Do you think he might have said *Vril* instead of Virile?"

"Oh. Yeah, I suppose that could be. Why? Is that important?"

Tal was nodding when she turned with coat in hand. He grabbed his cloak and swung it on, quickly fastening the hooks until he appeared swaddled in the thick wool. "Very much so. Vegre's minion mentioned they were based in Vril. Perhaps this Viktor had a method of reaching the city that would be quicker than making the journey up here. Do you know what sort of magicwielder he is? What guild he belongs to?"

She couldn't help but laugh as she pulled on her coat and gloves and reached for the door handle. "I don't remember Baba ever mentioning him using magic, but now that I'm thinking about it that way, some of the stuff he did that just seemed normal when we were kids, could well have been magic. And remember that until a few hours ago, I didn't remember magic existed and thought *geeders* lived in burrows like squirrels and were about this tall." She held up her hand and put her fingers about four inches apart while squinting.

He joined in the laughter with a deep chuckle that sent shivers up her spine. "It's sort of a shame we aren't that tall. Vegre would be a lot easier to manage."

The night wind rushed through the door when she opened it, icy cold and smelling of evergreen from the neatly trimmed bushes around the porch. She turned back to reply, but caught her breath at the sight. The breeze had set Tal's hair and cloak fluttering, and with the dark smile, beard-stubbled face, and glittering blue eyes, he appeared every bit the wild, untamed magician of every movie and video game she'd ever seen. Her stomach lurched quite pleasantly when his gaze caught hers and his expression returned to the one he'd had in the kitchen earlier. She couldn't help looking him up and down and letting out an appreciative breath. "Personally, I'm really glad you're not four inches tall. I like you just . . . oh, yeah, just like that."

Before he could reply, she turned and walked out the door, nearly tripping over her own feet to get to the car. Hopefully, by the time she got there, she could pretend the blush that was burning up her face was from the cold wind.

CHAPTER 9

$\mathcal{T}$he car turned off the main highway onto a side road that was thick with dirty slush from the recent snow. Mila slid to a slow stop when she reached the first wide spot, next to a pair of dilapidated letter boxes on an iron post. She looked out the windshield with worry etched on her face, drumming her fingers on the padded leather steering wheel cover. "We should probably walk from here. I've got all-wheel drive, but if it gets any colder while we're down there, this stuff is going to freeze and we'll be stuck. I'm not a great winter driver yet, so I tend to stick to the main roads."

It made good sense to Tal. While he didn't relish walking in the snow in the dark, Mila seemed confident of where they were going. Too, there were other vehicle tracks disappearing into the darkness, and with the letter boxes, the road obviously went *somewhere*. He unfastened the seat belt and lifted one foot onto the cushion to tuck his pant leg into his boot. She watched him with undisguised interest, so he explained. "The more clothing you can keep dry, the warmer you'll stay. I'd suggest you do the same."

She shook her head with a small smile. "It's not that. I was planning to do the same thing. But it's so weird to watch you." It seemed a strange thing to say, and his confusion must have showed in his body language, because she continued. "It's just that . . . I mean, you seem totally comfortable with cars, knew how to fasten the shoulder belt and the hospital didn't seem odd at all. But you have this sense of . . . *otherworldness* to you. Talking about spells and focuses and swearing by trees. They don't really . . . *mesh*, y'know?"

Ah. Now he understood. While raising his other foot to the seat, he explained. "The O.P.A. has been monitoring the overworld for centuries, sending agents up from Agathia, which is miles below where we're standing now. We're all assigned periods when we must live up here, keeping watch for problems. Denver was my last station, about five years ago. It's built up a lot since I left, and some technology has changed, but that's normal and it's easy to incorporate while we live here undercover. But after you've been back home for a while, you forget some of the social things—drop back into old slang, have the wrong body language. That sort of thing. It'll pass. I'll sound and act more *modern* each day that passes. Alexy just came back from being stationed in London, so he's already comfortable. He even adopted a British accent just through osmosis. He didn't used to have one. Mine's natural, even though it's mostly gone unless I'm chatting with someone from there. I was born in Brittania, before it was the UK."

She tried not to think about the fact that he might be a *lot* older than he looked. She considered Baba to be really old because she'd experienced World War II. But hadn't Baba said she didn't remember Tal from when the Parask split from the other Guilders? That would make them both centuries and centuries old, which was too much for her to wrap her head around at the moment. "Oh. That makes sense, I guess. But what sort of *problems* would make you guys need to be here?" She was trying to raise up her leg to tuck in her jeans, but the steering wheel was in the way. Finally, she just opened the door and lifted her heel to the armrest. "I mean, you said there shouldn't be any gates up here, so obviously not that many of you come here to get into trouble."

He realized he was staring at her again, for the umpteenth time since they'd gotten into the car. There was just something about her thick, shining dark hair and delicate features that he couldn't seem to get enough of. More than once he'd had to fight the urge to run his fingers through the strands or stroke that perfect skin. But now, with the door open and the dome light on, his attention was obvious enough that she noticed. He could feel the heat rise off her body from her embarrassment, warm enough for him to verify that she really did have some mage blood. "People like *you* are why we're here." That raised her brows and curiosity toned down the blush. "Frankly, I'm surprised nobody has approached you before now. The O.P.A. watches for the birth of guildercents like you. If they begin to show talent that could make officials here ask questions, we'll coax them down to train in a guild—help them find an acceptable outlet for their magic. After a few years, they can return home and live their lives. But some decide to stay in Agathia and live there. If so, they'll be deemed missing persons, or runaways. And if they later commit a crime with their magic, they'll either serve a sentence in a guild, or be wiped of knowledge of their magic by one of the kings. We can't really risk people discovering our world, so it's just better to have them forget what they saw and what they can do."

"So . . . what are you planning to do to *me?* When you said I'd just return to my life and forget this ever happened, what exactly did you mean by that?" He found himself nodding. Her mind was very analytical. She seemed to be able to take an idea to the next step, which said she had the promise of true talent.

"I'm thinking your mind would be too disciplined to forget your abilities. Criminal minds are easily swayed, but yours . . . I can see you have focus and determination. It would be a waste of my time, and magic, to even try. But I don't have the power to make an offer to bring you down to train. All I could do would be to petition the mage guild and see if the guildmaster would offer you an apprenticeship. But with your conjurer abilities—" He left the thought unfinished, not sure how to approach the subject of the general opinion of the Parask within the guilds.

"Oh. No, I wouldn't want to anyway. I like my life up here. I just wanted to hear you say that you don't plan to try to erase my memory or anything like that. I don't know tons of magic, but Baba did train me to defend myself. At the time, I didn't realize that's what she was doing, but I managed to fend off that Vegre when he tried to zap me. It was when I blocked his magic that it blasted the wall and made you guys come upstairs."

That made him pause. He hadn't really considered what had attracted their attention while talking with Candy in the living room, but it had indeed been the sound, and sensation, of magic. "So, you can defend yourself. Excellent. While I *could* defend you if Vegre showed up, I'd rather not have to. Can you attack or disarm, as well?"

She shrugged and wrinkled her nose in a manner that struck him as cute. He nearly smiled, but the conversation was too serious. "Magically? I haven't got a clue. I've taken plenty of self-defense courses, and I know I can kick butt on a mugger if one jumped me . . . even an armed one. And I suppose I *might* know some attack stuff. It's all such ancient history in my head, y'know? I mean, when Vegre said *'Moratay,'* the *'Avatay'* just slipped out, totally unconsciously. It was an old game Baba taught all us kids that apparently was so ingrained that it defeated whatever spell was put on me. Of course, that's the best time to teach stuff like that, I suppose. When it'll stick and be instinctive."

When he didn't respond for a long moment, she put the car keys in her inside jacket pocket and got out of the car. Honestly, he couldn't decide *how* to respond. Vegre, easily the most powerful mage in the world, had attempted a killing curse on her, and she *blocked* it? He'd had to fight back his initial reaction. The surge of undiluted pride nearly made him drop his jaw, let out a whoop of triumph, and give her a huge hug. Any Agathian she unknowingly told the story to would do the same. To avoid an intentional killing curse was reason to crow for weeks. But he didn't want to give her too much false confidence by doing that, because it could easily have been a fluke.

So, he held his tongue until he'd exited the car, locked his door, and was standing beside her in the snow. He tried to sound casual as she stared into the distance with hands on hips, trying to get her bearings. "Did he . . . happen to give any *reason* why he attacked you? Did he have some sort of grudge against you?"

She nodded just as she apparently decided on their path. "Not me personally, I don't think. I don't think he knew who I was. But yeah, there was a reason. I wasn't supposed to have known his name. He said I had to die for it."

He tilted his head and then turned toward her. "You knew his name *before* we came upstairs? How? Did Sela say it?" Even then, how would Sela know? She was never assigned to prison duty.

"No, it wasn't Sela. I just *knew*. It's a long story, but the short version is I collapsed in a restaurant, had a weird dream, and when Candy brought me home and I woke up, I knew his face and kept thinking that his name was really important to say out loud. Sela was in the dream, and so was Alexy. I can only remember bits and pieces though. There was a waterfall, and some guy was oozing black goo from his skin and I was running and falling and couldn't breathe—"

"My Tree spirit." The whisper came out unbidden. Tal didn't even realize he was thinking it, but there was no other explanation. If only Alexy and Sela were in the dream, and she could see Vegre, then he must have been the vehicle. She must have been the spirit of the Tree who had come to his call. A buzzing filled his mind as he tried to grasp the possibilities. His whole life had been built around having a link to the Tree spirit—to the essence of magic. What would it mean to his belief system to learn that it was all a lie? Mila was barely magical, nearly full human. How could he ask *her* for guidance on things she didn't even understand? In fact, how could he know that the advice he'd taken to date was valid?

Her eyes opened wider and her lips parted to release a startled breath as the realization struck home with her, too. There was something about that pose, the tilt of her head in the bright moonlight, her body just inches from his. She seemed . . . regal, and far too familiar. It was as though he'd known her forever. *Have I always had an im-*

age of what I imagined the spirit to look like? Is that why I'm so drawn to her? Because Tree help me . . . I can't seem to resist this woman.

Before he even registered the movement, he was kissing her, eyes closed and heart pounding. *Spirit of my heart, are you there?* He said the words in his mind, not really expecting a response. But when he felt the doorway open and light and sound flood his brain, aching desire flowed through his body—as though a physical connection to the spirit was all that had been lacking from his life.

I . . . I mean, you? It's been you all this time? All these years? Her voice was deeper, more resonant in his head than what reached air. No wonder he hadn't recognized it when they met. She leaned into him, relaxed into the curve of his arm, and ground her mouth against his as she clutched at his back. Finally his fingers could skim along the silkiness of her hair, warm against her heated skin as his mouth ate against hers hard enough to pull a moan from her throat.

She was no stranger to kissing, this one. Her tongue flicked lightly, then wound around his, filling his mouth with the taste of mint and honey. When her nails grazed his neck, and her knee moved against his swollen groin, he felt he would go mad. He moved his mouth to her cheek and then to her neck, savoring the scent of lavender flowers that made him nip her skin just a bit. Magic rose from her then, heady with fire and some other power he couldn't recognize. But his body recognized the mage magic and pulled, causing Mila to have a full body shudder. It apparently weakened her knees enough that she sagged. He had to tighten his grip to keep her standing. Her legs spread enough in the process that their hips met and the weight of her abruptly willing body made his erection leap against the fabric and zipper that kept it bound. The delicious pressure made him growl and find her mouth again. He ran his tongue slowly around her lips until they parted. He plunged it between her teeth, thrilling in the sensation of bone scraping against his flesh. Tal kissed her with something approaching desperation, and she did the same.

But there were too many layers of clothing, and his frantic hands couldn't find a way through to her bare skin. Short of throwing her to the snow-covered ground, or crawling into the backseat of the frigid car, there would be no easy relief he could think of. No, it was better to let this go before they went much further. They had many things to accomplish this night and it would be too easy to spend it exploring every inch of her body . . . listening to her screams as he pleasured her.

She pushed back first. "We have to stop." Her full lips, heaving breasts, and wild eyes said she didn't want to any more than he. "This is too . . . I mean, I . . . I need to think."

Tal nodded and took a deep breath. Only one thing would help at this point, so he grabbed a handful of snow from the hood of the car and held it to the back of his neck. His eyes squeezed shut automatically from the intensity of the cold against his superheated skin and it wasn't but moments later that warm water trickled down his neck to join the sweat she'd induced.

"Not a bad idea." She likewise grabbed some snow and rubbed it against her neck. She yelped and blew out several harsh breaths while blinking furiously. After a few moments, she made small helpless movements with her soaked gloves. "Um, that was . . . well, wow. You do that really good. So, Tree spirit, huh?"

He shrugged. "That's what I always believed. Apparently, I was wrong." He looked into those green eyes once more and realized it would take nothing at all for them to fall back into the same condition. He took a step back. Her face fell for a moment, but then a healthy dose of determination took its place and she nodded strongly.

"It's not a long walk, but we should get moving. The path is pretty tight in some spots. Stay close so we don't get separated."

Those weren't the best words for her to use while his

body still wanted completion. His voice deepened slightly as he responded. "I can't think of anywhere I'd rather be right now than *close and tight*."

He watched her hands clutch into fists as she fought against whatever she wanted to do. Her smile and laughter at the wording was shaky at best. "Okay, then. So, let's go."

*M*ila trained her flashlight on the rock wall, searching for the tiny spot of red paint that Baba had painted years before. She was breathing hard after the steep climb up the barely visible path near Castle Rock. Tal was right on her heels, and every time he brushed her, she remembered the kiss. Nobody had *ever* kissed her like that before. She'd been able to sense him in her mind, in her veins— like he was surrounding her and inside her all at once. It frankly scared the crap out of her to have such an intimate moment with someone she'd only known for a short time.

Or have I always known him? That was the part that was most frightening. The moment he'd mentioned the words *Tree spirit*, she'd remembered the voice in her head. Remembered asking questions he didn't have answers to. She'd been looking at the dream through eyes, touching things with hands, and yet had never asked *whose* hands and eyes. If they were Tal's, how did they come to be connected that way? She'd had episodes since childhood, but never remembered meeting anyone from the other place, except for Viktor.

Thinking of Viktor reminded her again of little Suzanne. Her mother must be terrified. Even with Tim going along, when Candy explained it, who knows how people were going to react? Part of her was furious with Baba for kidnapping a child, and part of her was very proud for risking her own freedom to save the girl. *And what am I going to do when I find her? Take her back? Turn her in? Or even worse, go against everything about the legal system I believe in to simply ignore it?*

But there was no ignoring the footprints that had suddenly

appeared in the snow ahead. Baba must have come from a different direction, but there was no mistaking the three pairs of prints—two adults and one child, that disappeared into the seemingly solid rock. "There." She pointed at what looked like just another boulder in a sea of boulders. The telltale bit of red dye was still vivid under the bright flashlight.

The moment she stepped behind the boulder and entered the darkness of the cave, old memories filled her. The sweet scent of spring blooms that shouldn't exist here in the bone-chilling winter blended with the faint fragrance that Baba always wore. The shirtsleeve warmth that hit her face was like stepping out into the summer sunshine and she raised her face and closed her eyes to drink it in after the long walk in the cold.

"It smells like a field of wildflowers in here." Tal's voice held both confusion and disbelief—which seemed strange from someone who certainly believed in magic. "But considering the location from the nearest plotted gate, this cavern *should* lead to the outskirts of Rohm. But there aren't any gardens left there. Everybody was evacuated to the second ring years ago. Even if someone managed to bribe an official to remain behind, there's not enough magic left in this area to maintain a flower garden."

She shrugged and started to unwrap the muffler from around her neck, shaking loose her hair as she did. "I don't think you're talking about Rome, Italy, which is the only one I know—although I'm sure there are plenty of towns in America with that name. And I don't have any clue what a *ring* is or how you evacuate someone to it, so I'm afraid I'm no help."

They walked in silence to the archway she remembered so well. Well, it was more that *she* was silent. Tal was muttering under his breath. But the words were too indistinct to understand and she got the impression they weren't for her ears anyway. She played her light around the cave floor. It was surprisingly tidy after all these years. No small animal bones, creepy-crawlies or cobwebs . . . just a smooth, uncluttered path, devoid of even stalagmites, even though their counterparts lined the ceiling.

"It's just through here." She pointed to the opening to their left which seemed to veer off the main passage, but ended abruptly with a rock wall. She reached back automatically. "Here, take my hand."

He didn't seem unwilling, but more curious. "Why?"

It was a logical question, and she didn't have a good answer. "Um, I don't know. It's just the way it works." Baba had always taken her hand, she'd taken Candy's, and they'd walked to the garden together, like crossing a busy street when the walk light came on. But she'd been a child then, so maybe it wasn't necessary. Still, there was magic involved. She knew that now, but in a different way than she'd known it as a child. Then it was just a source of wonder, no different than Santa Claus or the tooth fairy. Now it was a realization of reality that held as much danger as awe. All she could do was shrug and raise her brows. "I guess I'm not really sure how it works. We'd better stick with what I know."

He held his hand up, palm forward and then shook his head. "I sense nothing ahead. If this were a sanctioned gate, I should. And even if an illicit gate, there should be some magical signature."

If I shrug one more time, my muscles are going to cramp up. She wiggled her fingers with a bit of impatience. "It's there, trust me. At worst, we'll walk into the wall, and I'll admit I'm an idiot, okay?"

That brought a small smile and a breath of a laugh. He reached out and wrapped his fingers around hers. Again she was startled by how warm his hand was and couldn't help asking, "What's your guys' normal body temperature, anyway?"

He pursed his lips and tipped his head. "Same as you— ninety-eight-point-six. We're not another species, Mila. Just an offshoot that can do magic."

"Maybe it's me that's cold then." Amazingly, the next shrug didn't cramp her muscles. *Must be building them up—shrugging to the oldies.* She nearly laughed, but waved it off before he asked. "Never mind."

She stepped forward, trying to appear confident that she knew what she was doing. "It's magic. Why are you confused?" She remembered Baba's words when she'd asked how the door to Viktor's garden worked. It was after her eighth birthday, and Baba had told her Viktor had a gift for her. But she had become a *big girl,* and it seemed important to understand such things. Daddy had showed her the secret of pulling a coin from behind her ear, and she knew Santa was really just her parents. In some small part of her brain, she understood the garden shouldn't exist. But Baba was so stern, so matter-of-fact about the reality of magic, that she'd soon forgotten to question it, and then had forgotten it even happened at all.

Oh! That was the day I got the stone. Her last visit to the garden was when she'd been presented with the fire opal. It was the most beautiful thing she'd ever seen. She spent the entire visit just looking at it, catching the colors in the sunlight, watching the flames burn without any heat, except from the warmth of her hand. Even Candy's shouts to come join her chasing butterflies hadn't budged her.

She stopped, mere inches from the wall and looked back at Tal. "Could I hold the opal for a minute?" It was just an experiment, and it really didn't make much sense.

Without releasing her hand, he reached into his pocket and extracted it, holding it out to her other hand. She took it and stared at the stone. It was lovely and still bore the colors she remembered, but not the internal flames that licked and chased each other. But she kept staring at it as she walked forward, leading Tal toward the bower on the other side of the stone. A delightful shimmery sensation overtook her, followed by a rush of energy that was like the high of a double mocha espresso. The stone in her hand came alive as sunlight struck the face of it. "That's the way I remember you." She smiled and squeezed Tal's hand, not even noticing he'd been talking until then.

"This place shouldn't exist," he said. She looked up then

and the garden was exactly as she remembered it. The sky was the rich azure-blue of midsummer, and fluffy clouds floated by as the warm breeze hit her face. The riot of colors was more intense than a painting by Van Gogh. Every flower imaginable filled the landscape as far as she could see. Most didn't belong in the same soil, but she hadn't known that as a child. And some weren't even possible . . . like the glittering purple one that resembled an iris. But it spun and scattered stardust in a never-ending circle that would cover her clothing with multicolored glitter. Candy had been right. She'd loved that flower and had tried for years to find it at a garden center. *And I never believed Mom that it didn't exist. How could I have seen it if it wasn't real?* Was that why her mother took away her memories, because of her dogged insistence that magic was real?

"That gate shouldn't even exist." Tal was touching things, feeling the texture of flowers and leaves as though he'd never seen magical flowers. He noticed the spinning stardust flower and reached out to it, catching a bit of iridescent glitter on his fingers. He got an odd look on his face that was part smile and part . . . awe. "My mother had purple allurias in her garden, years ago. They were her favorites."

She held out the opal with a smile. "It's alive again. This is how I remember the stone." She tipped it so he could see. It took a moment for him to turn his attention to it, but when he did, the awe turned to something deeper, closer to respect.

He watched the flames dance under the thin layer of filmy blue that covered the stone and picked it from her hand to turn into the sunlight. "It responds to this magic, whatever form it is. Bloody hell, but I wish Alexy was here. Identifying the type of magic isn't one of my skills."

She shook her head and let out an exasperated breath. "It's just magic. The type doesn't matter."

"Oh no," he said while examining the wooden bower, trellises completely covered with rich dark vines and massive white flowers that smelled heavenly. In fact, she noticed that the garden never overpowered, nor had conflicting scents. It was as though the blooms were selected especially for their complementary scents, rather than the color scheme. "No, it does matter. In fact, it's *very* important. For something like this place to exist, outside of your reality *and* mine, speaks of a power that's extremely dangerous."

That made no sense to her. "It's a *garden*. Flowers, vines, grass. How can it be dangerous?"

He sighed and seemed to be trying to think of an analogy. "Think of it like energy in your world. If nobody had ever heard of . . . had never *conceived* of nuclear energy, but the world suddenly discovered that an unknown island country had devised a reactor, what would happen? If it was reported to be powerful enough to run everything on that island—no oil, no wind—wouldn't everyone want it? Good countries, bad countries, wild extremist groups?"

The thought was sobering. "So, you're saying that the mere *existence* of the garden makes it dangerous because the wrong people could try to steal the magic that makes it, for their own purposes?"

He nodded. "And the worst possible, but most capable person of stealing magic was in your house this morning."

She looked around again, tried to imagine someone sucking the very life from this place . . . seeing it wilted and dead and dark. "Oh God. We need to find Viktor and tell him about Vegre."

She didn't wait for Tal. She rushed through the garden, sprinted along nearly forgotten paths, under massive branches that held fruit for the picking at any time of year . . . across bridges over sparkling streams that she knew fat orange koi lived in.

Viktor's house was built into the remnants of a massive old tree, lovingly carved among the branches and gnarled roots and decorated with more flowering vines that always stayed well clear of the window openings and doorway, none of which contained actual windows or doors. "Viktor! Are you home?"

But no smiling man with tidy white beard and ring of

hair came to her call. Of course, he wasn't always home when she came to visit with Baba, either. He was always off, this place and that. But he always—"Left a message. We need to see if there's a message for us from him or Baba." She grabbed Tal's hand again and pulled him along, before he could protest or ask questions. They raced along again, through the formal English rose garden, past the wildflower meadow . . . finally ending up in the Japanese bonsai garden. After the tangle of conflicting colors and heights in the meadow, the precise order and careful lines of the rock garden and trained plants was a little startling.

Tal seemed a little out of breath. "Craters, but you can move when you want to, woman."

"It's a big place. If you don't run, you can spend hours getting from place to place. But I never seem to get tired here. Sorry I wore you out, though. Have some water. There's always a pitcher on the table over there. I need to check the pool for messages."

The reflecting pond had seemed so much larger when she was young. Now it didn't look much bigger than a family-sized hot tub. Slender reeds swayed in the light breeze and a leopard frog blinked at her from a lilypad in the center. "I hope you don't mind if I use your pond, Mr. Frog." She always used to talk to the animals in the garden . . . partly because Mom had read her *Mother West Wind's Children* too many times, and partly because Baba always told her that not everything in the garden was what it seemed.

"Do you often talk to frogs?" Tal's voice sounded slightly amused. But he also vibrated with curiosity. Apparently, he'd decided to just run with whatever was going to happen here.

She sat down on one of the orderly gray stones that surrounded the pond and ran her fingertips through the needles of the bonsai tree that grew right to the water's edge. It was far larger than a potted bonsai, but still tiny in comparison to even a shrub. She'd always loved this little tree and had marveled at the number of little woven nests among the branches. Viktor had told her they were hummingbird nests and each time she would visit, she'd check the nests to see if there were any babies. As tiny as the adults were, she couldn't imagine the size of a hatchling. But despite the fact that they visited at all times of the year, she'd never managed to spot a baby.

Then she reached a finger out to the frog, twitching it in a friendly manner. But that was too much for the little amphibian. It stretched out suddenly and slid down into the water, parting it without a single splash. "Hey, you never know. Maybe that was Viktor, watching us to find out our intentions."

Tal sat down on the carved wooden bench near the grape trellises. He reached out to touch the purple fruit, then lifted one of the bunches, as though testing the weight of it. "Not much danger of that . . . just so you know. While there are spells that can change someone's appearance, there's no such thing as shifting a human to another form—especially to something as small as a frog. Where would the mass go? A two-hundred-pound frog wouldn't be able to sit on a lilypad, unless it was made of iron and bolted to the ground."

She nodded in agreement. "Yeah, I always wondered about that. But you'd think magic wouldn't have to abide by physics."

He leaned back, crossed his arms over his chest, and let out a snort. "Wouldn't *that* be nice. Then we wouldn't have to worry about piping water to the cities. The water witches used to be able to simply pull the water through the soil, or raise it from the banks of underground streams and move it to fill the cisterns. But without sufficient magic, physics keeps the water just out of our grasp."

"But *why* can't you move it anymore? You said earlier that magic's being rationed where you live. But how can that be? Magic is . . . well, just *there,* isn't it?" She started to untie her left boot. It was soaking wet from the snow and she had to wiggle it to get it off her foot. Tal watched with interest but didn't comment about it. Instead, he actually answered her question.

"The Trees of Life are dying. They're the source of magic in Agathia. There's a Tree in each major city square, but they're *all* dying and we don't know why. So the kings of the various realms, who are generally the most magically powerful, have elected to ration magic. Each person can fill up their personal focus stone, plus a general household focus, once per day and when it's gone, there's no more until the next day when you can refill it." He raised up his hands and looked around. "That's why this place shouldn't exist. There's not enough magic left in the world to sustain it. If it weren't for the fact that some of these plants *can't* exist without magic, I'd swear it was just a normal garden, and the owner just happened to get lucky and find a fertile cave with running water, near a volcanic vent for heat."

She couldn't help but shake her head. "Boy, I'm just having a hard time wrapping my head around that idea. I mean, if all magic in the world comes from some weird species of tree, then why not just plant some more if they're dying? It's not like it's oil—where there's only so much of it and when it's gone, it's gone. Trees grow. They produce new seeds and the seeds grow . . . a never-ending supply. It just doesn't make sense."

"And yet it's reality, much like this garden. Neither make much sense." He finally pointed down at her pink cotton sock. "Is there a problem with your foot?"

She sighed and started to pull it off. "No. It's just another thing that doesn't make sense. I have to put my left foot in the pond to get the message to play . . . if there is one." She paused, sock halfway down her foot. "And please don't laugh. It's not my fault."

The introduction apparently made him curious, and how could she blame him? He leaned forward, eyes fixed on her foot.

Well, I might as well get it over with. There'd been plenty of time over the years to get used to people laughing at it. But this wasn't like the locker room in gym. She didn't *want* Tal to laugh at her. Not after . . . well, she just didn't want him to. Summoning up her courage, she tugged the sodden cloth off and wiggled her now-wrinkled toes. "Pretty stupid, huh?"

But he wasn't laughing. He slid off the bench and knelt down next to her leg. He was careful not to actually touch her, but she could tell he wanted to. "Were you born with these? You have birthmarks for *every* guild, plus one I don't recognize. What's that one?"

He was pointing at the symbol just above her big toe. The series of triangles attached to a long line, was the largest of the marks . . . or drawings, which is how they started out. "I don't really know what any of them mean. Baba painted them on my foot when I was about five. She just used regular egg dye. It was fun at the time—like getting my toenails painted. But they never came off. My mother's been mad at her ever since."

Tal touched the mark on her second toe. "So they're ink? This oblong mark with the dots is the symbol of the water witches. The straight line with spikes that looks like a comb is the mark of the dirtdogs—the earth alchemists. This one here," he said and raised his sleeve for her to compare his zigzag symbol with the vivid yellow one on her foot, "is the fire mage sign . . . although yours is complete, while mine is much fainter. The clarity of the mark is how magical strength is determined. While I'm an adequate crafter, the same symbol on Vegre is sharp and raised high above his skin."

"Then what's this one?" She pointed to the last mark, a short row of elongated curves. "These look like waves. Shouldn't that be the water symbol, instead of the little blob thing?"

Tal shook his head. "Water, like earth and fire, gain motion by wind. That's the flyers' symbol, for the air illusionists guild. And I suppose this last one is the symbol of your own guild, the . . . Parask." He seemed to struggle to say the word, but managed. Then he apparently finally got up the nerve to touch her foot. The sensation of his finger lightly stroking the skin over the marks felt *really* good. "It's odd. They don't look like tattoos, but don't feel like birthmarks. You're certain these were *painted* on? She didn't use a needle or magic to embed the dye under your skin?"

Mila pulled her foot out of his grasp, before the sensation of him stroking her skin made her forget why they were here. Already she was struggling not to throw him to the ground to kiss him and her heart was racing so fast that she should be able to see her shirt moving. Her voice had a breathless quality when she spoke. "Not—" She had to cough before she could speak again. "Not a needle, anyway. It never occurred to me she might have used magic, but I guess it's possible. Anyway—" She spun on the rock and raised her foot to dip it into the water. "We need to get the message and get moving. Otherwise, I'll never get any sleep tonight."

He raked her from bare toes to the top of her head with intense, dark eyes. Then he shook his head and muttered something she couldn't make out. She nearly asked him to repeat it, but she wasn't sure she wanted to know. Still, he backed up a bit to give her room to move. She hadn't done this since she was eight, and hoped she remembered how it worked. She slid her foot into the water. Not even breathing reached her ears for a long moment as they waited for something to happen. But the water remained still and warm. Mila shook her head. "I think I'm forgetting to do something. I'm still struggling to find things in my mind—" Frustration edged her voice and she wanted to scream. There wasn't *time* to forget things. "Hello? Viktor, are you there? It's me, Mila." Another pause, but still nothing.

She tapped her knee and stared into the still pool, desperately trying to remember back to the last time she visited. The memory came back so suddenly, and so strong, that she nearly fell face first into the water. She saw again her foot, much smaller—the symbols far larger than her toes. She twisted her foot, this way and that, watching as tiny fish came up to nibble on them. She felt a little bored, but had been assured that her foot was very important to the process. Then she heard Baba's voice over her shoulder and the identical words came out of her mouth in the present. "I am here, Viktor. We must speak."

A small glow suddenly lit up swimming fish from underneath, turning them Day-Glo colors. Her foot started tingling and she remembered that, too, a familiar pins-and-needles sensation like stepping into a hot bath after a long day in the snow.

"So, it requires both will and *specific* words. A useful safeguard." Tal was nodding his head, watching as the light grew brighter under the water.

It soon encompassed the whole pool, and then the water disappeared from view. In its place was a clear image of another cave—this one decorated with brightly painted murals and comfortable-looking furniture. "Greetings, Mila. You're looking well. And what a beautiful young woman you've grown into. You remind me much of Nadia when she was your age." Viktor looked like he hadn't aged a day since she was eight. His ruddy face was smiling, showing a dark space where one lower tooth was missing. He had a ring of tidy white hair under a patterned headband that had been very trendy when she was a girl. His neatly trimmed Van Dyke beard made his eyes look even bluer. They were darker than Tal's though and she found it odd that her mind was occupied with noticing it.

"It's good to see you again, Viktor. I'm hoping you can help us out. We really need to find my Baba. Did she come to see you here . . . maybe with a young girl and her father?"

Tal moved down to whisper in her ear. "I thought you said this was a *message*. Are you actually talking to him?"

She wiggled her hand back and forth and wrinkled her nose. "It's a little of both, actually. It's sort of an interactive message. He's there, and can answer questions we pose, but he's not *really there*, that we can go off target from what it's programmed to say. But he'll be able to watch it later to see our expressions and hear what we said. So it's recording as well as playing."

"Interesting." Tal leaned forward to stare at the image and was looking carefully around the background of the scene. Maybe he was trying to figure out where it might have been recorded.

"Who's that there with you, Mila?" The recorded Viktor's eyes narrowed slightly and it made her wonder if it really *was* a recording, or if he was sitting there live.

She looked at Tal and he shook his head. Just once, but she understood. If Viktor wasn't going to be forthcoming with information, then neither was Tal. It was common in corporate negotiations, so she was no stranger to handling it. "This is a friend of mine, Viktor, from Rohm. I didn't think you'd mind if I showed him your lovely gardens." She turned her head and raised her brows, encouraging him to give some sort of compliment.

He caught the meaning and nodded quickly. "Oh, yes. The gardens are beautiful. I'll have to mention to my mother that you have purple allurias. They're her favorites and these are splendid ones."

Whether recording or live, he was very proud of his flowers. The comment soothed him and his face relaxed into conversational lines once more. "Please, feel free to take one to your mother with my compliments. But I must ask that you not reveal where you came by it. I've gotten very used to my privacy."

Tal nodded, but his face looked odd, like he wasn't sure what to make of Viktor. He smiled anyway. "Of course. As you like."

"Viktor, have you heard from Baba . . . from my grandmother Nadia?"

There was a pause while Viktor looked off into space, as though looking behind the camera for instructions. "Nadia is here, with me. We've brought Suzanne and Tim to a place where she can be healed. It's better if you don't know where we are. You have more important things to be concerned with right now."

Tal apparently couldn't help but interrupt. He leaned forward, eyes flashing. "I beg to differ, sir. There's nothing more important than ensuring that *Tin Czerwona* doesn't become a pandemic over two worlds. You seem to be old enough that you were there for the last plague. You must remember why it's so important that—"

Viktor continued to speak over the top of Tal, as though he wasn't even there. So, perhaps this was a recording, after all. "It's much more critical that you concentrate on replacing the eggs. All your skill, all your effort must go toward that. There's little time left. It must be accomplished by midnight Sunday."

She looked at Tal, but he only shook his head and lowered his brows. "Eggs?" she asked the face in the pond. "Do you mean pysanky eggs? And replace them where?"

He looked at her with a sort of sadness, like he pitied her some great lack of knowledge. "Nadia should never have allowed your mother to cut you off from your heritage for so long. I wish we had known of her treachery in blocking your memories of your crafting talent. We can only hope you'll be able to *follow* the instructions once you've read them."

"I don't understand, Viktor. What instructions? What eggs?"

He sighed. "For me to answer that, you'll need to get the parchment scroll from the bookshelf in my den. It's the only scroll with copper handles. Could you bring it here, Mila?"

She looked at Tal. "If I take out my foot and break the connection, I might not be able to get it back. Sometimes the whole thing would erase if I got twitchy when I was little. But this is important. I don't know why, but I think it's *really* important that we listen to the whole message."

He nodded and stood up, and then bent down to whisper softly in her ear. Hopefully it was quiet enough that the recording wouldn't pick it up. "I agree. This is the third time eggs have been mentioned now, and after the one glowed at your house, I think we must follow up on this."

He stood and started to turn. She opened her mouth and pointed, planning to offer directions back to the house, but he waved it off. He opened his mouth to speak, but then remembered the still image of Viktor, who regarded them absolutely motionless in the pond, not even seeming to breathe. Tal leaned down again to dizzy her brain with puffs of warm air against her ear and the delicious, spicy scent of whatever cologne he was wearing. "I remember the way. I'll be back as quickly as possible. But, please— find out all you can about the girl's condition. I need some assurances that they've gotten her quarantined and know how to treat the illness. We can't be certain what all Alexy has told the O.P.A. or royal guard, and if they trace my magic signature and discover the illness like I did, they're going to hunt me down like a wild animal. I fear for you and your grandmother . . . not to mention the girl, if that happens."

And what chance would I stand if he's afraid of them? "I'll find out what I can. You find the scroll."

As soon as Tal was out of sight, she addressed Viktor's image again. "Could I see Suzanne, Viktor? Her mother is very worried and I'd like to say that I saw she was fine."

There was a long moment while the image stared off into space. "That would be a bad idea, Mila. The less you know, the less chance that people will try to find you to extract information." He looked at her then, directly into her eyes with an intensity that made her question again whether this was a mere recording. "It's for your safety that I ask you not to probe further. I could never live with myself if you were harmed because of choices that were mine and Nadia's."

He looked so worried that she couldn't refuse him. "Fine. I'll trust you and Baba. But please find a way to get word to Carole about Suzanne. Candy won't be able to hold her off from mounting a search party forever." That request met with a sincere nod, so she moved on to the next subject. "Could you please tell me about the eggs now?"

That request made Viktor hold up a finger and disappear out of the image for a moment. He came back with an elegantly dyed pysanka, which he held up to show her, perched on the fingertips of his left hand. He waved his right palm over the egg and it began to glow and vibrate, identical to the one on her mantel. But the decorations were completely different. She pointed to it. "I have one at home that does that same thing. How does it work?"

His brows shot up to disappear under the headband. "You've already created a *dushat?*" He smiled broadly. "But that's *wonderful,* Mila. I'm so very proud of you for taking your art to that level. This will make things much easier."

She'd never heard the word *dushat* before. She was pretty sure it was Ukrainian, so it was probably spelled with an *sz* instead of the *sh* she heard. "Is *dushat* the word for a glowing egg? What does it do? It stopped glowing after a minute and I couldn't make it work again."

He spoke the word again, this time putting in that little growl that told her for certain how it was spelled. "The *duszat* stopped glowing, you say? Was there a Guilder in the room with you by chance?"

She nodded. "Yes, Tal was in the room. He's the one who noticed it glowing, but he doesn't know why it stopped, either."

Viktor's image let out a small laugh. "He wouldn't have to *know.* His body, or his focus stone, would simply absorb the magic in the *duszat.* It's no different than a plant absorbing moisture from rain or you absorbing oxygen from the air you breathe. There's no conscious recognition of the fact."

"The glowing really *was* magic? How did it get inside?" She couldn't seem to take her eyes off the little glowing egg.

Now he smiled at her, the same smile her father and Baba gave her when she was seven—the night sooty wax was melted off the hen's egg she'd labored over for days to reveal the vivid colors and designs of her first completed pysanka. There was pride in that smile, mingled with innate knowledge of the craft that made the pride so much more profound to her. "You *put* it there, Mila. You have become a true Parask. While the other guilds take magic and utilize it, we *create* the magic to be used." He waved his hand again and the pysanka darkened, became just a pretty decoration once more.

"But Tal just told me that magic comes from *trees,* and that the trees are dying, so magic is dying too." It was hard trying to decide who to believe. Her mind said to trust Viktor, because she always had. But Tal seemed so sincere and *certain.*

But Viktor was nodding sagely. "Yes, Nadia told me of your Talos." The way he said it, *your* Talos, suddenly made her fidgety. "I remember the Onan family—they were powerful mages, and they'd expected Talos to be one of the greatest Guilders to be born in a generation. I wish one of our brethren could have been there to stop him from being mutilated by the prince."

Her eyebrows shot up. *"Mutilated?"*

Again he nodded, but didn't explain much further. "You would do the mage guild a great service by healing the damage, if you're able." She opened her mouth to ask for more information, but he held up a hand. "The prince knew he was not as magically powerful as his father, or as powerful as Talos would grow to be. But enough of this, we have little time, Mila, and that information can wait. But Talos is correct that Agathia's magical needs are served by the slave trees." He tapped the top of the egg and looked at her significantly before lowering his voice and leaning forward slightly. "The eggs are *inside* the trees, Mila. That is a secret that very few outside the Parask know. Each slave tree was carefully grown . . . trained just like my bonsai to have four identical main branches around a center trunk. Inside each branch was placed an egg—one for each guild. But occasionally these eggs must be replaced or the growing tree will crush the shells. It's an arduous task to create and replace the pysanka in each of the five trees." He tilted his head and gave her the same look as a teacher during a pop quiz. "Because what happens when a pysanka shell is cracked?"

She found herself nodding, remembering the words of her father. "All the healing leaks out, just like the yellow yolk." A slow smile came to her face. "So there *are* Trees of Life, then."

He chuckled and tucked the egg into a pocket of his fluffy patterned tunic. "No, no. Not plural. There is only *one* Tree of Life. The others are slaves, much like—" He pursed his brows, appearing to search his mind for an analogy. "Much like an electrical substation. They generate some small amount of power on their own, but mostly serve as amplifiers from the one true Tree. But you're correct that the Agathians *believe* there are four trees and that all are required." He must have noticed her questioning look, because he uttered a small, sarcastic laugh. "It would have been foolish on our part to tell the guilds there is only one Tree, Mila—human nature being what it is. Each guild would seek it out, battle to own it, to rule over the others. It was much better to have the kings each believe that there were *four* Trees of Life. By leaving that belief in their minds, it guaranteed they wouldn't harm the other trees for fear of destroying the magic in their own realm."

It made perfect sense—the ultimate cold war. Belief of a mutually assured destruction would keep people cooperating for centuries. "So where is this one true Tree of Life that needs eggs? And why hasn't anyone else made them yet?"

He sighed. "Nobody has made them because the members of our guild were banned from the underground— sought out and slaughtered centuries ago. Myself, the Penkin line that includes you, and a few others are all that is left of what was once a thriving guild." His face hardened, and anger glittered in his eyes. "After watching what they did to my family . . . and *your* family, and barely escaping with my life to live here in lonely solitude, I've had no desire to offer my services." The egg began to glow then. The light, yellow as a fresh yolk, seeped from around his closed fingers. "If it were left up to me, I would advise you to have nothing to do with the Agathians. I would tell you to create your own beauty and joy and leave them to the suffering their choices have wrought."

For a moment, Mila shared his anger. She'd seen images of Viktor's family—delicate paintings on porcelain, bone carvings, and faded photographs that were all that was left of the people he'd held so dear. She'd watched him walk by them, stroke the images gently and brush away wetness from his eyes. But she didn't know they'd been executed. Her anger turned to shock at his next words.

"I'm still firmly convinced the king's guard orchestrated your father's death." He nodded at her dropped jaw, but then shrugged. "But Nadia swears I'm being paranoid, and she would know better, I suppose. I was here, while she was there." He opened his hand again. "You can see how the emotions of the crafter affect the *duszat*. A Parask must be pure of mind, with joy and warmth in their heart . . . all the best qualities of life, to create a *duszat*. Any other emotion would taint the pysanka, and so taint the user. You see this yellow glow? It's a negative energy. Pure magic should be the absence of color, as white as an egg. I would doom all of Agathia, including those who have done me no wrong, by making the attempt." He waved his hand over the little egg again, and it went still and dark. "So, I have waited for centuries, keeping watch over the descendants of our guild, waiting for one who has both talent and a calm intellect. I believe you're that person, Mila."

A swirl of conflicting emotions and shock traveled through her, hand in hand. "But, I don't—"

He ignored her protest. "Nadia has convinced me that the situation is critical, Mila. While I say *good, and let them fall,* she has forgiveness in her heart and fears what would happen in this modern time if the Agathians are forced to move to the surface. That the great prison of Rohm has fallen tells me she's right. You must make the attempt to correct what I've allowed to fail. While I hate to put such a great burden on you, I know whatever you can do will make a difference, even if you only stave off the inevitable for a few years."

The enormity of what he was asking was finally starting to settle home in her mind. She tried to find the words, staring blankly as a covey of quail emerged from the meadow. The female and five chicks didn't even notice her. "I haven't a clue where to start. I've never even *been* to these places. I've never tried to make a *duszat*. I must have made it by accident. And, I've got a life, Viktor—a job, bills to pay. I can't wander around the world, making eggs, even to save the world. I just can't do it."

He reached out his hand in a comforting gesture. "Read the scroll, Mila. It will change your mind. It's only a few days of your life, versus an entire *way* of life for millions."

Already she was beginning to feel that annoying mix of anticipation and pathos for those she didn't know. It was that heady combination of shame and pride that made her reach into her purse as she passed by a bell ringer gathering Christmas donations at the mall. She *could* make a difference, like seeing the tree in the bank covered by paper angels—representing children who would have no gifts under the tree without her help.

Was this any different?

She let out a sigh of resignation and saw Viktor's eyes brighten. "*Fine.* I'm willing to give it a try. But I make no promises. So the instructions are in the scroll?"

He shook his head. "Oh no. I would never leave the instructions unguarded. There are those who seek such knowledge, such as the one your Talos came here to find. Vegre would have no qualms about enslaving guildercent Parask to create *duszat*s. No, the instructions were safely hidden years ago by Nadia. She said to tell you that they're in the vault in Mr. Sanders's office, where—"

A loud explosion made Viktor turn his head and then move quickly to avoid the scattering of debris that filled the screen. She leaned forward, panicked. "Viktor! Are you okay? What's happening there?"

A figure strode onto the screen, and she recognized him. Viktor apparently recognized the man as well, because he stood up proudly and began to brush pebbles and dust from his tunic. "You're too late, Vegre. They've gone, and even I don't know where."

Vegre sneered. He was in better shape than when she last saw him. His shaggy hair had been cut to a neat shoulder length and was held back in a ponytail. His inky shirt and slacks perfectly matched the stormy color of his eyes. It wasn't until he raised a threatening hand, palm out, that he looked like anything other than a modern, successful businessman. But then Mila saw again the stained dark leather glove surrounding the amazingly large faceted diamond. Something in the back of her mind told her the dark stains were blood. "I want those eggs, old man. I paid your price and now—"

Viktor snorted in derision. "*You* bought nothing. I sold them to another. You knew full well I would never have—"

But Vegre's attention had turned her way and she realized this was no recording. He waved his fingers elegantly, freezing Viktor in place with the same precision she remembered from being inside Tal's mind during the breakout.

But Viktor was more accomplished than that. After only a moment's hesitation, he broke free of the freezing spell and sent a blast of power that sent Vegre scrambling. With a wink Mila's way, he addressed the slender mage as he picked himself out from among the rubble. "You've grown slower while in prison, Vegre. Sad that you didn't die there, for all your sins. Unfortunately, I don't have time for a protracted battle, so I'll leave you to find your way back to the real world." There was a blurring around his tunic and he faded away into nothingness, leaving Vegre standing dumbstruck, while Mila smiled broadly. She expected no less of Baba's old friend. So, he really had been a recording, or he could work spells that Tal had no knowledge of. Either way, he was safe, and Vegre was mad enough to spit fire.

But then he stopped ranting and stepped closer to whatever was providing the image of her from Viktor's side and peered at her. She hurried to remove her foot from the pond, so he couldn't see where she was, but he was faster.

Another flick of his fingers, and her foot wouldn't budge. It might as well be encased in concrete. Thoroughly panicked, she grabbed her ankle and started to yank backward, but other than hearing her ankle pop and her skin stretch painfully, there was no movement. She wanted to get a better grip, but feared touching the water in case anything else got stuck.

"So, we meet again . . . *Mila.*" Hearing her name froze her and after a long pause, she looked into the pool to meet his eyes. He was staring at her calmly, all anger either gone or carefully buried. "I wanted to apologize for earlier in your home. I never meant to harm you."

A harsh laugh burst from her lips before she could stop it. "That is such bullshit. You *absolutely* meant to kill me, and you kidnaped my roommate. Now, let my foot go and tell me what you've done with Sela before I send the king's guards to pick you up and take you back to Rome. I've already got a lock on your magic signature." It was a bold lie, and her heart was pounding as she said it, especially with her foot trapped. She wasn't even positive what some of the phrases really meant, but Tal and Alexy had flung them around so casually that she hoped she could pull it off. Bluffing was something she did really well at work and she could say the words with a complete poker face.

It had an effect. Shock and fear played across his face for a brief moment, but then he let out a small laugh. "Very good, young crafter. You nearly had me believing you for a moment. But you apparently don't realize it was the king's guards who let me *out.* They're not likely to put me back. And as for what I've done with Sela . . . why, nothing at all." He waved his hand backward and another figure stepped past the rubble that had been one wall. Her face was calm, unafraid. When Vegre touched her shoulder, she didn't cringe or pull back.

"Sela!" Mila leaned forward, nearly touching the water with her knee. "Are you okay? What's he done to you?"

Sela chuckled lightly, without a trace of nervousness

and laid her hand over his on her shoulder. "He hasn't done *anything* to me, Mila. You've got Vegre all wrong. He was *released* from prison by the kings. It was a case of false imprisonment. They finally realized he didn't do what they accused him of all those years ago. It happens all the time. Like that guy we saw on the news special last week. You remember?"

It was true that new techniques for examining evidence had freed more than one prisoner, even from death row. But she knew better in this case. "Uh, I don't think so. He didn't exactly walk out the front gate of the prison with a new suit and twenty bucks, and you know it." Her absolute assuredness about the fact took both of them by surprise. But Sela tried to keep up the game.

"You're believing the lies my old partners told you. But it's *they* who are the criminals. They accepted bribes to break out prisoners, Mila. I was there. I saw it, and I turned them in."

There was no point in telling them that *she'd* been there, too. Plus, it wasn't something she wanted them to know. It would be far safer to play along at this point . . . appear to give in slightly.

"So why would you have to break in to Viktor's house, then? Free, honest men don't have to blast open walls."

Vegre actually managed to school his features enough to look contrite and embarrassed. "I admit it does look bad. I'm afraid I'm out of practice with modern society. Disputes in prison are handled in a less . . . civilized manner. But I bought some lovely pysanky from Viktor— beautiful art objects that I've long missed. Unfortunately, he never delivered them. In fact, he kept both money and goods. I was angry, and . . . well, overreacted. You're correct, though, that there are better ways to handle the dispute. I'll contact the authorities straight away and have them go collect Viktor to stand before his peers. That's the American method, correct?"

It was only through sheer willpower that she managed not to laugh sardonically and roll her eyes at the line of bull. But then she realized that until Viktor had explained the value of the eggs, she might have believed what they were telling her. It sobered her and made her realize just how serious this matter was and why it was critical that Vegre be kept from any possible *duszats*—because she had no doubt that was exactly what he was looking for.

"Then you won't mind releasing my foot so I can go on my merry way, right? I mean, if *Viktor* is the one who wronged you and you're sending for the police—" She left the statement hanging, seeing what he would make of it. *I'm no match for his magic. But if I could get Tal here— where the heck is he, anyway? It shouldn't take this long to get to the house and back. Could he have run into trouble?*

Vegre smiled, and even his teeth looked better. They were straight and nearly white, with no hint of the rotted stumps that she'd seen earlier. "Actually, I was hoping to convince you to make some eggs for me." His voice sounded soothing, but far too eager for her taste. "Sela tells me you're very skilled. I could pay you well—better than you'd make anywhere else."

Of that she had no doubt. While she still didn't know where the money was coming from, it was apparent from his clothes, and the designer outfit draped on Sela, that cash was no problem. "Well, see, that could be a problem. It's really . . . *busy* at work right now. I couldn't possibly find time."

He sighed, as though he knew her response was inevitable. "I was afraid you'd say that. Sela also told me that you value honor more than money. But you will craft for me nonetheless." He shrugged and then flicked one finger toward her former roommate. "Sela?"

Sela likewise shrugged, then gave her blond hair a little flip. Reaching her hand out as though to grasp something, she suddenly twisted it and clenched the fingers into a fist. *"Pusta!"*

Mila's foot was pulled downward so hard that she splashed into the pool. Water filled her mouth before she was able to reach up and grab onto one of the flagstones.

"Tal!" She screamed his name just as the water surged again, filling her mouth with more water that tasted just like it smelled, of fish and musty algae. She heard footsteps and brush breaking a distance away, but they weren't going to reach her in time. This was going to be up to her. She kicked at the seemingly solid mass of water that surrounded her, and pulled on the rocks, grateful that Viktor had thought to cement them together.

The water turned abruptly icy, nearly taking her breath away. She felt her movements slow in reaction to the bone-chilling temperature. *Warm. I need to be warm.* Her toes started to tingle, then burn, with white-hot intensity. She screamed in pain and another mouthful of water made her choke and sputter. Gritting her teeth, she called on every muscle in her shoulders and arms. While she hadn't made it to the gym much lately, typing and running up and down stairs with boxes of files had kept her arms toned. "I . . . am . . . sick of this!"

She pulled against the siphon of water, strained with every muscle until her head pounded. But she was winning. She was slowly, but surely, climbing out of the pond, wondering how her feet could be burning so hot while surrounded with frigid water.

She got high enough that she was able to flop her chest over the edge for better leverage to drag up her legs.

That's when the entire pond wall gave way.

CHAPTER 10

Mila's scream had spurred him forward, nearly making him drop the heavy scroll. It was as long as his torso and the platens were either solid copper or plated over an equally weighty metal. Birds took flight in a chirping whir of wings as he forced his way through the tangle of grass—foregoing the slowly winding path for a more direct route to the pond. He could hear her grunts of effort and the distinctive sound of splashing water.

He burst through the last flowering hedge into the orderly little space, just as the stones Mila had been sitting on tumbled into the pool and her head disappeared into a whirlpool that was sucking her down. As he approached the last few feet, a wave of bitter cold hit him in the face and he knew that the water had been magically chilled as a method to hamper her escape.

This was obvious water crafting. Either Viktor had betrayed her or someone had interfered and was using the message pool to attack her.

He dove face first and hit the ground, knocking the air from his chest. He reached down into the water to grab her, but she was in too deep, far past where the bottom of the pool should have been. Even when he ducked his head under, he could barely touch her fingertips. Thankfully, she'd managed to do a counterspell, so the water touching her had warmed to nearly skin temperature. With sufficient time, she could probably get the water to evaporate, but time was one thing they didn't have. Without help she was going to drown or be sucked directly to the caster's location. He had only seconds to act.

He looked around the garden, searching for something he could use to free her. But all the trees in this particular garden were stunted—barely as tall as his knees. It was obvious the stunting was intentional because of the careful trimming. He'd heard of this sort of decorative living art, but had never seen an example. The trees were pretty, but useless for his purposes. Still, one was close enough to the edge of the pond to serve as an anchor point—if it would hold his weight. One of the roots had been exposed when the soil gave way, and it was as thick around as his calf. When he shook it firmly, other than dislodging some tiny bird nests, the gnarled trunk didn't even budge. It must be very old, and deep into the soil to be so sturdy. But how to use it? He had no rope and no time to craft one from the surrounding materials.

Then he threw his hands in the air and rolled his eyes at his own stupidity. He'd brought along the perfect tool and had nearly forgotten about it in the panic. He smiled and reached for the solid metal scroll and quickly unwound one end of the lettered parchment, since he didn't know whether the ink would withstand being immersed in water. When he reached the end, he yanked the paper free of the narrow slot in the metal.

Taking a deep breath, he plunged face first into the pool, taking care to wrap his thighs around the sturdy old tree. He prayed that Mila would know what to do when she felt the scroll above her. Grasping firmly around the metal, just beneath the wide guard that kept the parchment even, he pressed it downward until he felt the tip of the other end hit something solid. He hoped it was her hand or head.

He couldn't speak under the swirling column of icy water to utter a spell. All he could do was to concentrate and throw energy into the deep hole and try to force it to his will. Unfortunately, fire magic didn't work well under water. He could turn the water to steam, but the resulting burns would make it difficult to hold onto the scroll end.

A surge of pride and hope swept through him when weight on the end of the scroll pulled him suddenly downward. He compensated by tightening his legs around the tree and pulling up. The weight remained and when he felt the scroll handle move from side to side, he realized she was using it to climb up out of the water. He pulled backward again, doing his best to aid her escape. His stomach muscles started to cramp as he struggled to draw his arms to his chest. Definitely time for more attention to keeping fit if they made it through this.

He was yanked suddenly backward and the scroll started to turn in a wide circle. Apparently the caster wasn't willing to give up the prize yet. But neither was Mila, because he felt the touch of skin against the bottom of his fist as she continued to climb, even though she was only moving inches at a time. He was impressed by her tenacity . . . and the power of her grip. Most people wouldn't have the hand strength to keep hold of the thick bar. He'd assumed she would just keep weight on the side guard and let him pull her up. He was surprised how pleased he was that she was trying to do it herself—including countering the caster's spell to bubble air into the water to push her upward. He could feel the bubbles popping against his face as she rose. Her claim that she knew no magic was quickly becoming a lie . . . even if she was only lying to herself.

He was almost out of air though so he lifted his head and drew in a great breath. But it was one he didn't need as he felt her hand grasp his wrist just before her head emerged from the water.

She gulped in great mouthfuls of air and then gasped. "Just don't move or lose your balance. I can do this."

He felt a smile pull at his lips from the fierce determination on her face. "Yes, ma'am. Not moving."

She let out what he could only describe as a primal yell and kicked one last time, then literally used his arms as a rope to scale the side of the pool before throwing herself sideways to collapse next to him on the disturbed dirt.

Once the prey had escaped, the pool stilled, returned to its former quiet state. But that didn't mean he wasn't careful to pull the scroll platen out of the pool and shimmy sideways away from the edge.

After a moment of both of them catching their breath, she turned her still dripping face to where she could see him. She smiled and motioned to his legs. "Always knew that tree was next to the pond for a reason."

*I*t wasn't until they were safely back in Viktor's house that he asked what happened. He was more concerned with checking her for injuries. He would have supported her as she limped back to Viktor's house, but she insisted he dry the platen and reroll the scroll. He had to agree, it was far too important to simply leave lying in the open. Still, it bothered him to see her moving with such obvious pain.

While she found some towels to dry herself, he started a fire in the small iron stove that sat in the corner of the kitchen. The fire had been amazingly easy to start, despite the lack of fuel. He hadn't been able to find any wood or coal piled near the house, and all the wood outside was very much alive and green. He'd managed to gather some dried grasses, but that wouldn't have been enough to last long. Yet, the focus stone in his pocket seemed to be brimming with magic. When he pointed the opal at the grasses and uttered the word *iska* the flames leapt high and hot—as though he'd filled the opal at a fueling station.

Soon the house was warm enough to dry them both before they returned to the frozen overworld. He found Mila in one of the many libraries in the house—which was far larger than he'd expected from the outside design because it covered three floors. "You can see why I had a difficult time finding the *den*. There are a dozen rooms fitting that description."

She chuckled. "Yeah, Viktor really likes to read. Books are what Baba always got him for Christmas." She looked up at the massive tree in the corner, decorated in a traditional manner—candles, glittering garland, and small glass ornaments.

"He seems to be rather fond of Christmas, too." There was a tree in every room—the kitchen included. Some had bows, while others were themed. "I've never seen a tree decorated with *shells* before."

She laughed lightly while running a comb through her thick damp curls. "You should see the place when he's gearing up for the holiday. About half the decorations have already been put away. We never minded climbing up to the cave when I was a kid, because it was like a Norman Rockwell painting when we got inside. Snowy hills for sledding, hot chocolate in front of the fire, sleigh rides, and Christmas music everywhere." Her mood sobered suddenly. "I hope he's okay. I don't even know where he was talking from. He could be *anywhere*."

Damn. He should have been there to see what happened.

Once again Vegre slipped through his grasp. But his anger dissolved at the look on her face. The pain and fear made him want to comfort her, and he had to hold himself back from walking over and pulling her into his arms. It would be too easy to get involved with this one, and an emotional entanglement with an overworlder, especially one from the conjurer guild, could be disastrous. But the information she had could be vital, so he couldn't simply keep silent, either. "Why don't you tell me about it." He sat down on the puffy leather couch and patted the seat next to him.

She sat, turned toward him with one leg on the cushion, and began to spin a tale that left him stunned. "*Eggs?* Our entire way of life is based on pretty colored eggs?" He didn't want to believe. The Tree of Life was everything to them . . . and especially to Sybil, his foster mother. Yet everything Mila said made perfect sense. This place, how she was able to energize him, the vibration of the egg on her mantel, how the opal focus stone brimmed with magic, and why Vegre would be gathering them up—even risking attacking Viktor to get the eggs. He shook his head, trying to wrap his head around the flurry of ideas. "It's just such a hard concept to accept."

So don't. The tiny voice in the back of his mind grew louder in his head with each passing second. *Circumstantial evidence and hearsay. That's all you're hearing.* When Mila spoke, she seemed to echo his sentiments.

She rolled her eyes and then shrugged. "For you and me both. To find out that eggs are the source of magic for the whole world is like telling me aliens have landed from Alpha Centauri. Yes, it's *possible.* But I want some solid evidence. Heck, I'm still trying to get a handle on the fact that my *foot* apparently has magical powers." She shook her head, tiny little movements that looked very much like a shudder. "I mean, I'm not completely oblivious to the fact that when I was cold, so numb I couldn't even move, and thought of heat, my foot got hot. Then, when I swallowed water and started to choke, thinking of breathing made air bubbles pop out of my toe. It tickled, so I looked." He remained silent, not really sure what to say. She didn't appear to want to be consoled, or taught. She just wanted to say the words. How he knew that still mystified him, but his mind and heart knew it was fact. "But," she continued. "We have to accept that *Vegre* believes it, and deal with it. And I promised Viktor I'd try to replace the eggs. It might well be the last thing he asked of me, so I can't dismiss it easily." She paused and then uttered a near snarl. "Traitorous bitch."

Had he missed part of the story? He didn't remember a woman being mentioned. All of Vegre's minions had been men. But perhaps popular slang had changed in the past few years. "Who is?"

"Sela." The flat statement caught him unaware and his face must have showed it. "Oh yeah. She was there. Sorry, forgot to mention that. She's the one who threw out that nifty spell to suck me under the water. At first, she tried to convince me that Vegre had been *released* from prison, not that he escaped. They both swore up and down that the king's guards let him out, so they wouldn't be in a hurry to put him back. But I wasn't buying that, so they decided to suck me under the water. I don't know whether they were trying to kill me, or—"

He wanted to defend his former partner, but the news simply bore out his and Alexy's earlier suspicions. "Most likely, they were trying to bring you to their location. And as much as I hate that my intuition was correct, Sela has enough water witch abilities to make the pond a temporary portal—like I could see the hospital in the fire. With enough magic, I might have been able to walk into the fireplace and appear where the image showed." He paused, not really certain if he could manage it. "At least, that's the theory. Whether I would have the skill to manage it is a question."

She acknowledged it with another movement of her shoulder. "So, what now? I'm exhausted, frankly. I haven't had dinner and feel like I could sleep for a week."

He motioned toward the scroll. "We still have that to read, but I don't see any reason why we can't take it back to your house. I don't like that the gate is unguarded right now, and I agree you need rest."

The look she gave him before she replied reminded him so much of Sybil's expression of motherly sternness that he nearly laughed. "Um, I think you mean *we* need rest. Last I checked, you'd had a worse day than me."

He stood and lifted his cloak from where it was hanging next to the couch. The heavy wool wasn't easy to soak, so it was often the first thing to dry. "Yes, but if I sleep, who will guard the gate? Do you believe your *foot's* up to the challenge?"

Mila sneered and opened her mouth to reply, probably with sarcasm, but then stopped. Her face dropped into serious lines. "No, you're right. Even if my getting out of the pond wasn't a fluke, I'm not trained in this magic stuff. But you won't have much better luck without sleep. Can't you set some sort of alarm or something, to wake us if Vegre tries to activate the gate? Really noisy, like a smoke detector that will get our adrenaline pumping?"

An alarm—He pursed his lips and considered the idea while he fastened his cloak. "An interesting idea. I'll have to think about it on the way back."

She smiled tiredly and stood. "I'm sure we'll come up with something between the two of us."

Tal had no doubt of that. As he watched her stretch and twist before putting on her jacket, he had to forcibly pull his eyes from staring at her curves and silken hair. *The only question is* what *will come up between us, and whether I can stop my own desire to keep her from getting any rest.*

CHAPTER 11

Mila walked out of the elevator, filled with determination and purpose. She'd been giving herself a pep talk since they'd left the house this morning and repeated the mantra again in a near whisper. "Just a few hours. Finish the Johnson brief. Find Baba's file. Pretend to still be sick. Meet Tal downstairs. Go make pysanky. Save the world." She nodded, then added, "No problem. Two hours . . . tops."

She kept breathing deeply, staring straight ahead as she walked down the elegant hallway decorated with bamboo-patterned wallpaper, poofy green-and-black carpeting, and tasteful, expensive holiday art that would be replaced with equally tasteful, expensive abstract prints come January third. The familiar metal letters spelling Sanders, Harris & Hoote came into view on one wall, peeking out from around the next corner. In fact, the foot-high polished brass words were around *every* corner, apparently just to be certain that visitors knew the whole top four floors of the American State Bank tower housed the firm.

A strong whiff of flowers from the massive arrangement on a corner table made her look up and caused her to bang one shoulder into the wall. The winter arrangement of calla lilies, poinsettia blooms, and swirling, glittered branches had been replaced since she left the previous day. In its place were fragrant, brightly colored spring flowers that were completely out of season. As she shook her arm to get the feeling back, she was abruptly reminded of Viktor's gardens. It fueled her resolve. "Johnson brief. Baba's file. Save the worl—"

At last her cubicle came into view, but the sight brought her to a stuttering, stunned halt that left the final word frozen in her throat. What had been a small, orderly pile of papers on her desk before lunch yesterday was now a crime scene. Files and loose papers were strewn haphazardly everywhere—across the patterned faux marble desktop, the entire length of the half-wall, and even lined up in neat rows on the chair mat covering the carpet. Most bore colored sticky notes, meaning they'd been placed there intentionally. Her center desk drawer was hanging sideways from one caster and an error message was blinking on her computer screen.

She closed her eyes and felt her shoulders slump, making her purse slide off her jacket to land on the floor with a thud. "Two hours? I'll be lucky to get out of here in two *days.*"

A double chirp from the phone as she was taking off her coat was followed by Rachel's voice from the front desk. "Mila? Was that you I saw sneaking in? What are you doing here so early?"

She let out a frustrated and very audible sigh. "Can I pretend I'm *not* in and leave now?"

Rachel's voice dropped to a warm, sympathetic alto. "Aww, you're still sick, huh? Poor baby."

As much as she wanted to play up the sick aspect, the first words out of her mouth wound up being, "What happened to my desk?" After stepping carefully over the stacks of papers, she plopped down into her chair so hard she heard air whoosh out of the hydraulic lift. Mila bent down and tried to figure out *how* someone had wrenched the drawer right out of the runners. These built-ins were hell for stout. She was a little afraid to touch it for fear the whole thing would collapse.

"Ah. You mean the drawer? That would have been the temp . . . some ham-handed loser named Bob who apparently didn't have enough dexterity to simultaneously push a button and pull—" Her voice cut off abruptly, and Mila looked up to see that a new light had appeared on the multiline phone set. It was understood by everyone here that the phones came first, so she was used to Rachel disappearing for long stretches in the middle of a conversation. While waiting, she tucked her purse in its normal home in the back of the bottom side drawer and started to gather up all the papers and files on the floor so she didn't roll . . . or *trip* over them. Her brow furrowed when she realized she didn't recognize half the client names on the papers. One note expected her to prepare a divorce petition! She didn't even know the *rules* for that kind of law.

Geez, guys! Are you asking *for a malpractice suit? Figures I'd get stuck with work for every department just because nobody in personnel knows how to schedule employee vacations.* She shook her head angrily as the chirp sounded again. Rachel began to speak as though never interrupted. "I don't know why Gail thought it was necessary to bring someone in just to type one brief anyway. I mean, I could have done it just as easily if I'd known you were out sick. Oh, and I called maintenance as soon as I saw the drawer this morning. But they said with the holidays—"

Mila nodded, even more irritated because she knew what *that* meant. Yet again she was going to have to put up with something broken until *at least* after the new year. But it would probably be February before she actually saw someone with a tool belt, if past history was any indication. And saints preserve her if she actually dared fix the problem herself. That was grounds for a reprimand. *Maybe if I stack all this work up under it to prop it up—*She felt a hysterical laugh bubble up, but managed to squash it before it reached air. It wasn't as easy to fight back the desire to throw the whole pile of papers across the room and storm out.

But then she caught herself and thumped her temple with one finger hard enough that it stung a little. *Focus, girl. None of this shit matters . . . not by comparison. Brief, file, save world.* She forced her face into a smile so it would come through over the speaker. "No big. I'll figure something out. Did the Johnson de novo brief get filed yesterday? Today's the last day to file or we'll lose the chance to appeal."

Rachel laughed bitterly. "Does your computer screen

look like it's been filed? Our buddy Bob managed to screw up the network so bad that *nothing* got filed yesterday. Why do you think *I'm* in at six thirty? The idiot downloaded some weird virus off a free music site that corrupted the server. Personally, I'd suggest you log off the network and save things to your hard drive today if you hope to accomplish anything."

Already her head was hurting. "But without network access, I can't reach the printer, so I can't scan the brief to electronically file with the court. Will they even *accept* a paper copy anymore? Does *anyone* have access to the drive?"

There was a pause where only background noise from people arriving and walking past Rachel could be heard. "Well," she finally said, "you might check Alan Lee's office down on the twenty-fourth floor. He hasn't been in since before Christmas, and I know he unplugged his laptop from the network before he left. The IT guys got the server itself running last night, according to the note on my desk. But they weren't able to get to the individual desktops."

It wasn't a bad idea. She'd worked with Alan long ago when he was an associate in the real estate department, so he wouldn't mind. And, if she was working down there, nobody could find her to give her new projects. Normally, she'd simply take the brief home, type it, bring it back for the signature, and hand-carry it to the court. But the only *Mr. Sanders* Baba might have known, who might have an actual *vault* that she felt confident Mila could reach was the very Myron Sanders who founded this firm. But she didn't have vault access and she couldn't imagine how to break in, so there was no leaving until things were sorted out. "I might do that. Just don't tell anyone else so I can get down there first. Oh and by the way, who is the great and sacred *keeper of the vault* while Devon's on vacation?"

Another pause and a flipping of paper over the speaker. "I can't find the memo, but I think Eunice in bookkeeping is the backup. Want me to find out?"

Mila shook her head, even though only Nicole in the

next cubicle, who had just arrived and was unwrapping a fluffy white muffler from around her neck, could see. "No, that's okay. She's on twenty-four, too. I'll just poke my head in on the way."

"Sounds good. I'll try not to bother you so you can get out of here. Hope you feel better."

Nicole, normally bubbly and sweet, gave her a wary look over the divider when Rachel said that. Mila took the opportunity to have a witness to her later leaving sick by letting out a chesty-sounding cough. The other woman grimaced and held up her hands, fingers formed in a cross, as though Mila was a vampire.

"Go *home,* Mila. Don't you dare get me sick. I have family coming into town for New Year's and I finally get to have a big party in my new house."

Mila held up a hand and waved it like she was surrendering. "Don't worry. I plan to. I'm even going down to work on the twenty-fourth so I don't breathe on anyone. But that Johnson brief has *got* to be filed today or Rick will kill me. Who's in who can look at it?" Mila's own boss was out for the week, but had dictated the brief before he left. All she had to do was make the edits the associate assigned to the case had made, attach the exhibits, get it blessed by one of the attorneys, and shoot the file to the court by e-mail.

Nicole sat down, carefully arranging her chair so it was against the wall, farthest away from Mila as possible. "Probably Mike Callendar. He wanted to talk to you anyway—something about a pleading that came in on your probate case. I think he put it on your desk just as I was leaving yesterday."

Mila's eyes shot down to the mess of paperwork on the desk. She'd hoped to ignore whatever might be in the stack, but horrified curiosity took hold of her. "There shouldn't *be* any more pleadings in the case. We had the final hearing, and are just waiting for a decision from the judge."

Nicole shrugged, already turned toward a similar stack of papers on her desk. "Dunno. I'm only repeating what I heard. He asked Gail where you were and was really concerned because he was leaving tomorrow—well, this afternoon, now—for Canada and won't be back until the middle of January. You might check to see if he left you a voice mail or e-mail."

She checked her watch again. Already an hour had passed since she'd dropped Tal off at the public library. Another O.P.A. agent worked there, and Tal believed he could trust him to find out what was happening down below. If she took the time to go through e-mail and phone messages before working on the brief, she'd be here all day. "Maybe I'll wander down the hall and see if he's in. I just don't feel up to looking through all this." That, at least, was the truth.

"Well, for what it's worth, I'll be happy to tell anyone who bitches how horrible that cough sounded. And I'll fit in whatever emergency stuff I can, if it'll help." She did look sympathetic, but was still firmly pressed against the farthest wall. Another inch and she'd be in the hallway.

"Thanks, Nicole. Appreciate it." She quickly reached for the red expandable file that housed the Johnson file. It was easy to spot amongst the other papers due to the sheer size and tattered appearance. A quick peek inside confirmed that the original brief was inside, covered with new wording and strikeouts in red marker.

Before anything else went wrong, she grabbed her purse from the drawer and gathered up her coat. "I'll be in Alan Lee's office, in case anything *really* bad happens." She put on her best pouty face. "*Try* not to call me, huh, Nic?"

The other woman opened her mouth to respond, but Rachel's voice sounded out of the speaker of Nicole's phone, so she simply nodded. Mila didn't wait, but took the opportunity to slip back out into the hallway. She took a left this time, instead of a right. *Okay, so now it's talk to Mike, finish brief, find file, and leave. That's not* too *bad. I can still get it done.*

She was halfway to the internal elevator when she saw a

light on in Mike Callendar's office and made a beeline to it. "Hey, Mike. You busy?"

The older man, dressed casually in black jeans and a comfy-looking burgundy sweater looked up from the document he was editing and smiled. "Hey yourself, Mila. Glad you were able to make it in today. You do look like crap, though, so don't come any closer."

Mila was quite pleased her makeup artistry was bearing up to casual scrutiny. It was an old trick her sister Sarah had taught her when they were less-than-ethical kids. Careful smudged liner made great dark circles under the eyes, and baby powder brushed on *under* the blush gave her a pale but fevered look that fooled most everyone—but especially her mother and the teachers. Poof, no math test. She'd outgrown that stage, but the success of it had given her the idea this morning. "No problem. Nicole said you're going to Canada. What's up?"

He smiled broadly and leaned back in his leather-backed chair with a squeak. "My wife gave me a great Christmas present—something I've always wanted to do. I'm going up on a photo safari to snap pictures of the snow geese migration. Personally, I'd rather be taking along my shotgun, but she doesn't really approve of that."

The thought struck her and she couldn't keep back the laugh, despite her supposed *sickly* state. He tipped his head, blue eyes twinkling in anticipation. They shared the same odd humor, which is one of the reasons she picked Mike to work on the probate. "What?"

"So she's finally sending you off on a wild goose chase, huh?" She grinned and waited for his reaction.

His laugh was loud and barking and he threw his body back against the chair so hard he nearly fell over. "I guess that's true. Never looked at it that way. Now I'll have to grill her about what *she'll* be up to while I'm off on it." Another shared chuckle, and then he dropped back into a more serious expression. "Well, you probably heard we got another motion from the Rankin boys."

Her brow furrowed and she let out a tense breath. "Yeah. What's that about?"

"Well, they *claim* they have new evidence that Lillian had a mental disorder. They want to depose you about the symptoms and bring in an expert witness to view the will-reading video to show she wasn't competent. I'm betting they'll also try to use the expert to show that you were somehow aware of this alleged *disorder* and took advantage of her. They want the deposition to take place before the judge makes his final decision."

The little frustrated scream escaped her before she could stop it. "Aah! Those men are driving me *nuts*. Lillian Armstrong was a completely sane, brilliant attorney. You know it as well as I do. I mean, I didn't *ask* to be her heir. I never planned to be anything more than her secretary."

He nodded, his salt-and-pepper hair catching the overhead light in flashes. "I know that. And, as the attorney who prepared her will, I'm well aware just how competent she was. She knew full well that they'd contest the will and did everything she could to counter their arguments beforehand. But, of course, if her nephews can prove incompetence, all the planning won't matter. Ordinarily, I'd suggest we ignore this and deal with it later if the judge approves the motion. But with me leaving for Canada, that sort of changes things. If anything were to happen to me it would take another attorney *months* to come up to speed on this. We need to put the ball back in their court so they're the ones delaying the process."

Mila found herself nodding. She shifted the weight of the file to her other arm, where her coat would cushion the sharp paper edges from where they were cutting into her skin. "Force them to *produce* this alleged evidence before the judge has a chance to decide?"

"And to produce any person they got the knowledge from for our own depositions. We won't let them speculate based on book definitions of the disorder without producing an independent witness who will testify they *saw* Lillian exhibit the symptoms. That takes it off your shoulders." He held out a tape with a sad sort of grimace. "I dictated it yesterday, but April left early yesterday with the same crud you've got. It's hit or miss whether she'll be in today. Can you hang in there long enough to whip it out? I'm only here until noon."

Another glance at her watch, another fifteen minutes gone. The minutes were swimming by, like someone was moving the dials while she wasn't looking. She needed to get out of here . . . but this was her *home,* not just a question of whether a business was going to be forced to pay damages for using a similar name to another company, like in the Johnson case. She sighed and stepped forward. "Of course I will. Can I use April's computer real quick?"

Mike shook his head as he tossed the tape to her. "That's close enough, thanks. And sorry, but her machine's down, too, because of that idiot temp. I hope the firm sues that agency. He shut the whole place down yesterday. That's why I sent her home early. She was willing to stay and get it out, but there was nothing to type *on.* I presume you found a machine?"

She nodded as she caught it, actually feeling a little sick now. "Alan Lee's office. I was on my way down there." While she knew logically it wasn't really her fault, Mila couldn't help but feel a stab of conscience. No, she couldn't have stopped having an episode, but she *should* have come back to work as soon as she woke up. Then there wouldn't have been a question of running around to hospitals and gardens and the whole firm wouldn't have been screwed by the actions of Bob the temp. She never would have gotten involved . . . with Vegre, with magical eggs and sinister plots, or—

With Tal— That stopped her cold and she realized she had a queasy feeling in the pit of her stomach at the thought. *I wouldn't have met him, wouldn't have kissed him, and never would have learned the* reason *for my episodes all these years.* She forced a smile and raised the microcassette to shake it lightly, listening to the click of the gears rattling. "I'll do it first thing, so you can get out of here. But there's not a transcriber in Alan's office. I'll have to use your handheld, if that's okay."

He nodded, dug under some papers, took out the tape inside, and tossed that as well. "It's not very long, maybe a couple pages. When you're done, just buzz me and leave it on the half-wall outside. I can get someone else to get the exhibits together and file it. That way you can finish your own work and get out of here."

She let out a breath she hadn't realized she was holding. "That would be great. I might be able to find my way out of the sequential vortex now."

"No problem. Now, if you'll excuse me, I have my own vortex to escape so I can pack and catch my plane. I had to bump up the ticket to miss the winter storm they're forecasting. First-class rates, so I shudder at the thought of missing it."

She was already turning to leave. "Color me gone." But then she paused and turned. "By the way, Mike." He raised his brows and waited. "Thanks. For everything. I know Lillian would really be pleased at how hard you're working on this, and I wouldn't have been able to fight it without you working pro bono for me."

He waved off the praise. "Hey, don't worry about it. You've pitched in plenty through the years. You've paid your sweat equity a hundred times over."

She smiled and walked away, feeling at least a *little* less guilty about the mess the temp had caused. Because Mike was right—she *had* worked hard over the decade she'd worked for the firm. She'd started as a file clerk right out of high school and eventually had found herself working as paralegal to one of the firm's senior partners—Lillian Armstrong.

I do miss you, Lillian. The white-haired firecracker had taught her to be confident, strong, and not take any shit from anyone. And for her to be taken down so suddenly . . . by a simple case of the flu. *If only I could have helped—but she was too proud to let me.*

It was a stark reminder of Suzanne's plight. As she

stepped off the elevator onto the darkened twenty-fourth floor, lit only by the few fluorescent bulbs assigned to after-hours security, she wished there had been some news from Baba—a phone message or note under the door. But although she'd immediately called her voice mail when they got home and checked her cell phone for missed calls, there was nothing.

Alan's office was cool and dark, except for the dancing electronic flames that decorated a digital picture frame on his credenza. She'd never seen one like it. The images of his family and life appeared and disappeared into the flames every few seconds. One picture in particular caught her attention. Alan was a good-looking man, but she hadn't realized just how similar he looked to Tal. That one photo, of Alan climbing a rock wall, his face intense and focused, reminded her so much of Tal last night it was a little frightening.

The whole situation was frightening. Yet, she couldn't ignore that she'd distinctly heard his voice in her head while they kissed and she finally remembered every bit of the conversation they'd held while he was under Vegre's spell in the cave. They'd talked about it and both of them had come to the uneasy realization that it had happened. There was simply no way to explain it away. Even if she wasn't a *Tree spirit,* she was *something* to be able to hear his thoughts.

Unfortunately, while she'd maintained delusions for several hours after getting home of continuing what the kiss promised, reality had wound up far different. Oh, there was sexual tension—no doubt about that. The air had practically crackled every time they were within a few feet of each other.

But Tal had been either unwilling, or *uninterested,* in following through. Yet it hadn't made her feel dismissed. It had been sort of . . . comfortable. She'd found it fascinating to watch him working with the opal. To see it used as a *tool,* rather than just a decoration sitting in a drawer, had been awesome.

And he certainly knew his stuff. Now that she understood how to sense it, she could *feel* the magic as he crafted. From putting guard spells on the wall upstairs where the magic portal had appeared, to simply moving her candlesticks around the room, she'd watched it all with growing respect for him.

And the things they'd learned from the scroll! Wow, was that an eye opener. But it wasn't just the recitation of the events that put Vegre in prison that had held her attention, but Tal's remembrances of that time. Like the difference between reading a news story in the paper to watching it happen on television, she could almost *see* the medieval world through his words.

"And thus it was ordered that houses of the afflicted should place dark cloths in their windows. The number which complied panicked the lords, for the magic which had served us became our enemy as *Tin Czerwona* laid waste to the guilds." She remembered him reading from the parchment. He let out a little sniff of derision. "That sounds so simple, doesn't it? So clean and neat. But it wasn't." He paused for a long moment and his eyes glazed over, remembering. "I remember women walking through the frozen mud with reddened, vacant eyes . . . skirts shredded and flashing their petticoats underneath. Revealing their shame."

She must have shown her confusion on her face, because he continued. "Oh, yes—*shame*. Average people didn't have closets of clothing to make hangings from, Mila. Cloth was precious, and all but the very wealthy had just the one outfit. To follow the law, one cloth at least two handsbreadths in width had to be flown for each of the afflicted. There were a lot of big families and eventually even the most skillful seamstresses couldn't hide the missing cloth. For a woman to show her undergarments was grounds for time in the stocks." He sighed and shook his head. "But eventually nobody pointed fingers or spoke of punishment because there were no families left to *point*. I was young, you understand, so I had a different view than adults might have had. I remember very clearly the tiny rows of stitches to fix damage after the dead were buried . . . the patchwork skirts that didn't quite match. Women would sneak into houses to strip cloth from the dead and dying . . . risking their lives so their families could retain a little dignity."

She didn't even know how to respond to that. Tears had burned her eyes, because as he spoke—some weird part deep inside her *remembered* those people.

"The smell was horrible, wasn't it?" She wasn't asking out of curiosity, but in confirmation of the phantom scent that burned her nose.

"Very. We had magic then, enough for all. But it . . . *permeated* our daily lives. You couldn't walk the streets for the stench of the dead and dying. And it was far worse once it mutated to infect the humans. Whole cities were laid waste by it. The humans called it the black plague because of how their skin would turn black. but we called it *Tin Czerwona*—red shadow, because of the way our magical aura would corrupt."

"Red and writhing. I know. I saw it attacking Suzanne, even though I didn't know what it was then."

He turned to her with horror etched on his face. "You didn't mention you *saw* the illness in the girl. How far along was it?"

All she could do was shrug. "I don't know how far it *can* get, so it's hard to judge. There were squirming tendrils of red and black. They seemed to come from a bruise on her neck. It was all over her chest. I beat it back a little by rolling eggs on her, but I would have needed a case to get rid of it fully. And the eggs stank when they exploded . . . filled with a blackish goo."

"Her *neck,* you say?" He got an odd look on his face and then put the scroll on the floor. Pushing the coffee table aside with one arm, he tossed the bottom roller hard with the other, making it spin across the rug to reveal the entire parchment. He crawled alongside it as it opened, finger tracing back and forth across the carefully inked words. She continued to sit and remain silent, because she didn't know what he was looking for and it seemed that interrupting would be a bad thing.

After a few long moments, he apparently found the right passage and tapped the parchment with a grim expression, then read it out loud. " 'And the prisoner doth further stand accused of intentionally inflicting *Tin Czerwona* on the great guild house of Cabal. Not a single illusion crafter family was spared owing to the prisoner's careful infecting of the children and elderly at the weakest point of the neck, forcing the healthy to remain exposed to the malady out of duty and familial affection. The council of elders, righteously indignant that those we have sworn to protect were used in such a heinous manner, then laid their judgment on the prisoner. It was adjudged by this august assembly that the prisoner Vegrellion David Peircevil would not be put to death, but would instead be stripped of magic and imprisoned in such place as would contain him for the remainder of his life, or for a minimum of one human lifespan for each guild member lost by the malady he created.' "

Mila's mind had swirled as she tried to follow the logic here. "So, you think *Vegre* infected Suzanne? For what purpose? And how would he even know who she was, and how did he find her?"

He rose to his knees and leaned back on his heels with a sigh and a shrug. "I wish I knew. But the circumstances bear a striking resemblance, don't they?"

"Well, yeah. But bubonic plague still exists in some animals, and it's not a big deal. We've got antibiotics now. How would infecting her do him any good? It just doesn't make sense."

A double chirp startled her and the image of Tal, shaking his head, disappeared into the flames with the other photos. "Alan's not here," she said to whoever was on the intercom. "He's out until after the first, and so's his staff."

Rachel's voice came out in a terse whisper. "Mila, it's me. Pick up."

She walked the rest of the way to the desk and put down the file, and picked up the handset. "I thought we agreed you wouldn't bother me." She tried to put some humor in the words, but a little growl came out nonetheless.

The words remained in a whisper and were now slightly muffled, like her hand was over the microphone attached to her headset. "I know. I know. But you really need to take this call."

"Why are you whispering? What's wrong?"

She sighed. "I'm whispering because Thomas Harris is standing over by the elevator talking to someone and I'm afraid he'll hear me."

That seemed odd. Normally Rachel got along fine with the elderly senior partner. But she didn't get a chance to ask further, because Rachel kept talking.

"The concierge at the Palace Hotel is on line four. He claims someone accidentally double-booked the lobby for Friday night and they're bumping our New Year's party."

Mila had heard of people feeling their heart stop for a moment after a shock, but she'd never experienced it. She sat down in the chair with a thud, her legs boneless. She'd spent weeks . . . no, *months,* planning this party. Every detail was perfect, intended to benefit and flatter every possible A-list client of the firm. Sparkling wine from one client's Australian vineyard, cheese produced by another's dairy cows. Crackers made from a particular field of wheat and even imported Beluga caviar for an expat Russian fishery owner. It had to be close enough for one of the partners to walk from his Lower Downtown loft, and have elegant enough rooms to house the entire staff of one Greek shipping magnate. Multiple grandfather clocks had to be rented, to chime the new year in each different time zone of the guests. Every delivery had been confirmed. Each agreement hammered out with a *damn the cost* mentality that was so unusual for the firm that she'd had to ask twice to be certain she'd heard right.

She reached for the button so fast she nearly overshot the whole top row. Taking a deep breath and letting it out slow was the only thing that prevented the words from coming out in a tiny squeak. "This is Mila Penkin."

The caller seemed startled that someone answered. "Oh, um. Yes, Mila. This is Jean-Paul from the Palace. How are you today?"

She looked at her watch again. It was barely 7:15. Why would he be calling at a time that was virtually guaranteed to miss everyone? It turned her voice cagey, yet smooth. "Always wonderful to talk with you, regardless of the *time,* Jean-Paul."

He made some odd noises that made her wonder if someone was standing over his chair with a gun to his head and she realized he was playing a game of chicken. First one to flinch won.

She let out a little chuckle. "The receptionist made the funniest joke when she buzzed me. She said you were canceling our reservation." She laughed again brightly. "But I *know* that couldn't be the case. We've had a contract in place for nearly a year. The lobby from eight to ten, the Arizona suite from ten-o-one to midnight and the entire top floor thereafter."

Jean-Paul cleared his throat nervously. "Well, you see—" he began, but she cut him off by continuing to talk.

"But really, wouldn't that be silly? I can't *imagine* what David Pierce would say at your next board meeting about that—not being able to celebrate in his own grandfather's hotel? Why, he'd be *humiliated.* It could ruin the hotel's reputation."

There was a pause, and then his voice dropped to almost a whisper. "Mr. *Pierce* is one of the guests attending?"

"Oh, he was one of the very first invited. It's why we selected your fine establishment to house the party." She kept the absolute confidence in her voice, feeling as though she was channeling Lillian—even though who would attend among the invited was far from certain.

"Could you excuse me a moment?" She smiled as she heard his handset being covered and then snatches of a terse, whispered conversation where Jean-Paul's voice lost much of its usual polish. He sounded downright snippy. "No, absolutely not . . . didn't you *hear* her? David *Pierce* . . . I don't *care* . . . what about the Long's Peak Room? Didn't that group from . . . canceled? No! Levi, that's *enough*. No more. We'll talk about this later."

Another pause and Jean-Paul was back, his voice once again the epitome of refinement and helpful courtesy. "Thank you so much for waiting. No, Mila. I merely wanted to call to let you know the strawberries you ordered had arrived. They're still a little green though. They *might* be ripe by Friday, but I wondered if you would prefer our chef find some fresher ones?" He laughed, light but forced. "Cancel your reservations? I can't imagine where your receptionist got that idea."

Another careful chuckle. "Oh, I'm sure she just hasn't had her coffee yet. I really appreciate knowing about the strawberries, though. *You* understand how very important this function is to our firm, and *I* really appreciate that. I'll be certain to let Mr. Pierce know how helpful you've been. Tell you what. Let's see how they look on Thursday morning. I'll make a note on my calendar to give you a call. We do want everything to be just perfect after all." God, her voice sounded so sweet it was making her teeth hurt!

He sounded like he was having a similar attack of sweet tooth–itis. "Of course. "I'm so glad we worked this out. Thank you again for your patronage of the Palace, Mila. I'm sure it will be a very special event."

"Absolutely, Jean-Paul. Thanks for calling." She hung up the phone, immediately planning ways to make *very* certain that was the case. With one press of the button, she powered on Alan's computer and crossed her fingers while it booted and found the server. She would have crossed her toes if she wasn't too afraid she'd start a fire or a flood with one of them. "Saints be praised! Houston, we have a network," she called out to nobody in particular. But it merited a chuckle from someone walking down the hallway outside. She became aware of life coming to the office—lights flickering on over cubicles, the scent of coffee brewing, and voices. Not many voices, but probably all that would be coming in today. She immediately logged off from Alan's account and entered in her own code. Soon she was back in her familiar work folders, scanning down the orderly list on her way to the Johnson subfolder. While she had every intention of typing her own motion first, she was a little worried about the brief still *being* there. So far, Bob the temp hadn't put in a sterling performance and since that was the sole reason he was brought in—

But it was safe, and she suddenly realized why. She hadn't really thought about it when she logged into her named network folder, but she'd entered a password. It was an additional level of security that she'd had installed by the techies when the network was first loaded. They'd agreed because her attorney, Rick Myers, was responsible for the firm's personnel files. *Bet he was digging through my desk looking for it when he ripped the drawer off. I really should tell someone what my password is one of these days.*

She set about transcribing the tape, putting the replay on the slowest possible setting. Even so, she had to type her fastest to keep up, and occasionally had to stop the tape and back it up to understand the wording. Mike had been right. It was only a couple of pages and when she finished, she saved it both to her folder and to Mike's, so whoever he found to finish it up, could. She quickly went upstairs to deliver it and return the machine. Mike was away from his desk, so she left it on the half-wall, promising herself she'd check back with him before she left so he didn't forget to sign it.

Then it was back down to Alan's office to start on the brief edits. Normally, she'd just make them and be done, but they were extensive enough that she was worried. Some of the passages the associate removed changed the whole context of the argument for the new trial. *If it's signed and sent in like this, it'll be denied.* She just knew it, and Rick would be furious. They might even lose the client. She sat there, fingers tapping lightly on the keys, trying to decide what to do.

"There's only one choice," she said to the empty room. While she hated going over the associate's head, she didn't really work for *him*. Picking up the phone, she dialed a number she knew by heart.

"Hello?" She immediately recognized the six-year-old girl's voice and as always, it was happy, full of recent laughter.

"Hi, Meagan. This is Mila. Could I talk to your dad?"

She had to pull the phone away from her ear as the receiver was dropped on the table with a clatter and Meagan yelled into the distance. "Daddy! Telephone!" Then the girl picked the receiver back up and started talking in a flurry of words. "He's upstairs but I think he heard me. Did you have a good Christmas, Mila? I did. Got a new dolly, and a pretty new dress—red velvet with lots of lace." Mila opened her mouth to reply, but there was no stopping the girl. "And I got a game, too! Have you ever played Trouble, Mila? I like the popper thing. Mommy won the first game but I won the second one!"

"That's great, Meagan, but—"

She heard a click and then her boss's voice broke in. "I've got it, Meg. You can hang up now."

"'Kay, Daddy. Bye, Mila." She put the phone down, but it must have been a portable unit, and she forgot to switch it off from the background noise of multiple children yelling and laughing that continued.

Rick sighed. "I'm going to have to train that girl better. What's up, Mila? I've got a houseful, so keep it short."

Mila nodded. "Just one quick question. I'm working on the edits that Robin made to the Johnson brief. I normally don't question stuff like this, but he pulled out paragraph six . . . the whole thing, about the judge's conflict of interest. Is that okay?"

Rick let out a swear that was loud enough for someone downstairs to notice the phone was on. There was a click and then the only voice was the one that was continuing to spout obscenities. "No. That's *not* okay. Are you done with the edits? Read me what changes he made."

She did, and could almost see his reaction in her mind. "What in the hell was he thinking? Damn it. I'm really glad you caught that. Someone else might have let this go in and we'd be screwed. Okay, let me find a quiet place somewhere and I'll dictate some changes."

She heard muffled scratching and a door opening as she turned on the speaker so she didn't have to bend her neck into an odd position to be able to type.

She nearly laughed when she heard a door shut and an odd echo come over the line. The only place that happened was in the bathroom. But she thought it better not to comment. The conversation was reduced to snippets: "Weren't, not wasn't," "Wouldn't you rather say *we believe* that he had, rather than *he had?*" and "Put six back in, renumber, then read it again." It wasn't the first time she'd written entire papers this way, and it worked because both minds were working in unison. Ultimately, the changes Rick made put the motion back to nearly the same wording as it started.

But typing the defendant's name over and over reminded her that Rick hadn't been in for a few days. "Did you see that bit in the paper about Johnson?" She tried to keep the worried tone from her voice.

She could almost see Rick nodding in her head. "Yes, but a grand jury indictment for embezzlement has nothing to do with this suit. Remember that he's our client. We have to stick to just the elements of this file. He's done nothing illegal in the case at hand."

Mila didn't like it, but it was the truth. "It doesn't do his image any good, though."

"Well, let's just say I'm glad the trial is over. We didn't have that jury sequestered to keep them from seeing it. Anyway, let's hear it one more time."

After she'd read it back to him and made a few tweaks, he was satisfied. "Okay, take that up to one of the partners for signature and get it sent in. Don't even run it past Robin. I'll talk with him when I get back."

"Mike's in until noon. Or should I track down someone else?"

"No, Mike'll be fine." He let out a frustrated but satisfied sigh. "I can't tell you how much I appreciate you calling about this. If there aren't any crises and the party's on track, why don't you take off?"

She breathed a sigh of relief. While she was *willing* to use her sick time, she'd much rather have the time off be of the approved variety. "That would be great, if you don't mind. I just talked to Jean-Paul about the party, and it seems that everything is on track. There was a little confusion when he first called, because it sounded to Rachel like something was wrong with the reservation, but we worked it out."

Rick let out a little growl. "Send him a confirming e-mail just to be safe. It wouldn't be the first time they tried to get squirrely on us. Copy me and Dave Pierce, just to get the point across to him that he does *not* want to piss us off."

It was a bold move that she never would have considered. "Has Dave confirmed attending? I haven't heard from him."

"Doesn't matter," Rick said with a dark laugh. "Dave pushed Tom really hard to get the hotel added to the short list of locations. Even if he doesn't make it, it's a big deal to him. Make it upbeat but firm. You know the drill."

So, the wording was going to have to be careful—not accusatory, not overt, conversational but with a veiled threat. "Yeah, I can do that. Want to see it first?"

"Nah. You're better at that stuff than I am anyway. I'm sure it'll be fine. Call me back if there are any problems with the brief though. I hate that we're this close to deadline as it is. But I've got to get back to my guests, so I'll let you get to it. Thanks again."

"No problem. I'll take care of it." As soon as she clicked off the speaker, she started pulling together the exhibits to be attached to the brief. Mike was picky, like Rick, and would want to see the entire package before he would sign it. Just to be safe, she buzzed him to make sure he'd be available to sign it, and let him know that Rick had approved the wording by phone. That would keep his own red pencil at bay. After she returned to Alan's office from delivering the documents, she composed the e-mail to Jean-Paul. Rather than just focus on this particular call . . . and, since it was going to also go to David Pierce, she decided to take the time to confirm *all* the details and add in reminders of when third parties would be making deliveries, like the clock movers.

She was just re-reading it for the fourth time when a double chirp made her jump. "Mila? You up there? It's Eunice. Rachel said you were looking for me."

Crap! The file! She looked at her watch to discover that two hours had come and gone. Between the party and the brief, it was after ten already. "Oh, hey, Eunice. Yeah. I really need to talk to you. You gonna be in the rest of the day?"

"Well, at least until noon. I'm trying to sneak out of here to spend some time with my granddaughter. She's in from Montana and I haven't seen her since she had the baby last year. What'cha need? Maybe I can answer it over the phone."

"I doubt it, but hey, it's worth a try." She tried to figure out where to start. "You've been here forever, haven't you?"

There was a small chortle. "Let's just say longer than you've been alive. Why? Is this on an old file?"

"Back when Mr. Sanders was alive." Like most older law firms in town, the firm name had been retained even though only one of the founders was still alive. Myron Sanders and Clarence Hoote had been dead for more than two decades, so if Baba had put something in Mr. Sanders's vault, it was *old*. "Apparently, my grandmother, Nadia Penkin, retained him at some point in the past and stored something in the vault. She left me a message, asking me to get it for her because she's out of town, if that's possible. But I don't know when or what—other than it's a document of some sort, and now I can't reach her on the phone."

There was a long pause where all she could hear was breathing and the clicking of keys. "Hmm . . . must have been pre-computer. I do *vaguely* remember the surname, because I remember wondering when you started here if you were a relation to an old client. Penkin's not a real common name."

"So you think there might be something? How would we find it if it was pre-computer?" She started to scan through her list of e-mail addresses to find David Pierce's to add to the CC line of the e-mail while Eunice thought.

"We used to have a handwritten inventory of the vault that carried over from the previous use. This was a bank long ago—Colorado State Trust. Don't know if you knew that. But it's how we managed to have a vault here, rather than just a safe. And, even after the bank folded, we kept a lot of things from the bank in there, waiting for people to come claim them. We've still got deeds and coins and stuff from the 1800s. Nobody ever claimed them so they just sit there. But if your grandmother was an actual *client,* then she's listed somewhere. I just need to think where that old list might be. When do you need this document?"

Mila sighed, because she understood what she was asking. "Last night, apparently. She asked me to get it and send it to her."

She could almost see Eunice wince. "Ouch. Well, keep in mind that the instruction filed with the document might not *allow* you to take it out. But if it does, then I *might* be able to find it for you. Probably quicker than Devon could. At least, I know where in the vault to start looking. But I'll expect flowers for this." Her voice had a smile attached to it, but Mila took it seriously.

"Hey, if you can pull this off for me, I'll buy you roses." It might set her back another hundred, but it would be well worth it. *Another hundred.* It reminded her that she still needed to pay the mortgage. She added it to the mental list on her way downstairs. Her loan was with American Bank, so it was just a matter of sliding into the bank on her way downstairs. "Is there anything I can do to help?"

"Sure!" came the immediate response. "You want to do some grunt work? The vault's pretty full right now and my back isn't what it used to be. We'll need to pull some boxes out to get to the very back where the old stuff is. I'm thinking I remember squirreling a copy of the handwritten inventory inside a pigeon hole in the old desk that's built into the back. It was shortly after Myron died and I moved into bookkeeping that I gave up handling the vault. Devon might have moved it, but that's where I'm going to start. I could definitely use some help getting to it."

Another check of the watch, but then she shrugged. It really didn't matter how long it took. This was her main reason for coming in. *However long it takes is how long it takes*. "Be happy to. Just let me finish up this brief . . . which *has* to go in today, and I'll come upstairs."

"Great. That'll give me a chance to finish up this batch of vendor 1099s. I'd love to be able to get them all in the mail before the tenth. Just come up when you're ready."

"Sounds like a plan." The intercom light clicked off and she started to read the e-mail to Jean-Paul one last time. It wound up being a *lot* longer than planned, but she couldn't pass up the opportunity to get all the details in one list that they could both check off during the pre-inspection the night of the party. Once more she read through it, looked for any tweak of language that could be construed as negative. But no, it was just right. She signed it, made sure David and Rick were copied, and crossed her fingers as she clicked the send button.

Then it was back to the brief, which Mike had now signed. While the *paperless* filing concept had indeed resulted in a leaner and meaner court, it had actually *doubled* the paper used in their office. The partners insisted on having the original signed document in the file, as well as the date stamped when one actually filed online. So, while it would be immensely easier to simply file the brief out of her computer folder, the attorneys required that she *scan* the completed, signed document and file it that way. Paranoid and overkill, yes. But the clash of the old ways with the new had been going on since the firm was founded. Eventually, Mr. Harris and a few of the other senior partners would pass on, or the court would demand they change.

But until then, the process would remain a pain in the pa-tootie for the staff.

She felt a surge of satisfaction as the file was sent and received in the court's system. While she was at it, she went ahead and finished up the probate motion and got that in, too. It was now eleven o'clock, but even if she got out of here at noon, that would still be okay.

Eunice was digging bits of paper out of the laser printer when Mila walked through the main door of the bookkeeping department. The older woman, her hair a natural silver that complemented the green-and-red sweater she was wearing, let out a frustrated breath. "Damn micro-perf paper, anyway. Get a sheet with one little nick and the rollers will rip it apart. Gums up the works until you get out every last scrap. It's times like these I long for carbon paper and a typewriter."

Mila leaned on the long countertop that separated them. "I can't even *imagine* trying to run a law office without computers. It must have been a nightmare."

Eunice shrugged as she yanked out another bit of paper and pressed the button to start the printer again. "It wasn't that bad, actually. Clients were more courteous. Nobody expected a multipage document the same day. The lawyers understood that billing would take a week every month instead of a few hours. And, we only took on the number of clients we could manage. It was still stressful—the legal trade just *is,* but it wasn't *more* stressful just because of the equipment."

The printer began to feed paper, but then stalled again, causing Eunice to let out a growl. She looked straight at the printer. "I *got* all the paper out, you worthless piece of plastic." Still, she opened the clamshell once more, took out the paper cartridge, and started to search for more bits.

Just wanting to fill the silence, Mila decided to indulge her curiosity. "So do you remember my Baba Nadia at all? What sort of work did she have the firm do?"

"She has a really thick accent, doesn't she? Mostly I re-member that it was tough to understand her. And no offense, but she was one of those pain in the butt clients, if you know what I mean. Everything had to be absolutely *perfect* which, when you were rushed and working on an electric typewriter—even a correcting one—slowed down the process a lot."

Mila smiled, part amusement, but mostly in sympathy. "Yeah, she's a perfectionist, all right." It made her think again of Suzanne and the ticking clock. "But she's got a good heart and is as hard on herself as anyone else. Her accent's gotten better, too. She's picked up a lot more English." Mila motioned toward the printer as Eunice pressed the button one more time. "Do you want me to get started on moving stuff until you can get that thing running?"

She let out a snort as the printer's light once again moved from green to red. Abruptly, she pressed the power button. "Maybe a time-out's what you need. Just sit there and think about the trouble you've caused until I get back." She shrugged as Mila smiled. "Hey, works for the grandkids."

Mila had only been inside the vault a few times in the entire time she'd worked for the firm. It wasn't visible to the general employees, the entrance being down a back hallway accessible only through bookkeeping. Rather than a modern brushed steel door with a time lock, this one was painted black and gold and had a massive dial set into the steel. Eunice stopped her at the outer glass door, about a dozen feet from the vault. "Stay here until I have it open. Company policy."

The glass door had an additional code lock, and the angle of the door made it nearly impossible to see the dial being turned once the authorized person was inside. "We can stack the boxes out here in the entry. We'll still be locked in, which is why they built this extra room. Betty used to get really claustrophobic working in the vault for hours, but Myron got really weird about having anything in the vault left in the open for more than a minute or two."

"Well, you just tell me what to do that'll make the partners happy and I'll do it."

Eunice proved that she was a manager for a reason. It was amazing to Mila how much trash was packed into the old vault, which when empty must easily be twenty feet square. It wasn't just boxes of documents inside, but old furniture, paintings covered in bubble wrap, and even a crumbling, water-damaged old globe. "What *is* all this junk? Who'd want to keep it in a vault?"

Eunice raised her eyebrows. "*You* need to spend more time watching *Antiques Roadshow*. That bit of *junk* in your hands is an extremely rare and valuable celestial globe. There are about five of that diameter in existence. The last one sold at auction for over ten grand."

Mila looked askance at the papier-mâché globe. "But it's ruined. Look at this—big chunks have disintegrated and fallen inside. The paint's almost gone and it smells like it sat in a musty cellar for a decade or so."

"It was still appraised at ten thousand, and it's in this vault to stay in good shape until an auction house is selected. So be careful with it, huh?"

"Oh, I'd planned to be careful with it either way. But geez! Who buys this crap?" She shook her head and carried it gingerly to the outer room. The room was filling fast, but they were nearly to the back. Just a few more boxes and Eunice would be able to open the rolltop desk against the back wall. That's when she noticed someone standing outside the glass door. The senior partner, Thomas Harris was watching the moving process with a very disapproving expression. He pointed to the lock and then to the door handle. Mila hurried to open it for him. It set off a little beeping noise inside the vault that she hadn't noticed before, and brought Eunice running.

She put a hand to her chest as though she'd been startled out of a year's growth. "Oh, hi, Tom. I hate it when that damn buzzer goes off in there."

"What in blazes is going on in here?" He looked furious, but if Eunice noticed, she didn't seem especially concerned.

"Devon's on vacation and I need to get to the old inventory. It's in the pigeon hole desk, so Mila's giving me a hand getting all this stuff out of the way."

He lowered a glare on Mila that made her want to bolt back into the vault and close the door. "I don't like anyone but you or Devon in this room. You know that."

The older woman snorted and put hands on her ample hips before looking into his face sternly. "Well, unless you want to pay the worker's comp bills for me throwing out my back, you don't have much choice." They stared at each other for a long moment, neither one budging. It startled Mila a bit when Harris let out a little smile. Then Eunice smiled too and winked at him. "Besides, you know Mila. She's been here over a decade and it's her grandmother's property we're getting out. Do you remember Nadia Penkin—one of Myron's old clients?" She paused and then put emphasis on the next phrase. "One of his *unique* clients."

Then Harris rolled his eyes and let out an exasperated breath. "One of his *witchy* clients, you mean. How could I forget?" Mila must have been wearing an odd expression, because he looked at her and continued. "I'm sure your grandmother is a fine woman, but there was no end of problems in this place every time one of them showed up. Either the plumbing would go out or the furnace."

Eunice laughed. "Oh, and how about the time the potted plant in the front office *exploded?*" She nodded at Mila, who froze and couldn't breathe for a second. "Yeah, actually exploded. The whole pot just burst into pieces when one of the witchy women walked by. There was dirt everywhere— even inside the typewriters. Old Betty Trophy, who was our receptionist at the time, quit that very day. Said the whole place was haunted."

"Didn't really mind losing her," Harris said with a small chuckle. "She was a bitter pill. That was the only good to come out of that group. Apparently, they were friends or relations to one grandmother or other, so Myron couldn't turn them down when they needed help."

Three days ago, she would have laughed along with them. But three days ago, magic wasn't real. It was something to scoff at on television. "So, what sort of work did the *witchy clients* have Mr. Sanders do?"

Harris shrugged. "Oh, all sorts. We were a general practice firm then. I do remember there were a lot of petitions for name changes. But in the late fifties and early sixties, that was pretty common all over—the McCarthy era, you know. Immigrants from anywhere in the USSR would want to *Americanize* their surnames. Rothschenko would become Roth, Kuryliak would be Curry. I remember doing that one when Myron was on vacation." He looked at the stacks of boxes, some five high, and let out a slow breath. "Anyway, that's beside the point and not why I'm here. I need a check, Eunice. Four grand should do me."

She snorted. "*Three* thousand will have to do you until January. Four would bump you into the next tax bracket and Gil would have my hide when he put your return together in April."

Instead of arguing or ordering her to comply, as Mila had expected from seeing his other interactions with staff—Harris merely sighed. "Well, you know best. I guess there's no helping it." He held open the door for Eunice and waved his other hand airily at Mila. "Carry on, then. I'll have her back in a moment. Don't let anyone inside except senior staff and do be careful of the breakables. I'd hate to have to find yet another insurance carrier if we have to reimburse someone again."

"Of course," she replied seriously. "I'll be very careful." She was just pleased he didn't suggest she was untrustworthy. That Eunice had said, *Oh, you know Mila* was a little surprising. She'd never really thought much about what the senior partners thought of her—so long as she kept her boss happy, she figured that was enough. Still, it was nice to hear.

Once alone, she quickly finished clearing out the boxes. It was easier with only one person working. As much as she liked Eunice, they had very different ways of achieving the same goal.

Mila stared at the closed rolltop. She *should* wait until Eunice came back. She didn't even know for certain what she was looking for. Yet, when she saw her hand reaching for the handle, she didn't pull it back. The slatted top wasn't locked, but it took some effort to make the rollers spin to raise it. The green leather desktop was covered with a scattering of loose papers. From a quick glance they appeared to be old bills to the firm—vendor invoices that had never been filed for some reason. But with dates of 1962 and 1963, she doubted seriously whether they were important.

Only a few of the multiple mail slots, or pigeonholes as Eunice had called them, were full and it was pretty obvious which one was the inventory. It was a bulky document, eleven legal-sized pages, with twin hole piercings in the top, as though it had once been housed in a folder or binder. She slipped it out and scanned down the top page quickly. It was actually a good system based on the boxes she'd already removed. Each document had a file number which corresponded to a box number. After the number was the client name, the file matter, the original document or item stored, and the date put in the vault. There were handwritten notations and initials on a line showing when someone had accessed the document. A strikeout line with the word *removed* made it obvious when something was no longer being held by the firm. It was the same system in use today, so apparently it worked.

Everything was in last-name order, but even after scanning each page two times, running her finger down the entries, she couldn't find a listing for Baba.

"Oh, you found it. Good." Eunice's voice behind her made her jump and let out a little yip. It was noticed and the other woman looked at her apologetically. "Sorry about that. You can see why the buzzer gets me. So, have you found the right box yet?"

Mila furrowed her brow and shook her head. "No, and I

can't figure out why. Did Mr. Sanders have any other *vault?* Maybe I'm looking in the wrong place."

"Nope. Just this one." She reached out her hand. "Here, let me take a look." Mila passed the stapled list over and watched as Eunice's finger sped down the page. She flipped sheets quickly, pausing once to stare at an entry, but then moved on. At the end, she tapped her fingernails lightly on the desk and then flipped back to the page where she'd paused. "I think this is our problem. We keep saying Nadia *Penkin.* But that was *after* the divorce. I remember now— that's why she retained Myron. I just need to remember her married name, 'cause that's what the file would be under. Give me a second." She started over on the list, looking at each entry where the document stored was an original Decree of Dissolution of Marriage.

Divorced? Mila was trying to wrap her head around the concept. Who did Baba divorce and why? It made her realize she really didn't know that much about her grandmother. She'd never really thought of her as anything other than . . . well, her baba. Yet she'd been someone's best friend, someone's lover, and a divorced woman trying to start over again—alone.

"Wow," she said after a moment. "You never really think of a *grandmother* that way, do you? Nobody in my family ever mentioned it."

Eunice smiled sadly. "No, they wouldn't have. It happened, but it was sort of frowned on. Like *having* to get married. Out-of-wedlock babies happened, too, but they simply weren't discussed in polite company. Not like now." She shook her head and returned her eyes to the list, then let out a triumphant, "Yes! Here it is. N. Zolota—d.f.d., my shorthand for decree of dissolution." She stopped and then moved her finger to the top of the page. "And here's another file for N. Zolota. All that's listed is *envelope.* We'd probably better pull both of them since you don't know what you're looking for. I'm betting she needs the Decree, but who knows. Grab Box 25, envelope 16 and Box 26, envelope 3, and we'll take a look."

Mila did as she was told, now incredibly curious. While it was probably unethical to look at the details of the divorce, it might also be pertinent. Each oversized manila envelope was sealed with shiny tape and bore a typed label with a repeat of the inventory index—name, contents, plus who was authorized to access it. Mila already knew that unless there were names shown, there were no restrictions. She was pleased when there were no names listed on the divorce file, and was quite surprised when she pulled out the other envelope. It was fairly thick. But even more interesting was the access notation on the front:

Zolota, Nadia (nka Penkin); Penkin, Sarah or Penkin, Ludmila, upon age of majority.

So, like Viktor said, Baba had *intended* either her or her sister to ask for this someday. As she moved the envelope to the side to return the box's lid, she noticed another envelope had gotten stuck to the tape of the bulky one. She unstuck it and had just reached back into the box to return it when she noticed the label.

PEIRCEDIL. VEGRELLION C.O.N.

If Tal hadn't read that scroll, she never would have spotted the name . . . or actually, the *change* of name. *But to what?* What did Vegre change his name to, and how could he have if he's been in prison for a century or more? Yet, she couldn't imagine two people having that same weird name.

She spoke the words quietly enough in the entry that not even Eunice would be able to hear. "And what the hell do I do now?" Should she open the file? Steal it and open it later? Leave it here and wonder about it for the rest of her life—which might be short if we can't find him before he does whatever it is he's planning.

Ethically, she had no right to look. Morally, she had a *duty* to look. She heard Eunice's voice from inside the vault. "Having trouble finding it?"

She put on a fake smile and answered lightly. "Just buried a bit. Bringing them in now."

What to do? What to do? She finally settled on folding up the slender envelope and tucking it inside her front pants pocket, even as the *Oh, you know Mila* was ringing accusingly in her ears. *If I just had a minute or two with it. That's all I'd need.*

As if in answer to her prayer, the buzzer sounded behind her. She turned to see Rachel standing on the other side of the glass. She held up her hands in front of her as though praying, mouthing the word, *Eunice?* Pleeease? She called into the vault. "Eunice, Rachel's at the door. I guess she needs to talk to you. Can I open it?"

Her white curls poked out again and she sighed as she walked toward the locked glass. "I'll take care of it. Take those envelopes inside and wait for me. *Don't* open them until I get back. We need to put an affidavit in the boxes to replace the envelopes and I need to sign it that I was there when you opened them."

"Not a problem. I won't peek." And she wouldn't—at least not in Baba's files. But as soon as the door latched behind the other two women, Mila removed the envelope in her pocket and carefully lifted the thick cellophane tape securing the flap with her fingernail. Only one tiny bit of the manila stayed with the tape, and it wouldn't even be noticed when she smoothed it back down.

There was a single-paged document inside . . . the originally signed copy of an Order of Change of Name signed by a judge from the district court down in Douglas County. It changed the man's name from Vegrellion David Peircevil to . . . David Rellion Pierce.

It wasn't possible, and yet there it was. *What are the odds that he would pick the exact same name as the CFO of the Palace Hotel?*

Mila couldn't find a way to squeeze the circumstances into the word *coincidence,* so she simply folded the paper and stuck it back in her pocket, and then resealed the envelope. She had to show this to Tal. Had to talk to him right away and figure out what was going on. She was just tucking the envelope back into the box when Eunice punched in the door code. Mila looked up, smiled, and flipped the file just before Vegre's to stand in the tall position. "Figured I'd better mark the spots where the files were."

Eunice nodded with a look of frustration. "Good. Because we'll probably forget before this is over—especially if people keep interrupting us. Sorry to make you keep waiting, but we've got to follow the procedures."

Mila didn't mind—even though it took another hour before they got the vault back in order and she could take her prizes back to Alan's office to examine them further.

Unfortunately, *Alan* was in Alan's office when she got back there. He had been a little surprised to find his station on and in Mila's files, but wasn't upset. Still, she couldn't very well kick the man out of his own office and didn't dare go back to hers. Instead, she stopped at the nearest darkened cubicle and buzzed the front desk. "Rachel? It's Mila. Hey, Rick said I could take off after I filed the brief, so I'm going to. I'm gonna sneak out the back way—through the garage elevator, so nobody notices. But I wanted to let you know."

"Did everything work out with the hotel?" She continued to keep her voice low, like when she'd first announced the call.

"Yep. Everything's still on schedule. Just a misunderstanding. But I sent an e-mail confirming, just in case. Still, call my cell phone if you hear anything hinky. You've got the number, right?" Then she remembered she'd given the phone to Tal in case she needed to reach him.

"Will do," Rachel replied, forcing Mila to interrupt her.

"Wait. Never mind. I just remembered I don't have my phone with me. Call the house if you hear anything. I should be there, but in case I run out for anything at the store, I'll call you back."

"Okay. Got another call now. Feel better." Then she was gone.

Now I just need to talk to Tal. She pressed an open line and dialed her cell number. The recorded message that was spoken into her ear made her furrow her brow, part curiosity and part worry. "We're sorry, but the mobile unit you've dialed has traveled outside the calling area. Please try your call again later."

Where could he have gone? He was just supposed to be talking with another undercover O.P.A. agent who worked at the library a few miles away. Her *calling area* was a five-county range, plus even farther when driving east of the city. It was certainly possible there was a problem with the phone—being the holidays, so she went downstairs and waited in the lobby as they'd agreed. Ten minutes passed, then thirty. At two o'clock . . . seventy minutes after she snuck out of the office, she finally left the spot by the building directory that she'd carefully described to Tal. She hurried to the bank entrance, trying to keep an eye on the front door in case he was running late. While she hated spending the majority of the money Candy had given her to pay the mortgage, it wasn't looking promising that Sela would paying her rent this month. And she definitely didn't dare make a late payment on the note or they'd refuse to turn it into a mortgage and lower the interest rate after the house deed was finalized.

She tried the cell again, using the phone at the building security desk after showing her employee badge. The same message played. Then she tried Candy's number.

"Hello?" Her voice sounded frazzled, which didn't mean good things.

She didn't have to introduce herself. They talked nearly every day. "Have you heard anything?"

Air rushed out of her friend in a frustrated snarl, or maybe it was just a car passed by. "Not a word. You? Did you make it to the garden okay? How's Viktor?"

"Gone. But he got Baba, Tim, and Suzanne out before *company* arrived." She had to be careful what she said on this phone. It was monitored. "Oh, and I'm on the phone at the guard desk downstairs, so we have to keep it short."

They did. There was nothing to talk about anyway, since neither of them was in a place they could talk. They agreed to meet later and tell each other everything. After she hung up, she tried the cell one more time. Nothing.

Curiosity got the better of her and she opened the first of the envelopes . . . the one about Baba's divorce. She was both shocked and yet not at all surprised to learn that it was Viktor Zolota who used to be married to her grandmother. So, a second marriage, and one that hadn't ended well. Yet, they'd always remained friends. Not unheard of, but it was strange she'd never heard a whisper of it.

Another ten minutes had passed. She couldn't afford to leave and miss Tal, in case he was following up on something important. She couldn't afford to go back upstairs and wait or someone would give her work. The only thing she could think to do was try something she wasn't positive was possible.

But it was her only option.

Mila got back in the garage elevator and got off on the fourth level. She unlocked her car and got inside. The cold had seeped into the car's interior and the darkness lulled her, put her into a relaxed state. *If you can reach me, I don't see any reason why I can't contact you.*

Closing her eyes, she took a deep breath of chilled air and let it out slowly. In through the nose, out through the mouth—over and over until she felt a light tingling flow over her skin. She reached inside her mind and felt for the door in the darkness, the one where the light was bright and hot—fiery as a mage's magical flame.

She stared with her inner eye at the light. She heard sounds from the other side of the brightness, but recognized them as screams and shouts of panic. Could this be where Tal was? Did he need her help? Or was she about to go to a different place, somewhere she'd never been?

There was only one way to find out. She pushed her way into the light, felt an invisible barrier stretch and then give with an inaudible *pop*. Her foot started to numb and her head pounded. Instinctively, she tried to back out, fought against going unconscious. But then the brightness faded, dimmed until it was almost dark. As the light disappeared, so did the screaming. It was cool and peaceful wherever she was, filled with soft footsteps and whispers in the distance. Mila tried to look around to figure out where she was, but she couldn't make the head or eyes move. Still, the calm confidence and swing of limbs was familiar and some weird muscle memory part of her recognized the sensations.

Tal! Tal, can you hear me? I need to talk to you.

But there was no reaction. No recognition of her presence like after the battle with Vegre. Instead, she heard the echo of him speaking to another person. It was a hiss of words, filled with outrage and fear.

"Right here in a *public library,* Jason? Are you *insane?*"

A light flicked on and Mila could finally see. Rows of bookcases surrounded her, covering every wall. There was a framed oil painting that reminded her of the Old West prints of Charles Russell—with a cowboy bulldogging a steer to the ground in a swirl of dust. The man facing Tal was slender with dark skin and closely trimmed kinky black hair. He was dressed casually in black slacks and heavy tan sweater. He crossed his arms, making the down jacket he was carrying poof up to nearly his chin. Then he rolled his eyes as though Tal's complaint was ridiculous.

His thick Irish accent surprised her. "Oh, don't get your knickers in such a bunch, Talos. It's not like a human could wander through by accident. It's fire keyed, and I'm the only mage in the city besides you. Besides, you said you didn't care *how* you got back. Are you coming or not? I've only got an hour for lunch." He motioned toward what appeared to be a fire exit with raised brows.

She felt Tal's head shake, which was an odd sensation. "I suppose. I've only got a few minutes as well. I've got to get back downtown to meet someone."

The way he said those words . . . it was warm, anticipatory, and it would have made her smile if she could have felt her lips. Jason apparently noticed the tone, too, because he raised his brows. "Found yourself a local bird, have ya? Poisoned candy, these topsiders, you know— dangerous to taste, but oh, so sweet."

She felt his muscles twitch uncomfortably and wished she

could see what he was thinking. But while he *was* thinking of her, she tried again, yelling as loud as she could with her mind this time. *Tal! Can you hear me? I have to tell you what I found out!*

Again there was no response, no recognition of her. *This is futile.* Apparently she didn't know how to make the connection work properly, and if someone came by while she was sitting in the car looking like a zombie, they'd probably call the police.

It was time to try something else. Thankfully, pulling out of Tal's head was easier than getting in. She'd never tried to pull herself out of an episode before, but then again, she'd never been conscious during one. She already knew how to close the door in her mind, so it was just a matter of concentrating and pulling backward. Unfortunately, it was like getting unstuck from a wad of used bubble gum. Pry and release, then pry again. Eventually she managed to shake off the tendrils that tried to remain attached to her. Good thing, too—because just as she was disconnecting the last thread of consciousness in the other place, Tal followed Jason through the doorway in a swirl of amber fire that stung her head like an angry wasp.

Mila's eyes opened abruptly. She rubbed at her temple where one vein was still twitching painfully. She realized her head had lolled against the window, and spittle was pooling on the windowsill from her open mouth. "Oh, yuck. Wasn't *that* attractive for people wandering by?" She quickly wiped the drool away with her sleeve and started the car.

She knew where he was, so all she had to do was go there. Of course, it was a big library, but there couldn't be *that* many cowboy prints in the place—even in Denver. She should be able to recognize it when she found it.

I hope.

CHAPTER 12

*I*t was the tension in the air that caught Tal's attention most as he stepped through the illegal gate into the storeroom of the butcher shop owned by Jason's family in Vril. Yes, he'd been warned it was bad before they activated the gate, but it was another thing entirely to hear the fading screams and smell the smoke of the riot's aftermath.

As the amber glow faded and became a freezer door once more, Tal shook his head—both grateful and annoyed. "I can't believe you've had this in place for over a *year.* Do you realize the penalties for having an illegal gate? I can barely convince myself to walk through it *once.* How could you do it a hundred times or more? Truthfully?"

Jason shrugged and took off his down jacket, despite their being able to see their breaths in the room. "Well, you must handle the overworld a lot better than me, 'cause twasn't a hard decision. The mattress in me flat is lumpy enough to bruise and I simply can't abide the food up there. Do you know you can't even *buy* mutton stew in a restaurant?" He reached over to hang up the jacket on a wall hook and picked a dark burgundy cloak to replace it. That was probably a good idea. The thick, puffy jackets favored topside weren't very common down here, so Tal likewise shed his, even though he'd be cold. Jason continued to talk as he looked around the room. "So I spend a few nights a week with me mum and da down here—have a good dinner, help Da with the shop. Who am I hurting? Not the O.P.A. Not the kings. Not even the bloke down the block." He motioned toward the coatrack. "Go on then. Take the black one to wear. It's Da's, and it's got a hood. You said you don't want to be noticed down here if you can avoid it."

He eyed the cloak longingly as another shiver caught

him. But he wasn't quite cold enough to deprive an elderly mage of the warmth. "Won't he need it?"

Jason was cautiously peeking through a window set high in the stone wall into the street above. He waved back one hand. "That's an extra. He and Mum took me advice and evacuated to Shambala days ago. That's why you don't see any meat hanging in here. Da decided to add his stock to my Uncle Fineas's store there."

Tal gratefully wrapped the thick wool around him as they walked up the stairs into the main shop, and felt heat return to his limbs. While he *could* warm the room with the remaining magic in the opal, he didn't know what they might encounter down here. Better to conserve the magic if he could. "It's *still* an illegal gate, though. You were risking both you and your parents going to the dungeon."

Again Jason shook his head in bemusement. "This isn't Rohm, Tal. Nobody *cares* about a little thing like a private gate in Vril. The way folks figure it here—if we want to use what precious little magic we get for such frivolity, we're welcome to . . . but we won't be getting any neighborly charity, either." He motioned toward the door. "Looks like most of the looters have moved to the next street. There's no magic left to steal around here . . . hasn't been for days. It should be safe to go outside now."

All the same, Jason slid on his battle glove, causing Tal to remove the opal from his pants pocket. He really needed a glove, but until he found his, or a replacement, he'd just have to keep a tight hold on it. But even the brief flash of it into the dim light made colored fire swirl around the room. Jason couldn't help but notice and let out a whistle similar to Alexy's of the previous day. "*Nice* focus. Looks old."

"It is. But it's only a loaner." He shrugged as though to dismiss it, but he couldn't help admire it, too . . . and admire the woman who *should* be wielding it. It was obvious Mila could craft magic, even if just basic defense. But he'd love to find out what she was capable of if properly trained.

His friend laughed and slapped his shoulder. "You've got that *look* again, lad. I presume it was *loaned* by the same someone you're meeting later?"

Tal cleared his throat and decided a change of subject would be in order. He motioned toward the front door, where the leaded-glass entrance to the shop lay in crushed shards on the floor. "What exactly happened here? When did the riots start, and why?"

Jason let the subject of the focus drop after a tiny smile. But his face dropped into serious lines when he followed Tal's hand and saw the glass. "Bleedin' hell! That wasn't like that yesterday. Aw, Mum will be heartbroken. That glass was specially crafted by Patrick Flannigan, the chief assistant at the local alchemists' guild. Da saved up part of the magic ration for the better part of a year for it." He walked to what used to be the door, then squatted down to pick up the largest piece with a look of sadness. The shard wasn't much bigger than his palm. "The raw sand and lead had to be gated three times, all the way from Germany."

There wasn't really anything to say. Still, it should be acknowledged. "Sorry—"

Jason raised angry eyes and snorted before dropping the glass back to the floor. "Yeah, I'm sorry, too. Sorry the bleeding kings didn't plan things any better. How could there *not* be riots, when there's no food, no water, and no way to get them? Arrogant sons of bitches, the lot of 'em!"

He stood in a rush and crunched across the glass out of the shop, causing Tal to throw up his hood and chase after him. Once outside, he couldn't help but stop and stare. The Vril he'd known just a few years ago was gone. Buildings were pockmarked by sledgehammer holes, and exquisitely carved masonry littered the streets. No grass left, no flowers; pet racoons, mole rats, and snakes abandoned to roam at will. Even the illusion of blue sky now existed only in snatches and grabs across the landscape—a patchwork quilt of seemingly endless air, chewed away by the dark stone ceiling that was the reality of Agathia. Fires burned wherever there was fuel, and the stench of cesspools long past overfull burned in his nose. "How long has it been like this?"

Jason turned around and let out a deep sigh, his brown eyes filled with worry and sadness. "It's never been this bad, but if you mean the sky, it's been like that for months. The king's counselors kept up the sky over the public areas as long as they could—bartering for magic at first, since we had a lot of water for trade. But since early summer when they had to evacuate the second ring and move everyone here to the city's center, they've resorted to begging and borrowing from the other kingdoms. That's about the same time the drought topside started to affect our reserves. King Kessrick hid the information as long as he could, but when the humans deepened their wells, eventually the guilds figured it out."

Tal shook his head. Riots had happened in Rohm, too, when they evacuated the third ring. Originally, the rings had been a perfect solution to the growing cities—and emulated how the humans managed their land. The city's center was the first ring, with roads laid out in concentric circles. The second ring just sort of happened, when the wealthy and powerful wanted private estates away from the city. But when growth continued through expanding families, they needed somewhere to go. *Up* wasn't an option because of the cavern's ceiling, so people moved further out. The second ring estates became suburbs and the wealthy moved again to create a third ring. It had stayed that way for centuries with the kings managing the populations to fit the space. "But of course, once the easy water was gone, the witches didn't have the magic to pull from deeper sources, so people had to move closer once again."

"Precisely," agreed Jason, now speaking louder to be heard over the yelling and racous laughter of what appeared to be a gang of witch apprentices. They were amusing themselves by crafting small water spouts from questionable trickles out of a storm drain and spinning them through broken windows to soak the floors and walls. "The moat worked for a long time, keeping the lower elements, like that lot—" He twitched his thumb toward the boys, probably not into their teens, "—away from the upper class. But then they had to drain the moat for drinking water. Once that happened, most of the middle class moved away and they put up the fences to keep everybody in the first ring. But you can't crowd a million people in an area scaled to house a quarter million, and not expect problems. Now most everyone is gone because all that's left is food, water, and skies over those who can afford to pay—the magic nearly stolen from those who can't afford not to sell." He let out a frustrated breath and stepped away, turning his back on the delinquents. "Well, come on then. You wanted to see where some of the other gates are, right?"

Some of the other. Tal was still trying to get that image firmly fixed in his mind. There should only be six gates to the overworld on the entire *planet,* but there might be double or even triple that just here in Vril . . . and right under the noses of the O.P.A. and the kings. "Yes, I suppose we should."

They walked together, keeping to the shadows, which wasn't too difficult. There was far more dark than light in the city. The only other people they encountered likewise didn't want to be seen, so they kept a good distance away from each other. It killed Tal inside to watch people destroying the property of others, looting focus stones and clothing from homes and shops, without doing anything to stop it. Even when he noticed a woman, clearly in O.P.A. garb, taking a measure of magic into her stone in exchange for turning her head, he couldn't intervene.

For, as Jason had told him, Alexy *had* walked back into a trap. He was in prison, no visitors allowed. Kris had been right about everything. He'd listened when Jason had checked in. Had *heard* Commander Sommersby calling for his capture . . . by any means necessary. That Jason trusted him enough to ignore that order—well, he couldn't risk turning his friend in for anything he might witness today. And he couldn't afford to make arrests for lawbreaking since he'd probably be taken away as well.

They hadn't gone more than four blocks when they came upon a form of graffiti. The sparkling red letters were over a meter tall, and hovered in the air near a pile of trash. A pair of racoons turned black button eyes their way, but then returned to their meal of discarded root vegetable peelings and what might once have been porridge.

Repent, for She is coming!

Another sign of similar style ran sideways up the side of a bakery.

Demeter's Children welcomes all!
Praise be She who will restore magic to the land!

He looked sideways to see Jason's reaction, but if the tall dark man noticed them, he gave no sign. After they'd traveled another block and passed two more such notices, he had to ask. "Demeter's Children?"

At last Jason acknowledged the nearest notice with a tip of his chin. "Latest in a series of cults 'round these parts. Best I can get is they worship some entity that lives in the magma, below the mantle. They claim the Trees aren't the real source of magic, and they have exclusive access to the *true* source. Fluff and nonsense, of course, but I have to give those boys credit for bollocks. They put their magic where their rhetoric is. Look at that glitter—takes magic to spare. Not subtle, but effective. They've loads of members now, and not just from Vril. Da nearly joined up just to get the business back in his shop. *The Children* only deal with their own . . . it's like they're a guild, but from before the joining."

Tal began to hear a low, droning noise that increased as it got closer. Jason elbowed him in the ribs sharply and then pulled him into the mouth of an alley. "Look, here comes a procession of Children. Looking for new recruits, I'll wager. Stay back here with me; watch how they work."

The group of men and women was certainly impressive to behold. Their scarlet cloaks had magical flames licking the cloth at hem and wrist, and white candles sporting multicolored fire floated at shoulder height on either side to light the way.

The chorus of voices was in perfect unison, the chanting rising and falling to where it was almost a song. "The earth is our mother. She means us no harm. Praise her and bless her and she'll keep us warm. The earth is our mother. Her magic has served. Praise her and bless her. She'll fill us with verve. Hail Demeter!"

Tal couldn't help but smile. *"Verve?"*

Jason likewise let out a small chuckle and shrugged. "Vim, vigor, and power, I suppose. Must keep that rhyme going, no matter the logic." He pointed toward the trio of witches that the procession was approaching. "Watch this."

Two members of the procession split off and walked toward the trio. They stopped what they were doing to watch, but their body language remained aggressive. The taller of the Children, a big man with pale, closely cropped hair, raised a hand in greeting. "Hail, young witches."

The oldest boy, red haired, his face sprouting a healthy crop of freckles, sneered at the pair. "Sod off, zombie. You'll not be suckin' the brain out of my head to follow your freakin' goddess." His pals chuckled and elbowed him in approval.

Then the woman spoke. She wasn't much older then the trio, but bore the serenity of age on her face and in her voice. "You're so young. You should be learning your craft. But here you are . . . wandering the streets, not even able to call up enough water magic to wash your filthy skin."

Another of the boys leaned forward with a leer. "I'll be happy to show you *all* my filthy skin, sweetling, if you wanna wash it. C'mon then, give us a kiss." He puckered and moved his lips, which set off his friends again into gales of laughter. But instead of pulling back in disgust or snapping a reply, she raised one delicate bare hand.

A roaring filled Tal's ears and water began to swirl

through the air, pulled out of nearby doors and windows so fast and furious that there was no time to react. The water twisted at the witch's mental command, surrounded the trio of boys and lifted them into the air until they were yelling for help. She kept them there for a long moment as they splashed and sputtered, and then dropped the spell abruptly, causing the boys to fall to the ground with a thud.

"Well, that was impressive," Tal whispered and Jason nodded.

"Like I said. Magic to spare and they're not shy about putting on a show." He motioned with his head back to the group. The boys were picking themselves up, their faces filled more with awe and excitement than anger and fear.

The young girl spoke and raised her hands skyward with closed eyes. "Now you are clean. Praise be to Demeter."

"Where'd you get all that magic, then? How'd you learn to do that?" The redhead was smiling . . . no, more *grinning*.

The woman smiled gently and reached out to touch his hand. "We are the chosen. Demeter blesses us with magic so we can show others the path. We have many master witches among us, who are happy to train young believers." She held out her hand. "Come. Be filled with food and magic. Elevate yourself to your potential in the craft . . . as I have. As we *all* have."

Jason shook his head as the boys eagerly followed the pair to the procession and were handed robes which materialized from thin air. "And so three more join their ranks. You see how easy that was? The equivalent of a street corner half-pence show and they're suddenly true believers. But the Sacred Tree has abandoned us, so people scrabble for something . . . *anything* to provide hope that we're not yet another endangered species about to end our time on this planet."

Tal furrowed his brow, thinking. "But where is the magic *coming* from?"

The other man shook his head. "Dunno, mate. That's the question, isn't it? If I didn't worry I'd be bargaining with the devil, I'd consider joining up me own self. They're certainly a happy lot."

"So, where do we go next?" The procession had started on their way again, with two new voices joining in on the chanting.

"Next we go visit my cousin Chauncy." He reached into the pocket of his cloak and then got a panicked expression, suddenly patting his hands up and down his body.

"Lose something?"

"Damn it! I must have left the box in my other jacket. We've got to go back to the shop. Bleedin' hell." He started walking that way, not stopping to see whether Tal was going to follow. He lifted the sweater from his wrist to check his watch and then started muttering under his breath angrily.

"Anything I need to know?" Keeping the suspicion from his voice wasn't easy, but this was no time to be so trusting of *anyone* that he wound up the subject of an O.P.A. trap. "What's in the box?"

Jason must still have caught some note of suspicion because he abruptly laughed. "It's not like that, Tal. I haven't turned you over. But Chauncy's getting ready to take the next gate out of here and *he's* the one who knows where most of the illegal gates are here. After all, I *am* an agent. You'd be surprised how many of my old lads stopped talking to me after I got my glove. The box has topsider chocolate in it. He's got a right fat sweet tooth on him, that bloke. And if I forget the chocolate—" He tipped his head and raised his brows.

Tal completed the thought. "No chocolate . . . no information."

The other man nodded. They were now in nearly a sprint, boots pounding on the cobbled sidewalks and echoing down the silent streets. "Right-o. I gotta tell ya, though—I feel like a blinkin' idiot showing up at his door with a box of sweets every few weeks. Like I'm courting me own cousin."

Tal's laugh was abruptly cut off when the sounds of a

scuffle came from around the final corner. Three men were surrounding a woman menacingly, just outside the butcher shop about three blocks down. It was still too far to see much other than movements, but the fighting style of the woman reminded him very much of his sister. One man lunged for her but she sidestepped, grabbed his arm, and did something to it that made him drop to the ground screaming. It wasn't a move Tal recognized, but it was certainly effective. He rolled around, clutching at his hand as the other two moved in.

They'd already increased their speed, in an unspoken agreement to assist the woman, but when Tal heard *Mila's* voice echoing down the street, he put on an extra burst that left Jason struggling to catch up.

"You really don't want to do this," Mila said as she circled opposite the men.

"Oh, but you're wrong, sweetling. You and us . . . we're gonna have a *party*. And you're gonna *pay* for hurtin' Ralphie." He lunged forward and grabbed her arm. But instead of screaming, she lashed out . . . delivering a vicious kick to the side of the man's knee. It sent him to the ground, but he held on, taking her down with him.

Without a second thought, Tal raised the opal focus and shouted, *"Karalt!"* A blast of liquid fire caught the man in the chest, ripping his hand from her arm. "O.P.A.! Remain where you are." Mila turned in shock just as the third man decided he had better places to be and took off running down the street. Ralphie had likewise gone, when she had delivered the kick—rightly figuring she was a bit too much of a fighter for his taste.

Normally, he'd run after or cast a net of fire to contain them, but he really didn't *want* them to stay. He didn't have a place to put them.

"Tal!" Mila's face brightened and she rushed forward the last few steps, throwing her arms around his neck as he slowed to a stop. It surprised him, but he couldn't deny it was what he'd hoped she'd do. Both of their hearts were pounding from exertion and a fine trembling was running through her body that spoke of too much adrenaline in her system. He let himself take a few moments to just hold her until they were both calmer. The scent of her hair, the heat as their magic met and mingled—they overwhelmed his senses. *It's only been a day. It shouldn't feel like this.* But even as he thought it, he felt his arms tightening around her until she let out a sigh.

It wasn't until Jason cleared his throat uncomfortably that he realized he'd lost track of time with her in his arms. He pulled back and cupped her chin in his palm. "Are you okay?"

She nodded, moving his hand. "Fine . . . now. I was okay with the first two, but I was running out of steam. They generally don't throw *three* attackers against you in defense class. I should have conserved my energy a little more at the start. I was afraid I was going to have to start injuring them."

He let out a little frustrated breath. "You need to *always* be willing to hurt an attacker. You can't rely on them running off."

Her face took on a similar frustration. "No duh. But when you break skin, people get *mean* in return. It escalates really fast, and then they aren't *willing* to run away. Three against one is still really sucky odds."

He couldn't deny the logic, and was about to comment when Jason again reminded them of his presence. But this time his voice came from a different direction and he sounded slightly out of breath. "Tick-tock, mate. Thought you'd be done fussing with the bird by now. Got the chocolate. Let's go."

Mila raised her brows. "The *bird?*"

The dark man dipped his head in apology and gave a small bow. Tal couldn't decide whether or not he was being sarcastic. "The *young lady,* then. No offense meant."

"This is Mila, Jason. Mila Penkin. She's the *person* I was supposed to meet later." What he couldn't figure out was how she'd come to be here. And Jason apparently thought the same thing.

"She's a *topsider?*" He stared at her incredulously. "How did you get here?"

She rolled her eyes. "Long story." Then she looked at him with excitement and touched his cloak while she pulled a paper from her pocket. "Tal, you'll never *believe* what I found out about Vegre in the vault. It changes *everything,* and I might know where the portal is."

"Vegre?" Jason's face dropped into serious lines, and his arms crossed over his chest. "Vegre Peircevil? The dark mage in Rohm Prison? What does he have to do with anything?"

Mila looked at Jason then, apparently realizing she'd spoken out of place. She shut her mouth, but the tall man wasn't going to sit still for her silence for long. Tal sighed and backed away from Mila, then waved his hands quickly to settle everyone down. He'd hoped not to explain everything to Jason, since the lack of information might be all that was keeping his friend safe. "Okay, okay. We all need to calm down. We'll do this in order. Jason, is there anywhere nearby we can sit down and have some privacy? I'd hoped not to involve you in this any deeper, but—"

"But . . . I can assure you we won't be taking another step toward my favorite cousin until you do." Jason crossed his arms over his chest and stared for a moment. Then he turned and crooked his finger. "C'mon then. We can talk in my folks' flat above the shop." He flipped his arm again to reveal his black leather watch. "But try to make it fast. I can't afford to lose my job up there."

As soon as his back was turned, Mila shoved the paper in her hand toward Tal. He opened it as they walked, but while he understood what he was seeing on the document, he couldn't quite grasp the significance. He looked at her questioningly before passing it back.

She motioned with her thumb toward Jason and spoke out of the side of her mouth as they slowly followed him back to the shop. "Can we trust him?"

It nearly made him laugh, because he had no doubt Jason would ask the same about her. Of course, that left him considering whether *either* of them could be trusted. He'd been roommates with the Fomorian in the guild academy—yet never thought he was *capable,* either magically or morally, of crafting an illegal gate. And he'd known Mila for only a day. Or had he known her all his life? *I can't tell up from down, nor right from wrong lately.* "Yes, I think so."

At least, I hope so.

$\mathcal{M}$ila took another sip of juice while she decided how to respond, marveling at the taste and smell of the drink. It seemed to contain every fruit in the world in tiny sealed bits that she could individually identify.

What do I say to them? She wasn't certain Tal would want his friend to know about the connection they had. She was also reminded of the line from a Harry Potter movie about even in the magicking world, hearing voices wasn't a good thing. "Let's just say I found the gate the same way you survived the first encounter with Vegre."

Jason simply looked confused, but Tal . . . he looked abruptly shaken and somewhat panicked, his face growing ashen in the pale amber light from the stone. "You were able to reach me?"

She shook her head. "I couldn't communicate. I could only see and hear. But yeah." There really wasn't any way to convey the feeling of helplessness and frustration she'd had. "I tried to talk to you when you were near the fire door, but it was like you couldn't hear me. But I was able to recognize the painting on the wall near the gate once I got to the library."

"What in bleedin' hell are you two talking about?" Jason pointed at her. "Are you saying you eavesdropped on our conversation in the library? How? I shielded that room from listeners. What did you use to break through me best spell?"

His Irish accent was increasing the more agitated he got. "How do you have an Irish accent anyway? I thought *black Irish* just meant dark hair and eyes."

He shook a finger in front of his face. "Oh, no. You won't be shakin' me teeth from this bone with fluff and nonsense questions, lass. What spell did you use?"

"It wasn't a spell." Tal's voice was quiet, nearly a whisper. He was staring at the opal's swirling colors, but then looked up and blue eyes met the other man's brown ones. "Mila is the Tree spirit, Jason. She's the voice in my head. She saw the library *through* my head."

Apparently, Jason understood what Tal was saying, but scoffed after a moment of thought. "Bollocks, mate. You've heard the Tree's spirit in your head since you were a boy. That was in the fourteenth century. This lass is a guildercent. She can't be more than twenty-five or thirty. Who was speakin' to you before her? Answer me that."

The *fourteenth century?!* She tried not to gape as she stared at him again, trying to place Tal in a morning coat and top hat, or in serf clothing. But even a zoot suit was too much for her brain to handle, so she tried to focus instead on the conversation.

Tiny movements of his head and hands spoke his confusion. "I can't, Jason. I only know that she *is* the voice in my head—the voice that has always been from the Tree. She *is* where I drew power from to free me from Vegre's death curse."

Jason thought about that for a moment and then pursed his lips, as though accepting it. He hopped down from the counter and grabbed his cloak from an iron hook on the wall. "Well then, let's go and reunite the spirit with her vessel, shall we? I'm afraid I'll have to see this to believe it."

Tal looked at him askance. "We don't have time to go visit Tree Square. We need to find the gate Vegre used to reach Mila's house and close it. To do that, we need to visit—"

Jason let out a bitter laugh. "Me cousin, Chauncy? Bleedin' hell, Tal. You are so freakin' trusting. I don't have a cousin with that name. Think on it, mate. *Chauncy?* What sort of name is that for a self-respecting Fomorian?" He stared at Mila as he fastened a wooden dowel through a loop of cloth at the neck of the cloak. "Ireland via Africa, lass. Me mum's clan were fierce warriors—dirtdogs with a taste for steel and a love of gold. They didn't merely arrive in Ireland, they *conquered* and claimed part of it. I might have inherited me da's magic, but the love of the finer life? That was me mum's legacy."

She looked around the room, trying to compare his words with the furnishings. The apartment was nothing special. It was small and tidy, but there was nothing to give her the impression of exceeding wealth. He laughed, apparently understanding what she was mentally doing.

"Not *this* place, Mila girl. This is just here to keep up appearances for the customers. There's another gate just outside that opens to where Mum and Da *really* lived—out in the third ring where there was plenty of splendor and a gate to keep out the curious. I did well by 'em, as a son should. In fact, I crafted *all* the gates in Vril, Tal. Me and me alone. There's no mysterious cousin. I crafted them for the highest bidder . . . and there were plenty of bidders when the evacuations started."

Tal looked floored and Mila started to wonder why he was suddenly revealing this. Apparently, Tal was thinking the same thing. He flicked his fingers and the opal dulled and then he picked it up, all the while watching Jason with suddenly suspicious eyes. "Why tell us this now? What's changed in the last five minutes that you're suddenly willing to risk me turning you in?"

Jason laughed again, this time a bright and happy sound that didn't match his earlier words. "You really don't see it, do you? Can't even *imagine* the profit potential in the lass?" He reached forward and tapped her on the head. "Demeter's Children wouldn't have anything on the *true* spirit of the Tree. The kings would pay *anything* to learn what's wrong with the Trees, and even more to *save* 'em."

She brushed off his finger like she would a biting insect, suddenly glad she hadn't revealed the information from the scroll to him. "*I* never said I was the Tree spirit, did I? I haven't a clue why I can connect with Tal's mind, but I wouldn't recognize a *Tree of Life* if I ran bodily into one."

"Ah, but that's exactly what I was planning to do, lass. Run you bodily into one." He grinned darkly, but then turned his head at Tal's single word.

"No."

Jason tipped his head, still amused. "You haven't much choice, lad. It's my price to show you the gates."

"No." The word was said with more force and Tal stood in a rush, his eyes flashing.

Jason likewise steadied his stance, keeping the glove he wore turned stone side up. The narrow gem slab, which could either be a ruby or garnet, glittered menacingly from within. "Think about it, *old friend.* Think carefully. One word in my mind to flash Commander Sommersby about your location is all it would take. I've no love for the man or how he's corrupted the department at the kings's behest, but I want life back to the way it was . . . at any cost. The overworld is no place for me, lad, and I don't believe an Agathia ruled by Vegre Peircevil would be to me taste." He opened his arms wide, but with a calculating look. "Now, I'm more than willing to keep your confidence, turn me head to your little journey, and even share me own small secrets. All I ask in return is for your lady friend to tell me what's wrong with the Trees and how to fix them . . . if she can. She doesn't even need to stick around to be later identified. I'll take it from there. And really, Tal—don't *you* want the Trees fixed, too? Don't you want the world back to the way it used to be?" He pointed to the window, where dark and false light met. "*Look at that.* Is that what you want for our people? So what if I profit, or you profit? The guilds would be safe, the land free, and Vegre returned to prison."

Smooth bastard that he was, she couldn't find any way to disagree with the underlying truth. The message wasn't any different than Viktor's speech—only the motivation was different.

She spoke at the same moment as Tal, her "Fine," tearing his "Absolutely not!" into bitter, angry shreds.

His face was horrified, indignant. "Mila, no. You can't give in to this, this . . . *blackmail.*"

She sighed. "Tal, I work in corporate law. A lot of our clients live their lives in the gray area—between the *letter* of the law and the squishy morals of the *spirit* of the law. If I refused to work with everyone who wasn't lily-white the firm wouldn't have many clients." He started to interrupt, but she cut him off with a raised hand. "This is my decision, not yours. I *came* here to see the Trees. I could have waited in the library for you to get back, but I promised Viktor I would try to save your people. I don't know if I can, but I said I'd try. If Jason's willing to help us, great. So far as I can tell, he's a gray area sort of guy, versus the lock-em-up-and-throw-away-the-key sort like Vegre."

Jason gave her an odd look, as though he wasn't sure whether to be flattered or insulted. Frankly, she wasn't sure herself. "Thank you, lass . . . I think."

She pointed a finger at him and raised her brows. "But I don't trust you as far as I can throw you, so don't expect me to take anything you tell me at face value. And, I'll expect you to help us find a way to clear Tal's name."

"I don't need *his* help." Tal was almost too furious to speak, and each syllable was delivered to inflict the maximum insult.

She blew out an annoyed breath at him. "Oh, would you get *over* it, Tal? Look, Jason was willing to help you before he even knew about me. Yeah, he might have been planning to rob or kill you at some point, but I'm betting not. Great, fine. You discovered he's not all sunshine and light. But he's not *all* bad, either."

Jason's voice was quiet when he spoke, his words serious and seemingly heartfelt. "She's right, mate. I'd planned to help you because I owe you. Maybe *all* those words you spouted about honor and charity didn't sink in at the academy, but a lot of them did. I could easily have been in a cell beside Vegre if given me own head."

"Terrific," Tal said sarcastically. "I taught you how to *outsmart* the law. That's something to carve on my gravestone."

"No. You taught me *respect* for the law . . . and the reason for it in the first place. I might not buy into the notion that to be honorable I must do it in *poverty,* but I *have* limits, and you put 'em there. I'm a good son to me folks, and good to me mates." He took off the glove from his right hand and held it out. "You used to be one of those mates. Have I completely ruined that or can we start over?"

Tal stared at the proffered hand for a long moment and then shook his head. "I don't know that I can forgive you just yet. Maybe when this is over and I'm still free and Mila is safe, I'll consider shaking your hand."

The look on Jason's face mingled regret with insult. Finally, he swallowed both inside and offered a stony face, lowering his hand with a nod. "I guess I earned that, and I don't know if I've it in me to live up to the standard you do so it may be that we never do shake."

They stared unblinking at each other until Mila could almost smell the testosterone in the air. "Let's just give it a rest for right now, and go see the Tree. None of this may matter once we do, because I haven't got a clue if there's anything I can do." She hooked her thumb toward the freezer door. "But won't you get fired if you don't get back?"

The grin reappeared on his face. "Nah. I actually had the rest of the day off anyway. I just told Tal that so I could get back and party with me mates. But this sounds like a much more interesting way to spend the evening, so—" He waved his hand and gave an exaggerated bow. "Shall we?"

Mila nodded agreement and Tal grudgingly did, as well. "Is it far from here? Does one of you have a car?"

Apparently, she'd either said the wrong thing, or the right one, to cheer them both up, because they let out nearly identical chuckles. "No cars down here, luv." Jason looked her up and down quickly, but with no interest attached. "And that jacket has to go. Too noticeable. That's why those men thought you an easy target. It's obvious you're not from around here. They just didn't know where you came from. I think me mum has something in the back that might work. She's a bit shorter than you, and broader . . . but since the magic's nearly gone, few can claim to be fashion plates."

The garment he handed her moments later was a beautiful hunter green, and though heavy as wool, was silky smooth. But when she put it on, she realized it was a confusing mass of cloth with holes and fasteners that made no sense. After two failed tries at wrapping herself in it, to Jason's supreme amusement, Tal finally came to her rescue.

"Here, let me. This goes across like so and ties under here." He reached under her arm with exquisite slowness and slid his hand from shoulder to waist while staring into her eyes with a look that made her breath catch. She didn't even realize he was attaching one long length to a fastener until the cloak suddenly balanced and stopped making her feel as though she was tipping forward. In addition to the shivers his hands provided, he stayed close enough to smell his wonderful cologne each time she took a breath—a lemony sage blend with some sort of musk. "And then this flap comes across the shoulder to hook here. You see?"

He stepped back, looking as flushed as she felt. He stepped to the table and slugged down the rest of his juice, as though dying of thirst. When she lifted her arms, she realized that the various folds had become sleeves. It all made sense now, and she experimented to see if she could later undo the mess and reattach it. While still feeling swallowed in the thing, it made her smile because it reminded her of when she used to disappear under her father's coats in the closet during hide-and-seek.

Jason looked on approvingly as she lifted the hood onto her head and then twirled to get a feel for it. "That would look right smart on you if not for it being a bit too short."

She looked down at the hem, which came to about mid-calf. "Is it too short? It looks about right to me." But then she looked at theirs, and realized that it should just touch the top of her shoes. "Oh, I see what you mean. Well, I sort of like it this way, for what it's worth. Easier to walk in."

"That's good," Tal commented, "since we'll be walking several miles." He looked at Jason, his jaw clenching and then loosening after a deep breath. He was trying to make nice, which she appreciated. "Unless you happen to have a gate that will get us there quicker?"

Again that fast grin from behind dark lips, showing brilliant white teeth with just a few crooked bottom ones. "As a matter of fact, I do. It comes out a few blocks away, anyway. See how valuable it is to know me?"

Tal snorted with equal parts annoyance and amusement. "Well, let's have at it then. Lead the way. And while we're traveling—Mila, you might as well explain what the paper was you showed me earlier."

Jason hadn't seen it yet, so she pulled it out once more and passed it over his shoulder as they descended to the lower floor of the shop. He shook his head when he passed it back at the foot of the stairs. "If this has significance, I'm afraid it's beyond me."

"Well," she said as she tucked it back in her pocket on her way out the door between them . . . since she had to return it to the vault eventually. "Either there are two men in the world with that singularly unusual name, or somehow a man who should be confined in the tightest prison in your world managed to pop topside in 1964 to change his name and then wander back behind his bars. The courts here used to require the physical appearance of the person before the judge in name changes."

That made both men stop and stare at each other for a long moment on the sidewalk outside. Tal spoke first, but it was pretty obvious Jason was thinking the same thing. "That's not possible. It must be coincidence."

She nodded and stepped past them just to get moving again. Jason corrected her direction by turning her shoulders with firm guidance. "I would have thought that, too, at first. But this particular person happens to be an heir to a major hotel in the city—except the hotel owner didn't know he *had* an heir until David showed up. And David Pierce is the only client of our firm who has *never* been inside our offices. The partners always go to visit him . . . wherever he might be at the time. I'd never really thought much about it and had just *presumed* they went to see him at the hotel, but now I'm wondering. According to Tom Harris, one of the original partners in our firm, Myron Sanders had a lot of *witchy* clients who were shoestring relatives. Apparently, there were always problems when they came in—with the plumbing, furnace, and with potted plants."

"Sanders," Jason mused, turning his head back slightly from where he'd walked past Mila. "Could be descendants of the house of Saunders mage clan from down near Brighton, I suppose."

Tal shook his head as they followed Jason to an old iron gate near what looked to be a stone dumpster—or maybe it was an incinerator. "I suppose. There were probably a few from that clan who didn't come down after the joining decree."

"But to what end? Did he somehow get out and later get captured again? Wouldn't there have been news reports, or at least *rumors?*" Jason stopped in front of what looked like a padlocked door through a high stone fence. He started forward again, but then got an impish look on his face before waving his hand in invitation to Tal. "Care to go first?"

Tal shrugged and stepped past her, then walked forward with authority . . . smack into the iron gate with a thud that made her wince and fight not to laugh.

"Oops," Jason said lightly before winking at her. "But you've no alchemist blood in you, have ya, mate?"

Talos gave the other man a sarcastic grimace while rubbing his nose lightly. "Funny."

Jason bit his lower lip in an impressive struggle not to laugh out loud and Mila found herself fighting not to giggle. "Yeah, actually it was." He held out his hand and wiggled his fingers. "C'mon then, lad. Hold me hand like a good boy so we can go through."

He growled low and glared, making Mila realize he'd had his pride bruised. "Oh, c'mon Tal, he's just teasing you a little." She reached out and grabbed his hand and then put her other one in Jason's waiting one. She was starting to like Jason despite her better judgment. He reminded her a lot of Candy's brother Tim when they were young—always the prankster. Well, she'd lived through that, and had managed a few in return, so she could do it again.

Jason grinned and winked at her again and then looked at Tal with raised brows. "Oh, I *like* this one, Tal. She's got spirit." As he popped his fingers outward and the gate began to glow an eerie brownish-black, he looked down at her once more. "Sure you're not Irish, lass?"

She shook her head and squeezed his hand lightly. "Ukrainian. We're where the Irish *learned* it." The resulting laugh from both men was lost in the roar of sound as they stepped through the gate. She'd noticed it when she went through the gate in the library, and wondered what made it. Was it wind rushing by from moving incredibly fast to span the distance? Or could it be that there was something between here and there, some magical location that they stepped *through?* She'd asked Tal the previous night, and he'd confessed having never thought much about it.

They emerged at the edge of what had once been a park. But the grass was unkempt and had gone to seed, the carefully pebbled paths overgrown and littered with animal droppings. It made her realize she hadn't seen many animals down here. Just a few raccoons and what had looked like hairless hamsters. No cats, no dogs . . . not even birds. It contributed to the eerie sense of this place, and made her wonder what it had looked like when it was normal.

Whether the wondering caused it, or she just finally noticed it through her mulling, she heard the sound. Her head raised and turned to the choir of voices that weren't voices at all. It was similar to the sound the *duszat* had made on the mantel, but this was deeper, richer—like comparing a first-grade chorus to the Mormon Tabernacle

Choir. Her heart sped up as the sound filled her. She had to get closer.

She tightened her hands on the others and moved forward quickly, pulling them along. "C'mon. I need to go see what's making the sound."

But apparently Tal and Jason couldn't hear it because they just stared at her quizzically. Tal shrugged and looked around. "What sound?"

Mila just shook her head and pulled her hands free of their palms, knowing she'd never be able to describe it. "Never mind. But I know where the Tree is."

It wasn't until she felt the hood fly from her head that she realized she was running . . . racing toward the Tree with the same enthusiasm as she used to dash for the playground. Joyous, eager, and with the firm knowledge the effort would be worth it.

It wasn't what she expected—even though she hadn't realized she *had* an expectation. The Tree of Life was massive, the trunk as big around as a sequoia, yet with branches far too short and frail for its size. The leaves were in places broad and wide as an elephant's ear, and in other places as small and delicate as a rosebush. *I don't even know what species this is. And if this is a slave to the real Tree, does the parent look the same?* She couldn't even imagine where she might find it, since she'd never seen anything like it in a tree species book.

Arrangements of flowers, now-rotting fruit, and other items were heaped around the Tree's base, offerings from people who had fled when their prayers weren't answered, and tromped on and scavenged by those who remained. Jason and Tal reached her as she stood and stared at it while catching her breath. Both of them let out whooshes of air that said how fast they'd been running. "See what you mean 'bout needing a shorter cloak, lass," Jason said between gasps. "Didn't imagine those little legs could move that fast."

"I do a lot of walking," she replied absentmindedly,

before reaching out one hand toward the Tree. She could feel the life here, sense it the same way as a wall in the darkness. She closed her eyes to allow her inner eye to see more clearly. They were right that the Tree was dying. She could see it in the pale blue bands where leaves had withered and wounds gaped in rotting bark. "It's not dead yet, though. It can be saved." She muttered the words, not taking her gaze from it as she searched for what Viktor had claimed was here—eggs in the branches that she needed to replace. She wasn't even positive she'd spoken out loud until she heard Jason's pleased response.

"Brilliant. Absolutely bleedin' brilliant. Go on, then. Tell us what needs doin'."

She stepped forward, hearing the crunch of leaves and wilted flowers underfoot, smelling the sickly sweet scent of rotten fruit. Her inner eye searched each branch in turn, looking for the egg. She had to find one, or she couldn't even hope to start. The manuscript Baba had left had only revealed the recipe for the dyes and steps to create a *duszat,* but without any indication of what *designs* to put on the eggs. Perhaps that was knowledge she was supposed to already have . . . but she didn't. If she could just find one of these, somehow see what they looked like through bark and wood, she could reproduce them.

Wait. There! She saw a flash of a rune as she reached the nearest limb and passed her fingers over the rough bark. Yes, a double straight line that cut across the pattern of growth rings. "The ribbon of eternity." But there was a jagged breaking of the image, where a secondary branch had sprouted out. She tried to turn it in her mind, moved around the branch, trying to see what else was on the egg.

"Blimey, Tal. Would you look at that?" Her ears heard Jason speak, his tone reverent, but she couldn't be distracted from her task enough to turn to whatever he saw. She could only hope they would keep her safe from any problems until she was done. She dropped to her knees under the branch, shuffling through the scattered gifts until she touched ground. She followed the cracked edges of the fragment with her mind and fingers. *Dots inside circles, over a basketweave. But what's the main theme?*

She extended her focus, reaching further around the branch, realizing the egg must have broken and moved long ago. Finally she found it near the trunk where it was put so long ago . . . the mostly whole shell. The runes glowed bright in her head, so close she could nearly touch them. *A sun pattern with trees and crude stag outlines. Heat, warmth, and life. This must be the mage guild's limb.* It was a complicated pattern but elegantly done. The artist who'd made this egg was obviously extremely skilled. She only wished she could see the *actual* egg to know what colors they'd used. But she'd have to rely on the manuscript and hope for the best.

But wait! There was one tiny piece that had worked out of the branch over the years. It was just at the edge of the bark. She reached forward to yank it out with her fingernails, being careful not to break it. But when she tugged, the fragment pulled back. A tingling flowed over her fingers, strong enough to pull a gasp from her throat.

"Craters! Help me get her out of there, Jason!" She heard Tal's panicked voice and her eyes shot open. What she saw made her gasp and fight not to scream. Her hand was deep inside a crack in the branch, her fingertips still clutching the egg fragment. But the Tree had reacted and had closed bark over her hand. Even as she watched, rough scales were crawling up her arm toward her shoulder, as though the Tree was trying to absorb her inside it.

Tal grabbed her around the waist while Jason got her feet and they both began to pull her away. But the Sacred Tree wasn't to be denied that easily, for the pressure on her hand increased, tugging her in. She tried to release the egg fragment, in case this was some sort of self-defense spell the original Parask artist had put in place. She tried the counterspell Baba had taught her. *"Avatay!"* and heard both Jason and Tal spout words that had no meaning to her.

"Arasht!" from Tal, and *"Meeyelk mesha!"* from Jason. Heat flowed over her with each casting, and at last the

combination of them pulling and casting, along with her frantically yanking her arm in circles cracked the bark. They all flew backward to land in a smelly pile of rotten squash, breathing hard and fast.

Her arm was still mostly covered by bark, and she peeled it off with her other hand, revealing skin that was pink and shiny, like a healing scar.

Tal helped her get the rest of the wood stripped from her fingers, and she realized she still had the bit of shell between her fingers. She dropped it into her other hand to see her prize. Even after all the years, the colors were still brilliant. Lacquered black, ruby red, and yellow bright as the sun were cut across with lines of white. She nodded her head, staring at the patterns, her mind already on the task of re-creating it. But Tal's flat, hollow voice dragged her back to the present.

"So it's true then." He was staring at the bit of eggshell in her hand, his face a mask of conflicting emotions. She didn't know what to say . . . how to make better something so devastating as the end of his whole belief system.

She opened her mouth to say something—anything to get that pained look off his face when a faint voice came from the distance. "Help me! Oh someone please help me with her!"

It was obvious that both Tal and Jason were trained police officers, because their entire demeanor changed into alert professionals. She followed their gaze to a pair of women—one fair skinned, one dark, in long red cloaks, stumbling toward them. The pale, elderly woman was supporting the other, who was having a hard time keeping her feet. She was obviously ill, and Mila closed her eyes once more to read their auras. It wasn't just what she saw that panicked her, but the worried voices of the men on either side of her that revealed their identities.

Jason's voice came first as she watched his energy aura shift in her mind's eye. Patterns swirled and flowed as he raced forward to catch the dark woman as she collapsed. Her robe opened as he turned her over, revealing the dark

red tendrils of *Tin Czerwona* crawling over her body.
"Mum?"

Then came Tal's voice, also filled with dread. "Sybil?
Mom, what's wrong? What are you doing here?"

CHAPTER 13

*S*he heard the jumble of voices as the men tried to find
out what was happening from their mothers. But she wasn't
listening. Instead, she was watching the tendrils carefully,
with a sort of fascination. The sickness was looking for
a place to expand, someone else to infect. But it couldn't
attach to the others—she watched as tendrils reached for
them, only to shrink back abruptly.

Then it occurred to her . . . they were *mages*. Tal had
said he lost his parents and was sent to a foster family—
also mages. Jason's mother was earth clan, but he had inherited his *father's* talent. "It makes perfect sense."

Tal must have been waiting for a reaction from her because he pounced on her words. "What does?"

"Of course he wouldn't create a virus he could *catch*.
You're all immune." But as she watched the squirming
threads of the sickness grow stronger, even as Jason's alchemist mother got weaker, she knew she had to do something. She opened her eyes and managed to get to her feet
among the smelly vegetables and brushed off the sticky
seeds as best she could. *But this cloak is never going to be
the same, and I need a shower.*

Jason was helping his mother rise to a sitting position.
But she couldn't hold it and fell backward. In that brief
movement, panic flashed in Mila's mind. She saw a wisp
of a tendril . . . seeping *down,* into the ground. *Magic. It's
a magical illness. But can a* Tree *catch a virus?*

"We have to get her out of here! *Now!*" She hadn't realized she'd yelled as her eyes opened, but everyone silenced

and turned with wide eyes. Mila didn't want to panic them, but something told her if they stayed, the slave Tree was going to catch *Tin Czerwona* and send it straight to the Tree of Life. "Somewhere, anywhere. But we need to get this woman *away* from the Tree."

"We can't move Mum. She's horribly ill. We need to find a healer to come to her." Jason looked at Mila as though she was insane and his voice reflected his anger and worry.

But Tal took in the whole scene before turning his face back to her and rumbling a question. "What's the problem?"

"She *is* sick, Tal—with the same thing as Suzanne. And she's about to infect the *Tree*. We need to get her *away*." She stared at him strongly, willing him to understand. She tried to push the words into his head. *Please figure this out so I don't have to say it, Tal. It's* Tin Czerwona, *and it's contagious. C'mon, you're smart enough.*

Whether he heard her, or figured it out on his own, she watched as confusion turned to panic, and then to action. He rose to his feet, away from his mother and picked up the other woman in his arms. "No time for talking, Jason. We need to get back to the shop. Mila, do you need to stay here to fix . . . anything?"

She closed her eyes again and stared at the ground. Thankfully, as soon as Tal had picked the woman up, the tendril had broken off. She nearly slapped her forehead. *Duh. This was the mage branch, so likely the roots were filled with fire magic.* She shook her head. "No, our luck is holding. But we need to hurry, and keep away from other people on the way back." Jason started to open his mouth, reaching to take his mother from Tal's arms, but she held up a hand. "Please, Jason. Once we get back to the store, I'll explain everything. I know you don't have any reason to trust *me,* but please try to trust Tal for a few more minutes. I swear it's important."

Tal nodded once at his former friend but didn't wait for a reply. He took off at a fast walk, carrying the heavyset woman with obvious effort. But then he muttered a word and she felt a blast of warm air swirl around her ankles as she followed. A shimmering appeared around him and she could see his shoulders relax under the cloak. It took a moment to put it in place but she smiled when she did. *Well isn't that a nifty trick? Hot air rises, so she's not as heavy.*

Jason's voice came from behind her. "Can I give you a lift there, ladies? I dunno what Tal's all about, but it seems important. I've not much magic left in me focus, but enough for this. Let's have us a little boost, eh?"

She felt herself rising from the ground and struggled to keep her balance, twisting and turning as she quickly moved forward a foot or more above the bricks. "Whoa whoa whoa—"

A light hand touched her shoulder and the woman chuckled in a warm British alto. "You're not used to riding the currents then, are you, dearie? It's jolly good fun."

Jason leaned over to whisper in her ear. "That's why there are no cars down here. Never used to be a need."

Tal's foster mother must have heard. Her face was filled with open amazement. "Cars? You mean autos? Are you from the overworld, then?"

"This is Mila, Sybil. She's a friend of Tal's." He looked at Sybil with raised brows then hooked a thumb toward her. "This lass wandered through that gate you're not supposed to know about near Mum and Da's flat . . . by *herself*."

Sybil likewise raised her brows, and looked at her with a new expression, but Mila couldn't quite tell whether she was surprised, impressed, or disapproving. Her own mother used to give her that sort of look when she would finally reveal something outrageous she'd done, long after the fact.

By the time they got back to the butcher shop, Jason's mother, who Mila learned was named Dareen, was unconscious and moaning lightly. She didn't even have to use her inner eye to see that the virus had spread. Tal placed the woman on the couch at the edge of the tiny kitchen, backed away carefully, and turned to look at Mila. "Can you help her?"

She shook her head and shrugged. "I honestly don't know." She looked out the window into the darkness of the cavern and threw up her hands. "No sun, no moon—which are who I call on for strength and purpose. And, it kicked my butt last time. I passed out before Suzanne was healed. This is even further along. Of course I'll *try*. Like Baba said . . . we don't refuse to heal just because the way is difficult."

Jason wasn't even listening. He'd knelt down by his mother's side and was holding her hand firmly while trying to revive her by calling to her softly. Tal nodded and touched her shoulder with a look of gratitude.

But she was surprised at how Sybil reacted to what she said. Her expression darkened, making her eyes glitter angrily. The flames that decorated her robe leapt higher and crackled, as though tied to her mood.

It wasn't in Mila's nature to just ignore a glare like that, so she turned fully toward her and cocked her head. She tried hard not to put any particular emotion into her voice. "Is something wrong?"

Sybil's features twisted into a look of loathing and barely contained rage. She clenched fists until her knuckles were stretched white. "It's no wonder you've never ridden the currents . . . no wonder Dareen's fallen ill." Mila reared back, struggling to figure out what she was talking about, but in the next moment it was made clear. Sybil turned all that quickly rising emotion on Tal, who regarded his foster mother with an expression of surprise and confusion. "How *dare* you bring a filthy *Parask* into our midst! We banished that disease-ridden guild to the overworld for just this reason, Talos." Holding out a shaking finger, Sybil pointed at her and spat words with a viciousness Mila had only previously heard in news footage of race riots. "Begone, enemy of Demeter . . . carrier of the red death . . . *whore of the dark mage!* I call on thee, blessed Demeter—" She paused and then her lips trembled for a moment, the final words finally rumbling from her chest to hang in the air with deadly intent. "Strike down this befouler of the craft!"

"*M*other! *No!*" Tal's hand shot out as though warding off a blow and he pulled Mila behind him frantically with his other hand in a vain attempt to shield her from the curse. But there was no stopping it, no counterspell in existence that could avert the weighing of the Tree's judgment against another guilder.

He'd never seen his foster mother like this. Her eyes were glittering with fevered intensity and a cruel smile was painted on her lips as the air grew heavy and still. He felt his heart pound with fear and a knot formed in his stomach that made him want to vomit. He clutched Mila's arm tightly as he waited to see what would happen.

It certainly wasn't what he expected. Mila yanked away from his grasp and came around from behind him, walking through the ozone-scented air as though it was nothing. *"Excuse me?!"* she yelled right at Sybil. "Who the hell are *you* to call me a befouler? I haven't *befouled* anything and I'm sure as hell not Vegre's *whore*." Mila stormed forward, not even understanding enough to be afraid. *I'll wager she doesn't even realize a curse has been laid.* She landed inches away from his foster mother with clenched fists, so close that their noses were almost touching. "Where do you get off calling me a *whore?* You don't know me, bitch . . . don't know a thing about me or my family." She turned one shoulder enough to point at Dareen's still form, but remained inches from Sybil's shocked face. Tal couldn't tell whether she was shocked that Mila was still upright, or that she dared to dispute her claims. "It's a damn good thing it's not *you* lying there, lady, because I'm not sure I'm a good enough person not to let you just suffer."

Mila shook her head before turning her back on them all to walk over and take Jason's place at Dareen's bedside. Jason had stood and backed away after the curse was laid. He was in the room's farthest corner, looking on the scene with mingled fear and confusion. No doubt he was also watching to see where the curse would land, and what effect it would have.

But Mila wasn't done yet, and Tal watched her in a sort of stunned admiration. She touched Dareen's forehead and shook her head once more before muttering to herself. "Geez, Viktor was right about you guys. No *wonder* nobody has wanted to fix the Trees for you."

Silence descended on the room as Mila pried open Dareen's lids to look into her pupils. She winced at whatever she saw and then closed her eyes. Her head and hands moved in unison, apparently *seeing* the illness with her other sight. It took a moment for Tal to realize the air had cleared. For the first time he'd seen, a befouler curse had dissolved without striking a target. Either the Tree wasn't able to raise enough power to punish, or it judged them all to be without fault.

Sybil apparently realized it at the same moment and opened her mouth. But he held up a warning hand and let out a growl. "Enough, Mother. It's the *Sacred Tree* who has judged here and your new goddess Demeter obviously has no power to override it. Mila is no befouler, so just *stop* this."

His words made her flinch and retreat into her robe, as though he'd struck her. He let out a frustrated breath. "Where did these strange new beliefs come from, Mother? When did you turn your back on the Tree's good ways?" He pointed at Mila, who was doing her best to ignore them all. "Mila hasn't harmed you . . . hasn't harmed *anyone*. Even the Tree knows she's good and kind and incredibly intelligent—and until the lot of us came into her world, had no idea she was even a guilder. Do you understand what I'm saying?"

Sybil had gotten her composure back while he spoke and he suddenly realized that the calm, rational woman who'd raised him had disappeared. She regarded him with what appeared to be sadness, but was merely a mask over the top of her delusion. "Yes. Of course I understand, son. She's *bewitched* you with the conjurer's soul-corrupting magic. He told us this might happen when the end of the days of the Tree came near. But once Demeter is returned to her throne over the guilds, She will cleanse the land of their kind. I can only pray that you'll be safe and will be returned to me when the era of fire begins."

Mila threw up her hands abruptly enough that he and Jason both flinched. "Oh for God's sake! This is getting ridiculous. I'm sorry, but you either need to get your whacked-out mom the hell out of here, Tal, or tell *me* to go. 'Cause I'm not going to stay and try to heal Dareen in the same room as her—she's ruining my concentration. And the *Tin Czerwona* is getting worse by the second, so pick fast. She won't last much longer."

Tal looked between the two women. He'd known Sybil most of his life . . . had believed everything she'd taught him about truth and goodness. So why was he favoring Mila's comments and believing that his mother was *whacked out? Am I bewitched?*

Jason spoke up before he had a chance to make a decision, and he couldn't say he was sorry. "That's about enough from the lot of you." He left his corner at last and walked forward with authority before pointing at Mila, but looking at Sybil. "I know what me own eyes saw earlier at the Tree, so I've no choice but to give some credence to the lass."

Tal agreed. There was no disputing Mila's healing abilities anymore. When she'd knelt beneath the Sacred Tree and touched it—well, it was like nothing he'd experienced before. He'd seen dozens . . . no, *hundreds* of Guilders lay their hands on the Tree—whether seeking guidance, praying, or just in reverence. But he'd never seen the Tree actually choose to *bond* with a crafter before. Her hands had just sunk into the limb in a glow of blue power, and warmth had flowed in a wide circle around the trunk. They'd been nearly too awestruck to notice when it had started to go wrong and it was only Mila's sharp gasp of pain that had brought them out of their stupor in time.

Dareen moaned just then and a rumbling came from beneath Tal's feet. He wouldn't normally notice the fine trembling of the floor or the swaying of the delicate china cups on their hooks under the cabinets because it was so faint. But combined with the possibility that a dirtdog had contracted *Tin Czerwona,* it spoke volumes. Once the disease began to progress, it would be dangerous to stay here, since even without magic, the very ground would react and try to bury them alive. Jason's face took on a new panic. He dropped to his knees beside the couch and yanked up the sleeve of her crimson cloak, baring skin for the room to see. Her alchemist birthmark, the same comb pattern as Alexy wore on his bicep, was swollen and glowing a deep rust-red. Jason dropped the sleeve abruptly and rubbed his hands on his pants with wide eyes. He turned his head again to Sybil, his words flat and final. "That tears it. Get out of me house."

"Jason, you don't understand what's happening here. She's—" Sybil pointed at Mila, her face already speaking the accusation that hadn't yet hit air.

The Fomorian stood firm. He clenched his dark fists and Tal watched as flames began to lick the air around his skin. But this was real . . . not mere decoration. "Me da's away, and me mum's in no state to speak. Until one returns to claim it, I declare familial right of this house. I claim the magic it contains and I revoke your welcome and your power here. *Get out.*"

Sybil's voice raised in a panic that was suddenly very real. Having Jason revoke her welcome had made her forever powerless in this place. It was an enchantment on every home by the kings to keep the peace, and didn't rely on an individual family's magic ability to maintain it. "You're siding with a *Parask,* Jason. It's *forbidden,* and dangerous! You don't know what you're doing. The legends speak of—"

"The *legends.*" Jason sneered and snorted loudly. "Those old legends are a flippin' joke. I've learned too much in the overworld to be frightened like a child. Frankly, I don't care one dosh if Mila's a soul-conjurer, an African witch doctor shaking gourds, or a naked mole rat in disguise. She's offerin' to help and, in fact, has offered nothing *but* kindness and charity so far. 'Tis only *your* words which concern me, Mrs. Onan. While I appreciate that you brought Mum to find help—which is the only reason I'm giving you fair warning, I say again . . . get out of me house before I *put* you out."

Then Sybil turned to Tal, her voice so weedling and needy it made him cringe. They'd done something to her, the *Children*. This tactic was beneath the woman he knew. "Tal, talk some sense into your friend. You wouldn't let him harm me, would you?"

Actually, he wouldn't, but he couldn't let her know that—couldn't let her try to use him as leverage. The ground rumbled again as Dareen moaned and twisted in growing delirium. He had no doubt Mila couldn't craft under this tension. Other than combat spells, he doubted he could, either. "I'd do as he orders, Mom. Having us *both* put out won't help your friend Dareen."

Her face moved through a dozen emotions before settling into a cold, distant expression that was unlike anything he'd seen her wear before. He needed to find out what they'd done to her, and how to bring her back to the mother he knew. *Soon, but not this moment.*

"Very well," she said at length. "I'll go. But we *will* be back to cleanse this place of the Parask scum, so be warned."

Mila let out a rude noise by vibrating her outstretched tongue, without even turning her head to acknowledge the words. It made Jason smile, which was apparently the last straw for Sybil. She turned and stomped down the stairs. She probably would have slammed the door if there was one. Jason moved to the window and after a moment the tension in his shoulders eased. He flicked his wrist with a flourish and Tal felt a pressure against his ears as the house's protection barrier covered over the open spaces. Only those invited would be able to pass, which was probably a good thing . . . especially if she decided to make good on her threat. Jason turned to him with raised brows and a shake of his head. "Your mum's gone crackers. You know that—right, mate?"

His reply came out angry and he realized his fists were clenched in frustration. "That's not my mom, Jason. That group's done something to her. Plus, we don't know that *your* mom hasn't gone crackers, too. One of us needs to follow her, keep her from reaching the other Children."

Jason chuckled. "No need, mate. Look outside." His friend . . . yes, Tal realized he *did* consider Jason a friend again, curled one side of his mouth in a wry grin.

Tal walked to the window and stared down into the street. Sybil was standing with furrowed brow, tapping her finger on her lip and flicking her eyes around the landscape as though searching for something. "What is she doing? Is she bewitched?"

"In a manner of speaking, yes," Jason said and returned to the couch to sit on the armrest next to Dareen's head. "It's part of the house magic. I've never really understood it, but if someone leaves here in anger, they won't remember why they were angry by the time they reach a block. She'll wander off and find her group and not have the vaguest notion of where she's been for the past few hours." He raised a hand as Tal's expression darkened, as though anticipating his objection that a memory alteration spell was incredibly illegal. "I know 'tis not proper. But not me doin'. This is house magic, not a spell. But I must admit it's been useful for the business. Never an angry customer that leaves our shop."

And house magic comes from the kings, so there was little Tal could comment about. But he could certainly wonder how it came about.

Jason touched Mila's arm after a shrug. "You just tell me how much magic you need, or what tools, and I'll bring 'em to ya."

She shook her head, obviously frustrated and yes . . . there was fear in her eyes, too. "Magic won't help. I can't use it. No, what I need to know from both of you is how important is she to you?"

Tal was surprised by the question, but when she continued, it became clear.

"See, I've searched the whole area for power to use while you guys were arguing." She looked at him and nodded with little tips of her chin. "You're right about those cult people, by the way. There's something really wonky about their life energy. They're not sick . . . not precisely, but there's *something* weird going on. I can't risk drawing on them for healing energy." She sighed and looked down at the woman on the couch. "But, unfortunately they account for all the humans I could find and, other than small animals, there's very little life left in this area . . . except *us*. So—" She touched Dareen's forehead and looked up at both of them with pain and worry clear in her eyes. "Which of us wants to volunteer to die to save her life?"

CHAPTER 14

*J*ason didn't hesitate, even though his muscles tensed. Mila hated that she had to ask, but the disease was too far along and she didn't know what else to do. "If that's what it takes." He shrugged and reached down to touch Dareen's thick long hair with a smile. "She's me *mum*, after all. I know she'd do the same for me."

It didn't surprise her in the least. She'd understood that was his base nature from the moment she met him. "I wish there was another way—"

Tal spoke up, his voice filled with the same frustration she felt. "Can't you take a little from the both of us? Spread the load so nobody has to *die?*"

She wished she understood the process well enough to explain it. "It doesn't work that way. I don't have that good of control over it. You saw what I did to the plant in the kitchen . . . and you were just *tired*. I don't know how I affected the hospital patients. I was too afraid to call and ask today. And Jason's mom is *dying*. I don't know how bad the damage is inside or what it's going to take to heal her. Once I pick a subject to draw from and start, that part of my brain shuts off and I just keep pulling until it's done. I don't really understand the process."

Tal knelt down beside her and reached forward to cup her face in his hands. She didn't know if he could feel her trembling, but she was. She'd never been asked to take on a healing like this . . . had never contemplated that there'd be a *need.* "If you don't understand the process, then you don't *know* it's impossible. Mila, there's a time in every crafter's life when we have to step outside what's comfortable. We all move from doing what's simple instinct to gaining control and crafting with *purpose.*" He obviously believed what he was saying and while she *wanted* to think it was possible, she wasn't really *crafting* . . . at least as he knew it. She opened her mouth to explain but he shook his head with a small smile. "I know what you're going to say—that you *aren't* a crafter, and don't use magic to do your healings. But I say otherwise. I saw you at the Tree and if that wasn't magic—" He paused for a moment, obviously trying to come up with an analogy.

Jason completed the thought, but probably not in the way that Tal might have. "If that wasn't magic then I'll be eatin' me da's stinky old boot. Not a crafter? Me right eye you're not. Bleedin' hell! With branches comin' to flower all around your head, and grass growin' up at your feet? If that's not magic, well—" He squatted down and tucked a finger under Tal's hands to turn her head. Tal dropped his hands, but took her free hand between his. Jason's voice was filled with admiration. "If I didn't know better, I'd swear you had dirtdog blood. No, 'twas crafting, lass, just of a sort I've not seen before. But Tal's right. You need to learn mastery of it. We'll do all we can to help. If that means me life in the process, then hell and be done with it. But do at least give it a *go* to stay your hand before I kick off, hey?" He smiled and winked before giving the tip of her nose a pop with his finger.

Branches flowering? Grass growing? "I don't remember any of that. I didn't do anything special . . . I was just—" She nearly screwed up and said *looking* for the egg, but didn't want to open up another whole discussion when Dareen was quickly failing. The way Tal had reacted, she was pretty sure he hadn't told anyone about the scroll from Viktor's. "Anyway, I don't know if I can, but I'll *try*."

"And we'll do our best to keep your attention focused. Remember," Tal said as he helped her get up and brought a chair for her to sit on. "Craft with *purpose*. Surround the flow with intent and you won't get lost in the moment."

She wanted to protest again that it *wasn't* magic, but these two men had known magic all their lives . . . for *centuries*, and swore it was. So what did she know? And, too, their advice wasn't much different than what Baba had tried to teach her, just using different words. "Think," Baba had said while tapping her temple. "Use the brain God gave you, yes? Plan the movements . . . like so—" Mila felt her hand rise, remembering all those lessons; hour after hour of healing the pinpricks on Candy's arms and legs that Baba had inflicted, struggling to concentrate each time Candy yelped in pain.

Pain . . . dear mercy, the pain! Dareen might not be conscious, but her mind was aflame with the onslaught of magical tendrils attacking sensitive nerves. Again Mila heard her grandmother's soothing voice from deep inside her memories. "Wrap yourself around the pain, Mila. Let it flow through and over you. Find the power . . . find your source and the healing will push away the pain, yes?"

She felt outward and found life and grabbed hold with her mind. It was pure, clean energy that pushed away Dareen's pain. She began to concentrate on the healing, moving each new pain as she did. Minutes passed as she tried to unravel the knot of infected tissue, one slimy tendril at a time.

Her throat began to feel dry so she swallowed and was surprised at the burning that followed. It even hurt now when she breathed and she couldn't seem to summon her voice to speak. She opened her eyes in panic to find Tal wrapped around her, one hand on her forehead pulling her against his chest while he uttered soothing words. "Shh. That's it. I know it hurts, but try to let it go."

Had she been screaming? Her throat certainly felt like it. She couldn't seem to move her body, as though she was still in her healing trance. Yet she was aware . . . could see and hear things outside of the ritual. *But I haven't even called on the powers. Haven't spoken the ritual to start the process.* Yet she could see Jason, bound to her with a glowing white rope as thick around as her wrist. He looked almost serene, but it was obvious the sensation wasn't completely pleasant.

She smelled flowers suddenly—roses and lilies and then it was like walking through Viktor's gardens. A riot of colors, smells, and sounds filled her head with life and warmth. "Concentrate on your crafting, Mila. Don't lose focus." Tal's words filtered through the other sensations. Was he experiencing the healing process, too? Could he see and smell the flowers, or was he just guessing and giving her something solid to cling to?

Either way, it *did* help her focus. She looked down again at Dareen. The squirming lines of red and black were no longer hovering on the surface of her skin. They'd burrowed inside and now stood out in sharp relief under her skin like a tattoo, but twisting and moving with purpose.

There was no time to lose.

She bent down to place her hands flat on Dareen's chest, and Tal moved with her—not obstructing or limiting her movement but instead giving her additional reach and support, taking her weight so she didn't have to concentrate on keeping her balance. She began to whisper hoarsely as she drew on the power from Jason. "*Vsi srakhy, vsi nervy, vsiu khvorobu.* All the fears, all the nerves, all the illnesses. *Z pasuriv, pazuriv.* Go out, out. *Vse bezson-nia zlo.* I send all away." When she uttered the last word, something hit her chest hard, like a line-drive baseball. It stole her breath and doubled her over so hard that Tal struggled to keep her from hitting the floor. The virus was reacting to her attack, trying to either push away the healing power or infect her. She tried to remember the right words, but the spells were getting jumbled in her mind. It was all she could do to keep an even flow of power into Dareen. Too much and she might do even more damage, too little and the virus would have time to react, to mutate. Damn it, what were the next words? *Come on, Mila!* Finally she let out a growl and opened her eyes. "Oh, screw the spells. You're going *down,* virus."

She started to send more energy in, cutting off each new path of the tendrils before they could get a foothold. But as the illness redoubled, she found the flow of magic to be fading. There was no *time* for that to happen. Another sharp blow came, but this time to her forehead. She heard Tal's voice as if from a great distance, but she couldn't hear all the words over the roar of the power in her head.

"Master . . . craft. Give . . . purpose." But she was so *close.* Just a little bit more energy and she'd have it beat.

"Too close. Have to . . . keep going."

A rush of wind and sound arrived in a burst of light that cut off all sensation. Tal's voice emerged from the brilliant void and she realized he'd found a way to mentally connect to her. *"Let Jason go, Mila. He's barely breathing. Control the power and cut the line. I'm here now. I'm with you and we'll finish healing her together."*

Jason? Who . . . what? But then she remembered, and knew her fear about killing someone had been well-founded. But Tal had reached her and she could think now. Again she was transported outside her own body to watch the scene from above. Jason unconscious on the floor, Dareen arched on the couch, her mouth open in a silent scream, and Tal . . . dear Tal, who was holding her so tight his muscles were ropes under taut skin. His lips were pressed to the side of her head, his eyes shut. When she concentrated she could feel the sensation, as faint and pleasant as a dream. She grabbed onto the new line of power, letting loose the other.

The power was a pure white needle of flame that burned through the foul bands of *Tin Czerwona*, creeping like an evil kudzu vine inside Dareen.

And then it was done. As quickly as the battle began, the last root of the virus was destroyed, right at the base of her neck, the infection point. It told her more clearly than anything that this illness was no accident. What she couldn't figure out was *why*. What was Vegre's goal in infecting random people? What tied Dareen and Suzanne together?

Before she let loose of the flow of power from Tal, she carefully scanned Dareen one more time, looking for any hint of the illness. But it was gone, dissolved away, leaving only pure tissue and blood.

Then her sight took her to the others. Jason was starting to revive, but he was very weak—lower even than Tal had been in her kitchen. But Tal had little to spare himself, having given his all to save his friend's mother.

That left only her. Normally, she would have called on her own life first, but Baba had always said it was better for the power to come from other family members. Once she got older, it made sense in the same way that doctors look first to the family for blood or organ donations.

But there was nothing stopping her from giving Jason a little boost from her reserves. She was full to brimming with the aftermath of the healing, so she connected to them both once more, long enough to fill their reserves until they were all equally tired, but functional. *A quarter tank of fuel each. Enough to make it until we can eat and rest.*

By the time she opened her eyes, still cradled in Tal's arms, Jason was up and at his mother's side. There were bags under his eyes as though he hadn't slept for a few days, but from the relief, and *joy* on his face, she doubted he cared. There was nothing quite like the aftermath of a healing, when everyone *knew* the patient would recover.

"Ah, Jason me boy." Dareen placed a gentle hand on his cheek, making him beam. "I knew ya'd find some way to make it right."

He smiled but shook his head. "'Twasn't me, Mum. Not one dosh. This was Mila's doin'. She's a—" He paused and Mila caught her breath. Would he start the argument all over again? But apparently, once was enough for him. "She's a friend of Tal's and a bit of a doctor, she is."

Yet her relief at Dareen's smile and nod was mingled with guilt. *What would Baba say to me being ashamed of who . . . of what I am?* She shook her head and gently pulled out of Tal's grasp, even as he tightened to keep her close. "I'm sorry, Jason. But I just can't. I appreciate you wanting to keep me safe, but I'm proud of who I am." Dareen's brows raised and she looked at her questioningly. "I hope you won't be offended, ma'am, but I'm apparently from the Parask guild. I didn't know it until recently, but . . . well, there you go. I'm a soul-conjurer and I used my talent to heal your illness."

Jason bit at his lower lip and Tal let out a small sound that she knew accompanied a wince. Dareen held one dark hand to her mouth, her eyes wide with shock. Her voice was muffled from behind her hand until she finally remembered to remove it. "So, there *are* conjurers left in the world. Bless me soul. I thought the hunt was just a way to keep the group busy so we wouldn't ask questions."

"The *hunt?*" That was never a good term for a large group of *anything* to use. Things tended to end badly.

But Dareen ignored her question. She grabbed onto Jason's arm, nearly pulling him down on top of her. "I must see King Kessrick right away. Help me up so I can get out of this robe, lad."

Jason and Tal looked at her incredulously, and Mila supposed their reaction was similar to her own mother expecting to be admitted to the White House. "King Kessrick? Bleedin' hell. He isn't seeing *anyone* right now, Mum. You know that. He's been locked in the palace, seeing only courtiers since the evacuation weeks ago. Not to mention," he added with a stunned note in his voice, "that you can't just expect to walk in the bleedin' *palace,* or be granted an audience, without stacks of paperwork."

She blew out a harsh breath and nodded her head angrily while tapping one finger on her leg. "That's right. Forgot the bloke's a bloody coward." She looked up again when Mila was forced to stifle a snort. "Well, he *is*. Hidin' away from his own subjects just because the world's gone a bit wonky. His da would have been ashamed of how he's actin'." She swung her legs to the floor briskly, as though she hadn't almost died moments before. "It'll have to be King Mumbai then." She looked at Jason, and disapproval spilled into her features. "I'll be expecting one of these gates of yours leads to Shambala? While I'm not pleased with you, son—not one dosh—those gates just might have some use. But if I were you, I'd be thankin' the Blessed Tree that you're not layin' over my knee this moment."

Jason couldn't meet her gaze. He began to study his hands while she kept the motherly evil eye on him and waited for an answer. "Well? Does a gate lead to Shambala?"

Tal cleared his throat before Jason could respond. He got to his feet and then offered Mila a hand to stand. She moved over to where Dareen was leaning against the counter and crossed her arms over her chest while he spoke. "I hope it's not too impertinent to ask, Mrs. Rockwell—but what do you need to see the kings *about?* Is there anything we can do?"

"Nay, lad. 'Tis far too—" She paused and then stared at the three of them, each in turn, for a long moment. "Bless me . . . now that you mention it, you just *might*. In case it's worse than I fear, or I don't make it back, someone else should know to get word to the kings."

"Mum, don't talk that way!" Jason nearly yelled the words and reached out to grab her hand. "I've just barely got you back. Cheatin' the devil once is more than most get."

She patted his hand, but her expression was no longer warm. The brown eyes had turned to black, steely with determination. "There are things in life worth dyin' for, boyo . . . and stoppin' that scoundrel Vegrellion is one of them."

"Vegre?" They couldn't have planned it better if they practiced, for all three voices said it simultaneously. It was Tal who continued. "I knew he'd come to Vril after escaping. Do you know what he's planning?"

She nodded. "Indeed I do. Why do you think he wanted me dead, then? He's the leader of Demeter's Children, though the others are too befuddled to realize it. Many of them are too young to recognize him—calls himself *Reilly* in the group. But I spotted his black heart at one of the rallies straight away and wondered what he was up to. So I stayed around to join up while Patrick left with the others. Our little town of Ryver was the first to be hit by the red death, ya know—when he was still full of himself and not afraid to be seen. But I never expected he might recognize me in return. Bad mistake on me part, and very nearly the death of me."

Mila found herself nodding. "I *knew* you'd been intentionally infected. It was exact same spot as Suzanne. But I still can't figure out why he'd attack a little girl up where I live . . . one who doesn't even know about any of you or this place."

Dareen's expression turned canny. "Don't ya, lass? Are you very sure you don't know why? Think on it for a bit."

She felt her head shaking no in tiny movements. "Not a clue. Really. I'd *love* it if you'd tell me."

She leaned forward and poked a finger into Mila's stomach. "He's *flushin'*, lass. Bringin' the conjurers out of the brush, he is. With every illness that's magic in nature, they come because they can't help themselves. It's in the blood, don'cha know. But 'tis an absolute disgrace, what he's doin', and I mean to put a stop to it."

Tal let out a harsh breath that said he'd expected the news, but also couldn't understand the rationale. "But why would he want to kill all the remaining Parask? Most of them don't have enough magic to fill a thimble and more than half probably don't have any clue about their heritage—like Mila."

"Are ya daft, boyo? He doesn't want to *kill* them." Her face was filled with surprise. "He means to *collect* them."

She nodded as they looked at each other in shocked confusion. "At first I thought he was blinkin' crackers, but if there are enough of you about still, he might just manage it."

"Manage what?" Mila had to ask. They were finally getting to the meat of what Vegre was planning and her curiosity was insatiable. She was just hoping that all of the pieces they'd discovered added up. But what Dareen had to say wasn't what she'd imagined. She'd expected to hear that Vegre planned to topple a government in a coup and become a despot, or bilk millions by starting an epidemic that only *he* could cure. But this—

"He plans to harness the very sun, lovey. The entire world would be at his mercy. He could freeze the equator or melt the poles . . . bake the land or deprive whole regions of warmth if the humans refuse to bow to his sorry hide. 'Tis an ambitious plan, to be sure . . . but with enough magic, anything's possible." She shrugged and threw up her hands. "While I don't claim to understand the connection with the Parask guild, there seems to be one, and he's usin' it to increase his own magic, and that of the Children. If the kings can't stop him, there's no telling what he might do, because it doesn't seem that he requires, nor *fears,* the Sacred Trees. That's why I have to see King Mumbai, so he can rally the others to stand against him."

Mila didn't say anything, and Tal likewise kept silent. He simply nodded noncomittally, the way she'd seen a hundred cops and another hundred lawyers do. She was having a hard time even wrapping her head around the enormity of the plan. Dareen was answering questions, all right, but raising so many more. Like, how were the Children involved, and what did the name change have to do with it? "Is there anything else about the things the Children have been doing that strikes you as odd? How do they fit in?"

She nodded. "You mean other than gatherin' up your other Guilders? Well, *Reilly* has been sendin' out groups to the outer rings in all the cities, collectin' root vegetables for some reason. Originally, I'd thought it was for food for the members because they've been rounding up birds, too. Chickens, turkeys, and the like. But we've gone hungry more than one night, even though I've seen baskets of onions, beets, and sweet potatoes being brought into the shelter. I'd expected at least *one* shepherdess pie to come out of the kitchen . . . or perhaps a nice chicken dinner, but not a breath of 'em have reached us. Same with the berries and flowers I helped craft in the bogs near the moat."

There was something about that list of ingredients. "Were they *crocus* flowers, by chance?"

She nodded and Mila couldn't help but feel a level of admiration for Vegre. "Damned if he hasn't got it all figured out. I suppose you're raising bees, too?"

Dareen tipped her head again, her look now curious. "Honey for our tea and made into sweets for the children. Why?"

Mila noticed Tal and Jason were staring at her as though she was mad. But she wasn't insane. In fact, this was probably the sanest she'd been in a long time. While she understood Baba would probably be annoyed if she revealed the secret she'd learned at Viktor's, there was too much at stake. There was no way she was going to be able to stop him alone. Hell, if she didn't spill the beans, Dareen might not even reveal where they were headquartered, and *then* where would they be?

"Mila?" Tal was looking at her curiously, obviously failing to make the connections in his head. It was no wonder, since he had no experience with pysanka.

"He's making dyes and wax, Tal. Vegre's somehow figured out what was in the scroll at Viktor's. Wrap an egg in yellow onion skins and it dyes red. The stamen of crocus is saffron, which is yellow. I wouldn't have thought you could get orange out of sweet potatoes, but maybe he's figured out a way. And berries—well, that's just obvious. Blue and purple. Mix 'em all together and you get black. I've never tried to make green, but I presume you could boil leaves."

The realization actually staggered Tal and he had to grip

the back of one of the chairs to keep his balance. "And with enough chickens and turkeys—we've got to stop him."

Jason and Dareen still looked confused, but they wouldn't be for long. "You both might want to make yourselves comfortable, because I've got something to tell you that's going to be hard to believe."

But while shocked, they *had* believed. By the time Mila and Tal finished explaining, Dareen and Jason were both sitting down on the couch with nearly identical expressions of shock. When Mila pulled out the bit of egg she'd pulled from the Tree, Dareen had crossed herself the same way Baba always did when she heard bad news, but sideways, like an X over her chest.

"So then," Dareen said after a few moments of silence. "The kings signed the death warrant of us all by puttin' the Parask out in the cold. I wish I could say I was surprised, but they're a damned stubborn lot."

"The problem, as I see it, is what do we do now?" Tal's voice was calm, but there was a level of frustration setting in and Mila understood why. It was a ridiculous scheme Vegre was planning—completely insane, and while she couldn't imagine it could work, it was obvious Vegre did.

She walked across the room to the window to look outside at the patchy darkness while she thought. "Even if he managed to pull together the power, though, there's no way people will believe him back home. They'd never bow to him. There's weird weather everywhere right now—droughts in some places, flooding in others. One side arguing that global warming is caused by the greenhouse effect of too much carbon dioxide, while the rest say it's just a natural cycle and there might be a new ice age. No matter what he did to the climate, the scientists would argue for *years* about the cause before they'd believe magic was involved."

Tal and Jason both appeared to agree based on their nods when she turned back from the window. "'Tis true," Jason said. "Humans are a skeptical lot nowadays, Mum. The few who don't consider magic mere fiction for books believe it to be evil and would fight to the death before they'd bow to it. And you'd be surprised at some of the weaponry they've created. You can't craft if you've no limbs left. Vegre would have to do somethin' damned impressive to bend their knees without risking being blown to bits."

"I wonder—" Dareen's voice was a whisper, as though she was musing to herself.

Mila turned to watch her as her eyes shifted from side to side. A pressure in her bladder told her it had been too long since she'd drank the juice. She hadn't gone since she'd walked into the library. "I don't suppose there's a bathroom I could use?" She looked around, but didn't notice a doorway other than the one that led down the stairs.

"Down the hall and to the left." Jason waved his hand and energy shivered her skin. A doorway appeared in the corner of the room. "We shielded it to keep out looters during the riots, but I haven't been in there recently, so I don't guarantee the condition. It *used* to be very modern. I do like the comforts you lot came up with topside."

He wasn't kidding. People must have paid a pretty penny for the illegal gates, because it was a bathroom most people can only dream of. It was larger than her bedroom, with a whirlpool spa, bidet, and even a heated towel rack under bright fluorescent lights. But the pipes clanked and groaned and while the toilet flushed adequately, the water came out only as a trickle when she washed her hands— reminding her that time was running out down here.

Tal was talking when she returned to the small living room. His beard stubble was darker on his chin and it reminded her to flick her arm over to look at her watch. Six o'clock! Yikes. They were going to need to get back pretty soon. "That seems pretty unlikely. I mean, where would the vent come out?"

"What seems unlikely?" She sat back down in the chair she'd vacated and leaned against the padded back.

"Dareen claims there's something being planned topside involving the Children. Vegre's convinced them that for the *age of fire* to begin, a sacrifice has to be made to Demeter."

"He's already sacrificed a few of the followers." Dareen's voice shook with anger. "I was supposed to be next, owin' to me knowing too much, but fortunately I still had enough of me mind not to consider it an *honor* to be tossed in a pool of lava. Beatrice and Nigel weren't so fortunate."

She tried to remember her earth sciences classes from high school. "Lava? Didn't you tell me Vril's under the Appalachians, somewhere on the East Coast? That's not a volcanic region . . . I don't think."

Dareen shook her head. "Not here. While there are lava vents pretty much anywhere if you know where to look, this is being planned to come up from under Rohm. I think Vegre's goal is to both destroy the prison and sacrifice a group of humans in a volcano. He wants something showy and totally unexpected to both Agathia and the overworld to show his power."

"Were you able to discover a location or time, Mum?" Jason's voice had changed into *cop* mode—flat, emotionless, and intelligent.

She released a slow breath. "The eve of the new year, I'm sorry to say. So we've little time to gain the ear of the kings. As for the location—" She shrugged helplessly. "The only thing I heard mentioned was *the palace.* But America doesn't have palaces to my knowledge so perhaps it's Buckingham or another place. I'm afraid I'm not much help."

Mila's breath had stilled as Dareen spoke. Finally, the last piece slipped into place. "The Palace Hotel," she said quietly. "*That's* what the name change was for." She pulled the paper out of her pocket to show Dareen, who looked at it with wide eyes before handing it back. "David Pierce owns the Palace Hotel in downtown Denver."

"And Sela told you the kings *let* Vegre out. What if they've done it more than once? What if he controls, or is in collusion with one or more of the kings, who are *encouraging* this attempt to invade the overworld?"

"'Twould explain why the O.P.A.'s out for your hide."

Jason was nodding while holding his mother's hand tightly, either giving support, or getting it. "If you spotted a government official getting Vegre out . . . but why come through the wall? They could just let him out by the front."

Mila shrugged. "Plausible deniability? Neither of them could really afford to be seen by their followers as courting the other. And invading the overworld would solve a bunch of problems down here. But I still can't figure out how we can stop him. If he's got a king in his pocket, and a group of delusional followers . . . what chance do we have?"

"If we can just unravel *one* part of the plan, he'll be finished. It's too intricate to hold up unless it all happens in order. If we can stop the volcano, and find some way to make it seem as if the Sacred Trees are responsible, he'll lose the faith of his followers. Or, if we destroy the eggs he's hoarding, he won't have the power to raise the magma. Any one of them will dissolve *all* of them."

"Just so, Talos." Dareen was nodding. "And since there are only four of us that we can trust, we'll have to split our efforts. Jason and I will visit King Mumbai to tell the tale and Mila—you will have to stay here to craft these eggs of yours to repair the Sacred Tree."

She shook her head and frowned so deep she could feel her eyebrows touch her lashes. "I think that's a bad idea. If I repair the Tree *now,* then won't Vegre have *more* power available? How will that help?"

" 'Tis a tall tale we'll be tellin' the king, lass. If we've a hope of bein' believed, it's going to be because the Tree returns to life without Vegre's aid. The kings are all tied to the Trees. He'll feel the slightest change in the energy and with the Trees healthy once more, there'll be four guilds of crafters, with magic a'plenty, to put him down."

"But what if he's in on it, too? Won't that just be a signal to move the plan forward sooner?"

The other three shook their heads, and even Tal scoffed at the idea. "Mumbai's the most outspoken of all the kings about keeping Agathia separated from the overworld and his mind is so strong I doubt even Vegre could gain access. He's also immune to blackmail. His people are warriors. If someone were kidnaped in an attempt to gain his cooperation, he'd consider they deserved their fate for not holding off their attackers. He's never bent . . . not in a thousand years."

"His Tree is also the last one with power," Jason added. "So his people will follow him to the end of the earth, believing it's his honor and temperate nature that keeps the Tree strong. But I've no idea whether he'll believe the bit about the . . . what did you call them? . . . dooshots?"

She shrugged. "Close enough. Frankly I'm not certain myself if I believe. I only have what Viktor's scrolls said and what I saw at the Tree. I've only made one of them . . . by accident, so whether I can do any good is still up in the air. But—" She looked again at her watch and turned her arm for them to see that it was nearly seven o'clock. "If I have any hope of getting this done, I've got to get back to the house and get started."

Jason's eyes went wide and he grabbed her wrist, turning his own arm over to compare. "Is that the time? Bleedin' hell." He took a deep breath and let it out in a sigh. "Well, I'm sorry to say we're all stuck here, then. The library closed at six tonight, owin' to the staff holiday party. They decided on an after-Christmas party this year because they couldn't find a restaurant with a large enough room. It was why I was trying to get back early. You're welcome to come with us to Shambala, though. I don't know if it's a good idea for you to stay here overnight."

"Stuck?" Her voice came out in a squeak. "We can't be *stuck.* My car's parked on the street. It'll get towed, and I've got to feed the cat. Don't you have a key to the library?"

He shook his head. "Only management has a key, and we wouldn't be able to walk to the front door anyway. The security alarm would go off. We wouldn't be much good at savin' the world behind bars."

Tal pursed his lips and tapped a finger on the table.

"There has to be another gate here. The one in Mila's house went *somewhere,* and I distinctly heard Vegre's minion Cardon mention Vril."

"Not one of mine, I'm afraid." Jason did look apologetic, but he raised his hands helplessly. "I only crafted one gate topside. Not even magic was enough to make me craft more. I do have *some* integrity. The rest of the gates here go to the other provinces."

"But I don't have tools or dyes or even eggs here." She hadn't felt this frustrated in a long time. "I was supposed to have dinner with my family tonight. If I don't show up, they're going to know something's wrong and call the police."

Jason shrugged and stood up. "They might *call,* but the police won't do anything for forty-eight hours. By then, we'll be back."

"And didn't I see you putting out a large bowl of food and water for the cat before we left your house this morning? I'm sure one night won't harm him." What Tal said was true, if not terribly supportive.

Dareen hammered the last nail in the coffin when she likewise stood. "If it's tools and eggs you're needin', I have both." She tipped her head to amend, "That is, depending on how long such things last. I've kept them dark and cool as he requested, but—"

"He?" Jason asked the same question Mila was going to. "What *he,* and what tools?"

Dareen swept past them toward the staircase. "Never you mind, boyo. I'll only say this: the Formorians once made friends with the Parask, and I wasn't born married to your da."

She swept down the stairs after a wink at Mila, which made her smile. But it made Jason scramble down the staircase after her, calling out an indignant, *"Mum!"*

Minutes later, they were all packed tightly into a small cellar beneath the shop—the entrance to which was likewise hidden from view by magic. Dareen emptied potatoes out of a stone bin carved into the bedrock and then knelt down next to it to reach far back into the wall. It took a little tugging, but finally she extracted a box about the size of a loaf of bread. She held it out to Mila but raised a warning eyebrow Jason's way. "Now, not a word of this to your da, hear me? He knew about Samuel, but not that I've been holdin' his craftin' tools all these years." She let out a small, sad smile that made Mila realize the man hadn't been just a *friend*. "I kept hopin' he'd come back one day, just to pick them up . . . so I'd know he made it through. But 'twas the death time, and he was so dedicated to the ill. When he didn't return, I—" She cleared her throat and squared her shoulders. "Well, that was a long time ago. I love Patrick with all me heart, and if this can help you save the Trees, then have and be done with it. It will have been worth keepin'."

It was too dark in the cellar to see much of what was inside the box, so Dareen led her back to the brightly lit kitchen. Tal and Jason followed more slowly and Mila could see they were talking, heads together while whispering and nodding. By the time they finally made it upstairs, Dareen grabbed for the green cloak Mila had worn around her, but made a face at the stains on it.

"I'm sorry—" Mila blushed. It was one thing to borrow something offered by the owner, but—

She waved it off with a small laugh. "Don't be silly, lass. I'd have beat his bottom red if he *hadn't* offered it. No guest of mine goes cold . . . or hungry, for that matter. And I have another." She re-hung the green cloak and reached up to snag a brilliant crimson cloak from a different peg. "I'll be expectin' you both to help yourselves to the pantry and icebox until we return. Eggs are there for the takin' and they're fresh. No more than a week old. I remember Sammy insistin' on fresh eggs. I just hope you can abide the dyes better than me own poor nose. 'Tis just powder in there, so you'll need vinegar. There's a bottle in the pantry." She spun on her heel and headed toward the freezer. "Come along, Jason. We must be off."

Jason rolled his eyes with a smile and then winked at Mila. "*Mums*. What are ya to do?" Then he sobered and reached out to grasp her arm before leaning in to kiss her cheek. "Thank you. Don't know what I'd do without her in me life. I appreciate it more than you can know. We should be back before morning. Mum knows Queen Krystella, so we should get an audience easily. The guest rooms are across from the bath." He glanced at Tal as he fastened the last hook at his neck. "Sorry you both have to stay over."

She heard Tal mumble something and hoped it wasn't what she *thought* she heard. But it made Jason laugh, so she feared it was. The sound of his dark chuckle reddened her cheeks as he turned and disappeared through the gate and she was left to hear the words echo in her ears.

"I'm not."

CHAPTER 15

*T*he blush on Mila's face made it fairly obvious he hadn't spoken softly enough. It nearly made him smile until she fidgeted nervously and lowered her eyes to the floor. A knot formed in his stomach. Was her reaction an admission of mutual attraction, or fear of a pursuer she felt trapped with? He'd been ready to lay with her, and *publicly,* in a roomful of strangers. He had been the one to kiss her, and had constrained her tightly as she screamed out Dareen's pain. Even now he wanted to gather her into his arms to carry her down the hallway to the nearest soft bed. *Am I missing something important in my lust to have her?*

Yet it didn't feel like mere lust. He'd known lust many times and while it could make him forget himself for a few moments, he'd always been able to set it aside to give attention back to what was important. It was why he'd never married, nor had any long-standing relationships. He never felt it was fair to shut the woman out the moment something more *important* occurred.

He shook his head while she stood there staring at the floor, sliding one finger over the edge of the old wood box. A tocking noise caught his attention and he realized she'd found a loose sliver and was flicking it with her thumb. Nervous . . . or trying to pull attention away from herself?

It would be a simple matter to just ask her. But would she lie if she feared him? He'd known far too many Guilders who would say anything—tell him anything they believed he wanted to hear—just to free themselves during an investigation. *Is that what I want from her?*

No, it was time for her to make the next move, if there would be one. He could wait to see if she had any desire for him. "So what's in the box? Is it what you need for your crafting?" She jumped as high as if a snake had bitten her, her eyes rising to his, wide and dilated. Whatever the cause, that reaction wasn't one he ever wanted to see again.

She stared at the box for a long moment, as though she'd forgotten she was holding it. "Oh! I mean, yeah. I suppose we should look in it." She put the box down on the table, pried open the latch with her fingernails, and looked inside. "Wow, it really *is* a pysanka kit, and a nice one. Come look." The note of admiration in her voice, combined with the invitation, made him curious enough to move next to her at the table. She took each item out and looked to him for reaction, but they meant nothing to him so he could only shrug.

"The block is just beeswax, of course. Nothing special about it. But see, the dark dust in these glass jars is powdered farba—dye. All I have to do is add vinegar. It'll liquify the powder and scar the eggshell enough for the dye to attach." Next she held up a slender wooden stick with an odd metal funnel on the end. "Now this is a kistka. You gather beeswax in the big end and then heat the metal with a candle flame so it comes out as liquid through the point. They have electric kistkas now, but I prefer these old ones." She must have noticed his blank look at the items, because her voice took on the tone of an instructor. "See, the whole process of making a pysanka is nothing more than painting wax on the egg, dyeing the egg, and then painting on more wax to hold in successively darker colors. The only trick is making it *pretty*."

Tal touched the tip of the kistka and felt the wax, dark with soot. It made him wonder how she could see what she was doing. "But by the time you've dipped it several times, how can you see what parts you made which color?"

She smiled brilliantly, her eyes filled with the same joy he got when he crafted hearth stones. "That's the fun part. You *don't* know until you melt off the wax. I always have an image in my head when I start, but it's a surprise every time. I never know what I'll end up with."

He shook his head and wiped the wax on his slacks. "That would make me insane. I have to see the process as I go or I couldn't do it. When I carve beads and hearth stones, I have to see the pattern emerging."

She raised her brows when he mentioned carving, but then shrugged—in a way that told him she wasn't offended by his opinion. "It's not for everyone. I'm the only one in the family who enjoys it, other than Baba. And you *have* to enjoy it to put up with the process. I'm looking at a long, painful night of cramped muscles and headaches from sitting in one position for too long. Plus, this isn't my regular kistka, so I'm probably going to wind up with blisters." She took his hand and guided his touch to stripes of hardened skin on her fingers. "Feel the calluses here, and here? That's where the kistka rides. But this one won't fit those grooves, so it's gonna be painful in a few hours."

He ran his finger lightly over the indentation in her skin. "It's very much like the calluses where the focus stones ride in our battle gloves." He turned his hand over to show her the whitened skin in the center of his palm. She got a curious look and reached out to play her finger lightly over the callus. A shiver caught him unaware. It quickened his heart and he was suddenly very aware of her—the feeling of her hand, the scent of her perfume. He had to force himself not to catch her eye for fear of getting lost in her gaze again. Unfortunately, he couldn't tell if this was her wanting to be close to him, or just scientific curiosity.

"That's interesting." She continued to stroke his palm as she stared at his hand, until he was forced to either pull it away or wrap it around hers.

"What—" He had to cough to clear the sudden dryness of his throat as he lowered his hand back to the table. "What is?"

"This mark. Isn't it just about the diameter of the opal? Are all the stones you guys use cut to the same size?"

He shook his head. "No, they're all individual. We usually have to get a new glove when we advance to a stronger stone." But she was right. It *did* appear to be the same size. He pulled the opal from his pocket and laid it in the center of his palm. The edges fit perfectly, as though it had made the callus. "It *would* fit the glove I have now. That's not very common."

Mila pulled out a chair and sat down, then patted the chair next to her. "You said a *more advanced* stone. But isn't a stone a stone? Does that mean a diamond is more powerful than, say, *granite*? I just don't know anything about how your magic works. I'd like to, if it isn't a secret."

He didn't mind, but there was already so little night left. "No, it's not a secret—at least from other Guilders. But are you sure we have time?"

She looked down at the jars and other items on the table and uttered a small snort. "I don't think we can risk not *taking* the time. This is for all the marbles, isn't it? But I'm still so worked up from everything that's happened today that I know I won't be able to get into a decent state of mind right now. I normally put on some quiet music, have some fruit or chocolate and a glass of wine before I start, but I don't think there's time for all that. And, I think it would help me keep a *purpose* in mind when I'm making the pysanky."

All of her points were good ones, and it made him think. "What purpose were you thinking of when you made the egg in your house?"

"See, that's just it," she replied while tapping on one of the glass jars with a fingernail and flipping that shiny black hair out of her eyes. "I thought about that all the way over to the library. But it's not like remembering you had a ham sandwich for lunch last Tuesday. Anyone can do that. This is like dredging up what precise *thought* was going through your brain when you bit *into* the sandwich. I remember deciding to try a simple black-and-white egg so I could finish it quickly and go to bed. I was halfway through one egg, but was out of red dye. I couldn't finish that one . . . but I wanted to do *something* because my fingers were all twitchy. They get like that after a rough day at work. But I can't imagine something like *magic* would have popped into my head. I didn't really believe in it until Vegre walked out of a glowing gate and dragged Sela through it. So, while I'm trying not to jinx the process of making the egg by thinking things I probably didn't last time, I don't want to overlook the possibility I *might* have had a random thought about healing or magic in a flash of inspiration." She made a face, like she didn't want to be thought crazy. "Does that make sense?"

He nodded. "Of course. Re-creating a particular intent consistently is the reason the guild academies were created in the first place. Teaching someone how to craft is no different than leading classes on writing the alphabet or adding numbers. It's based on memorization, repetition, and recognition. You learn what intent creates what result, what word best associates the intent in your mind and then you practice the intent with the word—over and over until it's second nature."

A light seemed to click on in her brain. "So, if you shouted the word 'fire,' and had the right intent, fire would appear?"

He smiled, because it was very much the question an apprentice would ask. "In a manner of speaking. But it would be very much like shouting just the word, 'five,' with equal intent, and expecting five apples to appear in your hands. Without training, I might see a drawing of the number five appear in the air, or perhaps five apples—buried in a nearby dumpster. Or . . . I might find five elephants crashing down through the roof. The devil's in the details. Five what? Apples. Where? In my hands. But you don't have time to say all that in a crisis, so your brain has to simply *know*. See?"

Mila mulled for a moment, chewing on her lower lip in a very cute manner before squinting her eyes a bit. "Okay, that makes sense. But if I called out, for example, 'candle flame,' then I *might* get that? Is that specific enough?"

Interesting. She'd transferred the question from what *he* did to whether *she* could. He pursed his lips. "Try it."

She leaned back in her chair, surprise clear on her face. "What?"

He pulled the opal from his pocket and set it on the table. "You've mage in your blood, and there's probably enough magic left in the focus for a small candle flame." He pointed to the wall. "There's a candle. Think on it for a moment, point the focus, and call your spell. No need to shout, though. It's quiet enough in here."

"Really? You think I might be able to do *magic?* God, I feel like Harry Potter."

Tal couldn't help but laugh. He hadn't heard of the popular overworld books until Jason brought them to his attention after he started working undercover at the library. They were certainly entertaining, if not entirely accurate. But the classroom scenes were very evocative of several of his harsher instructors. "Yes, but Harry already *knew* he was a crafter. Whether you are is yet to be seen."

She touched the opal gingerly, as though it might bite her, then clutched it in her palm tightly. "Just pick it up and point?"

She held it out before her, nearly pointed at the ceiling. He reached out and eased her arm down with a small laugh, since the candle in question was only about shoulder level, seated. "Like an arrow, darling, not a club."

The look that came over her face . . . pleased, yet amazed, made him wonder what he'd just said. He didn't remember anything unusual—he'd just told her to lower the stone. Once again heat rose to her face, but she didn't pull back her arm, so he continued. "Look at the candle. Concentrate on the thought of what a candle flame looks like—what color, what height, what width. Then say your words and mentally *push* the magic from the focus to the candle."

Once, twice, and then a third time Mila tried to light the candle, but he felt no taste of magic. "Do you think maybe the stone is out of magic?"

She raised her brows hopefully, even as he sighed and shook his head. "I'm afraid not." He didn't even need to take the stone from her for this. A flick of his finger was about all it took. He barely needed the word, but he wanted her to watch a proper crafting. *"Switlo."* A perfect yellow flame appeared around the wick just as Mila gave a little jump and looked down at the stone.

"Hey, I *felt* something when you did that. Was that magic?"

Hmm. Perhaps she had a bit of talent after all. He quickly pushed the hand holding the opal toward her lips. "Open your mouth, stick out your tongue, and close your eyes. Quickly now. Can you taste the magic residue? Breathe in through your mouth and tell me what you taste."

She hurried to comply and stuck her perfect pink tongue out, nearly touching the stone. It took only a few seconds and then she opened her eyes before smiling broadly. "I could taste something! It was like powdered sugar—or maybe cotton candy on my tongue. Really sweet."

He nodded, pleased. Perhaps it wasn't strong, but with more power available, and some training, she might be able to someday do minor crafting. "Very good. Fire magic tastes sweet. Earth magic is salty—like fresh potato crisps, water is sour and air is spicy."

She nodded absently and stared at the table—not really seeing it, her fingers sliding along her bottom lip. "Cool. That explains it, then."

"Explains what?"

Her eyes blinked rapidly, like she was waking from a dream and another blush painted her cheeks. "Nothing. It's nothing."

Just the blush told him what he needed to know, and she was right. Kissing a mage tasted sweet. Honey, chocolate, ripe fruit—the kind of sweet was based on the individual, and all slightly different. He couldn't pass up the chance, but it had to be on her terms. He leaned closer, until he was bare inches from her face. She froze and began to breathe fast with wide eyes. But this time he could tell it wasn't from fear. "You never can be sure if I'm right unless you try again . . . just to be certain." He paused and held her gaze, then whispered to her, so close now that the air bounced off her lips and tickled his skin. "If you want me, take me. Kiss me, Mila."

Her breathing stilled altogether and he watched her eyelids flutter closed as she leaned forward just that tiny bit, tipping her head slightly to miss his nose. Her lips brushed against his. As much as he wanted to lean in and claim her mouth, give her a kiss that would leave her breathless, he held back. *It's her turn to explore, if she's willing.*

Time and again she let the lightest hint of her smooth lips glide across his, soft as flower petals. With each kiss, he felt her skin growing warmer. Whether it was fire magic or mere human desire didn't change that he began to feel his body tighten and harden. He parted his lips slightly, hoping she'd take the hint that he was ready for more.

Mila took hints well. *Useful knowledge.*

Leaning forward abruptly, her jaw forced his open and she took her taste of sweet fire magic. He pulled some of the remaining magic from the opal back inside and let it fill him so she could get some measure of what passion used to be like among their kind, and what it could be again if she truly could do what the scroll claimed.

It was a struggle not to reach out and pull her into his arms. But the goal was to let *her* experience and fulfill whatever attraction she felt. When she finally pulled back, after a delightful mingling of tongues that pulled a groan from his chest, he couldn't help but give her a tiny bit of extra pleasure.

Eyes still closed, she gasped when his lips found the line of her jaw. As he traveled down her neck, kissing and licking her skin, her head flopped to one side bonelessly and her hand reached around to slide fingers through his hair.

When he took a small nibble of the hollow of her throat, her fingers clenched abruptly into his scalp and a hungry whimper found his ear.

She was more than ready for another kiss by the time he returned to her lips and this time he could sense she wanted to be the passive one.

It was pure, unadulterated torture to kiss her slowly, gently. But the goal was to relax, not excite. When he pulled back, she tried to follow, to continue the game. But he put a finger on her lips and pushed backward gently. "That's enough for now."

Her eyes opened and her brow raised. "No, it's not." But he pushed back his chair before she could finish wrapping her arms around his neck.

"You have" he tried to remember the proper pronunciation, "pusankuh to craft, and we need to eat. I'll cook us some dinner and if you're a very good girl," he said with a wink and a touch of her nose, "we can *relax* you more later."

She grabbed the finger and used the leverage to pull herself out of her chair and to her feet. "Just one more," she whispered before sliding her arms around his waist and leaning in until her lips hovered near his chin and her sofly curved body covered every inch of his—including the erection that was growing more urgent with every moment that passed.

"Maybe just one," he agreed, once again lost in those stunning green eyes. He twined his fingers into her curls to pull her close and then ground his mouth against hers. Jaws worked and tongues moved as the kiss deepened.

When she moaned, he felt his fingers dig into her strong back muscles and she moved her hands rather wantonly to his buttocks to cause a similar reaction in him. *This must surely be the sort of kiss that sent men willingly on dangerous quests.* Because he was nearly willing to take on Vegre himself if it would please her.

At last she pulled away with a gasp and he let her . . . reluctantly. She turned and grabbed the table's edge with near desperation, and he wondered whether she really did need it to stay standing. "Eggs. I definitely think I'm in a mood to make some kick-ass pysanky. Wow. And if they don't wind up being *duszats,* I'll be really surprised." She looked over at him to where he was regarding her with amusement and waved a hand as though to push him away. "Go. Shoo. Stop standing there looking so delicious and . . . *available,* so I can think."

Delicious. That one word dissolved his fears, and didn't harm his ego a bit. There were still problems aplenty, but for a few moments, he could relax and just enjoy a woman's company. It had been a very long time since that had happened.

Your problem is that nothing ever *seems like a dating opportunity.* Mila heard Candy's voice in her mind and it nearly made her laugh. Here she was, trapped in some strange new world for the night, with a gorgeous magician who was obviously interested in her, who'd called her *darling, and* who was making dinner for her in the next room. There was even the very real possibility that she might be having a wild romp later. *I'll take Dating Opportunity for five hundred, Alex.*

Of course there was the small matter of a demented madman wanting to take over the world, a horrible virus she'd just saved a woman from, and a group of people hunting them like animals—after *way* too much spiked Kool-Aid.

If this is a romance movie, it's being directed by John Hurt . . . or maybe Wes Craven.

She looked down again at the tiny bit of eggshell on the table as she mixed the dyes and vinegar in their various jars, trying to remember the patterns she'd seen while at the Tree. But the amazing scent of whatever Tal was cooking in the next room kept dragging her brain back to him, and to the kiss that had weakened her knees to the point she couldn't stand afterward. *Beard stubble scraping, lips nibbling, and a very talented tongue . . . wow. Oh, he could be a lot of fun.*

She shook her head to clear it, took a scoop of wax, and flicked the tip of the kistka through the candle flame. *Dots are easy. We'll start there. Big dots, tiny pinpoints, and then a bold sun—one on each half.*

What about tomorrow? The sun would rise in the morning and, if they were successful, a week from now. Where would she be then? Where would *Tal* be? He was like a biker who just rolled into town, or a sailor on shore leave. *But I'm not like Candy. I'm no good at one-night stands . . . or even one-week stands.*

Okay, that was plenty of dots. Sheesh! There'd barely be room for the basket weave and stags. The stag should be yellow, and so should the sun, so she dipped the egg in the first jar, thick and blue-tinted with tiny bubbles trapped inside the glass. She stirred it around lightly with the end of a fork, making sure no part touched the jar too long, which would prevent the dye from penetrating.

I don't know where he lives, or even what his favorite color is. And what about . . . "Tal? Do you roll up your toothpaste tubes, or squish them flat?"

He turned his head away from the flat stone on the counter, which wasn't attached to any electricity or gas, but which he'd sworn could cook their meal. He kept stirring whatever was in the glass pot. "Excuse me?"

She realized what a stupid question it was, but she couldn't say *never mind* yet again. "Toothpaste. I presume you use it when you're topside. Do you roll the tube or squish it?"

He tipped his head and then shook it slightly with a

supremely amused expression. "I use it down here, too. I press it flat. Why? What do you do?"

She nodded, oddly relieved. "Same. Sorry, go back to cooking."

His smile turned to a grin before he turned his head and moved the pot to a cool spot. After rubbing his hands on the towel that was draped over his shoulder, he spoke. "Nope. Sorry, you started it."

"What do you mean?" She blew lightly on the now yellow egg, dotted with black. Fortunately the dye was as fast setting as hers at home, but a much richer yellow—closer to marigold than lemon.

"Favorite color, food, hobbies—other than eggs, and . . . music, I think. Roll them out."

That stopped her cold and she had to raise the kistka or risk a big yellow spot rising off the stag's antlers. *He wants to know about me?* It both excited and terrified her. "Um, blue—that really vivid cobalt, like the candy-apple blue they paint cars with. Spaghetti with garlic bread, fixing up my house, gardening, and easy listening. You?"

He waggled his head and then pursed his lips. "I'll have to separate it into *up there, down here* choices. Up there . . . I like autumn-sky blue, Chinese stir-fry, searching for focus stones in rock shops, and classical music. Down here, I'll have to say the purple of ripe *majorica* fruit, shepherd's pie made with *squelk* meat, carving hearth stones to sell, and crystal chimes."

She looked up from where she was quickly drawing lines to hold in the images she wanted before dipping the egg in the red dye. "What is *majorica* fruit and what's a *squelk?*"

He started to rummage around in the cupboards. When he pulled out a shallow casserole dish and a bowl and placed them in front of the chairs, it occurred to her that there probably wouldn't be matching china and silverware after an evacuation. "Majorica fruit is what the Sacred Trees used to produce when they were healthy. Gorgeous color. The closest I can come up with that you might recognize is between heather and a plum, but glowing. A squelk is just what it sounds like—a hybrid ground squirrel and elk. Big and meaty, but burrowing. They love nuts, roots, and tuber vegetables. Great diggers. They really saved on magic and sore backs when we were expanding the rings in Rohm. They can even be trained to search for particular gems, like pigs dig truffles topside."

She tried to get that picture in her mind and failed miserably. She pulled the egg from the red dye, but it wasn't dark enough yet so she put it back in and continued to stir. "Squirrels the size of *elks*. Um . . . wow. You'd think someone from back home would have noticed something like that."

Tal smiled as he used the cloth on his shoulder to wipe dust off a pair of forks he'd found in a drawer. "I don't think you realize just how *far* underground we are, and we're not idiots. We originated the *leave no trace* concept your parks have finally adopted. But you're right that it's getting harder to keep our existence a secret. Your technology keeps increasing, while our magic is diminishing. That's a bad combination."

Of course that led to the big question. "What happens if I fail? What if Viktor was all wet and it's just coincidence that there was an eggshell in the tree?"

He stopped and stared at her for a long moment. She realized he'd been thinking about this for a while. "I don't know. More riots, I suppose. Maybe a world war or mysterious deaths around the planet that kill off large numbers of humans to make space for us." He picked up the pot and began to ladle the contents into the bowls. "I'm hoping none of the above, but I don't have a very high opinion of the integrity of my people when they're desperate."

She sighed and put the now dark red pysanka on the table and pushed back her chair from the table near the couch to join him in the kitchen. "I don't have a high opinion of *anyone* when they're desperate. So I guess I'd better not fail, huh?" She tried to smile, but knew it was tight from the tension in her cheeks. "No pressure, though."

They ate at a small wooden table. They sat in silence for long minutes but only because they were stuffing their faces. The dish Tal had cooked was amazing—with big chunks of chicken, potatoes, carrots, and some other root vegetables she didn't recognize in a spicy cream sauce. She hadn't realized how hungry she was until she put the first bite in her mouth. But her last meal, if it could be called that, was a hot dog from the wheeled cart outside the library. They talked a little more while they cleaned up the dishes. She finally got to find out what a hearth stone was and how the magic worked. "So, the Sacred Trees exhale magic as they grow like trees up here exhale carbon dioxide? The kings are somehow tied to the Trees so they can harvest the magic, and they can either use it right away or store it in stones. Right? And any kind of stone can hold magic, but some hold it better than others? Have I got it?"

He nodded while swirling a soapy cloth around the pot. "Right. For example, we give apprentices sandstone to craft with. It doesn't hold much magic because of the loose structure, and is easily destroyed. That teaches patience and caution, because parents of the children get informed if the student damages more than three stones in a term, and must pay for extras."

"So does that mean a diamond is the top stone? Can it hold the most because it's so pure?" She put the pot to dry in the rack with the others when Tal handed it to her.

He tossed her the towel to dry her hands as he removed the stopper from the drain to let out the water. "Not exactly. Actually, your heirloom fire opal is the most powerful stone, with the possible exception of cherry amber. You see, while gemstones like rubies, emeralds, and diamonds can hold a great deal of magic, to get the most of their power they have to be faceted. That actually makes them *worse* for crafting. It would be like—" He paused and looked around the room, as though searching for something. "Not cloth, not wicker . . . it's—" Then his eyes lit on something and he walked over to the window. Picking up the fringed tassel that was holding back the curtains he flipped it back and forth. "With every facet you put in a stone to hone the strength, you have another thread of magic to control, like a floppy tassel. Yes, you can braid the threads together and make a strong single beam, but it's a constant effort to do it. Get distracted for even a moment and the braid falls apart. Magic flies in every direction . . . except where you want it to. It takes a *very* disciplined mind to use a faceted stone."

She nodded grimly as she felt fear suddenly fill her. "Vegre uses a diamond, doesn't he?"

Tal nodded and walked back across the room, touching her arm when he reached her. "Rohm Prison was crafted *specifically* to hold Vegre, because of his discipline and abilities. His cell was filled with every method the kings could think of to negate his magic. Pure obsidian walls were raised . . . impervious to all but the most intense heat, and waterfalls surround his cell to dampen his natural fire. A magical vacuum behind the water was even specially crafted by King Mumbai so there wasn't enough air to feed a flame if he made it past the water. But somehow every one of those precautions—which we believed had held him secure for centuries, has been defeated. I'm inclined to believe Kris and Dareen that he was aided by one or more of the kings."

"But if he really did have a free pass in and out at will— to make an official human presence with the name change, to run the hotel, then why *break* out now?"

Tal shrugged and squeezed her arm before letting it go. "I wish I knew. Maybe the kings realized their folly and changed the deal? Perhaps the actions of his minions had nothing to do with the plan and he just decided to take advantage of the opportunity. I'd imagine if he was beholden to the kings for his release, he'd be allowed less movement, so true freedom would be worth the risk. But," he concluded, lowering is chin in mild reproach. "That's a topic for another time. You have eggs to craft and I have a focus to explore."

"Why *explore?* Doesn't it work now?"

He let out a small burst of breath, knowing she was stalling, but he answered anyway. "Fire opals are filled with inclusions of different stones. Their very instability, what makes them unable to be faceted, is what makes them very powerful. But each focus is like a maze with many correct paths. One path among the inclusions is the quickest, and most powerful. But any of them will get you from point A to point B, which is how I've been able to use it until now."

It finally made sense in her head. "But you want to find the most direct path. Okay, so it's like line loss on an electric cable. The longer it takes to get from the source to the object, the less powerful the signal?"

He'd already made himself comfortable on the couch, sitting cross-legged with the stone held in his open right palm. He nodded with an expression of admiration. "Precisely. You're a fast learner. Many apprentices take years to understand the process that well." He turned his head back to the stone and closed his eyes, a signal that he wanted to concentrate . . . alone.

She watched him for a moment, saw the colors swirl in the domed top of the stone. They faded after a moment and then she saw him move his finger slightly. Another swirl in a different pattern of colors. Then another subtle move of his fingers and he tried again.

She got the impression he was going to be at it for a while, so she returned to her eggs. There were a dozen of them in the woven reed basket from the fridge and Dareen hadn't lied—they were so fresh they were still slightly warm when she wrapped her hand around them. It didn't matter that there weren't enough for all the Trees. She wouldn't have time to dye them all today anyway. She just wanted to get this one Tree up and running before they left so Dareen would have some leverage.

There was something incredibly peaceful about making pysanky. Her mind blocked out everything but spinning the egg round and round, drawing line after line. Basket weave patterns demanded precision, requiring a sure hand

and quick movements, and that was all that was left to do before dying the background black.

As soon as the first egg was done, she held it close to the sample fragment to compare the colors. Either this kit was the very one used to create the original, or Samuel had used the same farba recipe, because they were identical, down to the same marigold yellow.

By the time she finished the second egg—a water theme with cucumbers, circles, and more basket weaving, a blister was starting to form between the first and second joint of her thumb. She was used to them, though, so she pressed on—doing her best not to let the rough wood of the kistka tear the skin to make it a wound. They didn't hurt bad until that happened, but afterward they were hard to heal because of the constant motion of her hands.

She'd just lowered the third egg into the yellow dye after making top and bottom borders of waves for an air egg, when she felt hands on her shoulders. She barely reacted, even though Tal's strong hands kneading her muscles felt amazingly good. But, frankly, she was just too exhausted to react to much of anything. Her eyes were burning from working in the dim candlelight and her wrist was throbbing from constantly twisting the egg in circles to paint the wax. She usually didn't do more than one egg a day, and had never tried to consciously *think* of magic the whole time.

"You should stop for today. It's nearly midnight."

She couldn't help but let out a small chuckle. "Then I *have* stopped for today. It's nearly tomorrow." He chuckled as well, but kept kneading, his thumbs digging into her shoulders in slow circles. She let out a small sigh and leaned forward until her forehead was resting on her wrists. "Don't feel compelled to stop that anytime soon."

He apparently took her comment as a command—which it sort of was. He began a full-blown massage from neck to lower back. Grinding, popping noises from her stressed muscles accompanied her whimpers of pain as he kneaded and pushed and pounded. By the time he'd worked out the major kinks and moved to include her scalp and biceps, her breathing had slowed. His hands were warm—so very warm. *Nice.* As she breathed in the scent of his cologne, she felt her eyes close.

"Wake up, Mila. Come to bed." Tal's voice was right next to her ear. She felt dreamy and warm, like waking up after a nap in the sunshine.

"Hmm? Did I fall asleep?" She felt leaden, but didn't hurt as he lifted her to a sitting position, hands on her shoulders once more. She saw the time on her watch. "Geez! It's been half an hour. Why'd you let me sleep that long?" She looked at the yellow dye jar in panic. The egg would probably be *orange.* But it was resting safely on a towel, dry and exactly the right color.

"You needed a rest, and still need *relaxation.*" He took her hand and pulled her up and out of the chair. She didn't expect to follow the pull, but her body had other ideas. She stumbled to her feet, her brain still fuzzy.

He backed through the room, pulling her forward and she looked back at the uncompleted egg more than once. "I really should finish the eggs. There isn't much time left."

"It can wait until I'm done with you." His voice was warm and filled with things that had nothing to do with sleep. The dark look in his eyes made something pull low in her body. It was then she noticed he'd showered and shaved, which was hardly fair considering she was probably sweaty and stinky. A quick flick of her tongue across her teeth confirmed there was a film that didn't speak well for her breath. "Do I get to freshen up before . . . whatever you're planning?"

He smiled, anticipation in the spread of lips. "Of course. Your bath's already drawn."

And wow . . . was it *drawn.* Flickering candles lined the ledge around the large room, and she breathed in the scent of oranges and ginger. The towel warmer filled the air with dry heat while steam rose off the tub in a wet cloud. He drew her to the center of the room and stopped. His hands fell off of hers and then slid along her jaw just as he stepped forward and tipped his head.

The kiss was everything the room promised—slow, sweet, and filled with the taste of cinnamon toothpaste and candy. He moved back just as slowly, but his languid movements were having an opposite effect on her body. "A toothbrush would be nice," she said hopefully.

"As you like," he said with a small bow of his head. "You just need to decide whether you want to bathe alone and then join me in the next room, or if you'd like someone to slowly . . . *ever* so slowly, sponge your back." He flicked his head sideways toward the steaming tub. "It fits two comfortably. Your choice."

Gee. Soak alone, or frolic with a gorgeous, and increasingly appealing fire mage? *Decisions, decisions.* She smiled with enthusiasm and sounded completely awake and far more chipper than she should be considering how tired she was. "Just let me give my teeth a quick brush. Don't go anywhere. And I do mean *don't go anywhere.*"

Again that little half-smile that was all male and then he was unbuttoning his shirt. She could almost feel the drool running down her chin as the tautly muscled chest she'd suspected was hiding under there was revealed. "Go ahead and brush. I'll just keep you entertained." He let the shirt hang open as he unbuckled his belt. The top button of his jeans was next. One flick accompanied a wink. The button popped open and so did her mouth. The smile broadened as he inched down the zipper, showing an impressive swelling beneath his underwear. Damned if he wasn't enjoying stripteasing for her.

It was definitely time to hurry. She wasn't surprised, after meeting Dareen, that there was a brand new toothbrush and several travel-sized hair products on the counter. She had finished her lowers and was moving the brush to the upper teeth when she let out a yelp that spit toothpaste onto the mirror. Warm hands had slid under her shirt from behind and were caressing her waist and tickling the bottom of her bra. She raised her eyes to the mirror and saw Tal's reflection. His eyes were intense, glowing with an inner light that could either be a reflection from the candle, or something about his magic she didn't understand. Either way it was impressive and more than a little sexy.

She could brush with him fondling her breasts under the shirt, although it made her writhe in pleasure. Even when he pushed her into the counter with his hips, she could still hold the brush. But when his lips and teeth started to nibble on her earlobe—

There's only so much a girl can take.

She spit into the sink, then slugged and spit a cap of mouthwash so fast she doubted the germs were in much danger. But minty fresh was her goal and by the time she turned in Tal's arms, she at least had that.

She wanted to touch that warm skin—had wanted to since the moment she met him. It didn't even make sense, but she couldn't deny the tingling, twitching *need* that made her hands reach underneath his shirt. If his moan as he kissed her was any indication, he didn't mind.

His lips moved away from her mouth and found her ear again. "Let's get you out of those wet things."

It made her brow drop down in confusion. "My clothes aren't wet."

Tal's hands were just suddenly on her hips. When he pulled her to him—grinding his very healthy erection against her stomach, a spasm between her legs weakened her knees and made her groan with need. "I'll bet *some* of them are."

Well, if they weren't before, they certainly are now. But he didn't wait for a reply, because before she could even open her mouth to reply, he'd tucked hands under her sweater and was lifting it over her head. Her arms had no choice but to follow suit, and soon only her bra covered her to the waist.

She was glad now that she'd dug into the back of the drawer this morning and put on one of the bras she'd been saving for her vacation next summer, because Tal's voice was nicely appreciative. "Mmm. Pretty." He ran a slow finger along the lacy scalloped edge and she felt her eyes flutter shut. There was just something about gentle touches that drove her insane. She never liked grabbing and pawing until the very last moment, which is probably why she never enjoyed the dating scene with Candy. "Hmm . . . I like that." She didn't mean to say it out loud, but he'd probably already figured it out from the sighs and goose bumps it was raising on her skin.

Something closed around her breast, pulling a startled cry from her. She would have opened her eyes, but the light flicks against her nipple kept them locked closed.

As amazing as his silk shirt felt against her skin, it was getting in the way now. She wanted his skin against her. When she tugged it down off his shoulders he finished the job, never taking his mouth from where it was suckling her breast. Hot desire awakened inside her, curling and stretching as though rising from a long sleep.

With his arms freed of the cloth, they moved to the button of her jeans. The zipper came down moments later and then the warm moist air joined the sweat that was already clinging to her like a second skin. "My boots are still on. I'll have to take them off." She whispered, because she feared breaking the mood.

His hands moved up her bare thighs in a slow line from knees to hips, where the thin lace panties that matched the bra indeed felt very wet.

She took her hands off him long enough to reach back and unfasten her bra. Tal had to move his mouth away as her breasts spilled out of the cloth. His right hand was scant inches away from slipping between her legs but he paused to sweep his heated gaze over her bare body. It had been a long time since someone had looked at her like that—probably since high school, when she was thirty pounds thinner . . . and ten years younger. "I've wanted to do this from the moment I met you, and it makes no sense. I don't even know you."

The front of his briefs was tented out so tight it must be painful and the need to straddle him, to feel that thickness plunge inside her, was growing too strong to bear. Her hand reached down to cover it, to stroke and tease the swollen cock. It jumped under her touch and his hand clenched down on her breast so tight that she cried out at the same moment he did. "*Why* doesn't matter. Nothing matters right now, Tal." Her voice was hoarse and needy and she struggled with every ounce of will not to wrap her legs around him and ride him to the floor where they stood. "I trust you, and that's enough."

His face went serious for a split second and he nodded, apparently unable to speak. Without another word, his hands grabbed her underwear and pulled them down. Then he reached down and picked her up before she could protest.

On the edge of the bath he set her down and began to untie her boots. The still hot water was strong with the scent of oranges as she breathed in. Her body was so swollen and tight that she wanted to scream . . . wanted some sort of release from the pressure. When she felt the last bit of cloth leave her skin she tried to sit up, reaching for him to pull him into a kiss. But he had a different plan and spread her legs, then lifted them until her knees rested on his shoulders. She was forced backward until her head rested on the wide marble platform surrounding the tub. The sensation of his lips and tongue on her sensitive folds was nearly more than she could bear. She cried out and scrambled for purchase on the slick stone as he spread the skin apart with his fingers and plunged his tongue inside her.

It was hot between her legs now, not merely warm, and she couldn't decide whether he was using some sort of fire magic, or if it was just her. She dipped her hand into the bath, planning to cup some water and ease the sweat on her brow when a hissing filled her ears. She turned her head to see steam rising from her arm, drying the water the moment it touched her skin.

She would have thought more about it, tried to figure out what was happening, but Tal took that moment to close his lips around her swollen clit and pull it into his mouth sharply.

Too much, too much! "Oh, God!" She cried out, felt her back arch as a powerful orgasm claimed her. It wasn't waves of spasms like normal, but one great clenching inside her that felt like it would never end. Felt so good she didn't *want* it to end.

She felt his fingers struggle to gain entrance through the tight, slick passage. He let out a growl that carried over into his voice. "Oh, I want some of that."

He was suddenly on top of her and she felt warm, throbbing pressure between her legs. It panicked her for a moment, finally relieving the intensity of the climax. "I'm not on birth control, Tal."

He nodded and leaned in to kiss her jaw. "Took care of that. It's why I was talking privately to Jason earlier. He helped me out with the spare condom in his wallet. I've been busy while you've been enjoying yourself."

No wonder Jason had chuckled as he was leaving. While it was slightly embarrassing to her mind, the need that still filled her body didn't care whether he was sheathed or not. He rose up over her, his face slack with hunger. It took rocking slowly and raising her legs up for a different angle before he could work his way inside her still clenched muscles. "So tight," he whispered with clenched teeth. "So hot. *Mila—*"

His wiggling and pushing added to the desire that still rode her and her breath started to come in small gasps. "Tal, oh God. Ohmygod, *yes!*"

He began to plunge inside her, opening her wide and making her so wet that she could hear every stroke. Her entire body was aflame, the heat so intense it was almost painful. She wrapped her legs around his hips to increase the feeling and he responded by claiming her mouth with his. It was hard to keep her balance on the smooth stone, forcing her to grab onto the faucet to keep from falling into the tub. Tal helped by bracing one hand on the wall as he ate at her mouth. Again she heard a sizzling sound and opened one eye to see that water was indeed drying on Tal's skin as she watched.

All the buildup had apparently taken him too far, because it wasn't more than three strokes later that she felt his free hand slide down to tighten on her hip. With a muffled sound that wasn't quite a word, he slammed inside her one more time and she felt him expand, opening her muscles just a little wider. It set off a chain reaction and another climax seized her, this time the more traditional series of frantic flutters that turned her mind to jelly. Her hips began to move of their own accord, seeking every bit of pleasure they could before she was spent.

She'd barely had a chance to catch her breath when Tal reached his hand between them to grasp the top of the condom and pull himself out. Then, without even taking his weight off her, he wrapped an arm around her right knee and swung her whole body around on the sweat-soaked marble. She dropped into the water with barely a splash, Tal riding her as she dipped below the surface to come up sputtering.

Steam rose with a violent hissing—the sound of forged metal being quenched. It made her look down both of their bodies frantically . . . searching for flames or charred skin. But Tal didn't look at all concerned. In fact, he was smiling with a contented look.

"There's nothing quite like a romp with another mage to get the blood boiling." He stroked a hand along the curve of her waist. "You may never be a crafter, Mila, but you're every inch a mage."

The room was a sauna, and the tub water had dropped by half. "You mean this is *normal?*"

He nodded. "My mother once admitted that I was conceived in a forest fire. Theirs was a secret tryst, when magic was freely available and they were too love-blinded to remember to use precautions." He dropped down beneath the water and came up again, pushing the water from his hair even as it steamed. "I thought it best that our first time be near a source of water, just in case one or the other of us burst into flame." He let out a little laugh that was part amused but mostly post-coital possessive. "But don't tell me you didn't enjoy the fire we shared, for I'll *know* you're fibbing."

She couldn't deny it, because even now her body was tightening, heating—just from his nearness. She couldn't remember the last time she wanted to have sex again ten minutes after she just had it.

It didn't take long to wash off from their encounter with the last few inches of water. They emerged from the roiling steam of the bathroom into the hallway, touching each other languidly—without the heat that had driven them earlier. He led her across to what was obviously the guest room. There was no *personality* to the room. It was nice, and tastefully decorated, but no one had claimed it and made it their own like the other two rooms.

Mila didn't sleep naked. Not ever. She just *couldn't.* And yet she found herself crawling between snowy white sheets without a stitch on, and snuggling up against Tal. She curled around him, trying not to dwell too much on why it felt so . . . *right,* so comfortable to be this intimate. Because it *felt* intimate, not in the way of sweaty bodies and lustful hunger, but of comradery and comfort after a long day. She promised herself that it would just be a quick nap. But as his arms wrapped around her and she felt herself mold against him as perfectly as if they'd been made that way, she stopped caring about the eggs, and the Trees, and everything else. Soon there was only warm skin, contented breathing, and the taste of candy on her tongue.

CHAPTER 16

I don't understand. Show me. Help me. Tal's eyes opened in the darkness as a thrumming of power filled his body. His hands touched something rough and cool. But there was softness underneath, and warmth grew the longer his hands were in contact. It was a comforting sensation, and he reached toward it almost eagerly now. Yes, it was important to hold that warmth, keep it close. He grasped, then tightened his hold but the warmth kept slipping away. It triggered something deep in his mind, a memory that he couldn't quite place. While by itself, the warmth wasn't frightening, he felt fear building in him nonetheless. He reached out to where Mila should be beside him, but she wasn't in bed. The mattress was cool to the touch, the covers neat and smooth.

His eyes opened and he felt himself frown. *But didn't I already open them?* Yet, now there was enough light to see, when before he'd felt blind. He threw off the covers and stood up, listening carefully at the door for sounds of movement before venturing out naked. Everything was still and quiet save for the chanting of a group of Children outside, far in the distance. *At least a block away.*

"Mila?"

There was no answer. But the lamp on the desk next to the couch was burning and Tal was surprised to see the surface clear. The bottles of dye had been put away, the eggs were gone . . . and so was she.

Another sensation vibrated his chest and the panic returned. He didn't know *why* this had something to do with Mila, but he was sure it did. *What are you up to, woman?*

Could she have finished the eggs? All the clocks in the house had been removed, so he went back to the bathroom and fumbled through his clothing until he found the watch in his pants pocket. Ten o'clock. Had he really slept that long? But it was plenty of time to have finished her crafting.

Hurriedly he dressed and put on his cloak, his actions fueled by a growing concern. Surely he would have awakened if someone had broken in to abduct her, but wouldn't she have awakened him if she'd decided to wander out into the city to find more supplies? Unless—*What if she's gone to try to somehow put the eggs in the Tree by herself?* But why wouldn't she tell him? They'd barely gotten her away last time. She would need help.

He flew down the stairs, trying desperately to remember the way to the Tree from here, since he wouldn't be able to open Jason's gate. Could Mila? Or was she wandering around the city, risking running into unsavory characters—and without magic to aid her?

Still, he mused, *she did manage to hold off those characters earlier rather nicely.* It made him smile slightly as he crunched across the broken glass on his way out the door. The sun shone bright where there were patches of sky, but it was still eerily dark where he stood.

It took a moment to get his bearings. He knew a *general* direction, though, so he started off. But he hadn't gone more than a block when he heard his name being called behind him. He skidded to a stop and turned, because even though it wasn't Mila, he recognized the voices—one male and one female.

"Alexy? Kris?" He raced back to where he'd started and threw his arms around his sister. She laughed and gave him a tight squeeze. He reached out his arm toward Alexy and his friend clasped it firmly, and warmly.

"How did you get out, Alexy? I'd heard they captured you."

He nodded, face filled with embarrassment and chagrin. "They did. I should have listened to you. The moment I stepped through the gate, I was in chains. I gotta tell you—I prefer the view of the palace from the *outside* of the dungeon bars. Although I did get some information along with my bruises."

He looked from one to the other, confused. "So how are you here now? Did you escape? Kris, did you—"

She pulled back in annoyed surprise, her slender arms crossing over the official burgundy cloak that marked her a palace guard. She dropped her chin down so far that her auburn hair turned into a curtain that she had to peer through. "I do *not* break prisoners out of jail, big brother. Alexy's just lucky that I took copious notes of our earlier conversation. It took a few hours to figure out what happened after I wiped my memory, but once I did, I took the evidence over Sommersby's head. Combined with King Mumbai's call to His Highness, it was enough to—"

"*King Mumbai's* call? So Dareen got through to him? You know about Vegre?"

She nodded, as did Alexy. "An entire squad is getting ready to capture Vegre as we speak."

Alexy clapped a hand on his shoulder, nearly knocking him off balance. "Can't thank you enough for telling Kris what *really* happened at the prison. You've been cleared as well, and the Commander's been taken into custody. They found magical traces of his signature, as well as Sela's, in Vegre's cell, and his explanation was . . . less than satisfactory. We don't know exactly how Vegre corrupted him and Sela, but it's being investigated and Sela will be behind bars too as soon as we find them."

"But what are you doing *here?*" The sun came from behind a fluffy white cloud in a nearby patch of sky, making it easier to see the others. Alexy definitely looked the worse for wear, despite only being in jail for a day. But Tal wasn't terribly surprised at the bruises on his face or the rips and spots of blood on his clothing. Plenty of the residents of the dungeon had good reason to seek him out and remind him they weren't pleased to be there.

Kris looked surprised. "We came to collect you, of course. His Highness was very impressed with your tenacity under pressure. You're being allowed to join us in the operation, when we capture Vegre and the others. But Blessed Tree, we need to get moving, so collect your gear and let's go."

Blessed Tree. He shook his head and stepped back. "I can't go. I have to stay here and find Mila."

Alexy reared back, his mouth open in surprise. "Mila? Sela's guildercent roommate? What in the name of the Tree would she be doing in Vril?" He glanced at Kris in explanation. "The one I told you about, from the Bakus mage line. Sweet girl, but a bit of an odd granny."

Tal sighed because he doubted *he'd* believe his own explanation. "It's a long story. But come with me. I might need your help in this."

Kris looked at Alexy and then at him, and shrugged. "I suppose we could spare a few minutes to help a overworlder get back home. This is no place for anyone other than enforcers to be. Any idea where she might have gone?"

He nodded, smiling. Alexy shouldn't have any problem opening Jason's gate, which would speed up the process immensely. "Follow me."

Kris was still growling about the gate minutes later when they exited a few blocks from Tree Park. "Jason has some explaining to do. I'll see him stripped of his rank the moment he shows his sorry face."

"Let it go, Kris." Tal's voice was a warning. While he didn't disagree that Jason deserved some sort of punishment for his activities, now wasn't the time.

"I will *not* let it go, Talos. I . . . what in the world is *that?*" She was staring at the massive Tree, which was now glowing with a bright blue light.

Tal raced forward, not even caring if the others followed. "Mila!"

She was kneeling beneath one of the branches again, her hands deep within the bark. The thrumming in his chest began again, and the sensation nearly dropped him to his knees. He reached the park's edge just as Mila started to tug her hands backward and it spurred him forward, heart pounding.

"I've got you!" Adrenaline raced through his system as he grasped her arms and yanked. Her hands popped free almost immediately and they both tumbled backward down the small incline. She'd apparently cleared a path through the offerings, so they didn't land in rotten vegetables again.

He wrapped his arms around her frantically, one hand in her hair to pull her close. "You had me worried *sick*. What in the world were you thinking?"

She pulled slightly out of his grip until his hands were resting on her shoulders. He realized his hands were shaking and his stomach felt queasy. "I didn't want to wake you. I finished the eggs and I was afraid that if I didn't get them put in the Tree right away, Dareen would be in trouble during her meeting."

Alexy and Kris caught up just then, while Kris walked over to the Tree, brows furrowed and Alexy tipped his head in greeting. "Bit strange to see you in this setting, Mila. But glad you're okay. How's your luscious friend Candy, then? Her niece better?"

Mila's face lit up and she rose to her knees. "You're out of jail! I'm so glad for you, Alexy. Or—" she added with a cautious look, "should I be worried that you're out of jail?"

"Relieved," Alexy said, his blue eyes twinkling. "You should be relieved. I was released, and Tal's been likewise cleared."

Mila turned from Alexy to look at him, with joy clear on her face. She threw her arms around his neck and let out a little squeal. "Yay! I'm so glad. I could tell that was bothering you." Tal accepted the hug and held her tight, a little worried that her well wishes meant so much to him, but trying not to think about it too much.

Kris raised an eyebrow at their embrace and then went back to examining the Tree. She poked and prodded where Mila had been attached, and seemed to be examining the bark closely with an odd look on her face.

Mila gave him a quick kiss on the cheek as she moved back and then motioned to the Tree. "I've got three of four installed. One more and Dareen will be set for her meeting."

"Actually, the meeting's already happened." He nodded his head toward Alexy. "That's part of why Alexy was released. King Mumbai called King Kessrick. I don't know if the Tree had anything to do with it. But how did you manage to install the eggs and get your hands out by yourself?"

"Gloves." Kris's voice was odd, and she was staring at Mila with an expression of concern that bordered on fear. "There are *gloves* buried in the bark of this Tree."

Mila nodded and then winked. Speaking to Tal softly, so that neither Alexy nor Kris would hear she said, "I like to think I'm smarter than the average Tree. I did feel a little bad about sneaking in that shop to grab them, but the window was already broken out and they were just lying on the floor. I don't mind paying for them. Do you use money down here?"

Tal got his feet under him and joined Kris under one of the branches. The wide ribbed cuffs of what were obviously men's light cotton work gloves were sticking out of the bark as though they'd always been there. No wounds or cuts marred the surface. They were just . . . embedded, with no apparent harm to the Tree. It made perfect sense and a rush of admiration made him chuckle.

"The Tree grabbed the gloves but because they were so big, your hands slipped right out. Brilliant." He turned and smiled at her and she preened.

"Yeah, it was, wasn't it? And like I say, there's only one left. Well actually," she amended with a small grimace. "There are really *two* left. But I haven't got a clue what the fifth egg should look like, and I couldn't find instructions in the papers Baba gave me. But here *has* to be a fifth egg— the life egg, because it mentions there should be one *duszat* for each guild and our guild should be represented, wouldn't you think? I'd imagine that would go in the trunk. But I couldn't see it, so I wondered if maybe it's in the roots or some such. Anyway, even if Dareen didn't need it, I've noticed there's more sky around the park so it's having *some* effect. Did you see that when you arrived?"

"Who would do something like this to a *Tree?* What's happening to the world? If I weren't a man of faith, I'd track 'em down and—" He didn't complete the thought, but Alexy's voice was shocked and outraged as he touched the bit of glove. Mila opened her mouth to reply, but he stopped her with a warning look and a frantic shake of his head. She looked confused but closed her mouth when she saw Alexy drop to his knees and put his hands reverently on the bark and begin to pray.

"Blessed Tree, maker of all things, forgive those who would violate the sanctity of your home."

Now Mila looked taken aback, especially when Kris joined him on her knees and whispered similar words with eyes closed. They'd always been devout in their beliefs, and a part of Tal wanted to follow their lead. Mila had used her brain in putting on the gloves, but not her *heart*. It was the equivalent to Alexy and Kris as embedding a chunk of metal through a stained-glass window in an overworld church. Even if it didn't harm the window, it was a violation of the spirit of the place. "Where's the fourth egg?" he whispered while holding tight to her hand.

She motioned to the fluffy cloth they'd cleaned the dishes with, spread open at the base of the tree a few yards from where the others knelt.

Alexy and Kris didn't even notice him slide sideways and pick up the egg. He handed it to Mila. It was when she started to put it in her pocket when Kris finally noticed. "What's that?"

"It's—" She paused and looked at Tal for guidance. "An egg? I dye eggs as a hobby." She held up her fingers to show the mottled colors decorating them.

Kris nodded and smiled, her face showing the same calm reverence it had when she and Mom used to return home from Blessing Ceremonies. "That's a lovely offering. I'm glad your parents taught you the proper values, even so far away."

Offering? Well, *that* had some possibilities. "Yes, Mila has always wanted to make an offering at one of the Trees, haven't you?"

She caught on immediately. "Oh! Yes, that's why Tal brought me down. He thought there wouldn't be as many people worshiping at this Tree."

Alexy stroked the bark like you would a sick pet and sighed. "A shame, that is, but you're right. I only wish someone could figure out why they're doing so poorly."

He nudged Mila, hoping it was enough of a hint to hold her tongue, and she gave him a look that nearly spoke words—*do I look like I'm stupid?*

"We'll leave you to your worship. I'll go around to the

other side so I don't distract you. Tal, could you come with me?"

"We'll just be a minute," Kris agreed and then turned back to stare at the trunk. "We need to get you home and back to normal before Tal joins us to catch Vegre."

Mila stared at him and spoke from the corner of her mouth. "*Back to normal?* What's she talking about, Tal?"

Tal's breathing stilled as the realization came home to him. Alexy must have explained to Kris how they came to meet Mila. Naturally, his sister's first thought would be the security of Agathia, as it should be, but that would mean . . . she intended to wipe Mila's memory of the entire event—from seeing the gate to living with Sela and . . . *meeting him.* He needed time to think. Things were happening too fast for him to both deal with the moment and imagine all the possibilities and implications that might occur. "Which branch is left?" He spoke softly as he pulled her away from them.

"What is *back to normal?*" Her voice was likewise a whisper, but a tense one. Still, she followed him and pointed to the branch that was farthest from the others. They shouldn't be able to see her craft, and he could stand watch to make sure they didn't get too close.

"We only have a few minutes for you to finish. We can't let them see." Because he *had* noticed the sky over the park, the *entire* park—when just yesterday it didn't extend beyond the farthest branch.

She stopped and shrugged off his hand on her arm. "No. Not one more step until you explain. What does that woman intend to do to me?"

Bile rose into his throat as he stared at her face, filled with a mix of anger and worry. *It was just one night. Just one. It shouldn't matter. She'll go back to her life and I'll go back to mine.* No, it shouldn't matter.

But it did.

He felt his muscles unclench as determination filled him. He squared his shoulders and put a solid hand on her arm. "*That woman* is my sister, Kris. And I don't care what she *thinks* she's going to do, she's not. Nobody is going to lay a hand on you or do *anything* to you. Okay?"

She looked at him for a long moment, searching his face and eyes. Finally, she nodded. "Okay. I said I trusted you, so I will. Let's finish this egg and then we'll start planning how to capture Vegre."

He held his tongue on that one. Just like he had decided that Kris wouldn't wipe her memory, he'd decided that he couldn't risk her being involved with Vegre any further. *Nobody* will lay a hand on you or harm you. Not while I live.

"Oh, hell. We left the gloves over there." She started to turn around but he stopped her.

"No gloves. I hadn't considered how sacrilegious it might seem to others. Can you perhaps place the egg just under the surface, rather than deep inside the branch? Then we can pull you out easier."

"*Sacri*—" She paused and then winced. "Crap. You actually worship the *Trees?* I thought it was the spirit you worshiped and the Trees were like . . . I don't know . . . like *churches.* Places to worship."

He motioned her forward frantically, continuing to speak in low tones. "It's both, and the gloves were like kicking over an altar. I didn't think about it, but I understand why they're upset."

She nodded and hurried to the branch. The egg was a pleasing mix of blues and yellows, bearing the wave symbol of the illusionist guild among the dots and circles and tiny, precise diamonds. Mila closed her eyes and the little egg began to glow and hum. He'd forgotten about the shrieking hum. He heard the voices and footsteps of the others, hurrying toward them. *Craters!* There'll be no hiding that sound. "Just hurry. I'll do what I can to stall them."

Blue light began to fill his peripheral vision as he hurried toward Alexy and Kris. But by the time they rounded the corner, both the sound and light were gone. He stumbled to a stop and turned. Mila was sitting under the branch with a racoon-ate-the-corn look on her face—full of guilty innocence. She wiggled her bare fingers, without a trace of bark on them, and smiled at him.

"What was that? I heard a noise from over here." Alexy and Kris both had their gloves on, and looked around frantically, their postures battle-hardened, prepared to take on Vegre himself.

"What noise?" He tried to look calm and curious.

"Bloody hell," Alexy said. "You *must* have heard it."

He shrugged and looked over at Mila, who was the picture of calm indifference. "Did you hear anything, Mila?"

She was patting the ground where she'd apparently dug a small hole and then filled it in. "No. Just you two saying your prayers. Maybe the spirit was speaking to you?"

It was the perfect thing to say, for Kris and Alexy both blinked and stared at each other—awe plain on their faces. Alexy couldn't seem to quite grasp the implication, but Kris did right away. She clutched his upper arm with an amazed light in her eyes. "Don't you understand, Alexy? We were *chosen*. The Tree *spoke* to us . . . rewarded us for our faith in this trying time." She looked at Mila with warmth but then noticed her cleaning the dirt from under her fingernails. "Why have you been digging? Didn't Tal tell you not to dig near the Tree?"

Mila was a wonderful actress, for she put on a sad face, but filled with hope. "I buried my offering. So many things have been taken from here and it's so fragile." She held up her hand and spread her thumb and first finger just a bit while squinting her eyes and looking pathetic. "It's only a *little* beneath the surface. I hoped it would be okay."

That caused Kris to look around at the mangled, scattered offerings and sigh. "I can't argue with that. It was a pretty thing. Someone was bound to take it if left out in the open." She shook her head. "Such a shame so many have lost their way—like Mom. I fear for her, Tal. I haven't heard from her for days. Not since that . . . *cult* came and befuddled her mind. I've looked *everywhere* in Rohm but she's nowhere to be found."

"She's here in Vril. I saw her yesterday. But you don't want to find her, sis. She's not . . . *herself*."

Kris nodded, her face filled with both sadness and anger. "I know, and I can't believe it's natural, even though every spell trace I did on her was negative. But she was a *gatherer,* Tal—one of the church leaders, since I was a child. I just can't imagine she would betray the Tree for a false goddess who'd never even been mentioned in ancient texts."

They'd started walking back toward the gate. "Well, they certainly turned her into a harpy," Mila said with obvious distaste. "I'm sure she's normally a lovely woman, since I can't imagine someone with that temperament could have raised people like you and Tal. But I'd imagine that Vegre has methods the average crafter *couldn't* trace. Otherwise he probably would have been caught before he started the plague. Right?"

Kris and Alexy looked at each other with wide eyes and then at Mila. It was Kris who spoke. "What does Vegre have to do with Mom?"

Of course, that made Tal and Mila look at each other before he responded. "He's the leader of Demeter's Children, sis. Didn't you say that King Mumbai called King Kessrick?"

Mila nodded. "That's why Dareen went to Shambala to see the king in the first place. She went undercover into the cult because she recognized Vegre as the cult's leader, Reilly."

Kris stopped cold and waved her hands in front of her, green eyes confused and frustrated. "Wait, wait. When did this happen? How could Vegre, who just broke out of prison two *days* ago, be leading a religion that's been around for two *years?*"

Well, this complicated things. "What exactly were the details *you* heard about the call from King Mumbai?"

She'd crossed her arms over her chest and was tapping her boot on the cobbled brick. "I was *there* when the call came in, Tal. He said that a dirtdog from Vril, mother of one of the O.P.A. agents—which we later figured out was

Jason—had come to him with a wild tale about Vegre attacking Buckingham Palace on New Year's Eve, to assassinate the queen. Mumbai asked for at least a squadron of our best agents to infiltrate the palace and capture him before he could get to her. He said his own guard was too stretched keeping the peace there, because of all the evacuees. So, that's what we're doing."

Tal sat down on a small stone wall that surrounded what used to be the pretty flower garden of a residential building. "No mention of the Children? Nothing about the volcanoes, or sacrifices? Nothing?"

Mila was shaking her head and reached out to touch his shoulder. "Something must have happened to her, Tal. That's not the message she went there to give. She was so *adamant* about what was happening here."

"Or," he mused, in total agreement, "Mumbai wasn't as innocent as we hoped." He looked at Kris and raised his brows. "The call *was* from the king . . . *personally?*"

She shrugged and rolled her eyes. "His defense minister. Same thing." Apparently she noticed his immediate suspicion and anger because she let out a frustrated breath. "The kings *never* talk directly to each other, Tal. That's *why* they have staff. But it's the same as talking directly to the kings— the ministers have all taken oath spells of allegiance and truthfulness."

He nodded and let out a small, bitter laugh. "So had Commander Sommersby . . . and Sela."

Mila let out an exasperated breath and threw up her hands. "But if the kings don't know about the plot, they're not going to send people to the right spot. It's not Buckingham Palace. We already know that. It's the *Palace Hotel,* right in downtown Denver." She paused and the realization of the gravity of the situation came home in her face. "Geez, if all the *best agents* are halfway around the world, Vegre's going to be able to do anything he wants before anyone can stop him."

Alexy frowned while Mila was speaking. "That doesn't make any sense. Why would Vegre attack a *hotel?*" He shook his head, revealing another long cut on his forehead that his hair had been hiding. "No, I'll buy him attacking Buckingham. After all, it was King Charles II who insisted that the guilds intervene and capture him when the red death spread to the humans."

"It *is* the Palace Hotel. We worked it all out—how Vegre has been getting out of prison off and on for decades. He even has a human identity up there, and *owns* the Palace Hotel. Tell him, Tal."

He kept his eyes on the ground, trying to work things out in his head. It had sounded so good last night when they were all sitting around the table. But this morning . . . he was inclined to agree with Alexy and Kris. It just didn't make sense that Vegre would raise a volcano in Denver. "We never did come up with a reason *why* he'd pick that location, Mila. And, too, we don't know if Mumbai got independent information after Dareen left. I can understand why you'd worry, considering the documents you found, but—" He hooked his thumb toward Kris. "I'm going to have to go with them on this. I think he's after bigger fish . . . whether it's a seat of power to rule from, mass chaos among the world's rulers, or some other reason. Denver just doesn't seem . . . well, *vital* to anything."

Alexy nodded. "I know you've reason to want to chase him, Mila . . . possibly every bit as good a reason as us, since you probably lost some ancestors at his hand. But you don't know our culture . . . our ways, and as a guildercent, you—"

She let out a harsh angry breath. "Y'know, I'm really sick of hearing that *guildercent* word from all of you. Apparently, you see it as the equivalent of being a little . . . slow. Well, guess what? I'm *not* a guildercent." Tal looked up in horror and grabbed her arm to stop her but she yanked it away. "No, Tal. Damn it. I don't give a shit about what these two think of me. I'm Parask, okay? Half-mage, and half-conjurer. And I just worked my butt off for the better part of a day trying to save your precious Tree and *did*. Look up. Enjoy your sky, and don't tell me that I'm stupid or foolish or *misguided*. Look, Tal. I told you last night that I trusted you, and I'm only asking you to trust me in return. I *know* this is right. I don't understand why or how, but I *know* just like I knew how to fix the Tree. Please, believe me. *Trust me.*"

He closed his eyes, trying to think. But there were too many things to consider, too many consequences. He felt his head shaking and when he opened his eyes again, hers were wounded and filled with tears. "Fine. I know where I stand. Go do whatever the hell you want, go wherever you think is best to save your world. But I'm going back to Denver, and to the *Palace Hotel,* to try to save mine."

"Mila, wait." He stood up, wanting to say . . . something, but she stormed off down the street, muttering under her breath. While he watched, open-mouthed, she walked up to the gate—a *dirtdog* gate, and passed through as though she'd crafted it.

The others were looking up, and up, into the vivid blue sky that was chewing away at the stark stone roof with each second that passed. Warm sun began to shine down on them, and the few people remaining in the city came out of buildings and homes to stare . . . and then to cheer and dance.

"Tal?" Kris's voice was filled with a stunned sort of awe. "What exactly did she mean that she *saved the Tree?*"

He sighed and wondered if there were any shops left that had ingredients for coffee or tea. Because this was going to be a *long* conversation.

CHAPTER 17

"*S*tupid, stubborn—" She searched for the right word as she stepped through the gate into the library. "—*man!*"

An older gentleman, sitting at a table flipping pages of a large reference book, involuntarily jumped and turned wide eyes to her.

"Oops. I'm sorry."

His wide eyes narrowed in annoyance and he whispered with a small growl, "Weren't you taught any manners, young lady? *Some* of us are trying to concentrate."

She felt heat flood her cheeks and lowered her eyes to the floor, properly humiliated. But at least he hadn't noticed her walking out of a glowing gateway where the fire door normally was. Better he was mildly annoyed than racing screaming down the hallway. *That's something, I guess.*

Still, her gratitude didn't last more than five steps before her annoyance and frustration returned. *I can't believe he'd pick them over me! Who do those people think they are? We were going on, perfectly well—*

Of course, she'd never been able to have a decent rant even in her own mind without her voice of reason arguing—always in Candy's best sarcastic voice. *Sure, Mila. Why in the world would he stay with his partner, who's also a detective, and his sister? I mean, after all— he could stay here with* you . . . *the woman he's known a whopping two days.*

"Three. And I'm right. I know I am." At least her voice had lowered to a quiet murmur. Always a good thing when talking to yourself. *Then prove it.*

Well, why not? This was a library, after all. If there was a reason why Vegre was going to attack Denver, it should be in here. She looked down the long hallway, shelves of books in wide rows as far as she could see. *Yep, somewhere, in one of these books on one of the floors was probably the answer.* It made her laugh, albeit with a slightly hysterical edge. More people looked up and she covered her mouth.

She put her hands on her hips and let out a deep breath. "Well, okay—let's think about this logically. If I can still do that after all this." She rolled her eyes and started to walk toward the nearest librarian station.

If he's planning to raise a volcano, then . . . geology. "Excuse me?" A petite, elderly woman, who was typing at a computer station behind the desk looked up. "Where would I find books on Denver's geology?"

The woman raised brows and chuckled. "You aren't anywhere close to the right section. This is Western History." In moments, Mila was holding a tri-fold map of the stacks and heading toward the elevator. Her feet stuttered to a stop when she overheard someone talking at another reference desk. A middle-aged man in an expensive business suit, with a red power tie, had been tapping his fingers impatiently on the desk as she approached. But there was no one behind it, so he started looking around. Finally, he spotted someone wheeling a book cart slowly toward the desk and walked toward the man with clipped steps.

"Pardon me, but where do you keep the Colorado statutes, and are they up to date? Someone took *both* copies of Volume 7B out of the law library and I've got twenty minutes before court. Do you have one?"

Law. Court. *Shit.* I should be at *work!* Her eyes moved up to the clock over the elevator doors. *Eleven? Geez, half the day is already gone!* But her cell phone was in her purse, which was locked in the trunk of her car. Her musing was interrupted by the dinging of a car arriving so she got inside. As soon as the door closed, she felt a gurgling in her gut and bile rise into her throat. She'd *never,* in the ten years at the firm, taken such a cavalier attitude toward being at the office on time, and it really made her wonder where her head was.

Another gurgle and a cramp. Nothing like the intrusion of reality to make a person's stomach go insane. Instead of pressing the button for the floor she'd planned, she pressed the Lobby button. She fished in the pocket of her coat and found two spare quarters that had worked through a tiny hole and were now clinking together near the zipper stay.

"Pay phone?" she asked the woman at the information desk on her way past.

"Down the hallway near the bathroom." She pointed

across the wide-tiled entry toward a small sign on the opposite wall.

Work first. Then get to the car, get the cell phone. Call Mom and call Candy. While she hadn't forgotten about Baba and Suzanne, and wanted to know if anyone had heard from them, Mom must be frantic.

But another cramp made her add *use bathroom* to the list before making the call, which was fine, because someone was using the telephone when she rounded the corner into the small entryway. Five minutes later, she was feeling a little better, and calmer, as she finished drying her hands on the front of her jeans and dropped the coins in the slot of the now vacant phone.

"Good morning, Sanders, Harris & Hoote . . . how may I direct your call?"

She let out a sigh of relief, her mind hurrying to come up with a sufficient lie. "Rachel? It's Mila. Man, I *really* overslept. Damn cold medicine. I still feel like crap, though. Is anything going on?"

Her friend snorted. "Hardly. It's just me and the crickets today. It's a tomb in here, other than up on twenty-four. Bookkeeping's going full bore, trying to get paychecks ready since we'll be closed on the first. Really. Nobody's here to care if you stay home. Please . . . *stay* home. I feel pretty good for a change. I'd like to stay that way."

She nodded, relief flowing through her. But then a crazy idea occurred to her. "If any of the partners ask, tell them I'm spending the afternoon at the Palace to make sure everything's on track for the party." Maybe there was something about the *building* that made it important. She had a free pass to wander around there . . . especially today. Nobody would even question the woman with the clipboard being followed closely by the banquet director and concierge.

"Will do. Can't imagine who would ask, except maybe Tom Harris. But even Mr. Anal-Retentive hasn't shown up yet, so I doubt anyone will care. But I'll tell them. Feel better, sweetie. I'll see you at the party, right?"

She nodded, even though Rachel couldn't see it. "With bells on." *And possibly a variety of other weapons.*

That thought made her nearly drop the handset. *Weapons . . . yeah right.* She began to bonk her forehead lightly against the stainless steel plate covering the phone workings as she hung up the receiver. *What* weapons? What the hell was she going to do, even if she was right? She didn't *own* a gun, couldn't use knives beyond chopping vegetables, and couldn't even raise a candle flame with magic. Hell, he could probably burn her shoes to a crisp before she could kick him. And she could just imagine the laughter if she walked into the party with the police and announced, "Officer, arrest that man!" and pointed at one of the political elite of Denver.

And even if she could get him to reveal his plan, what then? It'd be the best joke of the party. "Why yes, Mila. I *am* the dark mage, Vegre. I plan to use glowing chicken eggs to raise a volcano right here in *my* very own hotel, and then harness the sun to turn the planet into a winter wonderland so all the magical people underground can come live here. Yep. That's me. What are you going to do about it?"

She couldn't help but beat a fist against the wall and laugh, even though it came out as nearly a sob. "Crap."

It was no good. It was completely hopeless to try to save Denver without the people who could fight against him.

But that didn't mean she shouldn't try.

She squared her shoulders and followed her map to the Earth Sciences section. It wasn't long before she was seated at a table, surrounded by books on geology. Unfortunately, by the time she'd seen words like *pluton* and *tertiary* a dozen or more times, she was completely confused. She was definitely going to need more time to decipher the language, so she made copies of the pages that offered a "geologic tour of the Front Range" and then returned the books to where she'd found them.

As she walked out of the library, a stack of papers rolled up and tucked in her pocket, she realized the city was blanketed with white. Another storm had come sometime during the night, and snow was piled high down the edges of the sidewalk. *And me without gloves.* She should have tucked a pair in her pocket before leaving the Tree, but hindsight being what it was, all she could do was zip up her coat a little higher and tuck her hands deep into the down-filled pockets. The temperature wasn't really very cold, but the brisk wind was enough to take her breath away.

She was just glad she'd parked in a lot rather than on the street, as she passed by yet another tow truck removing vehicles illegally parked in the snow route where they'd get in the way of the plows.

She'd just stepped up to her car and pulled her keys from her pocket when she heard her name from down the next aisle of parked cars. "Mila?"

She froze, desperately thinking what to say as her mother and sister approached her. Baba was probably still missing, and there might be a warrant out for her arrest by now. And what to even *say* to her mother, who cast a spell on her to make her forget most of her childhood? All she could think to do was smile and bluff. "Hey, Mom. What are you guys doing downtown?"

Her mother put her hands on her hips, head buried so deep into a poofy hood that she could be a character on *South Park.* "I should ask you the same thing. Where in the world *were* you last night? We were supposed to have dinner. I called and called."

There was no reason to fake being embarrassed. "Sorry, Mom. I got tied up." That was at least the truth. Then an idea occurred to her. She pulled out her dye-stained hands. "I was teaching a friend how to make pysanky. Time sort of got away from us, so I stayed over."

Her mother rolled her eyes. "Oh for heaven's sake. You and those eggs. I thought you'd given up that silly hobby years ago. It's nothing but a waste of time and money."

It wasn't a *hobby* and she knew it! The anger roared back

in a flash and she felt her hands clench into fists. Her mother's actions might well have doomed the entire world. Why should she protect her from that knowledge?

She took a step forward, and saw their eyes widen at her aggressive posture. "Hobby? *Hobby?* You know damned well it isn't a hobby, Mother!"

"Mila!" The shocked tone of her voice didn't match the sudden discomfort in her eyes. Her sister could only stare open-mouthed at them both. But she too was noticing that their mom's outrage didn't match her face. It made her eyes narrow with vague suspicion.

"You want to know where I was last night, Mom? I was in *Agathia,* doing my best to prevent the next great plague." The discomfort on Clara Penkin's face turned to panic and her knees started to buckle, causing Sarah to grab her arm to help support her. A part of Mila wanted to rush to her to keep her standing, but she was just too angry. She could only step closer and stare down at the woman whose stricken face had turned ashen.

"How *dare* you steal my memories—all the times with Baba and Dad! What about Sarah? Did you do it to her, too? Is she Parask, too?"

Sarah's eyes widened in shock, before she turned to look at their mother. She opened her mouth to say something, but her mother spoke first after a single shake of her head.

"Mage. Sarah took after your father." Then her chin came up, and tears began to flow down her cheeks. "They killed your father, Mila. They *killed* him! You don't understand what they're capable of. I had to protect you from them. Had to protect you *both* so I didn't lose you, too."

She'd sunk down until she was crumpled in the dirty puddles on the concrete and began to shake with quiet tears.

Sarah didn't know what to do, with her mother clutching her leg, sobbing and snuffling. She looked up, concerned and confused. "Mila? What's this about? What are you guys talking about?"

"You used to start fires when you were little, Sarah. Do you remember that? Not playing with matches, but starting fires with little stones that Dad gave you."

Sarah's brow furrowed and she stared down at the sand-covered sidewalk while stroking her mother's hair. "A little. I remember playing with Dad out by the old barbeque in the backyard. We'd start fires and then cook dinner. I like fire. It's why I cook with a gas stove. What does that have to do with anything?"

"But you're not pure Parask. You can't be." Her mother's voice was a whisper, filled with pain and fear.

Pain and fear wasn't enough, because Mila was starting to realize just how selfish her mother had been to cast the spell. It wasn't to protect Mila and Sarah, it was to protect *her.* If her kids didn't remember their heritage, they'd never leave her to train in the guilds. She demanded calls every day, and dinner twice a week. How could she have that if her children left the surface world? Forever together with a simple spell. "I was pure enough to make a *duszat,* Mom. Pure enough to save the Tree in Vril this morning. But if not for a total *fluke,* I never would have known. I never would have *remembered,* and I'm so pissed off right now that I could *spit!* Suzanne could *die* because you broke your vow to Baba! She has the red shadow. Did you know that? Do you even *care* about your people anymore? Haven't you heard them calling in your veins? They *need* us." She grabbed her mother's arm, a little harder than she'd planned by the expression.

But it galvanized her mother's response and Mila realized just how deep her pain went as her words turned cold and bitter. "They *need* to die, Mila! They *deserve* to die." She shook off the grip angrily and was off the ground and standing to her full height.

Mila could taste the magic now, and it tightened the glands at the back of her jaw. Apparently even her mother wasn't pureblood. Didn't Tal say water magic tasted sour? But Mila refused to back down even when her mother began to spit the words in nearly a yell . . . while people stepped around them, trying to ignore the scene. "They cast us out! Killed our people, our entire guild. You're too young to have any idea what it was like. Mikel's family took us in. They elected to stay topside because they were tired of killing and death. But even then the kings couldn't stop. They had to track down the *traitors* who wouldn't buy into the lies. They drove and pushed him until he had a heart attack. It's all their fault, and I *refuse* to let them destroy you both, too! I will not save the life of any Agathian and I forbid you to as well!"

Mila stared at the woman who'd raised her, open-mouthed. Was this the same mother who taught her to love and respect your neighbors? To not care where a person came from and to treat every person as a brother, regardless of what they looked like or what they believed?

Apparently, even Sarah was shocked. "Mother! You can't mean that. You think little Suzanne deserves to *die?* She's only ten. Why would you say that?"

Maybe it was time for some shock therapy. She felt a calm flow through her. "You can't *forbid* me to do anything. I make my own choices. The dark mage Vegre's broken out of Rohm Prison, Mom. He's here in Denver. If you want Guilders to die, you're about to get your wish." Her mother's eyes moved through a dozen expressions, but ended up terrified. "Feel free to sit in your ivory tower of vengeance and ignore it as we all start to keel over. But now that I remember the spells, and with some help from my new friends, I'm going to be out there in the trenches, trying to keep people alive."

Mila turned and started to walk away, but paused long enough to look over her shoulder. "I'll even save you, when the *Tin Czerwona* comes knocking. I can only hope and pray to the Blessed Tree that you'll do the same. I also hope that you'll love . . . and *trust* Sarah enough to let her remember, because she deserves that much."

Maybe it was calling on the Tree, or maybe the realization that the plague wasn't just a memory of the past, but she was gratified to see the beginnings of respect in her mother's eyes for a brief moment before she walked away.

She half-expected her mother to follow and continue the argument, but she didn't. Part of her was sorry, but part glad, because there just wasn't time. Thankfully, the day was warm enough that most of the ice had melted on the windshield, so that all she had to do was brush the towering pile of snow off the hood and roof. As she settled behind the wheel and started the engine, she began to think of the thousand things she needed to do before tomorrow night. If things went well, she could talk with her mother another time.

And if things go bad, I won't have to worry about anything at all.

Next stop needed to be home, both to feed Mr. Whiskers and try to scrub some of the dye from her fingers before going to the Palace. She tried to call Candy on the way, but the cell phone had sat in the cold trunk too long. The battery was dead.

She parked in her usual spot and started up the sidewalk when her feet started to slow and a buzzing filled her head. There were footprints in the snow, leading right up to her door. And not just one pair of prints, but several—coming and going from various directions, as though there'd been a party. *But I thought Alexy sealed the gate and Tal put a guard spell on it. Of course, why use a gate when Sela still has a key? Stupid, stupid! Why didn't I change the locks?*

Or, could it be Tal? Could they have found the other side of the gate and come to the house?

Either way, she decided it would be prudent to cautiously look in the windows before simply walking in the house, into a trap. She stepped off the walk and sank into the fresh snow to her knee, hoping she wouldn't have to do any fancy maneuvering, since that wasn't likely to happen.

The living room was dim, with only the table lamp on . . . just like she left it. Mr. Whiskers was curled up on his favorite noon perch, a fluffy yellow towel on the horsehair love seat. It was a couch for show, rather than comfort, but Whiskers loved that couch. Mila was sure it was because it was where Lily used to sit and pet him.

"Heya, Mila!" She jumped a foot and nearly fell on her tail in the snow. She turned her head sharply and saw her neighbor, Jeff Hopkins, headed her way—his arms laden with all manner of boxes, bags, and small wooden crates. "Forget your key?"

She shook her head, a small measure of relief filling her. Jeff was a former cop and now worked as a bouncer at a local pool hall. He was the *perfect* person to walk in the door with her. He might not know magic, but he was an awesome fighter. He'd taught most of her defense classes, which was how they'd met. "No. I was just channeling you, I guess. Saw all the footprints in the snow, and I knew *I* didn't make them. So I figured I'd look around before sticking in my key."

He smiled and nodded. "Good girl. But you don't have to worry about the prints. I made most of them. I guess you didn't make it home last night, so I've been collecting these for you and keeping them in my house." He motioned toward the odd assortment of containers in his hands. "You planning an art show or something?"

"Huh?"

He motioned with his head toward the door as a gust of wind nearly took the top box off the stack. "Let's talk inside before I drop something."

As she stuck her key in the lock and opened the door, he explained. "Whole bunch of people started coming by your place yesterday. When you weren't home, they knocked over here. Mostly old Russian ladies—from their accents. They said they were all delivering these boxes so you'd watch over them and keep them safe. I'd presumed you knew what they were."

She shook her head and took off her coat. It was chilly in the room, colder than it should be with the furnace going. Or had she turned it off yesterday morning, because it was supposed to warm up? She couldn't remember. But it wasn't so cold that anything would have frozen, so she wasn't too worried.

Jeff held out his arms, as though waiting for help in taking the packages from him. "Bryan loaded me up when we saw your car. I can't get them down without dropping something. They're pretty fragile."

Fragile? She took the top two boxes and the bag that was hanging on his wrist, giving him the second hand he needed to balance the rest and put them down on the coffee table. She opened the top box after placing her burdens, and the paperwork from the library, carefully on the love seat. They were close enough to Mr. Whiskers to make him lean over and take a sniff. Whatever they smelled like didn't agree with him, though, because he stood up and stretched in a tall arch before leaping lightly to the floor with an indignant expression.

"They're absolutely gorgeous. I had the hardest time convincing Bryan not to just *forget* to mention them to you."

She opened the first box and felt her breathing still. It was a pysanka! An absolutely beautiful egg with alchemist motifs—rakes and stags and grains, in the exact colors she'd been using down below. She could even match the blue on her fingers to the blue on the egg. "Wow." She didn't know what else to say, and couldn't figure out why they were here. "No, I don't have a clue why people would deliver these to me."

Unless . . . if Vegre really *was* doing what Dareen suggested and "collecting" Parask to dye eggs for him—*Word might have gotten around to other artists to dump all their stock. But how did they find me?*

"There's about a dozen and a half of them. If you decide to get rid of any of them after the show, let us know. I know Bryan will buy at least three of the blue ones. They match the drapes."

Show. Well, it's as good an excuse as any. "Oh! the *show*. I remember now. Geez, can't believe I forgot. It's something the firm's planning. I don't know much about it, but I'll check to see if the artists are willing to sell after it's over."

As she continued to open boxes, she realized the symbols were exactly the same as the ones she'd seen in the Tree.

What if some of these were *duszats?* Maybe there would be time to fix *all* the Trees, before Vegre could make his move. "This is great, Jeff. Thanks a bunch for keeping them safe for me. And hey, if any more people show up while I'm out, could you grab those, too? Just make sure that *nobody* but me picks them up. These are real works of art and someone might pretend to be my assistant or something if they happen to see one. It's just *me,* unless I tell you otherwise, 'kay?"

Jeff nodded firmly and then his face tightened. "No problem. Frankly, we've been sort of *wondering* about that guy who's been spending time with Sela lately. He trips my radar."

It was the first she'd heard that Sela had been spending enough time with anyone for the neighbors to notice. But if it was Vegre, she knew what he meant. "Tall, thin guy with bad teeth?"

Jeff nodded. "That's the guy. A few times he's showed up in a really nice suit and either caps or dentures. But you can't hide that look, Mila. He's been *hunted* at some point. He's too wary. Keep an eye on him, huh? I wouldn't be in the house alone with the guy."

She opened another box, with a royal-blue and red mage guild egg nestled inside. "Seen him in . . . the past day or so, by chance?"

"No, and we've been watching. We were sort of surprised when neither you nor Sela came home last night, so we took shifts keeping an eye on the place." That was really sweet of them, and it made her smile. Who said there weren't any good neighbors anymore? "No visitors at all have made it inside. Either Bryan or I would always come meet people at the door or as they were leaving, and there aren't any tracks to the back door or any windows. Unless someone showed up while we were asleep, I think it's okay. But if you'd like me to check before I go, I'd be happy to."

She did, so he did, which made her feel a lot more comfortable about staying in the house. It was hard to look around her house and suddenly *not* feel safe, but who'd have thought that someone could step inside without using a door or a window?

Once Jeff was gone, she sat down at the computer to start searching the Internet for anything she could think of that might make Vegre blow up Denver. Then she read through the photocopies. Neither was much help. The whole city was a saltwater sea for most of the prehistoric era and, in fact, they'd discovered large coal beds when they'd built the airport. The nearest potential volcanic activity was either in Fort Collins, nearly an hour north, or Golden, which was at least twenty miles west.

She scrubbed her face and did her makeup while she read the documents she'd printed from her Internet search. Nothing was any help—even looking at the history of the hotel. It had just been a cheap tract that nobody wanted during the silver rush years, an odd shaped parcel that wouldn't fit a traditional square building.

"So why, then? Why spend the time or energy to blow up a hotel?" She didn't have an answer and it was making her start to doubt herself. Maybe the others were right. Buckingham Palace might be the place after all. *But I know it. I can just feel it in my bones.*

But Tal was half a world away by now, and there wasn't any guarantee she'd ever see him again. If he and the others were right and it was England, they'd simply go back to their lives after they caught Vegre. If not, then Denver would be a smoking crater with her as a part of it. Either way—

She felt her jaw start to tremble and shook her head to fight off the emotion. *No. I won't cry. He'll come back or he won't. It was one night . . . probably just, like he said, a romp.*

Pfft! You're lying and you know it, came the Candy voice in her brain. *You know damn well you're hating this, and would go straight back to Vril if you thought they were still there.*

The phone rang at the same moment as the doorbell,

bringing Mila's head out of the clouds—the dark gray ones that screamed a storm was coming. She bolted down the stairs from the small office that had once been Lillian's sewing room.

She clicked the on button while she peered through the peephole of the solid wood door. "Hello?"

Candy was waving on her front stoop with a broad smile, so she opened the door as a voice spoke in her ear. "Mila? This is Jean-Paul from the Palace."

She motioned Candy inside just as a frown overtook her and she walked back into the living room. "Hi, Jean-Paul. What's up?" She knew her voice sounded suspicious, but there was no helping it. She was. "I don't remember you ever calling me at home before."

Candy's face brightened at the male name and pursed her lips with a small ooo-ing noise. Mila shook her head and rolled her eyes. Not in a million years. "I'm pleased not to have any bad news for you, Mila. I was simply following up on the strawberries, as we agreed, and your receptionist mentioned you planned to visit the hotel this afternoon for a last-minute inspection. Unfortunately, I already have a meeting scheduled out of the hotel. In fact, I'm already late. But I'll make my assistant, Denise, available for your walk-through. I think you'll find we've taken care of everything."

He really did sound apologetic, rather than nervous. But having an *assistant* available might actually work to her benefit. She might not know where Mila could and couldn't go. It would make it perfect for searching for clues. "That's great, Jean-Paul. Will she have access to the whole hotel? We have some pretty famous people coming, so I'd like to tell the partners I looked at security and safety arrangements, too. You know how picky they can be." And she'd made *sure* over the course of their negotiations to remind him of their pickiness, even when it was actually *her* attention to detail he was satisfying.

"Of course. I'll let her know that you'll have the run of the place—except for guest rooms which are still occupied, of course."

That grabbed her attention. Was Vegre already there? "Oh, of course. Have any of our guests checked in yet? It might be nice if I personally welcomed them—maybe with a fruit basket or champagne?" Making it a question would let him know that the *hotel* was being expected to provide the gift, and then add it to the bill.

She heard clicking in the background, probably him checking arrivals on the computer. "Mr. Pierce arrived last night, but he's out right now . . . and, let's see . . . Mr. Popolous and his entourage just checked in. I don't believe they're in their room yet, though. Would you like me to send up room service, or wait until you arrive?"

Okay! *Mr. Pierce* was there. So, she was right. *Unless you're wrong, and it's not the same guy.* But no, she wouldn't consider that possibility right now. "Perfect. No, wait until I arrive. I was going to come in casual clothes, but I think now I'll change. Let Denise know I'll be there in . . . say, an hour?" She glanced at her watch. Two o'clock, so three by the time she got there and she should be out of there by five. She could report back with a voice mail to one of the partners and hopefully, she'd have some idea of how to ambush Vegre before the party. It's all she could think to do. Maybe knock him out or tie him up in a bathtub or some such. Or maybe she could sneak into his room and see if he had any *duszats* she could steal or destroy. Frankly, there wasn't much else she *could* do if nobody from the O.P.A. planned to show up.

"That will be fine. I'll see everything is ready. Have a pleasant day, and thank you for patronizing the Palace." He hung up without waiting for a reply, which meant he was either annoyed she was going to do the walk-through, or he really was late for his meeting.

Candy had already made herself comfortable in one of the recliners that Mila had bought with the leftover money from the roof loan. Mr. Whiskers was perched delicately on her lap, happily shedding fine gray fur all over her dark pants and rumbling noisily in approval of the chin scratching he was getting.

Her friend raised one carefully plucked eyebrow and waved a hand to the opposite chair for Mila to sit. "I'll presume that wasn't a social call, so I won't bother to grill you. I'm much more interested in where you were all night. You mom must have called a half-dozen times. When I finally got worried enough to actually get in my car and drive through a blinding snowstorm, your car wasn't here, you weren't here, but there were footprints all over the place. So spill. Where are the magicians, where is my niece, and why aren't you at work for the second day in a row?"

She did sit down, mostly because she was too stunned to stand any longer. God, where to start? The last time she'd talked to Candy was when she left work yesterday and they hadn't really *talked*. "Um . . . wow. Where to start? It's been . . . *wild*." She shook her head and stood up again. If she was going to explain it all, it might as well be while she was getting ready. "Follow along. I'll try to bring you up to date."

As they quickly climbed the stairs, she decided it would be a good idea to explain *how* she was going to explain things. "It'll be easier to tell you whole threads at a time. If I try to do it in order of what happened when, we'll be here all day. First, I don't know how Suzanne is, except that Viktor told me they'd been moved somewhere safe."

Candy's face took on a frantic look. "Did they cure her? Where's she been this whole time? Carole has been *insane* and has been taking it out on me."

Mila waved her hands in front of her to wave off the questions fluttering around her head. "No, no, no. No questions, or we'll *never* get through this. The short answer is *I don't know*. Third-party information, remember?"

Candy took a deep breath and closed the toilet lid before sitting down as Mila plugged in the blow dryer and tied back her hair so she could wash her face. "Okay, I get it. I'll have to wait to talk to Tim. Where's the magician guy?"

She always did suck at names. "Tal. His name is Talos Onan and he's—" She couldn't decide how to end the statement. *He's awesome? He's a total jerk? He's great in bed?* "Actually, I don't know how he is right now."

Candy's brows rose a fraction and she tilted her head. "*That* was an odd tone. I'd say you had a lover's quarrel and were on the outs, but that would imply things I can't quite believe about you."

She had a few seconds respite while she scrubbed and then dried her face. "Let's talk about what's happening with Sela, instead. That's a lot more important, and why I'm going over to the Palace."

"Look at me, Mila." It was a casual request but she found herself trying to school her features as though she'd just broken her mother's favorite vase. It was only seconds that she was under her friend's scrutiny when Candy's jaw dropped and her hands fell off her lap. "Oh . . . my . . . *God*! You did! You slept with him. I cannot believe this. My best friend *finally* got lucky. Let the bells ring and the choirs sing!"

She blushed such a dark red there was no way she'd be able to put on foundation and get it even, so she grabbed a brush and flipped her hair over her head. "It's not what you think."

"Oh, it's what I think, all right." She snapped her fingers so loud Mila jumped. "Girl, I can spot a woman who's gotten some a mile away, and *you* got some. Is that where you were last night—at his place?"

That started the conversation about their adventure at Viktor's, and in Vril and why she was back. Candy didn't ask a single other question while Mila primped and preened to go to the hotel, and followed her like an obedient dog while they moved from room to room—finding her best St. Laurent suit, ironing it, digging the matching shoes out of the back of the closet, and then blow drying her hair with a fat round brush to get out some of the weird kinks from sleeping on it wrong. She took a sip of the soda Candy had brought her while she ironed, now at the front door. Mila was very nearly hoarse. "So, that's where we're at. Now you know why I need to inspect the hotel, and now I've got to go."

"Actually, *we* need to go and you need to take *those* along. I'll drive." She pointed at the boxes of eggs and then started to pick up the nearest bag.

"I'm fine with you coming along. I could use the company. But why take the pysanky? We'll be back in an hour or so."

Candy tapped a finger on the front of her purse and then shook her head, tiny worried movements that started to chew at Mila's stomach. "We need to take those along because when I went to get the sodas, I figured I'd grab the eggs you sold me. But they're gone, carton and all. And since you didn't mention taking them, and *I* didn't take them, then—"

She hung her head and let out a frustrated breath. "Then either Sela or Vegre took them. So, they've been back here. Crap, crap, *crap!*" Was the gate open upstairs? Jeff hadn't mentioned it, but she remembered now that she and Tal had left Sela's door *open,* but it had been closed when she and Candy walked in the bathroom. Without waiting for her friend, she sprinted up the stairs, but switched to a tiptoe as she approached the door. There was no sound, no voices, so she opened the door. The closet was bare and the suitcases gone. *Yep, they've been here all right. I suppose I should be glad they didn't strip the place.*

"Need any help up there?" Candy's voice came from the bottom of the stairs. Apparently, she wasn't real interested in running into either of them again.

She spun and grabbed the doorknob, intending to shut it again when she left, when something sparkled on the floor, out of the corner of her eye. Furrowing her brow, she leaned over the cart that held Sela's stereo system and game console. The item the sun had glinted off of looked like a driving glove, made from black suede. It was snagged underneath a wide splinter in the bed frame, and it took a little tugging to unhook it. She turned it over to see the clear green faceted stone that was nearly the diameter of a soda can. *And exactly the diameter of my opal.*

Could it be an emerald? Was this Tal's glove? She'd only seen it for a moment before he threw it into the gate. She raised it carefully to her nose and inhaled. The same spicy grass tones she remembered from his skin clung to the leather.

A spark of something that felt frighteningly like joy filled her with a speed that matched the thought sailing through her head. *Now he'll have to come back.* He'd been looking for his glove, and here it was. It was a shame it wasn't connected to Vegre anymore, but she supposed he made it back through the gate when it got snagged.

She tucked it in her coat pocket with a smile. *I'll just keep it safe until he gets back.* She was halfway down the stairs when Dareen's sad face came into her mind. *Will I be waiting forever? Hoping he'll come back until I finally put it in the basement—hiding it away from whoever I eventually marry? Is that what I want for my life . . . to always hope, to always—* She couldn't even finish as she joined Candy at the door. Her friend noticed her abrupt mood shift and didn't ask questions . . . yet.

Her hands were windblown and cold by the time they got the eggs loaded in Candy's vehicle, and she put her hands into her pockets until the heater began to blow hot air. She felt the glove under her hand. Actually, she felt the *stone.* Rather than icy cold, it was warm to the touch, radiating with the same heat as when Tal was near. She opened her mouth and tasted . . . sweetness, and it made her heart pound and her skin ache.

"Candy," she asked in nearly a whisper as they pulled out into traffic. "Is it possible to discover you need something . . . truly *need* it with every ounce of your soul, even though you didn't realize it existed until a few days ago?"

"Accept it, guv. You need Mila." Alexy took another casual sip of fragrant herbal tea in which he'd poured about three times the normal majorica fruit sweetener. He raised his cup and winked. "Or, at least, the rest of us do. Once she makes a few more of those pretty eggs, we won't have to ration the juice at all."

They were sitting in the lunch room at the O.P.A. station in Vril, surrounded by a growing number of agents who were gating in to investigate the *phenomenon* of the Tree. Both the kings and Demeter's Children had claimed responsibility for the new life of the Tree . . . *naturally*. So it was being tasked to the O.P.A. alchemists to figure it out. If, and *only* if, the alchemists came up empty would he give hints about what he knew. Both Alexy and Kris had agreed with him about that—just for different reasons.

Kris shrugged and took another drink of steaming dandelion root and chicory, her preferred drink. She'd gotten more than one appreciative glance from arriving agents. One didn't often see the royal burgundy of the palace guard in a lowly O.P.A. office, and his sister was a striking woman even without the cloak. "I'm not willing to make a judgment on what Mila might or might not have done. I mean, I saw the gloves with my own eyes, but I didn't feel a trace of magic come from the woman, Tal. She *felt* like a human and it's my *job* to sense magical ability—searching for threats to His Highness. And while the evidence you showed me does support some of what I already knew from our search for Vegre, I still can't get past thinking that there's no cause to attack *Denver*." She leaned back in her chair and set her cup on the table again.

"I know," Tal admitted, rubbing his forehead with his fingertips, in a vain attempt to relieve the pressure. "That's what's making me crazy about this. But, I can't ignore the fact that Sela was in Denver, the gate she crafted . . . or Vegre crafted, was in Denver, I traced my *glove* to a hospital in Denver. The same hospital, I might add, where I first spotted the *Tin*—" He paused, not wanting to panic anyone in the room. "*Teeen* . . . aged girl. There's not a single British connection. Either Vegre is exceptionally good at throwing us off the track, or we're being exceptionally dense."

Kris reached out and touched his arm. "Look, big brother. It's obvious that there's something between the two of you. It might be that your judgment's clouded."

He frowned. The way she said that—"What do you mean, *it's obvious?*"

Alexy let out a bark of a laugh and then shook his head. Kris rolled her eyes before responding. "Talos Onan, I've known you all my life. I've met every one of your girl-friends. Craters, half of them were my academy class-mates. But I have *never* seen you look at a woman like that before. So yeah . . . it's *obvious.*"

He tried to shrug it off, and even to him it felt a lie. "I've known her for three days. It's nothing."

"You *met* her three days ago. But from what you've said, you've *known* her for a lot longer. Like your *whole life* longer. Didn't you say she was in your head during our battle? That's not real normal—even in our world."

He shook his head and fingered the carved handle of the intricate cup he'd found to pour his coffee in. "No, Jason was right. What about before she was born? She's not even thirty. Who was the voice before that? The Tree has been inside me my whole life." *And if it hasn't been the Tree spirit, then who . . . or* what *has been in my head?*

Kris released his arm to pat his hand. "Call it whatever you like, brother. I only know what I saw, and what I saw between you and Mila at the Tree wasn't the embrace of a concerned O.P.A. agent for a crime witness, nor a devoted acolyte for a deity. You've bedded her, haven't you? Or is it even more than that?"

The blunt phrasing took him aback and his reply was defensive and more than a little angry. "That's none of your business."

Alexy tipped his head toward Kris. "Yep, he's bedded her. Can't blame you. I'd be more than happy to give that friend of hers a go."

They made it sound like a frivolous *romp!* But . . . well, *wasn't it?* Wasn't it supposed to be just a relieving of the sexual tension between them? When did it become more than that? When did he start to *care* that her favorite color was blue, or she liked to work in her garden? Apparently, the others realized they struck a nerve, and Kris shook her head with a sad look. "I'm not saying it's wrong to feel something for her, Tal. I'm just saying your logic might be affected. Happens to all of us." She winked and then flicked her eyes to Alexy. "Well, *most* of us, anyway."

Alexy flipped his blond hair like a girl and stuck his nose up toward the ceiling. "You're just sorry I'm not available, so you can't date me."

She laughed and it made Tal smile for the first time since Mila had walked away. "*Glad* you're not, you mean. My sympathies are with Olga for having to put up with you."

They continued to banter for a few minutes while Tal tried to think. *Was* his logic affected? It didn't feel like it. Soft hair and hot skin couldn't explain away the legal paper, nor his glove. And where *was* his glove? He never did take the time to look for it in Vril, which was foolish.

"I should do another search for my glove. Maybe that'll give us some answers." He scooted back his chair and Alexy followed suit.

"Now you're thinking. With some of the magic restored here, we should be able to craft a right powerful tracking spell."

He was halfway out of his chair when a sound filled the room. Chimes, bells, and every manner of horn sounded in one clarion call. It was an announcement—a member of the royal staff had just arrived. Before Alexy could even get his feet fully under him, his allegiance spell activated and forcibly dropped him to one knee, so abruptly that the bottom of his jaw slammed against the ironwork table, nearly knocking him out.

Well, that answered which palace, because Alexy answered to the Shambalan king. A dozen or so of the other agents likewise dropped and bowed their heads in reaction to the spell, dropping cups and food trays all over the room.

Even Tal was forced to bow his head to the dignitary—a

side effect of his own allegiance spell to show respect and modesty. Only Kris was immune as a member of another royal guard. It would be a deadly mistake for a king to be killed because the palace guard couldn't move, or for them to be taken out of action in time of war. Yet, she stood as well and tucked her chin to her neck. But she kept her eyes fully on the door to see who was arriving. One hand was already under her cloak, likely putting on her glove.

Occasionally, a general or defense minister would visit an O.P.A. office to follow up on an investigation, so that's what he was expecting. But when a tall, dark-skinned man with a broad face and thickly muscled bare arms swept into the room, without a single courtier or attendant, his golden laurel crown glowing with enough magic to burn the eyes, Tal was frankly stunned.

Kris immediately dropped to a knee next to Alexy, and slapped one fisted arm across her chest in the traditional salute of the guard. "O great and noble King Mumbai, ruler of Shambala. I bid you welcome on behalf of King Kessrick. My pardon, Your Highness, for our lack of tribute, but we were not informed of your visit."

Of course, Tal couldn't speak even though he opened his mouth to try to pay his respects. A king may only be spoken to by other kings, or when directly addressed. His sister could offer welcome on behalf of her ruler, but Tal and the others had become mute, as well as awestruck.

The king dipped his head toward Kris and made a tiny movement of his fingers. She must have understood it because she rose and stepped back a pace to stand at attention—eyes forward and blank. But he also noticed her delicately bending her middle finger to touch her focus, no doubt to mentally inform her commander of this surprise visit.

Mumbai spoke, and his voice was the rumble of the earth itself, low and powerful enough to shake the blood in his veins. "I seek the mage commander Talos Onan. Let him approach me now."

Tal was released from the spell so abruptly that he stumbled and nearly fell over Alexy. His heart was pounding like a caged animal as he stepped forward and presented himself with a similar salute. "I am Talos Onan, Your Majesty. How may I serve you?"

The king stared down at him for a long moment. It was hard not to flinch under those dark eyes, glowing with the rich color of fertile new soil. "The Kingdom of Shambala is indebted to you, Commander Onan. May your king and your peers praise you in song and word for your foresight in averting a great wrong. The news you sent us—" Tal noticed that the king was very cautious not to mention *what* news. "Allowed us to rescue a number of hostages . . . guildercents who might have died but for your actions."

Now he was confused. What guilder—? But then he remembered. Dareen had talked about Vegre *collecting* Parasks. Had the king found them? Had they found his hideout? Again, he wanted to ask, but the spell kept sound from passing his lips.

Mumbai noticed and lifted the spell with a nod of his head. "You may speak freely to me for now, Commander." That turned Kris's eyes his way in surprise before her discipline kicked in again. But a fine trembling had overtaken her, that curiosity and intelligence that had made her a guard at such a young age.

"Highness, may I inquire if you have indeed found . . . *his* stronghold?" That should be vague enough not to break too many taboos.

The king nodded and crossed his arms, the golden bands surrounding his biceps twisting as the powerful muscles flexed. "We have indeed, and we never would have considered that location if not for your message." Then he took a deep breath and let out a frustrated rumble of noise that vibrated every glass in the room. "But we need your help once again."

His help? A king, surrounded by the best minds on the planet, needed help? But it wasn't his place to question the word of a king, even though he couldn't imagine how he could assist. "Of course, Your Highness," he said with another bow of his head. "Anything I can do."

The king nodded and walked toward him and then clapped an arm around his shoulders. "Walk with me, Talos."

His heart rose into his throat from the blast of power that pressed against him like an avalanche of stones. He could even smell earth now—plowed fields and the ripe, fresh scent of harvest day. He saw a golden light and then all went dark for a moment.

He blinked and he was suddenly topside, or in an amazing facsimile of it, on a hillside of blowing golden grass. A deserted stone building was mere steps away. Tal had heard that the kings could gate at will, wherever in the world they wanted to travel. But he'd never seen it before. He wondered what the others would think to see a gate appear in the middle of the break room, or whether they were still bound by the spell.

"This is Silberdag," Mumbai said as though it explained everything. When he realized it didn't, he continued. "This is the guild house of the Parask clan, the soul-conjurers. It was burned to the ground by our human neighbors and deserted by the guild shortly after. This land is part of what was once the *original* Shambala, before we were exiled to Agathia." He walked toward the building, apparently expecting Tal to follow.

So he did.

The original doorway had collapsed so long ago that the stones were half-buried under the grass. But there were obvious signs of recent occupancy once he stepped inside.

"It was your mention of the Parask that made us realize that Vegre might have returned here. Perhaps he thought us still filled with foolish pride . . . or too *afraid* to venture close." He swept his hand around the room. "The trouble is that Vegre was gone when we arrived, having left his captives to starve behind bars. There are clues aplenty here, but we can't read them. Unfortunately, in our attempt to bury the Parask in obscurity . . . we *did.* But Lady Rockwell informs us that you have knowledge of their ways . . . that you have met and watched one or more of them craft." Mumbai sat down on a bare stone and sighed. Without an entourage or golden light and flowers raining down upon him where he walked, he looked just like every other agent Tal knew—as frustrated as a man surrounded by water, but with no way to drink. "We are asking . . . no *I* am asking for your help, for the human queen of this land relies on me to protect her from our kind. If you cannot read these clues, or give me some hint of where to go, then our centuries-old agreement may finally be lost."

The kings had binding agreements with overworld leaders? He opened his mouth, but no sound came out—even though it wasn't the spell. Rather than think of a response, he decided to simply do as he was asked.

There wasn't much left of the building. The fire-scarred granite was moss-covered and crumbling. But here and there were spots of bright colors—brilliant reds and blues that stood out in sharp relief against the pale brown of the dried grass.

Dye. It must be dye. So, confirmation then of their theories. But the king already *knew* the Parask were here, since they rescued the captives. He turned his head while still in a crouch, twirling the blade of blue-stained grass in his fingers. "I'm not certain what you wish of me, Majesty. Did you seek confirmation that it was really Parask who were held here?" For there was little more to be seen in the open room. A little dye, some bits of crushed eggshell—nothing that would tell him Vegre's location, nor his true plan.

"I knew your father, Talos. Knew him well and he was a brilliant investigator . . . absolutely without equal." He let out a small smile. "But he was not one who worked well with an audience—considered most people supreme fools." Now a small chuckle as he fell further into his memory. "Me included, I've no doubt. But I called Khevdir *friend* in a time when there were few to be had." He stood up and walked over to Tal and likewise squatted near the colored grass. The light of his crown was so great that it hurt his eyes and he had to squint and drop his gaze to the man's neck. Mumbai looked chagrined for a moment and then swallowed that great mass of power inside, until he was just a normal man, wearing an unusual cap. "You see, I was once an investigator like you, and your father was my partner."

Tal was taken aback. Sybil had never mentioned any history between his parents and one of the kings. He'd thought Father a simple crafter of heat and light. "I didn't know that."

"Well, the O.P.A. wasn't organized then . . . not as such. And kings weren't exalted nobles, to be catered to. We were expected to earn our keep—bring lawbreakers to justice, protect . . . or *avenge* the innocent, and always, but always *seem* to be more intelligent than the average crafter." He winked at Tal and let out that rolling chuckle again which moved the very ground beneath them. "Your father made me look damned good for a very long time. I'm hoping you'll do the same, because I admit I'm at a loss. I see colors staining my ground, but it means nothing. I see bits of shell and remember the flocks of birds which used to call Silberdag home. Yet there are no birds here now. What am I missing, Talos? Before I must face my people and admit my own stupidity."

So that's why Mumbai was being so casual with him—taking him away from the pomp of the courts and the fawning of his staff. He needed help to be seen as the *king*, with all the knowledge of the world—and was willing to get that information however he had to. Including plying the son of his old friend with flattery.

Yet, even Tal's own knowledge was stolen, taken from the scrolls entrusted to Mila. And there had been *hundreds* of scrolls in the secret garden, likely revealing the entire history of the soul-conjurer's guild. *Trust me.* The words seemed to echo in his head . . . burn through his chest. She claimed to trust him and had proved that trust with the sweat of her brow. Could he do any less? Was he willing to betray her trust by offering up stolen knowledge as though his own?

He shook his head. He couldn't take Mumbai to Viktor's home. But he could reveal the information he had so far. "I will tell you what I know, on the condition that the knowledge not be attributed to me . . . because it's not truly mine."

King Mumbai stood and brushed off the front of his golden robe. "Your father had that same humility inside . . . an odd sort of ethics which was cold as steel, and hot as fire when betrayed. He couldn't be bought, nor bullied. It made him a valuable advisor, and worth the rather frequent bruising of my ego. I see in your eyes and stance you inherited that. I don't know if you're his magic equal, but he could . . . well, let's say I ruled over my warriors because he had no desire to lead."

It was fascinating to hear his father spoken of this way. He'd had no clue. And whether Tal could live up to the king's memories of the man—time would tell.

He explained what he'd seen of the egg dying process, remembering to call them pysanka, as Mila had done . . . but being careful not to mention her by name. He didn't want the king to suddenly pay her a visit in a fit of frustration, nor endanger her to Mumbai's court, since he wasn't certain they could be trusted. "And once the eggs are fully dyed, they can house magic inside to be used by any crafter." He explained what he'd seen of the egg on the mantel and how his focus stone had filled itself without aid. "And so I believe it's Vegre's goal to create large masses of the pysanky to aid him in his conquest of the overworld."

Mumbai was listening . . . truly *listening,* and trying to work things out in his head. He tapped his jaw with one wide finger and began to walk around, examining the bits of shell scattered around the room. "This wasn't all achieved in two days. Those people were nearly starving. What I'm hearing is that Vegrellion has somehow been able to command his people to capture the Parask and force their labor from within the walls of Rohm."

That furrowed Tal's brow. "No, Majesty. I'm telling you that Vegre hasn't been *in* Rohm, or has been getting in and out at will. I'm betting it's been at least two years, since he formed Demeter's Children."

The reaction was enough to tell him that the king had no idea about that aspect of Vegre's plan. It made him sigh. "You didn't speak with Lady Rockwell directly, did you?" When the king shook his head, Tal was forced to break the bad news. "I fear you've a traitor close to your throne, Majesty . . . or at least someone who's been bewitched."

Mumbai frowned and then waved a hand. A pair of chairs appeared—thick-cushioned but simply crafted of wood that seemed right at home among the crumbling stones. "Then perhaps you should start at the beginning."

CHAPTER 18

"*A*nd that is the private door to the fire escape for our Presidential Suite, where Mr. Popolous is staying." Jean-Paul's second, Denise, pointed at a sturdy fire door, up the final flight of cement stairs. Mila grabbed the handrail and twisted so she could see the red emergency bar with the words DOOR OPENS OUT printed in bold letters. It was handy information, because the fire stairs accessed every floor. It would make it easier to move around if she need to track or *escape* from Vegre the night of the party. But if the door only opened *out*—

"What if, for example, a fire started in the basement. Sending the top floors *down* could kill people. Is there guest access to the *roof* for helicopters or ladder trucks to pick them up?"

She nodded professionally. It was actually nice to be taking this tour with Denise. Jean-Paul would be rolling his eyes at her *paranoia*. "Absolutely. Right this way."

Denise spun around and tripped down the stairs past

Mila and Candy. Fortunately, the woman didn't realize Candy didn't work for the firm, so she hadn't asked a single question about her following along, taking notes when Mila pointed to her. She was actually starting to hope that Candy really *was* taking notes. It was a complicated building, for the small size.

Denise had just walked through the fire door on the fifth floor and Mila was about to follow when Candy tapped her on the shoulder. "Um . . . is that what I think it is?"

She turned her head and followed Candy's finger, but couldn't see into the dark space under the stairs where she was pointing. So she stepped up to where her friend was standing and peered into the spot. "Is that a pysanka back in there?"

It *was*. She motioned down to the door. "Go block that door with your boot and pretend it's stuck for a minute." Candy nodded hurriedly and sprinted down, bracing her body against the metal just as Denise started to open it to find out what was keeping them.

"It's stuck!" She shouted the words at the assistant concierge and peered through the glass. She rattled the handle and tugged while adding her knee to her weight against the door. Turning her head, she whispered back. "Hurry up! She's stronger than she looks."

Mila wrapped one arm around the handrail and swung wide into space. The little pysanka was crudely drawn, a lot like the ones she'd made when she was just a child. It seemed to be a mage egg, and an overkill one at that. Multiple interpretations of the sun and stars covered the face, along with jagged saw patterns around the top and base which weren't anywhere close to even or straight. Only red and black had been used for some reason, which wasn't very typical.

"*Mila*—" Candy's voice pulled her out of her inspection. Should she take it along or leave it here? If Vegre had placed it there, he might come back to look for it. On the other hand, it could be vital to learn how they were crafting them. She tucked it in her pocket. If they spotted any more of them, she'd leave them, but mark the locations to come back and destroy later.

Because that's something she *could* do. If his plan was to put eggs all over the hotel to draw the magic from, then the more of them she destroyed, the less he'd have to work with. Maybe she could even stop the whole process if she broke enough of them.

She caught Candy's attention and mouthed, "Okay." Candy put on her best, most fierce face and leaned back with all her might, simultaneously releasing her weight from the door. Denise burst through the entry and slammed into Candy and only Candy's grip on the knob prevented them from bouncing down the next flight of stairs.

Denise's voice was horrified. "I am *so* sorry! I'll have maintenance look at this door immediately." In fact, she pulled a black radio from her back pocket and did just that. While Mila felt a little bad about the extra work they'd probably go to trying to fix a problem that didn't exist, it had been worth it. She knew more about what he was planning and she had been *right*. There was no reason at all why there'd be a pysanka in the stairwell, and it had only been here for a day or two. Someone would have spotted it during a regular inspection, just like Candy did.

Now that they knew what they were looking for, they spotted six more eggs hidden around the hotel. It was like an Easter hunt. They were tucked into little-used spots— from the top of the furnace to the center of an artificial flower arrangement and even wound into the garland that still decorated the bannister. Someone had been pretty darned creative. Once or twice she'd looked over at Candy's pad to verify that she'd later be able to follow the directions to the eggs.

But despite looking in every room she could, on every floor, she *still* couldn't figure out the burning question— *why here?* In the long run, she knew it didn't really matter. One place was as good as any other for a catastrophe. *It would just be nice to know if there's something I'm miss-*

ing . . . some tiny detail that would make the difference in figuring this out.

And then the tiny detail walked in the door, while they were standing at the top of the grand staircase on the second floor.

Sela walked across the lobby, dressed in a blue designer pantsuit. On each side of her was one of the Guilders she remembered from being in Tal's head at the prison. Following behind nervously were several people who were staring at the decorations as though they'd never seen a hotel.

And maybe they haven't. For one of the entourage was Tal's mother, Sybil. Mila stepped back abruptly and looked up as though admiring something. But the move put her behind a large potted tree, hidden from the lobby. Candy stared at her oddly until Mila pointed down. Then Candy likewise dove behind the tree, but not with nearly the subtlety. "Is there a problem?" Denise looked all around her, probably still spooked from the sticking fire door.

"I was just admiring the stained glass. The sun's not so bright back here."

Denise nodded, pleased and proud. "Oh yes. That's our pride and joy. The original owner had—"

While Denise was talking and pointing up, Candy whispered in her ear. "That was my client down there with Sela. The one who ordered the eggs—Terry Cardon."

Why was she not surprised? But then Denise's voice cut in again. "—designed and made by the finest craftsmen in England and flown here in pieces to put together. At night we even backlight it so people can see the intricate design."

The phrasing actually made Mila *look* at the window. She really did have a good vantage from this location and stared up at it. The center of the hotel was open all the way to the roof, where the stained-glass skylight sparkled color across the rich gold-and-blue carpeting in the lobby. *Made by the finest craftsmen in England.* But what if it was made by the finest *crafters,* instead?

Denise looked down over the railing and pointed. "Oh, look. You were asking earlier who'd checked in. That's Mrs. Pierce right there. Would you like me to introduce you?"

She and Candy looked at each other with raised brows. "*Mrs. Pierce?* I hadn't heard Veg . . . that is, *David* had married." She waved it off with what she hoped was a nonchalant expression. "No, that's okay. We really need to get back and she looks busy with all those people. I'll meet her at the party tomorrow." She held out her hand. "Thank you so much for your help today. I'll let Jean-Paul know how much I appreciated your knowledge of the hotel."

As expected, Denise beamed and shook her hand amiably. Now the only trick was getting out of the hotel without Sela seeing. It was Candy who came to the rescue.

"Any chance we can take the elevator down, Mila? My feet are *killing* me from climbing those concrete stairs in these heels." She bent down to rub one ankle just for good measure. Mila could have kissed her!

"If you'd like to take the service elevator, it comes out right next to the garage, so you won't have to walk all the way around the block. It's right over there. Let me unlock it for you." Ah . . . wonderful, helpful Denise. And she didn't even realize just how helpful she'd been. It was definitely worth talking her up to her boss—if she still had a place to work come next week.

Once they were settled in the front seat of the SUV again, Mila let out the breath she hadn't realized she was holding. "So what do you think?"

Candy started the engine and backed out of the parking space so fast she nearly hit the car behind them. "I think we were lucky to get out of there in one piece. But I won't feel better until there's a few miles between us and Sela." Mila couldn't agree more, so she just sat back to let Candy take care of the driving. She pulled the egg from her pocket and looked at it in the bright sunshine that came through the windshield. There was something familiar about the design, but she'd be damned if she could remember what.

"I also think you were lucky I was in there with you." Candy's voice was laced with enough smug satisfaction to choke on, but Mila could hardly blame her.

"True. You found the pysanka. I didn't even notice it. And you managed to get us into the staff elevator so Sela didn't spot us. Good job on both counts. Now, if you don't have any plans, I need to make a couple of stops. Otherwise, run me home so I can grab my car."

"Oh, no. I'm sticking to you like *glue*. I'm out a thousand bucks with no eggs to give the client. And I'll just bet you've already given a chunk to the bank. Haven't you?"

Mila winced and nodded, but then a thought occurred to her and it made her laugh. Candy turned her head briefly in acknowledgment before going back to watch traffic. "Technically speaking, I'm out of the loop. I made the eggs. Your client *got* the eggs. We both know darned well they're hidden *somewhere* in that hotel. We just didn't have enough time to search."

Candy let out a frustrated breath, followed by a snort. "Well doesn't *that* just bite. But you're right. I can't blame you when the client stole them from you so he wouldn't have to pay *me*. What really sucks is I can't even file with my insurance because who'd believe me?"

Mila reached over to touch her friend's hand. "Candy. I'm kidding. Of *course* I'll get the money back to you. But could it at least wait until payday? That's just next week. Of course, that's provided I've still got a job then . . . *and* there's a next week at all."

"Point, that." She flipped her fingers in the air, still holding onto the steering wheel with her thumbs. "So, where to next?

"We need to stop at that weird candle shop on Third Street we found on Halloween. Remember it?" Then she allowed herself to smile, but it wasn't a friendly one. It made Candy visibly shiver. "After that, I think it's time I made damned sure *nobody*—human or Guilder—gets in my house unless I want them to."

CHAPTER 19

$\mathcal{T}$he news that Demeter's Children was being led by Vegre sent shock waves through the O.P.A. office. Nearly every agent knew someone who had converted and it was growing more difficult to keep the news quiet.

King Mumbai had returned to Shambala later in the day and was making all his reserve magic available to the O.P.A. He'd even persuaded the other kings to do the same. While few knew what Tal had actually said to the king, the other agents and commanders were certainly treating him with kid gloves.

Even Henry Ordos, who had never been particularly friendly, apologized openly. "No offense, Tal—yeah? It's just that Sommersby made it sound like there was such strong evidence against you. You do understand, don't you?"

Both Alexy and Kris had snorted at the idea Henry was really sorry. It was more likely he was embarrassed at being one of Tal's leading detractors, now that he was a favorite of a king. When there was a spare moment after Mumbai left, Tal sat down and told the pair what had happened, especially the events after the chairs appeared from thin air. That part had been interesting because Tal had never known a Guilder to be able to move matter. It was one thing to craft items for use, but another thing entirely to *move* them without touching.

"He listened to the whole story. And he asked some very pointed questions about what could be *proved* versus what was mere speculation. But he seemed to believe me."

Unfortunately, much of what Mila believed fell into the speculation category and Mumbai couldn't be persuaded to send even a single man to Denver. "He also shared the evidence his own men found at the guild house. I can't say that I blame him for believing there's a threat to the residence of the queen." It was certainly compelling and even Tal was swayed.

"I'm sorry, Tal, but I have to agree." Kris really *did* look sorry. "The evidence is just too strong. I can't reveal what *I* know, but trust me. It's compelling."

He shook his head in frustration. "Anyway, that's when he gated us both right back to the center of the lunch room."

If Tal had thought the king's *first* appearance had raised eyebrows, showing up midsentence in a pair of chairs was going to be the talk of the office for months to come.

Alexy let out a slow whistle. "That was something all right. And what about that communication viewer he made from a tree? I mean, I can talk through soil, but to make a plant into a viewing gate? Wow." Tal nodded. He distinctly remembered when the king stood and it was a good thing he followed suit, because the chairs disappeared before he had fully unbent his legs. Mumbai's crown started to glow again but this time nobody was being forced to kneel or bow. It was as if he could put aside such trivialities in times of need.

The potted tree in the corner of the room had indeed become a makeshift communication viewer. Leaves wove together at the touch of his finger, and then the image of a room filled with flowering vines and leaves appeared. "Lady Rockwell, may I speak with you?"

Dareen rushed to whatever in the room was providing the image of the king and dropped to both knees. She had cleaned up and was now dressed in the traditional golden robes of Shambala. She'd styled her hair in a complicated pattern of braids with golden leaves and flowers woven in that was quite beautiful. "Your Highness! Long may ye reign."

He chuckled, and this time the rest of the agents got to experience the rumbling of the ground underfoot. Even the dirtdogs like Alexy seemed impressed, so it must not be a common thing. "The last time you said that to me,

Dareen, was the day I wed Krystella. And you were laughing at the time, because you *knew* I would never *reign* a single day thereafter in my home."

Her eyes twinkled but she didn't even crack a smile. "I was very clear when you asked me whether I thought Stella was strong-willed enough to be queen. Was I wrong?"

The sniff he let out wasn't quite a laugh, but Tal could tell he was fighting not to grin. "She does what a good queen *should* do. She forces open my eyes to see past my blindness to the whole truth." But then his jaw tightened and the twinkling turned to flashing anger. "I need to know who in my staff you told your story to, Dareen. I apparently make a mistake by not meeting with you myself."

She shrugged. "You're king. 'Tis hard to see every visitor who gates in off the street."

"I should have seen *you*." The king turned his head and caught Tal's eye. With a twitch of his finger, he summoned him forth. Tal couldn't have withstood the pull even if he'd chosen to, and he had no idea how the man was managing it. *I'm not alchemist guild, nor Shambalan.* Yet Mumbai was doing it.

In seconds, Tal was standing before the window into the palace. "Do you know this man?" the king asked Dareen.

"Aye, m'lord." That was the first time she'd referred to him that way, and it seemed to Tal that was how she was *accustomed* to speaking to him. "'Tis Talos Onan, son of your dearest friend and friend to me own dear boy, Jason. He was the one who confirmed my suspicions about the dark mage. He and the Parask girl, Mila. Is she there with you, too?"

No! Not Mila! He didn't want her involved. And yet he couldn't speak and could barely move his body enough to breathe.

Mumbai raised his brows and turned his head slightly with a disapproving expression. "I see from your discomfort that you *intentionally* chose not to mention this girl. Why? What secrets does she hold? What have you withheld from me?"

Dareen shook her head and then waved a hand at the viewer. "Oh, leave him be, Mumbai. Talos wouldn't have withheld anything from you, except perhaps the name of the girl. She's of overworld stock, newly introduced to our kind. He probably fears . . . and rightly so, that she would be too easily frightened of you. Besides," she said with a sly wink, "I seem to remember a few of your *omissions of fact* from your own dear da."

It was Mumbai's turn to cough uncomfortably. Dareen was standing up for him and Mila—to a king? But why? She noticed his expression and waved a hand before rising stiffly from her knees. "Bleedin' hell, but I'm gettin' too old for all this kneelin'. Kneel to get in, kneel to the minister, kneel to you. Fie on it all."

It turned the king's attention back to the reason for the call. Tal let out a sigh of relief. "Which minister? You need to be *very* clear, old friend, for punishment will likely follow. According to Commander Onan, I was *not* told the story you came here to tell."

Dareen's brows shot up and then her arms crossed tightly over her chest. Apparently, she'd figured out that Mumbai was calling from the O.P.A. offices, because her eyes kept flicking to the background, where agents were moving about. People were trying to ignore the king's actions, but there were still far more people in the lunchroom than normal for this time of day. "Weren't ya now? And it took Tal to bring you the news, when 'twas meself what traveled all this way? Well, then I've no issue with revealing *that* scoundrel to the light. None a'tal. T'was your defense minister, Lobota, who listened to me tale."

Things happened quickly after that. The king adjourned to another, more private room for several hours. Word eventually filtered down in whispers that after a nearly an hour of hanging upside down in charmed chains, the minister had coughed up a bespelled lapis stone. However, reports *also* claimed the king remained uncertain of Lobota's loyalty even after removal of the charm, and had gated rather quickly to the southern border, to review troop locations . . . *personally.*

Before Mumbai had left, he'd clapped a broad hand on Tal's arm and squeezed tight. "While I would prefer this hadn't happened, I'm pleased with your aid. You're welcome in Shambala anytime, m'boy. I expect I'll see you in England tomorrow. Have someone notify me when you arrive. Kessrick and I will be leading the operation personally, while Reginald and Laird will be looking into the problems at the prison."

So here he was, hours later, sitting in the Vrillian barracks, trying to decide what to do. Kris had returned to the palace to bring King Reginald up to date and ready the guard for action. He and Alexy were officially released from duty in Rohm to help in the operation.

"You missed that volley completely, guv. Where's your head?"

He blinked and looked up to see the frustration on Alexy's face. The small bubble of energy they'd been using to test the opal's precision was hovering up near the ceiling. He looked at his hand. The focus was now housed in a brand new glove gifted by Kris before she left, and it felt good. But it felt *wrong,* too. It wasn't really his stone.

He let out a deep breath and shook his head before popping the bubble and flopping down on his bunk. "My mind's completely befuddled, Alexy." He reached his thumb up to rub across the dome of swirling colors in the stone. "So many wonderful things have happened, and yet something's still not quite . . . right."

"Wouldn't have anything to do with Mila, would it?"

He slid his hands under his head and stared at the ceiling, the laughter and energy of the other agents seeming hollow and false. "I honestly don't know. Maybe. I mean, I wouldn't want her here right now. It wouldn't be safe. But it might not be safe where she is now, either. I just can't help but think she's right about Vegre."

"Tal—" Alexy's voice was disapproving.

He turned his head to see the voice matched the face. "I

know. I know. Everything points to England. I just can't help but think that it seems too . . . *easy*."

Alexy let out a donkey bray of a laugh. "You call this *easy*? Corrupting allegiance spells of several key officials, then sneaking out of prison to form a religion for the sole purpose of capturing guildercents? And let's not forget locking the captives in an old Scottish Guilder hall and forcing them to dye Easter eggs. You've uncovered an *amazingly* intricate plot, Tal. We're going to catch this guy because of you. We'll save the *queen*." It was obvious Alexy had spent a bit too long up in England. The awe in his voice for the leader of the British people should be reserved for only his own king.

"I know. And that's just it. Don't you see? It *was* an amazingly intricate plan. So why stop now? All roads are leading to England. A Shambalan minister with a bloody *map* to the palace in his quarters. A bit of paper found in the ruins with the queen's seal. An increased number of Demeter's Children members in London. It might as well be an engraved invitation. It just doesn't feel right."

"You know the problem with intricate plans, Tal?" He turned his head to see that Alexy had raised brows and was leaning forward, elbows perched on his knees, hands clasped together. "Hmm?"

Tal sighed. "Go ahead."

"Too many people are involved. There are too many chances for something to go wrong. If just one thing goes, the whole plan falls apart. Face it, Tal. *You* were the thing that went wrong. You wrecked his plan."

That made him shake his head and sit up once more. "Not just me, Alexy. Mila, too. And *that's* what's wrong. She doesn't think the whole plan's been revealed yet. There are still loose ends. The old name change in the vault, the gate in and out of her house. And what about the *Tin Czerwona?* Nobody's said a *word* about that. That's part of the plan, too. It has to be."

"Bollocks. It *doesn't* have to be. It's purely circumstantial. You don't *know* the name change is Vegre's. There's probably a Talos Vladimir Onan somewhere up in the over-world. Have you looked? Are you positive *you're* completely unique?" He didn't wait for Tal to speak. "No. Of course you haven't. *None* of us have. If there weren't coincidences in the world, there'd be no such *word*. You don't even know for sure that Dareen or the niece—Suzanne?—were infected by Vegre. Could just be a weird outbreak. Again, happens all the time topside." Alexy reached out and lightly punched his shoulder as a Klaxon sounded in the distance. "Let it go. Let's get back to concentrating on the operation at hand . . . right after dinner, that is."

It made him smile. Good old Alexy—always thinking with his stomach. "You go on ahead. I'm just going to sit and think for a bit."

His friend stood and then leaned down to whisper next to his head. "A man can think himself to *death,* guv. It's only *action* that moves the world forward."

And then he was gone, along with everyone else in the barracks. Dinner was expected to be exceptional tonight, owing to both the forthcoming battle and the availability of magic. Food had been gating in all day—meats and vegetables, spices and sweets. All afternoon the scent of roasting meat and baking pies had been making his mouth water.

But suddenly he wasn't hungry. He leaned back on the bed again to stare at the ceiling. He could still almost feel the sensation of her next to him, phantom tingles of heat against his skin, and the scent of citrus in the air. Was that what this was all about? Was he merely infatuated with Mila, and not seeing the obvious?

"Does it matter *why* I have to go back?" Hearing his own voice speaking in the empty room startled him. *When did I decide to go back?*

The answer was instantaneous. *When you realized she was right.* He could argue until his face was blue with the others about the possibilities and the *probabilities*. But he knew she was right.

Trust me. But he hadn't. It wasn't logical, so he didn't. Yet trust *wasn't* logical . . . any more than faith was.

In that one brief flash of the obvious it was suddenly clear. He understood. He lost faith in Mila the moment she took away his faith in the Blessed Tree—the moment the Tree came back to life by her hand. There was no spirit, no guiding force inside the Sacred Trees—it was all just pretty *eggs. Why believe in anything at all? Why not just let logic rule?*

He didn't have an answer for that. But it wasn't fair to let people *die* just because he was having a crisis of faith. That, in itself, wasn't logical.

And, too, he needed to see her, hear her voice. He hadn't been able to reach her even mentally since she'd left. Whether it was him or her didn't matter. Even now his fingers ached to touch her, his heart pounded at the memory of her drowning deep green eyes, the curve of her lips, the taste of her magic. *Love isn't logical, either.*

Again he could argue with himself that it wasn't love . . . *couldn't* be love this soon, or this strong. But his reactions when her name was spoken betrayed him.

Can there be love without trust? Without faith? As he began to gather his things, hoping that the gate in the butcher shop still worked, he let out a small sigh. *I guess I'm about to find out.*

*T*he iron eyebolt made an ear-splitting squeal as it slowly ground into the door frame. It was like fingernails on a chalkboard, amplified a dozen times by the narrow hallway. "Man, I don't know what kind of wood they made this place of, but it's hell for stout. How you coming with that other one?"

Candy let out a violent burst of air. The battery-powered drill went silent at the same time. "Broke another bit . . . *and* another nail. Next time you ask me to take you to the hardware store, remind me to say no."

Mila smiled. Candy could talk tough, but she was a hard worker when she put her mind to it. She proved it by cranking the second eyebolt into the hole she'd drilled without much effort. "We're almost done. That's the last bolt and then there's just the magical deterrents to spread out."

Her friend blew a few strands of hair out of her eyes. "I'm not even sure why we're doing this part. I understand installing the security system and emergency lights. Hell, you should have done that two years ago. I even see why you'd put a double-keyed dead bolt on Sela's door. But a *trip wire?* What good will that do? Her door opens *in,* brainiac. She'll spot it right away and just step over it."

"You'd be surprised how the simple things get people, Candy. You're the one who gave me the idea." The confused look made her point down the hall. "Don't you remember that statue that used to stand next to the table? The bronze one of the running girl with the foot that stuck out into the hallway?"

Her friend grimaced and stared at the spot. "I *hated* that damned statue. Hit my shin on it I don't know *how* many times."

Mila smiled. "Precisely. You hit it over and over, even though you knew it was there. People just forget to look at that height. You look at the floor, you look at arm and head level, but forget the shins. I figure I'll have ten . . . maybe fifteen seconds to wake up after they go crashing to the floor. That could mean my life, or my freedom." She flicked her finger against the nearly invisible piano wire tightly stretched across the doorway and listened to the high-pitched ting. "I don't know if their magic can open dead bolts, but I know Vegre can burn down the door. This won't burn easily and won't be affected by air or water magic. And," she concluded, giving the bolt one final twist, "Even if it doesn't work, it is worth a try."

"Well, I do have to admit it's hard to see, and putting the bolts on the outside of the jamb will make it nearly invisible from both directions. It'll also be damned hard to yank out. So how much did the security system set you back?"

Mila shook her head and shuddered before rising to her feet and starting to pick up tools. "I didn't even ask. I just handed Bryan my credit card and told him what I wanted. He said the motion sensors that came with the base unit would cover the house, but there are a *lot* of windows in this place. Putting those magnetic thingies on all of them probably won't be cheap. I'm just hoping he'll remember I'm a neighbor and be kind on the bill. I gave him the last two hundred to get him started. So now I'm broke again until payday."

"But at least you're likely to make it to the next payday. Definitely worth it, in my opinion." Candy helped her carry the tools downstairs and let out a low whistle when she saw the security command unit now attached to the wall near the door. "Wow, you got the *fancy* one."

Mila shrugged and put the tools back in the duffel bag before heaving it into the hall closet. "It's a commercial unit, which is a little overkill. But I got this model because it's the same one we have at work. I took a whole day of classes learning how to make that one sing and dance and jump through hoops. I know every code by heart and if a red button starts flashing anywhere, I don't even have to look at the chart to know what it means. Frankly, I just don't have *time* to learn another whole system."

A light caught their attention and they turned toward the front picture window. It was the new emergency light clicking on to illuminate the walkway. Candy pulled up her sweater sleeve and looked at her watch. "Wow. It's already dark? Man, I've got to get going. I didn't plan to spend the whole day here . . . not that I mind, of course," she hastened to add. She touched Mila's arm, worry making tiny lines appear between her eyebrows. "You going to be okay here . . . *alone?* I could cancel my dinner date."

Mila rolled her eyes and tried to let out a small laugh, even though she was wondering the same thing. "I've been here alone for two years now, Candy. Sela only spent a night or two here every week, remember? I'll be fine."

She nodded, still worried but then her eyes brightened hopefully. "Have you checked voice mail?"

The sigh that erupted from her chest spoke volumes and though she fought to keep it out, a small thread of hurt wound around the words. "We've been here the whole time, Candy. He hasn't called."

"But with the power tools running and . . . oh—" She finally noticed the look on Mila's face . . . the one that said she'd already checked. "Well, I guess he hasn't then, but he might still."

She had to face the truth, just like Candy did. "It was a fling. A one-night stand. No big deal."

Candy dropped her coat then and grabbed both sides of Mila's chin so tight it almost hurt. "No. It *wasn't* just a fling, and you know it. I don't know what it *was* exactly, but don't you dare give up hope this soon. You have a look in your eyes that—" Wetness appeared and she blinked it back. "That I pray every night I'll see in the mirror. It might not be love, but it's *something,* and it's worth hanging onto. Okay?"

She'd never seen her friend like this, had never imagined that there was a deeper meaning behind all the flirting and dates and lovers. "Candy, I didn't know . . ."

She smiled, but there was sadness in her eyes. "Everyone wants to find that perfect someone, Mila. At first you want it on your own terms, but eventually you start to bend. By the time you're our age, you start picking and choosing—'Oh, I don't really mind being a football widow,' or 'I suppose his friends aren't *that* bad.' " She let go one side of Mila's face to touch her hair. "You found one of the good ones—smart and brave and handsome. So he's a cop, so he's a mage, so he's hundreds of years old. Who cares? Of course," she amended with a tip of her head and rolled eyes, "the elk-squirrel is a little odd, but maybe they taste good. I like elk. One of Tim's friends hunted one once and brought back steaks. It was pretty good."

Mila reached up to pull Candy's hands down and held them tight for a moment. "You're babbling, sweetie. But yeah—I wish he'd call. I wish I knew he was okay. But I don't, and all I've got to hold onto right now is the thought that if I can stop Vegre, and keep the people at my work safe, then there'll be a tomorrow. And with a tomorrow, there's hope."

Now Candy really did smile. She let go of Mila's hands and picked up her jacket. "Hope's good. I like hope. Well, then, I'll *hope* everything will be okay here, and I *hope* he calls you, because it'll make you happy. And hey, sue me—you're my friend. I like it when you're happy."

There was no way to respond to her that didn't involve a hug. So she did.

But once she'd closed the door behind Candy and was alone, it was a different story. The house felt big and empty—in a way that it never had when Sela was out. An energy was missing, and she knew whose.

So, rather than concentrate on the energy that was *missing,* she decided to think about the potential energy in the eggs that had been delivered. She still didn't know if they were *duszats,* nor how to make them work. What she *did* know was the one on the mantel was. Thankfully, it hadn't been attractive enough for Vegre to take, or he didn't notice it. Either way, it still rested on the little block of wood.

But just as she was making herself comfortable on the couch with the egg, the bag from the occult shop vied for her attention. She wasn't going to do *everything* the woman suggested tonight, but a few of the things had made sense. It was just hard to take someone seriously when they were dressed like Morticia Addams, right down to the octopus fringe on the bottom of the dress and a black waist-length wig. But it couldn't hurt to pour salt on the windowsills, and she liked the idea of putting down a layer of painter's masking tape first, so the salt didn't eat the paint or dry out the wood. The best thing she came across in the shop, though, was the big old iron ladle. It reminded her of some of the old incantations Baba used to do to rid someone of the "black lady," the carrier of ill health and the evil eye. Since some of the other incantations had worked in the healings, perhaps this one could keep evil from the house.

She didn't bother with the old tongue, for the moon and sun wouldn't need to hear her. Plus, it had worked just fine underground without the words. *Purpose and intent.* Just like Tal had said. She climbed the stairs and walked up to Sela's door, feeling completely foolish. She lit the sandalwood candle and let the smoke fill the hallway with a warm, earthy scent. Gradually, the embarrassment passed and she began to breathe slowly, let purpose fill her. When she spoke, it came out as a booming command that echoed down the hallway. "Black lady, why do you come here? You good-for-nothing, you mustn't show yourself. You may not dwell here among the light. I give you three tasks." She held up the dipper and then placed it on the floor next to the door. "One task—fetch water for me from far away, where people cannot tread." Then she held up a tuning fork that had also come from the occult shop. "Second task, make the rocks hum, far from here where roosters don't sing." Then she held up a bamboo walking stick, a cheap one from the drugstore. "Third task, lean on this and travel to where the icy winds dance. Be gone and never return again."

She felt an odd sensation, like her ears popping, and the air felt clearer. Ozone mingled in her nose with the sandalwood. "Wow, did that actually *work?*" And if so, what did it do?

All she could really do was hope for the best and cross her fingers. She went back downstairs and had nearly resumed her place on the couch when her stomach growled audibly. It occurred to her that she hadn't eaten all day. Well, if she hoped to be able to do anything productive, food should probably be next on the list.

Sadly, the vegetables in the crisper weren't very crisp anymore and, if the black squishy spots were any indication, not terribly healthy, either. She was sick to death of TV dinners and frozen pizza, but didn't feel like cooking a real meal. That left the borscht her mom had insisted she take home as leftovers from Christmas dinner, even though Christmas hadn't really happened yet. It was always fun as a kid to have *two* holidays—the school one and the church one. Christmas wasn't actually held in the Ukrainian calendar until January because they still used the old Julian calendar. Plus, she *loved ushki*—the little mushroom dumplings, and Mom always put in lots, so it wasn't a hard choice.

Soon the house was filled with the wonderful aroma of spiced beets, and her hunger kicked into high gear. She ate the entire container that she originally figured would last two meals.

Then it was back to the pysanky. By the time she looked up again, it was after midnight. The score was *duszat*–1, Mila–0. No matter how much she poked and prodded it, waved her hand over it or thought, yelled and occasionally *screamed* at it, the pysanka just sat there looking pretty, albeit a little charred.

I've got to get to bed or I'm going to be useless tomorrow. Or today, or whatever. That prompted a yawn. Closing her eyes made them burn, meaning she hadn't blinked for too long again. It was a problem when she made eggs, so she recognized it, but it meant she definitely needed some sleep. She was halfway up the stairs when she heard a noise that sounded like the door handle being rattled. She leaned over slightly so just her head was out from behind the wall. That was *exactly* what that sound was. But it wasn't merely that the knob was rattling, it was *opening*. Her eyes flicked to the control panel, to see the comforting red light. *Great job, Mila. Arm the system, set the chain, and leave the stupid door unlocked!*

She stood, transfixed, as the knob continued to turn. Finally, it began to inch open . . . and the beautiful, wonderful alarm panel started to beep. If she didn't enter her code in thirty seconds, it would trip a silent alarm at the police station and let out an ear-splitting shriek that could raise the dead from the ground. Since she wasn't armed, she'd wait to see if the person left or broke in. There was always that handy iron ladle in the hallway if it came down to it. Mostly, she was content to see what happened, and that seemed really odd to her. But the system needed testing anyway and she couldn't imagine what could cause her to turn it off at this point.

"Mila? What's that beeping? Are you okay?"

"Tal?" Her jaw dropped and her legs felt weak. The beeping increased in volume and speed, to let her know there were only ten seconds left. She raced down the stairs so fast that she didn't remember touching the last three treads. Four buttons later and the beeping stopped and the system went back to standby. She looked out the small crack the chain permitted and couldn't keep a smile from her face. "It *is* you. Hang on." She shut the door so fast and hard it probably clipped his nose. And then the door was open and he was there. Just standing there staring at her as though lost for words. She motioned to the wall with her head. "New alarm system. Thought it would be a good idea . . . considering."

There were bags under his eyes and his shoulders were slumped. Still-wet mud decorated his cloak and the small bag he was carrying in a way that made it look like he'd been crawling through a wallow. He didn't take a single step forward but he did raise his brows and ask in a soft, worried voice, "Can I come in? Or are you speaking to me?"

Had she been mad at him? She couldn't really remember anymore. Nor could she think enough to speak. She did the only thing she could think of—she launched herself at him, her lips and arms finding him at exactly the same time.

She heard the thump of the bag on his shoulder hitting the stoop and then his arms were around her, with the same fierce need that she felt. Her feet weren't even touching ground so when he kicked his bag and stepped forward, she went with him. Another kick and the door slammed closed.

She pulled away after her lips, tongue, and hands had their fill, breathless and struggling to get her heartbeat back to normal. He smiled brilliantly and those deep dark eyes began to gleam with amusement. "I'll take that as, *yes, please come in.*"

"Yes, please come in . . . and don't spare the lips." He apparently accepted those terms, because she found herself bent backward at the waist having the daylights kissed out of her. It wasn't frantic this time, but instead slow and thorough. It weakened her knees and made things pull urgently deep in her body. "Will that do?"

She smiled and sighed. "That'll do nicely. You came back."

He nodded his head once, almost a bow. "I came back."

Then she remembered and her words took on a worried tone. "Not just for your glove, I hope?"

His brows raised and he stepped back one more pace so that her hands barely reached around his neck. "You have my glove? Where'd you find it? I've been trying to track it for hours but haven't had any luck." She looked down and finally noticed he already had on a glove, and the opal rested nicely in the hole. He looked around for it eagerly and she felt a bit of sadness invade the happiness when she walked to where her jacket hung on the hook and took it from her pocket.

"Here you go. It was in Sela's room. They came back while we were in Vril. Took all the eggs from the refrigerator, and left this stuck on the bed frame." She really didn't want to consider *how* it came to be stuck there, since . . . well, *eww!* With *Vegre?* "Is that all you needed? I have a bunch of new information, but I don't want to tell you just to have you laugh at me."

His face moved from amazed to stricken as he took the glove and then he picked up her hand and pressed it to his lips with eyes closed. It was less than a kiss, and more. Just that expression and action did more to lessen her annoyance with him than if he'd brought a dozen roses.

He kept holding her hand even after his lips left it. "You were right all along, so I want to hear *anything* you have to say. I want to stop Vegre, and the only way to do that is here in Denver . . . with *you.*" She opened her mouth, but he held up a hand. "I have to warn you, though. I left without permission. I'm supposed to be gating to London just about now, but I needed to be here to prove you right, so I snuck out. I don't know what they'll do to me if they catch me. I can't guarantee I'll survive a king's anger. The O.P.A. is part of the military, and they don't treat deserters very well."

He went AWOL? Just to prove her right? "Oh. Um, I—"

He shook his head and put a finger to her lips. "Don't say anything. I made my choice, Mila. If it turns out we're right, all will be forgiven . . . I *think.* But there's a really good *chance* it'll be forgiven, so I'm going with that." He looked around the room, probably noticing all the small details that had changed while Bryan and the others were installing the magnets. "What's been happening here? Why are you still even awake at this hour?"

He took off his cloak and heavy sweater to reveal a form-fitting uniform that looked like it was silk, but was too thick. The sleeves ended just below the elbow, leaving those lovely, muscular forearms bare. She pulled her drooling gaze away long enough to show him the eggs that people had delivered. A few of them started to glow the moment he was near. That's when Viktor's words came back to her and she slapped the palm of her hand repeatedly against her forehead. "He asked whether *you* were in the room when the first one went off, not *me!* The eggs respond to *crafters,* magicworkers, not the artist. Duh."

It gave her hope, because the pysanky that had responded to Tal had mage symbols nearly identical to the ones she'd made for the Tree . . . and to the one on his arm. And since he didn't have blood from any other guild, which Jason had mentioned, the others naturally wouldn't react to him. She started lining up the eggs with similar patterns and yes—there were four of each. That would repair the other three Trees, plus the master Tree—wherever it was.

She yawned again, involuntarily and with her hands full she had no choice but to let him see the fillings in her wide open mouth. "God it's been a long day."

"What all have you done around here? It looks like you've been busy."

She nodded, because she *had* been. She gave him a tour, including Sela's door and the trip wire, and even explained what had happened when she'd said the healing incantation.

He picked up the iron ladle and shook his head. "I can't imagine *how* it would work, but a great number of our spells are from the region. I bear a name from that stock myself, although I'm not aware of any full humans in my family tree. Just to be safe, though, I think I should cast a few protection charms on the doorway."

He brought his hand forward, stiff-armed like she remembered Sela doing on that first day. "Oh!" Mila exclaimed loud enough for the sound to echo. Tal turned his head before he could cast. "That reminds me." She told him all about her visit to the hotel with Candy, and seeing Sela. But especially seeing *Sybil*. "I'm afraid they might be planning to use her as a hostage in case you arrive."

He let out a growl and drummed on the wall with his fingertips. "They'll try to use her as leverage, at least. But finding the pysanky around the hotel has given us valuable knowledge. I think our best bet is to go straight to the hotel and see if we can destroy those eggs."

She nearly whimpered as her shoulders dropped. "I can barely *move* after everything that's happened today, Tal. Remember that I was up *hours* before you, making pysanky."

He stopped and looked at her then, *really* looked. She knew what he was seeing because she'd already looked in the mirror last time she went to the bathroom. Her skin was pale, and there were wide, dark bags under her eyes. Every inch of her felt like great weights were attached that she would have to drag forward with each step she took. "You're right. You need sleep. Go to bed. I'll take care of it. I can use a cloaking spell to avoid being seen by the hotel staff."

She looked him up and down. "Um, have I mentioned that you look like shit, too? You have mud all over your cloak and there are bruises on your face and arms. What exactly happened to you on the way from Vril to here?"

He rolled his eyes and looked at one particularly nasty bruise near his elbow that also was covered with tiny abrasions, like it was a rug burn. "Sheer stupidity on my part, I'm afraid. I underestimated the security system at the library. The gate from the butcher shop still worked, but I didn't want to wait until morning to get out."

She winced. "You really didn't go out the fire door, did you?"

He shook his head. "Thought about it, but it was locked. I figured a simple cloaking spell would be perfect to reach the front door or an employee entrance." He chuckled with self-deprecation. "Not so. It didn't occur to me that they would protect mere books with a laser grid that would trip a silent alarm."

Her eyes widened. "Wow. Wouldn't occur to me, either. So the cops came?"

He nodded. "Fortunately, they have no magicwielders on the force, or someone would have felt the spell. But in my hurry to leave, I slipped on a patch of ice and went face first into the street. Nearly got hit by a passing snowplow before I could roll out of the way."

It was one of those stories that got funnier the more she tried to visualize it, so she forcibly banished it from her mind before she laughed openly. But she couldn't erase the smile. "Sorry."

"It's okay," he said with a shake of his head and frustrated chuckle. "In a day or two it'll be funny to me, too. But for now it just hurts, and neither of us have the strength to heal it. So I think you're correct that I should get some sleep, too. Let's get the spells laid and retire."

And let's get the Mila laid, too. Before *we retire.* She didn't say it out loud, because he had already returned to his casting pose. *"Trywoha . . . ataka . . . bezpeka."* She saw color glow in the opal and felt a gentle wave of warmth flow over her. It was a soft, comforting sensation and made her mind a little fuzzy. But it was during that moment she noticed Tal's birthmark glowing. But it flickered oddly in the middle, where it was only a shadow, rather than a solid line.

She didn't want to distract him until he was done casting, but the moment he lowered his arm, she stepped closer and picked it up. "Does this always glow when you're doing magic?" He nodded and she felt her brow furrow as she fingered the mark. The skin where it was faded felt *different* than the surrounding skin, and she suddenly recalled Viktor's words. "Has there ever been a king named Reginald down there?"

He looked at her oddly. "That's the king of Rohm, where I live."

"Has he been king since before your parents died?"

Tal pursed his lips and shook his head. "No. His father, King Edward, ruled until I was about thirty. But Reginald's had the throne ever since."

She wasn't really speaking to Tal, but her words reached air anyway, instead of just appearing in her mind. "Then why would he want to mutilate you?"

Now Tal pulled his arm away and looked at it, as though searching for whatever she was seeing. "What are you talking about?"

She let out a deep breath and tapped the side of her mouth as she thought. "When you went to get the scrolls at Viktor's, he told me that he knew your parents and that the guild was thrilled when you were born because they had high hopes for you. But then Prince Reginald *mutilated* you and everyone was sad. Have you ever noticed the skin feels different where your mark is really faint?"

Now he was staring at it, too, and touching it lightly with a curious look on his face. "I *have* noticed that, but never thought much about it. I can't imagine why the king would do something like that. I'm not in line for the throne, and none of my family has even a drop of royal blood. Reginald's family has reigned over the mages since the world was new, and became ruler of Rohm when Agathia was created. As far as I know, there's never been an attempt to overthrow him, nor any scandals that might make him see me as any sort of threat. But—" He, too, was now musing out loud. "It *would* explain why I'm so long lived. Nobody has been able to adequately explain why a mage of my limited ability has existed for centuries. Normally, long life is reserved for the powerful born."

That gave her an idea. "Well, Viktor suggested that I'd do your people a great service if I could heal you. But I haven't a clue *how*. I would have thought that'd happen when I healed you earlier. But when I gazed you, I didn't notice that area as *needing* healing."

He shrugged. "I can do magic just fine. I'm not a particularly powerful caster, but I'm above most."

"Still, if we *could* bring you up to full power, we'd have a better chance against Vegre and Sela. Right?" She shook her head, her thoughts growing muddy. "But my brain isn't working right now, so let's sleep on it and try a healing again in the morning." She yawned again and this time it was catching. Tal's mouth opened wide enough that she heard his jaw pop lightly.

He winced and rubbed the area. "Falling face first to the pavement didn't help my physical condition. I may take you up on the offer of a healing in the morning. But for now—" He reached out his hand and wiggled his fingers, so she slipped hers into his waiting grasp. "I want to feel your skin against mine while I fall asleep."

She couldn't think of anything she wanted more, either. All they had to do was follow the trail of gray fur that ended with the fluffy lump on her bed. She doubted Mr. Whiskers had moved all day—he'd even slept through the security company invading every room in the house with noisy power tools. She'd swear he was dead except for the content rumbling that made the fur rise and fall. But he was soon interrupted by Tal picking him up gently and setting him on the floor. "I fear there won't be room for you tonight."

The cat looked at both of them indignantly before baring white fangs in a yawn and walking out the door to begin his nightly patrols. She'd put food down for him when she fed herself, and he'd find it when he was hungry.

"We should probably leave the door open so we can hear . . . *things.*"

Tal nodded. "I placed spells of security, alarm, and attacking on the door. Since they already defeated the wards Alexy cast, they'd be expecting new ones on the *room.* I'm hoping they won't notice them on the door. The alarm of clarion trumpets should wake us and we should be able to get to them before they can stop the door from assaulting them."

"Can you guys get through a dead bolt? I wasn't sure what all to do to the door."

He shook his head. "We can *create* physical items, but can't really affect those that already exist, except by sheer destruction. Guilders can't manipulate a lock without picks, but someone could *craft* the picks and then use them, which is why putting a block on magic in the room seemed prudent."

A movement of light caught her eye as the red digital numbers of the clock changed to one A.M. She couldn't even *remember* the last time she'd been up this late—and after waking in Vril at three. Sheesh!

Tal closed the door until there was just a crack showing, about the width of the cat and then shrugged at her raised brows. "We might need some small measure of privacy, after all." He walked toward her, pulling his shirt over his head as he did. She'd never gotten the chance to really *look* at him last time, since she'd been too busy *feeling* his body to bother looking. Her body tightened just watching all those muscles flex. When he reached out his bare arm toward her, she noticed a small design on his upper arm—a stylized sun. She couldn't help but touch it and he let out an appreciative sigh as she stroked her fingers over the mark. It wasn't raised like the one on his forearm, but didn't look like a tattoo, either.

She planned to ignore it, wanted to, but her mind switched tracks, moved from fun back to work. "Is this a birthmark, too? Does it glow when you craft?"

He looked at it and gave a small shrug that moved her hand. "No, it's just a tattoo. It's the symbol of the mage guild, given to me when I entered the academy. Everyone got one, so the instructors would know at a glance that a student had been tested and what sort of magic they could craft. I don't really know whether it glows. I can't say that I've looked. Normally, I'm crafting with clothing on . . . or at least not in front of a mirror."

"Do some magic, then." She pointed to her dresser. "Light those candles." This time he did magic without a word. He simply flicked a finger, the opal glowed, and flames appeared inside the cobalt glass holder. But she saw all that from the corner of her eye, because she was watching the mark. "Yeah, it glowed a little." A smile pulled at her lips. "Perfect."

He shook his head. "What? What have you thought of?"

There was no time to explain, and she really didn't think she *could* explain it. She patted him on the arm and moved past him. "Stay here. I'll be right back."

Her studio was on the ground floor, near the kitchen so she could wash up in the sink and not get dye all over everything. She lifted the light switch and started eyeing her jars of dye. She couldn't get her mind off the memory of her foot heating up when the water in the well was sucking her down, or the bubbles that rose *from* her foot to give her air. The designs above her toes had never disappeared, even though they'd just been painted on. "Let's see—" she muttered softly, remembering that pretty rhyme from long ago, when Baba painted them. "Blue for the water where life was born, yellow for the sun that keeps us warm, green for the leaves that fill the air, and black for the earth that's never bare." She reached for the yellow dye bottle as well as the slender pointed paintbrush she kept around for touch-ups. Then, almost as an afterthought, she added the bottle of red dye to the pile. It was the color on her foot of the fifth design, the meander road . . . the symbol of the Parask. A road with no end, eternity—from where evil could never escape to harm.

Burdens in hand, she started back up the stairs. *Time to see if I can make a little magic.*

*M*ila walked in the room, carrying a pair of bottles of colored liquid, and a paintbrush sticking out of the front pocket of her pants. "Wouldn't it have been easier for me to go downstairs than for you to drag all that up here?" He looked at her askance, wondering what she was up to. "Are those *egg* dyes?"

She swept a hand across the dresser, pushing small bottles and knickknacks to one side so she could put the jars down. "Room's too small for two. I barely fit in there myself with the bench and shelves. And yes, they're dyes." She started to unscrew the tops and pointed at an elegant chair in the corner of the room, heaped with clothing. "Bring that over here and have a seat. You can just dump the clothes on the floor. I forgot to bring the laundry basket upstairs last time I did a wash load."

Her voice had changed from warm and soft to commanding, businesslike. He crossed his arms over his chest and didn't move toward the chair. "First tell me what you're planning."

She let out a harsh, frustrated breath as if every moment he took to understand was wasting time. But when he didn't move except to raise his brows purposefully, she leaned one arm on the dresser and regarded him. "I'm going to fix that birthmark. The same way Baba did my foot. So if you could *please* sit down? I'm tired and trying hard not to sound as cranky as I feel."

Seeing her like this was a valuable insight, for it said she was willing to show less than her optimum personality to him. Kris had once told him that a woman has to feel very comfortable with a man to show her . . . *aggressive* side if it's not her normal state. But it raised his own, because he refused to be bullied. He wondered how she'd react to having her own words thrown back at her. "No. Not another step until you explain what you're intending."

If she recognized the reference to when she was at the Tree, she gave no sign. "It's not rocket science, Tal. I thought you could figure this out. Baba *painted* my foot. Paint that stuck and has remained unchanged for over twenty years." She pulled the paintbrush from her pocket. "I dip this in the dye and darken the line of your birthmark. Although, maybe it would work better if I first outline it in hot wax, like a pysanka. Not sure about that part yet. Anyway, I do it *with purpose,* like you said. If it works, you should go up to full strength. If it doesn't work, you have a little dye to scrub off in the shower. No big deal."

If his face revealed any of the outrage or fear that filled him, he must look horrified indeed. "Yes, big deal. *Not sure? Should? Maybe?* You are a magicwielder, Mila. Those aren't words you dare use to begin a crafting, and certainly not on *my* body. What if instead of just rinsing off dye, I'm no longer able to craft at all? What if it kills us both?" He shook his head and took a step backward, almost involuntarily. "No. It's not important enough to me to risk it."

She sighed and lowered her head with a small shake. "Would you please just *trust me?*"

"The last time I trusted you, you stole my faith." He didn't intend for the words to slip out, but once in the air he couldn't take them back. They were bitter, accusatory, and made a great tightness in his chest form. He thought he'd gotten past it, but apparently he hadn't.

She looked up then, her mouth wide with shock. "What?"

He turned away from her to stare at the door, unable to look at that expression—so surprised, so completely unaware of the effect she'd had . . . the damage she'd done. "For centuries we've believed the Trees are sacred, born fully formed of the earth itself and possessed of a pure spirit that guides us. They called us *home* from the overworld to begin a new life underground. They led us away from the corruption of mankind, to where we wouldn't have to hide our crafting from view or bury it amongst the *science* that humans favored."

He threw up his hands in frustration and turned around to find her sitting on the bed, a look on her face that was close to tears. But he wouldn't hide from this nor shy away because of a little discomfort. "But then along you came, with no knowledge at all of our ways, took our truths and spit them back as lies. The Trees are just trees, magic we felt was Tree-given is just pretty eggs made by other Guilders and stuffed inside the branches. Our guiding spirit is nothing more than smoke. So you tell me—why should I trust you in this . . . *painting* session that could end everything *else* I know?"

Tears were now rolling freely down Mila's face. Her voice came out in a whisper. "Oh, Tal—" She cleared her throat and then stood. Her hand touched his and while he didn't pull away, he wasn't sure he welcomed her touch. "I had no idea. This is all so new to me that I never gave your history a second thought."

He nodded and couldn't help the bitter laugh. "And that's the hardest part to bear—*knowing* it was all an accident for you. The scroll from the garden could have been any other fairy tale, until it came true."

Now she let out a little sniff that carried a similar bitter humor. "Or *geeders* who live in burrows like squelk coming to life and stepping out of a glowing gate in my spare room? In that, I *do* know how you feel." But then her face filled with something close to wonder and she squeezed his hand. "But don't you see, Tal? You're taking the bits of what you know that have just been altered as proof positive that the whole story, the whole belief system, is false. It's throwing the baby out with the bathwater. There's nothing in that scroll that said the Parask *planted* the trees. I read it again, so I *know*. I mean, who ever heard of underground trees that give off magic instead of oxygen? And illusion aside, what trees can live in darkness and still produce green leaves and fruit?"

The question was a good one, but he didn't have an answer. "But it's . . ."

She smiled then, and it was filled with hope and something that tied his stomach in knots and made his heart beat faster. "Who *says* the spirit doesn't exist? Who says it, or he or she didn't create *both* the Parask and the other Guilders in a sort of check and balance, to teach humility and cooperation? Conjurers can make magic from life energy but can't use it . . . you can use it, but not create it. I mean, I was raised to believe in another God, but the principle isn't all that different—we're all the same, yet all unique, so be nice to each other because we all have to live together and depend on one another." She leaned in and kissed him gently on the cheek. "I don't think I proved your spirit doesn't exist, Tal. I think I proved it *does*." She winked and let go of his hand. "Now, I'm going to run down and get my kistka while you mull that over. Then I'll do your mark if you want me to, and think you can *trust me* to do it. If not, then you know where the spare room is. I'll just go to bed and we'll see how we're both feeling in the morning."

He stood there, blinking like an idiot as she walked out, trying to wrap his head around the concepts she'd raised. Was this why Alexy had seemed so excited when he'd learned of Mila's healing? Could his friend's faith have made the leap to the logic . . . the leap he himself hadn't until this moment? Because she was right. Someone or some*thing* had given her people the gift of creating magic. Why not the Tree spirit? For they were called home to Agathia, too. It was only the other Guilders who pushed them away in arrogance and fear. Could it be that the guild priests who had later become Tree gatherers had done it intentionally? What had crafters believed in before the Trees? Was it the same God that Mila did? They lived and loved among one another once, after all.

What was it King Mumbai had said to Dareen—that Stella forcibly opened his eyes to see the whole truth? "What a good queen *should* do."

"I'm sorry . . . *what?*" Mila had come back in the room, carrying a well worn red kistka, paint flaking off beneath the blackened metal tip.

He shook his head and smiled. "Just remembering some good advice." He grabbed her arm before she made it past him and kissed her gently on the lips. "Thank you for helping me see past my blindness."

She smiled and licked her lips, as though reaching for the last taste of something sweet. "We all have blind spots. Sometimes what it takes is a little outside perspective. Are you better now, or should I just put this stuff away?"

He nodded and realized that everything in the room seemed a little brighter, as though a dark filter had been lifted from the colors. His heart was beating not just faster, but stronger. "Yes, I think I'm better now. Better than I've been in a very long time." He looked at his mark and while he felt the fear beginning to creep in once more, it was softened . . . tempered by something. *Trust.* Her skill was undeniable and her instincts sound. He could do far worse than to have her mend him, and now couldn't imagine any harm befalling him. "I've still no idea if this will work, but I do trust you." Another smile that reflected the sensation that was growing in his chest. "How could I *not* trust the woman I seem to have fallen in love with?"

Again those wide green eyes and dropped jaw that made her mouth look so kissable. So he did. It was worth being stabbed by the sharp metal in his ribs as he took her into his arms and tasted the sweet fire of her mouth. He rained kisses from her mouth to her ear and then to the curve of her shoulder while cupping her breast and flicking a thumb against her hard tight nipple. He wanted to lick that nipple again, pull on it, bite it and hear her moan and grow wet and ready for him.

She went limp and pliant in his arms. He let out a small, possessive growl and slid his teeth along the pulse in her neck, which was quickening wickedly, throbbing in time to the urgent pressure of his cock. "The only question is whether I can stand to wait to be inside you again until after you do your crafting."

She shivered hard enough to raise bumps on her skin and let out a nervous chuckle. "I might forget how if I don't do it now. I seem to lose my mind every time you touch me."

He leaned back just slightly, inches from her face, and let his lower lip slide across hers while he continued to tease her breasts. "I like that," he whispered. "I like that I drive you mad. You drive me nearly beyond my limit of restraint."

She stared at him strongly, her eyes intense enough he couldn't help but look. "I love you, too." She touched her lips to his softly and ran a slow hand across the swelling in his crotch, weakening his knees. "It doesn't make any sense, but I do. And I swear I won't do anything to hurt you. I'll make you *better.*"

He pulled her hand away from him before he couldn't turn back from the need and released her breast with a final pinch that pulled a gasp from her. "You already have."

Once he got used to the sensation of the hot wax on his skin, it wasn't too bad. The trick was that they had both gotten so aroused that it was difficult to make the wax *cool* enough to be a barrier for the dye. Finally Mila resorted to going downstairs and retrieving a tray of ice cubes. After that, it was no trouble at all to finish her crafting. She dipped the funnel of the kistka right in the scented candles on the dresser and shrugged when he raised brows. "They're beeswax, and I didn't feel like hauling up that huge block in the studio."

He wanted to say that it felt amazing or that magic filled the air. But it just looked like yellow dye, his mark darker for the intense brightness of it, so when she asked, "Feel anything?" he could only shrug.

"Nothing at all, other than my arm's cold. And what are you doing now?" She had moved the kistka to a new spot, just below his guild mark.

"Oh, nothing. I just thought I'd do a couple more pictures while I was here and in the mood. This one will be an oak leaf, which is the pysanka symbol of spiritual strength—in case you ever feel lost again." It was done in seconds, before he could really react—her hand moving swift and sure now that she'd figured out how to make the drawings on skin. "And this one is our symbol—the Parask road, so evil gets lost and can never reach your soul."

"Not, of course, as any sort of reminder of you?" he said dryly, which made her smile.

"Of course not. But it is sort of common—artist's license. Call it a signature of my work." With a chuckle, she blew out both candles, apparently done with her crafting.

By the time she rubbed off the wax to reveal the bright yellow markings, he was laughing along with her. It didn't last long, though. Not after she turned those wide eyes to him again and parted those luscious lips a tiny bit. He leaned in and kissed her again, moving his jaw against hers until he heard the kistka clatter to the wooden floor. Then it was just a matter of pulling her off the rolling desk chair she was sitting on into his lap. The weight against his sudden erection made him moan and shift until he found a spot that wasn't so sensitive. He pulled back and pushed back a long curled black hair that had fallen across her eye. "I think it's time for bed."

He reveled in the way she squirmed as he slowly unbuttoned her blouse, kissing his way down her chest with each bit of skin that was revealed. She kicked off the light slip-on shoes she wore—much better than the heavy boots that required unlacing. She helped things along by standing up to pull off her pants and underwear. "I'd do it slow, but my poor body's just about worn out. I don't want to waste what energy I have left."

He couldn't argue, since he felt the same. So he just smiled and followed suit. She reached for his erection after he was fully nude and his brain stopped trying to think. Slowly she stroked him until every inch in his body was screaming for release. He heard the ripping of plastic and then a new, wet sensation over the sensitive nerves. His eyes opened and he saw that she'd found the box of condoms he'd bought on his way here and had put one on.

Mila smirked and tickled the hairs on his legs, which nearly made him drop. "Pretty brazen to buy some on the way, when you thought I was mad at you."

His tongue flicked out over his dry lips. "Hope springs eternal." She rose to her feet and took his hand, pulling gently toward the thickly piled bed and turned off the light. When he followed her under the covers it was like sinking into a cloud, buoyed in a way that made him feel like there was nothing above or below them. "What sort of bed is this?"

"Down mattress. But they don't make them anymore." She stifled any more questions with her mouth over his and then she pulled him over on top of her.

There was no question of her readiness. She was so wet and swollen that he nearly fell inside her. And then there were only sounds and sensations as the need rode them both.

Tal felt her body tighten around him just as his own climax found him and then they were locked together, cries reaching ears that could barely hear. But then he felt a burning sensation in his forearm that grew in intensity the longer he erupted inside her. Moments later, his other arm began to burn until his cries were a completely different variety. He struggled to pull his arms from under her to see what was wrong but by the time he could, the pain had dimmed to nearly nothing.

"What's wrong?" Her voice was still breathless with pleasure, but she sensed all wasn't well with him.

"Something stung my arm." He rolled off and turned on the lamp. She leaned over the top of them and both of them just stared. The astonishment he felt was mirrored on her face at the image on his arm. The yellow dye was gone. In its place was a new mark, darker than it had ever been and whole—unbroken and still glowing slightly.

"Wow. The other arm, too!" Mila stared at her own hands like they were some sort of weapon that had discharged without her knowledge. But she was right. The oak leaf and Parask symbol had burrowed into his skin, raised a welt that was now skin instead of ink. He didn't think it would be going away anytime soon.

She bit at her lower lip. "Can you still do magic? Can you light the candles?"

She'd taken off his focus glove—wonderfully slowly with her teeth, and it was still buried somewhere beneath the sheets. But he didn't need it for this. He flicked his finger, like always, but what erupted from the candle was a blast of blue-white flame that nearly reached the ceiling.

Mila let out a shriek and pulled the blanket up to shield her bare skin from the heat. He immediately put out the flame, but his heart was pounding like a hammer against a forge when he did it. His voice sounded a little hollow and more than a little shaky when he spoke. "I'd say you fixed my mark."

She nodded, her head moving slowly at first and then speeding up until she was bobbing. "Uh, yeah. You could say that. But is it a good thing or a bad thing?"

"That is the question."

That was most *definitely* the question.

CHAPTER 20

*M*ila walked into the party, a tense smile painted on her face. She tried desperately to make it seem like she was just distracted with making sure the party ran well, but it was a lie.

Oh, she was distracted all right, but not because of the details. Every pysanka she and Candy had spotted were now *gone*. She'd felt her heart in her throat when she'd taken Tal to the first location in Candy's notes and discovered it missing. By the time they'd reached the sixth hiding place on the list and found it empty, her heart was no longer in her throat, but sitting like lead in her stomach.

"Mila! Glad I finally found you." She turned to see Rick and his wife Lydia entering the room, dressed to the nines. She broadened her smile until her lips felt like they would rip, but her jaws were clenched tight. God! She *knew* these people. They were her friends, her colleagues. She couldn't just watch them burn to death in an explosion of lava!

Lydia touched her dress. "That is so *lovely* on you, Mila—and I must say you've done a terrific job with this party. Rick's told me all about the weird things the other partners wanted to add, and I know how frustrating it must have been to try to please everyone." Lydia was being kind about the purple-and-black sequined dress. Yes, it was pretty and, in fact, her favorite party dress. But it was not in the same league as the designer originals being worn by some of the other women and Mila knew it.

"Thanks, guys. So, you're probably just here for a few minutes before you jet off to the next party, huh?" Lord, she hoped so. She'd worked with Rick too long, and knew all his kids. They deserved to have their father for a lot longer.

But Rick shook his head. "Nope. Just one party this year. We decided after last year's blizzard that stuck us on I-70 for two hours that making the rounds was just asking for trouble. We even rented a room here so we don't have to brave the traffic until tomorrow morning."

Mila fought with every breath not to break down and cry. But then a voice hissed in her ear and the tears disappeared, to be replaced by a rush of adrenaline. "Mila, dear. We need to talk. *Now.*"

Tal put a hand on her lower back and started to guide her away. But it wasn't that easy. She skidded to a stop which made him have to turn to see why. "Tal, this is my *boss,* Rick Myers, and his wife Lydia. Rick, Lydia, Talos Onan." She started to attach a relationship to him, to explain why she'd brought him, but it was sort of obvious. He was her New Year's date, and looked good enough to eat in dark slacks, a fawn turtleneck, and sports coat that matched the pants. It had taken a frantic trip to the mall before they closed in order to find him something suitable. But it was worth it. If this was any other New Year's party, she'd already have dragged him to a dark corner to start the midnight kisses early.

But since it was instead the New Year's from hell, all she could do was admire him from afar until they could stop hell from arriving.

"A pleasure, folks. Mila's said some wonderful things about you, but I *really* need to take her away for a few minutes. It's a bit of a . . . crisis." The way he said it made her believe him and she turned wide eyes to him.

Rick noticed it, too. He always was good at reading body language and voice intonations. His face sobered, turned serious. "Of course. Go. We'll cover for you, Mila. I hope everything's okay."

She hurried away with him, trying to seem somewhat casual as they wove through the arriving guests.

"Hi, Mila! Glad you could make it." Rachel waved and motioned her over to the small group of other support staff.

She called words over her shoulder as she sped past. "Be right back. Have to take care of something."

Thankfully, nobody asked questions since they all knew she was the planner. Stop the party planner and you might stop the party.

When they finally made it to a quiet corner near a waterfall near the front window, she grabbed his arm and stopped to catch her breath. "What's the crisis?" He looked devastated and seemed to be trying to find the words. "Just tell me, Tal."

He took a deep breath and let it out slow, then put a hand on her shoulder. "Alexy and Kris showed up a few minutes ago, wanting to help. They covered my tracks in Vril and then gated in through the library. I sent them to start searching the hotel, looking for either Vegre's or Sela's magic signature, or any sign of the pysanky. But they're all gone."

"Do you think they've found out about the ones at the house? I *knew* we should have brought them along to guard them."

"Thank you—" The pleased musical tones drifted down to them. She and Tal looked up to see Sela, dressed in a shimmering silver gown and sparkling diamonds, leaning over the balcony above them. "Just what I needed to know. I knew you weren't nearly as tough . . . or *smart* as your grandmother, Mila."

"What do you mean, as *tough* as my grandmother?"

Tal tugged at her arm, trying to pull her away, which didn't make any sense. Why wasn't he racing up the stairs to capture her? She looked back and forth between them. Sela was acting too smug, and Tal seemed suddenly uncomfortable.

"Talk to me, Tal. What's happening?"

"Go ahead, Tal," Sela's voice taunted. "Feel free to tell her. We got what we needed. Or would you rather *I* told her? I *really* want her to know, and I'm sure your version would be . . . kinder."

Mila stared at him, fingers digging into his arm—willing

him to be honest. He glared up at Sela with a look that should be able to kill, and might have killed her in another place that wasn't so public. "I didn't plan to tell you, so you wouldn't worry. We did search the basement, Mila, like I said. We didn't find any pysanky, but we found something else instead. We found . . ." He took a deep breath and let it out slowly while Sela leaned on the railing, enjoying herself as thoroughly as if she was watching a movie. "We found your grandmother locked in the furnace room. She's . . . not in good shape. She's been beaten and tortured with magic."

It was a good thing she was holding his arm or she would have fallen to the ground. But when he felt her legs start to go, he grabbed her arm tightly and lowered her to the bench that surrounded the waterfall. "Baba? But . . . *why?*" She looked up at Sela, unsure whether to plead or scream. "Why?"

Sela shrugged, as though torture was no big thing. Mila had never *hated* a person in her life until that moment, but it was all she could feel for the woman who had once shared her home. "Because she had information we needed."

"But you didn't get it." There was a cold satisfaction in Tal's voice. "She told us that you got *nothing* from her. She told us instead. We already know how to stop you."

Sela was suddenly beneath Mila's notice. She could call her all the names in the world, or go up and kick the shit out of her, but it wouldn't change what was already done. The only thing she could think of was her grandmother. She could feel the pain flow through her as she thought about her, and knew it wasn't just her imagination. She grabbed his arm and pulled him toward her. "To hell with the party. To hell with Vegre and Sela and to hell with Denver. Take me to her, Tal. I can heal her and we'll forget all of this ever happened."

He shook his head and despite her panic, she couldn't help but feel comforted by his look of sympathy. "I can't do that, Mila. I promised Nadia I wouldn't tell you where she was taken."

"*What?!* Why would you do that? Why would *she* do

that? Tal, she's my grandmother. I have to help her." She
stood up, not even certain where to look. But she *had* to
look.

Tal grabbed her jaw, forced her face to turn to him.
"Mila, you made me see my own blindness. Now I have to
help you through yours. This is *exactly* what they want."
He pointed up at where Sela still watched them, arms
crossed and looking supremely amused. "Look at her!
They want you confused, and distraught . . . so you can't
think. That's why Nadia wanted to go, so you could concentrate. Listen to me—our healers will do everything
they can for her. *Everything*. With the Tree in Vril back up
there's enough power to take care of almost anything they
could have done. But *you're* needed here. You're the only
one who can figure this mess out. I need your mind here
with me, Mila." He searched her face and she knew her
tears were getting his sleeves wet. He pointed out to the
lobby with his other hand. "I *need* you if all those people
are going to live through the night. We can figure this out
together. But only if you don't react to this. Don't let them
win."

There must have been an incredulous look on her face if
it matched what she was feeling. "You must be *joking*.
How can I not react to this? I already want to launch myself at that bitch . . . beat her head into the floor until she
stops moving."

Sela's voice was calm and amused. "Even if you could . . .
which you couldn't, I'll have you kicked out of the hotel
or even better, tossed in jail. I would right now if there
weren't so many lawyers around. Remember that you're
not the one in power here. We are. And we'll be in power
for the rest of eternity, so get used to it." She wiggled her
fingers over her shoulder. "Tah. I need to get back to the
house before the party starts."

There was no way to reach her in time to keep her from
leaving, and Tal blasting her with magic would only serve
to bring the others. No doubt there were Children scattered among the guests, and Mila had already spotted Tal's

mother posing as a server. That's when it occurred to her that he was fighting his own battle with worry and anger. If he could remain focused, then so could she. Sela and Vegre must have wanted information about eggs, and she just bet that Sela was going back to search for more . . . maybe they hoped Baba could provide the names of the artists who delivered the eggs to her. "Don't you want to know about the security system, Sela?" She made her voice taunting. Tal stiffened beside her and looked at her as though insane for mentioning it.

The metallic rustle from above paused and she waited, offering Tal an open palm lightly moving in the air. She gave him a confident look, and got a worried *I hope you know what you're doing* one in return.

"*What* security system?" Sela's head had poked back over the rail. "I don't believe you."

She shrugged. She'd lived with Sela long enough to know what tripped her triggers. Curiosity was one of her weaknesses. "Then don't. But Bryan installed it yesterday. Doors, windows, motion sensors, plus silent *and* onsite alarms. The works. And you *know* how often the cops drive through our neighborhood." She did know, because she'd been the one to mention it. At the time, Mila had thought it mere curiosity on her part, but now she knew that the noticing was born of guilt and fear. Who knew how many O.P.A. agents were also overworld cops? It sure would be handy for the agency. "Oh, and did I mention the double-keyed dead bolt on *your* room?" She tapped her chin with one finger and appeared to think. "Hmm . . . can you find the pysanky before the police get there? See, I already had Jeff tell them that I kicked you out for stealing and that you or your friends might be back." Actually, that part was a lie, but she *should* have, and Sela would probably believe she'd think of it. She knew both Jeff and Bryan . . . knew that Bryan worked for one of the big two security companies and how close Jeff still was to his buddies at the station.

Her eyes narrowed and she let out a small growl that was barely audible over the sound of the party. "Tell me the code, or I swear I'll come down there and rip it out of you. I can, you know."

Mila spread out her hands helplessly. "I don't doubt you can. But I don't know it. I'm not the one who set the system. *Tal* did." She flicked her eyes over to him. He was smiling darkly now, one brow raised as he stared at his onetime partner, arms crossed over his chest. The dark suit made him look every inch a mage, and a cop. Yummy. "Somehow I doubt you'll get it out of *him*. What do you think?"

She believed, and her face twisted, turning her careful makeup into a mask, a parody of the elegant lady she wanted to be. *"Bitch."*

Mila stuck out her tongue. Yes, it was childish, but she felt like doing something immature at this moment. *"Witch.* You'd better hurry, too. There are agents all over the hotel, just waiting to tighten the noose on you and Vegre . . . *Mrs. Pierce."* Part truth, part bluff. Would Sela know which was which? Her former friend's head moved almost involuntarily, eyes searching the crowd. Looking for a familiar face, perhaps? Then the eyes widened and her hands tightened to white on the rail. Mila followed her gaze and spotted Alexy just stepping off the internal elevator from the basement. What incredible timing! He, too, was dressed in a suit, his blond hair carefully styled. He looked quite elegant and perfectly at home in the hotel.

She did exactly what Mila expected her to do. She turned and bolted. No doubt she'd go running back to Vegre to tell the tale, which was precisely the point.

Tal had raised his hand to catch Alexy's eye, who noticed and started weaving through the crowd toward them. "Well, that was fun . . . but I don't know what good it did. Now they have time to prepare."

She nodded and stood, smoothing her dress as she did. She suddenly felt a little more confident. "Yep. And now they *have* to prepare. Nothing like forcing the opponent to put their defensive squad on the field to keep the score down." She had no idea whether Tal followed football up here, but if he'd been stationed here at one point, he should at least understand the reference.

He raised his brows and nodded with a surprised expression that soon turned to admiration. "They'll split their resources. If they believe the *duszats* are at the house, they'll *have* to send someone there, and will probably send quite a few to effect a search before the police can arrive. I notice you didn't mention the defensive spells I laid."

Mila opened her mouth as though surprised. "Oh, *didn't* I? How careless of me." A small chuckle escaped her. "Frankly, I'd *love* to be there to see the bedroom door slapping one of them around. Those are damned heavy things. Maybe it'll even be Sela."

Tal likewise chuckled just as Alexy joined them and then spoke to him. "What news do you bring, old friend?"

They clasped forearms in greeting. "Kris has been trying to reach you. Seems she can't get through to flash your mark—keeps getting feedback and static, like her call is just bouncing off. I expect it's a result of your new power." He tipped his head to Mila, taking in her outfit with an appreciative glance. "Amazing talent of yours, Mila. When this is done, I'm sure the kings will be courting your favor. That is—" he amended, "if Tal doesn't blow himself up first. Try not to get startled again." He jerked a thumb toward Tal with a grim smile. "Nearly took off our heads, he did, when we first arrived. We barely got shields up in time and the basement still smells of smoke. We had to take away his focus in self-defense."

She didn't really hear much after the kings wanting her favor, and just nodded blankly. She hadn't even considered the possibility of what it would *mean* that she fixed Tal's mark. While it was flattering, it was also worrying. "Do we *have* to tell them? I can't imagine a *king* would be willing to take no for an answer."

He shrugged noncommittally. "I've no idea. But I'll keep it mum if you wish. Though I think you're a bit crackers to not take advantage of it. You could have your heart's desire, just for the askin'."

"The only *desire* I have right now is waking up tomorrow, safe in my bed. Is Baba okay? Has she been healed?" She realized she was twisting her fingers nervously, and shook them to make herself stop. Part of it might have been that Alexy's other comment had finally sunk home. They'd taken Tal's focus away because he couldn't control his new power. It was a side effect that had never occurred to her. He'd spent most of the day working with both focus gloves and was damned glad she hadn't gotten the extra option of the smoke detector with the security system. As it was, he'd been concentrating so hard he hadn't noticed the several small fires he'd started in various places, and she had to take to keeping a bucket of dirt from the backyard handy. No way was she going to spray a fire extinguisher around the house or drown the expensive antiques until she had a deed in her hot little hand.

Alexy nodded but his face didn't light up with relief which dragged her attention back to him. His expression went blankly serious, and Tal reached around her to pull her close. Mila let him—drew on his strength to hear the news. "She's not out of the woods, not by any means. She's stable, because the physical damage was quite easy to repair. But some of the curses they laid on her were bloody complicated. The healers fear that even a simple counterspell will set off something else, like triggering a bomb in a crowded market. It might be that Vegre *wanted* you to find her. We just don't know yet."

That made her think. "It's possible. I didn't get that impression from Sela just now, but I suppose *she* might not know the entire plan, either. Once a betrayer, always one, so Vegre might be keeping her out of the whole plan."

That made Alexy look around with an angry expression. "You've seen Sela, then? Where is that traitorous witch?"

Mila pointed up to the balcony. "You just missed her. And she knows you're here. Spotting you is what made her bolt."

Alexy snorted and clenched his fists. "She *should* run. She knows I'd bury her alive and leave her there."

Tal was tapping her on the shoulder with the hand around her. She looked up at him, but he was staring off into space, which didn't surprise her. She'd noticed that habit today while they were making plans—deciding who would do what. She nudged him with her hip. "What are you thinking?"

He jumped slightly and blinked. "Hmm? Oh, um . . . I just tried to flash Kris and couldn't reach her from this end, either. I tried you, too, Alexy. You didn't get any tingle?"

Now Alexy's brow was furrowing. "No, and that *is* odd. Even if the connection is fuzzy, I should get *something*. He turned his arm palm side up and stared at it. Then he shook his head. "And now I can't reach Kris, either. But the signal was just fine outside."

It actually made Tal smile. No, more . . . *grin*. "Only one thing I know that blocks mark flashing."

Alexy clapped Tal on the shoulder, also grinning. "Squelk. He's got squelk around here somewhere. *That* must be how he's planning to divert the magma."

She must have looked as confused as she felt, because Tal turned to her, his face animated. "Sometimes when you alter nature with magic, odd things happen. One of those things is squelk. They're big and tame, like cattle, except during rut. Then they chatter to attract each other, so high pitched our ears can't hear it. But the magic we use to contact others through our marks is affected."

Alexy nodded, tapping his hand on his leg. "And they chatter *constantly*, like echolocation."

"Okay," she said with a shrug. "So how does that help us? He couldn't have them hidden in the hotel, cattle or not. They're just too big. So how will knowing change anything?"

Alexy winked. "Alchemy, luv. What magic created, magic can turn. See, I worked a digging crew in my . . . misspent youth."

"Community service, you'd call it here," Tal whispered, while Alexy coughed and looked away.

"I prefer *service to the crown*. Anyway, I got familiar with how the squelk work and why dirtdogs had to be assigned to the crews."

Tal removed his arm from around her shoulder and moved to sit down on the slatted wooden bench, still keeping his voice down because of the people walking by. "Squelk *can* dig through anything, but *won't* go near some things. One of those things is *coal*. Whether it's the taste, or the smell, or the feeling under their claws—nobody really knows. Dirtdogs have to either swing the squelk around the coal bands or use alchemy to turn the coal into something else."

Now she had the idea! "And Denver used to be a swamp in prehistoric days. I'll bet there's coal around here somewhere."

Alexy lifted his foot onto the bench and rested a hand on it. "I'll be *making* the coal, luv. No need to find it."

Then a thought occurred to her and her shoulders dropped a bit. "But coal *burns*. It might stop the squelk, but it wouldn't stop the magma. It'd eat right through it."

Alexy's head nodded slowly, but he didn't seem bothered by the idea. "Eventually, yes. But I can make the coal hard enough that it'll be *slow*. It might take days, maybe even *weeks* to get here. Now, there'll be some damage up here, some pavement cracking as the ground shifts, but nothing drastic. If geologists find the coal at all, it'll only make them scratch their heads that they didn't notice it before. But there's plenty around here already, so it won't be really noteworthy." She could almost see the gears turning in his head. "I'll need to do some probing in the basement—see if I can get to all the exterior walls to try to sense which direction they're coming from. They could still be miles away, or right underneath. But I can't craft the coal without some idea or I'll wind up making the whole area settle a foot or more."

Tal let out a slow breath and then slapped the back of

his hand against Alexy's calf. "And don't forget that this is Vegre's homestead. You'll be fighting to get through that."

"Homestead?" The word had a particular meaning in real estate law, but she didn't know what it had to do with magic.

"Magic's always more powerful in your own home." Tal rose back to his feet, apparently getting ready to end this session. "Just like Jason could make Sybil leave his house. This hotel is *Vegre's* house, which makes him most powerful here."

She was trying to remember that particular moment. Mostly, she'd been concentrating on making sure Sybil didn't attack any of them. "So Jason invoked some sort of special magic to make himself more powerful? Can Vegre do that, too?"

"He won't need to invoke it, luv." Alexy had likewise gotten ready to move and was smoothing his slacks, tugging them back into place. "So long as *others* acknowledge his right of ownership, there's no need."

Tal nodded. "Jason had to invoke it because he wasn't the owner of the property . . . just a resident. You told me Vegre wormed his way in as heir so he could own this place legitimately. Once the state acknowledged his ownership, his homestead magic was secure."

That brought back the question in her mind. "But why *this* hotel?" Again, it was rhetorical, but there had to be an answer. She looked up and around the room. There was no denying the beauty, from the waterfall to the stone walls and the stunning stained-glass windows. She stared at the small round window in the wall that matched the massive dome over the lobby. Her eyes narrowed for a moment, and she left Tal and Alexy to walk across the entry. She moved aside a couch a few inches so she could squeeze herself right next to the wall. The men followed, but she wasn't even sure yet what she was seeing. It was a pretty mix of typical stained-glass colors, sort of in an abstract design. It wasn't until she actually looked at the *pieces* of glass, rather than the entire window that her heart started pounding and a gasp escaped her. In that moment, a thousand tiny pieces fit together in her head, shards of information that also formed a picture. "I've got it! I know why he's *here,* instead of England. I know what he's planning!"

Tal opened his mouth and she was certain he'd have a dozen questions. But she didn't want to lose her train of thought so she held up her hands and waved them quickly. "Shh, shh, shh. Let me talk or I'll lose this."

They both looked at each other for a moment, and shrugged. They sat down on the couch and simultaneously waved her to a chair. But she couldn't sit. This was too exciting, and she began to pace. "He followed the *windows* here." They both stared up at the little round opening of colored glass, trying to see whatever it was she was seeing. "The concierge said the stained-glass dome was made by the *finest English craftsmen.* I wondered at the time if it was really made by *crafters,* because the colors are so very similar to the farbas for pysanky. But that didn't make any sense until I started thinking in terms of the *glass,* rather than the picture. Look at each individual shard. Stained-glass windows are *always* made from odd-shaped glass. That's part of the charm. But these bits are in particular shapes. Look at this one." She reached up to point, but she was too short. She looked around and pulled one of the long bird of paradise blooms from the table in front of her to use as a pointer. "Why put this bit here? It's shaped like a butterfly wing. It doesn't match the diamonds and triangles around it. Sure, it could be abstract, but it also could be a completely different picture, just mixed up like a jigsaw puzzle."

Tal was struggling to understand. His frown wasn't from anger, but from confusion. "But he couldn't manipulate it back to the original picture with magic. I already told you we can't do that with magic."

"See, but with pysanky the order doesn't matter that much. Eggshells get broken. They're useless for healing after they break, but the pieces are still valuable. My mom always used to bury the broken shells around the house foundation as protection from evil. Like you said, it's *intent*. Once the picture is made, it's *made*. Forever. And what happens when you dedicate roadways, sidewalks, and easements on a triangular lot?"

Alexy just shrugged and leaned back against the cushions. "I'm afraid you've lost me, luv." Even Tal was shaking his head, unable to make the logic leap.

Instead of explaining it, she licked her finger and smeared spit on the smoked-glass coffee table. Once the triangle that the hotel sat on was drawn, she narrowed the lot by where the walkways and roads were. "Dedications in real estate mean you're deeding bits of the land to the city for the public good. Alleys to get delivery trucks in, sidewalks for patrons, roads for drivers. So the owner doesn't *own* them anymore. No more homestead on those bits. What does the lot look like *now*?"

It was Tal who said it first, in a voice filled with both awe and fear. "It's an egg. Blessed Tree, this entire *property* is egg-shaped!"

She slapped her palm against the tabletop, startling them both. "*That's* why he's doing it here. The rune designs became part of this egg when they were installed, and they circle the building. The skylight is just part of it, and I haven't ever looked at all the smaller windows as a *whole,* to see if there's a larger picture made by them." Every single bit of evidence was flowing into her head, attaching like they were suddenly magnetized. "Remember what Dareen said? He wants to harness the *sun* to blackmail the world. That would require a massive amount of power, and a pysanky this size, filled by a hundred smaller pysanky, would dwarf the power of the Tree. And controlled by him through homestead magic, he could do it."

The two men were trying to wrap their heads around it, blinking repeatedly and staring at her with slack jaws. It was when Tal finally spoke that her balloon hissed and dropped a little. "But then why the squelk and the magma? Why *destroy* the hotel he worked so hard to get?"

She kicked her toe against the leg of the table aimlessly

and crossed her arms. "Well, I haven't worked out *every-thing* yet. I also haven't figured out why *now*? If Vegre really has been coming and going for years, why did he pick tonight? There's so many people out and about celebrating tonight. I'd think that would make it much harder to plan everything so it goes smoothly. Or is he *anticipating* the chaos? Maybe that's the thing he needs—lots of confusion so nobody notices anything until it's too late. Then he can start the New Year with a bang."

Something about what she said made both Tal and Alexy sit up straighter. Alexy raised one finger in the air, but then lowered it and shook his head in tiny movements, as though whatever he was thinking was such a preposterous idea that it was too much to actually say. But Tal was willing to say it. "The Time of Cessation."

Unfortunately, Mila had no clue what that meant. She rolled her hand, hoping one of them would provide an explanation. Alexy shook his head and tried to smile, but it faltered more than once before he gave up. "Just a myth. Claptrap to scare the poppets—a way for the kings to enforce the New Year's curfew."

"I've thought that about a *lot* of things lately, Alexy. But it's mentioned too often not to at least consider it." He looked at Mila. "Remember what I just said about homestead magic? It's old magic—based on generally accepted belief of a thing." She nodded and he continued. "Well, the Time of Cessation is older still . . . goes back to pagan times, and claims that there's some sort of mystical clock in time and space that resets itself each year. It used to be during the celebration of Samhain in the old Celtic calendar, what's currently celebrated as Halloween. But when most of the world adopted the Gregorian calendar, the last day of the year moved to December thirty-first."

Alexy nodded. "The old myth claims that on the stoke of midnight on the last day of the year, reality ceases . . . just for a split second. Anything that happens during that moment *becomes* the new reality when the next year begins. If enough people *believe* that the old is gone, and the new begins, it does and they'll never know the difference—won't even remember the old world."

She'd say it was ridiculous, but nothing else made sense. "But wouldn't the entire world have to believe it about that particular thing? Wouldn't the world have to acknowledge Vegre's plan knowingly?"

Tal's face went through a dozen emotions. "I just don't know. But I *can* imagine that Vegre would try to use any advantage he could. If it worked, it would be just that much less work to take over. But it still doesn't explain why he'd make a volcano in downtown Denver."

"Maybe there's some other way to fill a pysanka? I didn't read all the scrolls at Viktor's and Vegre was there. Maybe there's something else going on—some sort of backup plan?"

Alexy nodded, his eyes still on the smeary drawing on the table. "It's a pretty theory, luv, and I'll give you marks for thinking of it." He raised his head to look at her. "But the squelks are something that's easily proved, where this . . . it'll be something I'll have to believe when I see." He used the cuff of his jacket to clean off the spit art. "That's not saying I won't watch for signs. If I see an egg, I'll destroy it. Every one that's destroyed is one less to be used. But for now, I'm going to cloak myself and head for the basement, or a lower point if there is one. If I sense any squelk, I'll flash—" He paused and sighed. "I'll find a way to get word to you. For now, though, I think you should find a way to contact Kris to let her know what's going on. And Mila needs to keep tabs on Vegre and his motley crew and see if she can find any reason why it has to be *tonight*. I don't suppose he's fool enough to leave a written plan around, but maybe there's *something* to be found."

She nodded, and so did Tal. It wasn't the *best* plan, as plans go, but at least it was movement forward. They just needed to find some way to score before the offense got back on the field.

"Mila!" She turned sharply to her name and saw Mike

Callendar waving near the staircase. As he moved closer, he continued to talk. "They sent me to come find you. We're about to go into the main room."

"Mike? I thought you were headed to Canada on your goose chase . . . *hunt.*"

He gave a rueful laugh. "Missed my flight. I'm heading up day after tomorrow to join them late. So, tonight, I'm here at the pleasure of the firm, and *we* need to get going."

She looked at her wrist only to remember she hadn't worn a watch. "Is it eight o'clock already?"

Tal nodded, his eyes on the watch under his sleeve. "Very nearly." He stood smoothly and stepped around the coffee table before offering his arm. "Shall we?"

Alexy leaned back as Mike stepped close to her, just a passing acquaintance chatting with two strangers. "Nice meeting you both. Have a happy New Year."

Tal nodded and turned his head as they started to walk away. "Good luck with your project."

"Never a need to worry about me. You just take care and keep that pretty girl safe."

Tal closed his eyes and set his jaw before nodding and tightening his grip on her arm. "I'll take care of her. You can wager on it."

Mike looked at the interaction curiously, but didn't comment beyond raising his brows her way. She just rolled her eyes at him and shook her head as if to say, *Men.*

That made Mike chuckle and he offered his arm so that she was sandwiched between them. He leaned closer. "Came to get you because I wanted to be the first to tell you the good news. The judge denied the motion and the clerk says there's a good chance the judge will sign the order finalizing the probate before the end of the day. He starts a three-week vacation on Monday, so he's burning the midnight oil tonight, clearing off his desk." He looked at her with a note of caution. "But it's just rumor at this point, so keep your fingers crossed."

It shouldn't make her so ridiculously happy, but it did.

Suddenly she *knew* everything was going to be okay. Baba would get better, Vegre would be stopped, and Tal—he could come live in her house with her. *Don't get the cart ahead of the horse, girl,* said her Candy voice, but she shooed it away. *I get to have my moment, even if it gets stomped on later.*

"Thanks for telling me, Mike. I'd *love* to start the new year with the house in my name. Lots of things to do that I've been putting off."

He chuckled and winked. "At least *you* have an excuse."

It was walking through the door of the banquet room that made her stutter to a nervous stop. Mike, his mission accomplished, let go of her arm and kept walking toward his wife with a small wave good-bye. *Boy, that moment of happiness didn't last long.* All of the firm employees were lined up along the walls, drinks in hand and eyes wide as they surveyed the dozens . . . no, *hundreds* of pysanky that filled the room. They were lined up side by side like toy soldiers along a low shelf that encircled the room. They rested on the buffet tables among the chocolate-covered strawberries and caviar. There were even little tree-shaped holders, like would normally bear deviled eggs, up on the podium. She could only look at Tal helplessly, seeking some advice on what to do.

Vegre had trumped them both. There were too many people in the room to just start walking around the room, destroying eggs. And some of them might be booby-trapped, just like Tal had done with Sela's door.

Her dismay was complete when she heard a tapping on the microphone and looked up to see Vegre himself staring down at her and Tal. He was in a full tux, with a bloodred cummerbund that had various pysanky designs embroidered on the fabric. Sela stood behind him now, the lights catching the shimmering silver floor-length gown she wore that so flattered her blond beauty and was accented by a stunning necklace with a center diamond the size of a pigeon egg.

Vegre looked down at Mila with open amusement. The

smirk he wore was shared by the two mages from the prison. They were dressed as hotel security, complete with dark sunglasses and black fingerless gloves on *both* hands. They flanked the stage on which the podium sat, looking annoyingly capable.

"Shit." It wasn't a word she'd heard very often from Tal, but she couldn't deny it fit the circumstance.

"Ladies and gentlemen of Sanders, Harris & Hoote— I'm David Pierce, and on behalf of myself and the staff and management of Peircevil Holdings and the Palace Hotel, I welcome you." His voice was smooth, without a trace of the lofty British accent she'd heard before.

All of a sudden, the lights dimmed and she felt the heat and blinding light of a spot on her. She looked around frantically but then understood when he spoke again. "Please join me in a round of applause for your own Mila Penkin, who both arranged for this affair and was the . . . *inspiration* for the lovely decorations you see scattered around the room. Mila is quite an artist herself, and several of the eggs you see were made by her." Everyone obediently clapped, hollered, and looked at her but she only had eyes for Vegre. His smile was self-satisfied and turned briefly to a sneer before settling back into more civilized lines.

He gestured to one of the waiters she recognized as one of Demeter's Children. "Fetch Ms. Penkin a drink." When the woman failed to move, to even react, his brow furrowed, but Sela covered for him, "Yes, do." As if in a daze the waitress brought a tray of champagne flutes, offering one each to Tal and Mila.

"To the oh-so talented Mila Penkin."

To Mila's horror she was the center of attention as everyone obediently raised their glasses. "To Mila."

Pierce flashed a venomous smile. "Now everyone, please, eat, drink, be merry."

᠂ The old toast continued on in her head, *For tomorrow we may die.*

Vegre stepped off the stage and was immediately surrounded by the partners of the firm, many of whom had never met him. His guards stood just in front of the crowd, keeping a close eye on Mila and Tal.

Mila set her flute on the nearest table. A sense of hopelessness filled her and she stared around at her friends, wondering what it felt like to burn to death in lava. Would it be fast, or agonizingly slow?

Tal's voice whispered in her ear. "I tried to talk to my mother."

Mila blinked at him, but didn't say a word. She wasn't sure *what* to say.

"She didn't even *recognize* me, or Kris, either, for that matter. She's completely bespelled."

"I wonder if they all are?" She nodded toward a long line of people—dressed as waitstaff, even though last time they'd been wearing red robes with flickering flames. They barred the exit as well as if they were iron chains. Oh, they moved aside easily enough for the other members of the firm, but she was fairly confident the two of them weren't going *anywhere*.

But Mila still had a few tricks up her sleeve. She whispered to Tal from the corner of her mouth, "We need a little privacy. Stay with me and don't ask questions."

He nodded, his face worried but trying to show confidence. She began to walk around the room, waving and chatting with people as she surveyed the room. Mostly she was looking for a particular place along the curtained wall. It was possible, just *possible*, that Vegre didn't know about the side exit from this room into the adjoining one that was hidden behind the fabric. While it was obvious there wasn't a person standing there, it could be chained. She spoke as she turned, so it wouldn't seem like they were plotting. So far, just being party guests wasn't attracting attention. "See if you can block me from view for about five seconds."

Tal nodded and glanced around. He spotted Mike standing with one of the intellectual property attorneys, Trixie Sang. He and Mila were both equal to Mike in height, which was about a head taller than Trixie. In seconds, he had managed to strike up a conversation with them and kept moving by inches until Mila couldn't see the door guards. And if she couldn't see *them*—

She grabbed the opportunity. She pulled down lightly on the curtain so it wouldn't rustle and be noticeable and then poked her head behind the fabric. It *wasn't*. No locks or chains on the push-lever door. Casually she pulled her head back out and went back to inspecting the various pysanky with an overly critical eye. She nodded to Tal when he looked over and he ended the conversation smoothly before moving back over to her side.

"I found a way out for *one* of us. We can't both go missing or they'll know something's up."

Tal nodded and responded, his lips hardly moving. "I'll go. I'm better prepared to fight if it comes to it—" he paused and then added, "magically, that is."

Apparently, he'd *noticed* how she'd kicked butt on those guys down below. She'd been proud of herself for that. She hadn't had much chance to use her defense skills since she took the class, and was glad they really had sunk in as instinct. It was nice he considered her to be capable of taking care of herself. "Thank you." It was worth mentioning.

He bent to look at one of the pysanky that she'd actually created, a stunning blue-and-yellow with a harvest motif. "Do you have a plan beyond me getting out?"

She really didn't. But just then, she noticed Rachel standing up after having been bent over an egg, her nose wrinkled and an odd look on her face. She felt a smile growing inside that finally erupted on her face. "As a matter of fact I do."

As quickly as she could, she went to where Rachel had been standing near a large potted plant with psanky arranged around the base. She took tiny little breaths near the wall, trying not to be noticed. "Block me again."

Tal did as instructed and soon she was palming two of the pysanky and holders and had moved the surrounding eggs to where they covered the gaps. She gingerly slid one into each of Tal's jacket pockets by stepping around him casually to see the next batch of eggs.

She straightened, just in time to hear a whispered conversation between two of her co-workers.

"Money isn't everything. *I* wouldn't marry the man. Did you *hear* the way he ordered her around? 'Sela *you* will go and fetch them. No other. *Now!*' " Nicole's voice mimicked Vegre's perfectly enough to send a chill up Mila's spine.

"And she *did?*" Rachel's voice held surprise. "I mean, she didn't strike me as the submissive type."

"Oh, she went all right. But she didn't look too happy about it."

Mila shook herself. Grabbing Talos by the hand, she led him away from the women and the overheard conversation. When she'd managed to find a place where they could speak without danger of eavesdroppers she explained her plan.

*I*t hadn't been easy to make it this far. Mila had to barge her way onto the stage to get to the microphone. But then she'd proceeded to discuss all of the food and drink that was the product of one client or another and soon all eyes were on her—including Vegre and all the Demeter's Children in the room. It had been a simple matter to slip out the door she'd found. Tal wound up in a masquerade party in the next room and simply had to apologize his way across the room as needing to find a bathroom.

Mila's idea was brilliantly simple and could be the ruin of Vegre's plan. Tal made his way to the basement after casting himself invisible, somewhat surprised that the spell actually *worked* in Vegre's stronghold. He looked briefly for Alexy, but didn't find him. Either he'd been captured or had found a lower point of the building. But it didn't matter if he found him, for the plan only required he get to the furnace room.

Tal did his best to ignore the bloodstains on the floor when he entered the room. He prayed that Mila's grandmother would recover, but she hadn't looked good. Far worse, in fact, than he'd been willing to admit to Mila. He found a spot to hide and waited until a thermostat on the ground floor triggered the furnace to fire. When it did, he identified the duct that carried the air out of the basement and went back to waiting until the furnace turned off.

Then he went to work, using a coin from his pocket to loosen the screws on the duct. He only needed two of them out before he could easily manipulate the steel with heat. When he heard the click that would make the machine fire, he took the eggs from his pocket, shook them up a little, and heaved them against the inside of the duct with a silent prayer of hope. "Here goes nothing."

The scent that billowed out of the weeks- or months-old pysanky was enough to make him retch. He turned, covering his face with his arm, and caught the gleam of light refracting off something in the far corner of the room, half-hidden by a stack of boxes. Despite the growing stench, he had to investigate.

He bent down, and found Mila's fire opal in its new focus glove.

What in the blazes? How did this get here? He shuddered. Alexy had taken this from him not an hour ago. Had his friend been captured?

A part of him desperately wanted to hunt for his friend, but there was no time. They had to stop Vegre, and the plan needed him to take as much advantage of the stench as possible. Saying a swift prayer, he left the furnace room and hurried back toward the party. There were already shouts and people racing around when he reached the lobby again. The doors to the banquet room where the attorneys were meeting burst open, as did the doors of several other rooms.

"My God! What is that smell?!" Women in heels and men holding noses raced for the exits. Mila was at the back of the crowd, pushing them out and calling for a maintenance staffer. She winked as he approached and kept moving past him.

In moments, only Vegre and his cronies were left in the room. He looked livid as Tal steadied himself in the doorway, but there was grudging respect in the mage's eyes. "Bravo, young crafter. Well played."

Tal smiled, just a slight twist of lips. "Thank you. But I'm not so young as I might appear, Vegre. I remember you of old."

That raised his brows. "Do you now? Well, you might as well close the doors. I presume you mean to settle this, and I'd hate for my staff to see your charred body staining the carpet."

Apparently even Vegre wasn't quite willing to have the world know of their kind until he was good and ready, so Tal knew there wouldn't be any trouble until the doors were closed. He wished Alexy was here, because his powers were still completely unmanageable. He didn't even dare put on the glove—not unless or until he had no choice. Because it wasn't that he *couldn't* do spells. They were just too powerful—a sledgehammer when only a pushpin was needed and the opal merely amplified the problem.

The first blow came when the door clicked shut. He barely avoided the searing blast of heat that scorched the floor. Vegre had on his glove now, and Tal felt naked without his. He only hoped he could do offensive spells without it . . . because he had no idea where the power that filled him was coming from. *"Ataka abo!"*

A blast of pure white light erupted from his hand, as though there was a stone there. He could feel the magic flow through his fingers and bind into a powerful beam that nearly threw him backward onto his rear.

Vegre blocked the attack, but the others weren't so lucky. Cardon the witcher was screaming and the fact that nobody came running told Tal there was likely a silencing charm on the room. Naturally, it would make all the people he anticipated dying in the room much easier to hide.

A loud crash sounded from the wall and then a wave of water knocked him off his feet. A pipe was sticking out from the wall, moving around like a snake to follow him as he moved. The water quickly turned into icy daggers that sliced through skin. He pulled over one of the banquet tables and ducked behind it while simultaneously sending searing fire their way again.

The draperies behind them caught on fire, and the witch was forced to turn the water away to put out the blaze.

"I stand corrected," Vegre said, his voice tightening from smug satisfaction to something approaching annoyance. "You've more skill than I gave you credit for."

Tal remained behind the table, keeping an eye on them in the convex mirror near the ceiling. He didn't know why it was there, but it was certainly handy for watching multiple attackers.

The smell of the rotten eggs was burning his nose and it reminded him of the other pysanky lining the walls. He took a moment to send a blast of fire toward them and watched with satisfaction as they exploded and covered the walls with blackened, rotten goo.

"No! Stop him, you idiots! Garack . . . now!"

A baritone he recognized as the alchemist minion, who must be named Garack, spoke. "*Bereh . . . boloto.*"

Abruptly, Tal felt himself sliding, felt mud forming under his body. He scrambled to get away from it, but it sucked him down quicker than he could move. He'd seen Alexy using the swamp charm before, but had never actually had it done to him. The more he struggled, the quicker he sank. He concentrated, making his body heat to dry the mud. He'd just about climbed out when the side door behind the curtain opened and Mila stepped inside.

Vegre was to her in moments, his arm around her neck. "Give up, mage, or the woman dies." He put the diamond right next to her head and sneered. Tal's heart sank and he was nearly ready to do as commanded.

But then Mila grabbed his arm with both hands and dropped. Just let her entire body weight fall. It threw Vegre off balance and he bent forward, just in time to receive a sharp kick to his jaw that threw him back again. *"The woman* doesn't think so, asshole." She rolled quickly away from him and shouted *"Avatay!"* the moment she saw the witcher's hand rise. Whatever the spell had been passed sideways shattering even more of the eggs, causing Vegre to roar with rage.

Mila laughed and Tal couldn't help but smile. "Keep it up, boys. We got lots more shells to break."

"Enough of this!" Vegre raised his hand, his diamond flashed, and movement in the room ceased. But instead of being completely frozen, Tal could move . . . just a little, but it might be enough. He waited until Vegre's attention was elsewhere and began working his hand toward the focus and glove. So . . . close.

Vegre stared at Mila for a long moment, disgust written on his face as he touched his lip and came away with blood. *"You* have been an annoyance of extraordinary proportion. I'd hoped to save you, bring you over to see that my plan is the only way to save this world." But then he shook his head. "Your skills are valuable, but not worth the price. *Moratay."*

She mouthed the word, but no sound came out and he watched as shock flowed over her face. He was suddenly frightened, panicked in a way he'd never been before. He closed his eyes and reached out for her, threw open the door in his mind until he touched her. *I won't let him kill you. Hold onto me.*

Her mind grabbed hold, but her words added to his hurry. *I'm losing consciousness, Tal. If I black out, I'll let go.* He began to whisper every counterspell he could think of, struggling to hold her against the slow death that Vegre had cursed her with. But even as he felt her heartbeat start to steady, her face remained slack. Hopefully that would keep Vegre off guard enough that when the old mage turned his back on what he thought was a victim, he wouldn't know she still lived, and still plotted.

"And now that your lover's dead, mage, it's your turn."

There was only one chance, one hope. It would kill him, he knew that, but Mila would live, and the world would be safe from Vegre and his evil. Tal had just enough movement to turn the opal focus stone toward Vegre and put all of his will into a single word that spat from his mouth with all the venom he felt. *"Befouler."*

Blinding light and the shriek of a chorus of angels . . . or *devils* filled the room as egg after egg began to explode and release wild magic into the air. Tal covered Mila's body with his own, dropping to the ground. Vegre's containment spell was destroyed as the lights began to chase him and the others while they threw magic and curses and blasts of power to attack the bolts of energy.

The villains' hideous screams joined the cacophony as wild magic assaulted the three crafters. It was like watching a death by a thousand cuts as each bit of magic took its measure, tearing at the men until they were screaming and crawling on the floor.

He could feel Mila's heart beating frantically against his chest. He held her close, waiting for the death curse to claim and drain him, knowing that this embrace would be his last.

Pain, hot and intense, burned at his arm, as he watched the sleeve of the jacket he wore begin to char in the image of the meander pattern she had drawn on his arm.

The pain faded, the screams died. It was done. What used to be three men was now a pile of expensive clothing covered with black goo that smelled much like rotten eggs.

And Talos was still alive.

A new voice came from above them. "Bravo! Talos, I didn't think you had it in you." Sela's voice came from the . . . thing that hovered above the open door, filled with dozens of Children in red robes.

"Sela? My God, what happened to you?" Mila's voice was horrified, and for good reason. Sela's short mop of golden hair was now long and stringy black. She wore a ttered black dress that seemed to be more skin than cloth that flamed at the edges. Her nose was misshapen and covered with bumps and moles that made her features twist.

"*You* happened to me, thrice-damned *bitch!* You cast something, *did* something at the house that made me look like this. But I'll change it back again as soon as the plan is done."

She pointed at what was left of the bodies. "But Vegre's dead. There *is* no more plan."

Sela shook her head with a disgusted expression. "I *told* him that stupid pysanky thing would never work. But it kept him busy and out of my way while I was working on the real plan."

Sela was the mastermind behind all this? No wonder they couldn't connect the two pieces. They were entirely different plans. Mila spoke before Tal could. "So the squelk and the magma is *your* doing? Why would you want to blow up the hotel? What purpose will that serve?"

Sela looked at her as if she was insane. "What are you talking about? I don't plan to *blow up* the hotel. I plan to use life energy to awaken the goddess in the magma."

Mila let out a little laugh. "No . . . *really.*"

"You're a naive fool, Mila. Do you think you're the only Parask in the world?" She raised her flame-ridden sleeve to show the meander road symbol on her arm. "I've just used illusion to cover it all these years. Didn't want anyone to discover me while in the academy. Since I already had two marks, nobody looked for a third. But there really *is* a goddess in the ground and all it will take to awaken her is a big enough sacrifice." She smiled as the Children filed into the room. "Why do you think I lured all the agents to Buckingham Palace? There's a domed window, just like this one, buried inside the ceiling—hidden away for all these centuries, waiting for just the right moment. I'd *hoped* to use the additional souls in the hotel, but you ruined that, so I'll have to settle for my faithful followers." She waved her hand and the men and women filed in. There were more than the dozen Tal had expected. There could be close to a hundred of them—including his mother and the three boys who had joined in Vril. "But I want to make sure you have a front-row seat. Hold them!"

The combined force of magic that blasted them from the focus stones of the Children hit them both in the chest. He felt hands grabbing him . . . clutching and clawing, just before he blacked out.

CHAPTER 21

It was hot. Hotter than she could remember ever being. Did she have a fever? Was she sick in bed? She couldn't seem to focus. When her eyes opened, Mila realized they were in a cavern of coal bisected by a red . . . blinding light that wasn't eased even by squinting. But then she heard Sela's voice and it all came back to her. She was bound to a chair, back to back with Tal, less than a yard from a vicious slash in the ground that glowed red and hissed ominously. Alexy lay bound and gagged on the floor at their feet. He'd accomplished his crafting and stopped the magma, but had paid the price.

"Oh goodie, you're awake. I was hoping you'd get to see this. It's nearly midnight, and my Children have surrounded Buckingham Palace. They're beginning the spell that will pull the souls from the people inside . . . souls that will be captured by the images in the glass and will send them here . . . to *me*."

"You're insane." It was hard to talk. Her mouth was so achingly dry. She could barely open her lips.

"Not insane, Mila dear. Merely about to become a *goddess*. At exactly midnight on New Year's, there will *truly* be a new beginning. I plan to offer the power my form, and my purpose and then I will control all that is—the water, the earth, the air, and the very fire that makes the planet exist. I will *be* the planet and the sun will do my bidding. A new world will be born from the ashes of the old."

The Time of Cessation. She believed in it, too. There would be no talking sense to her if that was the case. She was beyond sanity. A flash of light caught her eye and a object appeared near Sela's feet. She noticed it and threw it angrily into the vent. "And stay there." She turned, pushing one of the pliant Children out of the way violently and muttered, "I am getting so *sick* of that thing. Why in the hell does it keep showing up?"

But Mila recognized *that thing,* and while it was impossible, unthinkable, it might just be real.

She whispered the words, her voice so cracked from the heat it was almost gone. "Fetch me water."

Sela screamed and dropped to her knees. The iron dipper flew up out of the molten earth and smashed into her, welding to her hand. The scent of burned flesh and sound of screaming filled the air as she disappeared . . . like *magic.*

The scream woke Tal. He looked around frantically and struggled to free himself. He was making a mmm-ing sound that made her turn her head as far as she could. Sela had taped his mouth, probably to prevent him casting spells. There was also something large and glowing around his neck. It looked like . . . the diamond necklace Sela had been wearing earlier. Did it carry a charm of some sort? She felt his voice in her mind for the first time in days. *Mila? I need you to speak for me—to cast a spell to free us. I believe I can use you as a focus of my will.*

But then her toes started to tingle. "Oh God! I can't black out now. I can't finish the spell if an episode hits." She slammed her head backward, hitting his skull with a crack. "*Tal,* no! Don't try to connect to me. I have a plan and I don't *dare* black out."

He paused in his struggles to free himself, and she knew how hard it was for him to trust her enough to remain tied and helpless.

Sela appeared again, holding the now cool ladle. She

was still screaming, and struggled mightily, but was forced by an unseen power to hold the metal lip gently, close enough that Mila could drink from the cool water. It was enough for her to talk again. Mila opened her mouth and the little tuning fork appeared and likewise forged itself to Sela's other hand as if glued there. She couldn't believe she was about to say it, but she knew she had to. Something had happened when Sela went back to the house. Some freak of magic had transformed Sela so that she now *was* the black lady. But if Mila didn't give the orders fast enough, if the clock hit the last stroke of midnight the spell would dissolve and Sela would be free to finish her plan. "Second task—go and make the rocks hum far from where the roosters sing."

Another struggle and the hag disappeared in a blink of light. Tal's eyes were wide over the strip of tape that covered his mouth. Again he tried to reach her. *What have you done?*

"She tripped the spell I cast to keep out evil. The only thing I can think is that the judge signed the order to make the house mine, and—"

Homestead magic. It amplified the spell. Again her feet started to tingle and now her head was hurting. A loud noise began to sound, low and echoing though the narrow cave. She looked with vision that was flickering with tiny pinpoints of light to see that Sela had brought one of the grandfather clocks down. Both hands were nearly touching. The second bong sounded.

A wave of dizziness washed over her. She shook her head quickly to fight it off. "You can't talk to me, Tal. I'm about . . . about to pass out and you . . . don't know the rest of the spell."

He let out a harsh, frustrated snort of air through his nose but nodded, eyes flashing with both worry and anger. She doubted it was directed at her but instead at the third chime of the clock. He knew what it meant as well.

Sela appeared once more and the walking stick appeared to join the tuning fork as part of her right arm. Mila stared in horrified fascination while the clock chimed. She could actually feel time slowing, moving toward that delicate moment, when time ceased. Finally Sela was as bent as a hunchback, leaning on the cane as though her life depended on it. As the tenth chime sounded, Mila raised her voice and screamed the words. Sela tried to stop her, tried to beat at her with the stick and the ladle but it hit a solid mass of air in front of Mila's face. As the eleventh chime sounded, icy wind began to whip their hair and Sela's eyes were suddenly frightened. The final strike of the clock came as the words hit air. "Third task—lean on that cane and travel to where the icy winds dance. Be gone and never return again."

A crack of light and sound slammed into their bodies, dumping the chairs over, frightfully close to the lava. The Children were still frozen in time, waiting for the return of their mistress . . . their goddess—who would never return. Sulphur smoke made her cough until she couldn't catch her breath. Tal was moving his head back and forth across the sharp rocks and she finally realized why after he scraped the tape away and she finally heard his voice. "We've got to get out of here!"

"Good idea," she said, trying to keep the sarcasm from her voice while she struggled with the tight ropes and tried to blow away the splatters of molten rock that were making her hair sizzle and smoke. "Any idea *how?*"

"One." His voice sounded uncertain and worried. "But I don't think you'll like it."

She shrugged her shoulders and kicked to spin away from another splatter. "Try me. I'm becoming more adventurous by the minute."

"Can you reach this amulet with your teeth?" He nudged the glowing stone of the necklace her way. Obviously he needed it off him to do magic, so she threw herself into the task. It took four tries but finally she got her teeth around the chain and yanked while he twisted his head. The glowing stone went flying, to land in the lava with a loud pop. She heard his voice call out with authority. *"Areszt!"*

At first she didn't notice anything but then she heard voices. Unfortunately her head wouldn't turn that far and while the noise filled her with panic, Tal was quite calm. "We could use some help here, folks."

Suddenly, there was yelling and footsteps and she felt herself being lifted. She squeezed her eyes shut and gritted her teeth, trying to think happy thoughts. It was only when she felt the ropes loosen that she opened her eyes.

Tal was holding his mother tightly against him and she was crying. The air began to cool and she saw Guilders of all descriptions, frantically casting spells to return the lava to where it belonged. "I couldn't help myself. She was making us *do* things and we couldn't stop."

He stroked her hair gently as the red light dimmed to nothing but a tiny glow. "I know, Mom. I knew that wasn't really you." He saw Mila standing there, looking uncomfortable and held open one arm with a smile. She went to him, snuggled in against him and felt her heart finally slow and another arm, a *woman's* arm, reach around her to hold her close.

And then the world went white.

CHAPTER 22

Mila woke and sat up from where she was lying in a field of flowers, wearing a snow-white dress that reached her knees. She heard a voice and seemed to recognize it, but yet she'd never heard it before. It was either a contralto or tenor, not quite male or female, but part of both. "It must be now. There is no more time."

Her brow furrowed as she stood and looked up, trying to find the source of the voice. "Who are you? Where am I?"

"You know where you are. You must hurry. Everything is prepared." She blinked again and looked around. *I know where I am?* And then she did. She recognized that path, and the little bridge that went over the koi stream. "This is Viktor's. Viktor? Baba? Are you here?"

"There is no time, conjurer." Finally the voice had direction. She stood and walked toward the pond. The voice came from just beyond, in the tidy little bonsai garden near the pond. A quail rose from a nest, revealing four perfect white eggs. "Take them. Help me."

Take them? Take the eggs? She found herself carefully collecting the tiny orbs and walking toward the garden. As she entered, she stopped and could only stare. Her favorite little tree, the tree that had supported Tal as he plucked her from Vegre's clutches, was withered and brown. "Hurry, conjurer."

You'll recognize it when you see it. Hadn't Viktor said that? Is that why she'd always been so drawn to this little tree—to the Tree of Life?

A kistka and dyes were already spread out on a blanket near the pond. She recognized the slender black length of wood and metal. "Baba," she whispered.

"Mila?" Tal walked into the garden, also dressed in white, as though the color had been bled from him . . . from them both. "What's happening? How did we get here?"

"The Tree brought us," she replied with a smile. "The spirit of the Tree. It needs to be healed. It needs *me.*"

Whether he understood or not, she finally did. The other eggs would be too big for these tiny branches. No wonder there were so many quail that lived in the garden. She couldn't believe that Viktor could live here so long, listen to the Tree growing weaker and not step in. But he had admitted his failing and moved on. Whether Baba could or couldn't make the eggs, she didn't know, either. Mila didn't blame them. They had their burdens, just like all people. But now was her time and she *would* do it.

Tal sat down beside her and stared in wonder as she quickly re-created the eggs she'd done in Vril. The kistka had the narrowest point she'd ever worked with, but it was perfect for working on the tiny, delicate shell.

She didn't remember how long she worked, just that Tal kept gently rubbing her shoulders, keeping the tension down. She would have expected that it would make the lines jiggle, but instead they came out sure and straight, no matter how hard he rubbed. Yellow, red, blue, black. Line after line, egg after egg.

Finally they were done and she held the painted eggs up for Tal's inspection. "They're beautiful. But there are only four. Didn't you say there had to be *five?* Where's the egg for the conjurer guild? Did you ever learn what it looks like?"

He hadn't figured it out yet and she hated to tell him. But she knew. She'd tried so hard not to think about it while she was crafting, but now there was no escaping the reality.

"The fifth egg is *me,* Tal. The life of the Tree *comes* from the life of the artist. In a way, you were right. I *was* the Tree spirit in your head . . . the *future* Tree spirit. Not yet born."

Shock filled his face, and then horror. Finally his eyes filled with tears. "No! No, there has to be another way."

She touched his face gently and then motioned to the old tree. "A way that won't doom your people? The Tree is dying. You can see it with your own eyes. The slave tree in Vril, and Shambala will soon fail and even if I replaced every egg in every tree, they won't survive without this one. You know this has to happen. You know it in your heart."

He grabbed her and held her tight against him and she felt the first of his tears on her cheek. She didn't want to go, either, but there was no other way.

"It is time, conjurer." The voice sounded tired and impatient, as though nothing mattered anymore except passing on to the next place.

Mila nodded and pulled away from him. He let her, except for the hand he refused to let go of. His was shaking and she couldn't blame him. She was scared, too. But it wouldn't be death. Not really, and she'd always be in contact with him. It was he who had been the key all along. He really could talk to the spirit. It had guided him his whole life and she vowed that would continue for as long as he lived.

She picked up the first tiny egg—representing the air guild. She felt her fingers slide easily beneath the bark. The egg settled into the wood and she felt a spark, awareness awaken something in her mind. With the second egg came the sensation of the other Trees, the slaves that kept their people strong—*their* people, hers, too, even though they were shunned. The water egg was next and she could feel all the streams and the oceans of the world like a pulse against her throat. Water was everywhere, in places where neither Agathians nor humans knew existed. Mankind could survive infinitely if only they knew.

The mage egg was last. Tal gripped her hand furiously, refusing to loosen it even when she tried to pull away. But he would eventually have to give up, for the Tree would have its way. She settled the last egg into place and felt a warmth fill her. The world shifted and air became light became motion.

She was welcomed joyously and all the Trees of the world hummed and reached for her. She realized this was the mother of *all* trees, those topside and below. Every pine and oak knew her, recognized her as their mother.

Blessed Tree, hear me! She felt fire burn in what used to be her feet. *Do not take her from me. You live again . . . you are healed. You do not need her.* A pause and then a choking sound. *But . . . I do.*

"I know you." Mila heard another voice. It echoed through her mind. It was the peal of laughter, the cracking of lightning on a hot summer day, the blowing of winter snow. "I know you, mage."

"Yes." She recognized Tal's voice now, speaking in the air instead of her head. She realized she could think a little more clearly as herself now. "You know me, spirit. I have always trusted you, believed in your goodness and light. Don't do this. Don't take Mila from me now that

I've just found her. She deserves to laugh and love and bear children of her own before she takes on the cares of the world."

There was a long pause. It was the slender ribbon of time between night falling and dawn breaking. "But I am tired."

Now his voice was angry. "And just because of your weariness you would doom another to your fate? Weren't you once human? Once Parask to breathe air and heal bodies? There is still sickness among us, Blessed Tree. The red shadow has found us again. Please . . . do not take one of the last healers from us in our time of need. All the magic in the world will not replace the lives of my people."

Mila felt another pause and then felt roots searching, seeking . . . *confirmation.* A fever here, a glowing mark there—dark red and throbbing. Magic disrupted, the future only chaos without quick action. Vegre had indeed spread the illness, looking to become the one and only magicwielder in a world of lowly humans, who would have eventually worshiped him as a god but for their efforts.

She felt again, searched for another of their kind. Another Parask. She found her mother, mortified and shamed that she hadn't herself taken on the mantle of the Tree, when she knew that the Tree was sick. Then Mila sensed Baba, her hand cool and frail in Clara's larger one, wounded in body and spirit. But she could be healed . . . was being healed. There were healers all around her. Jason and Dareen sat at her bedside, looking worried, and a tall dark-skinned man with a wreath of gold on his head was creating a gate to bring in even more healers. She knew it, could sense the intent. Even Sarah was there, dressed in party finery that said she had come from an event somewhere. Viktor was there—dear Viktor, her once and future Dido, grandfather. She could feel it in their hearts as she swept through the air past them. Baba's eyes moved up under closed lids as she went by, as though she could see or sense Mila's presence. Perhaps she could, because a tear glistened in the light as it trailed down her cheek. She abruptly felt her mother's resolve to return to their people, to restore Sarah's memories, and teach her to craft properly and restore the Parask guild.

She would miss Baba, miss her mother and family. Most of all, though, she'd miss Tal. How had he become so important so quickly? Why did it stab her in the chest to think she'd never again know his touch, or hear his laugh? Had the Tree ever lived, ever known pleasure or family or . . . love?

"Can't you remember a time when you walked among us? Is it because nobody speaks your name anymore that you have forsaken us? Did we forsake you so that you punish us? Should we have worshiped you by name?" Tal's voice in her ears sounded sad now, and Mila couldn't help but remember the ruined fruit and scattered flowers. She remembered her own sadness, even though she didn't understand what the offerings meant at that time.

A stab. Pain. Sharp and intense, so powerful that she couldn't draw in enough air. And the voice was there again, stronger now. More confident. *I remember . . . remember . . . my people.* A name flowed through Mila's mind—*Eva. I was Eva.*

Eva. It was a good name in the Ukrainian language. It meant *the mother of all the living,* and Mila could see an image now, of a young blond woman not that different from her, but in brightly colored garb with embroidery on the apron, her hair in coiled braids under a pretty kerchief. Her family had died from *Tin Czerwona,* and there was nobody left to heal. The past opened to Mila as she watched and she could see Eva stumble into a cave, exhausted from healing, seeking a place to simply lie down and die. The cold wrapped around her, as though there was no warmth left in the world. She felt her pulse slow, weaken until the light became darkness.

Then she awoke to see a beautiful tree. She thought herself dead, so when the tree spoke to her, Eva answered. The Tree was just a tree in that bygone era, but it bloomed with magic that could heal her people. Eva shared her love of her people with the Tree, and it responded by offering to help.

She became one with the Tree, with a strength of purpose that would save all their kind. The purpose of *love* and health.

Tal saw the story along with Mila and she could feel him squeeze her tight. "If you remember love of your people, then don't do this. As you have healed us, we can heal you. We can renew your purpose without taking an unwilling life."

Eva's voice hesitated, as though confused. It echoed through the air uncertainly. "She is not unwilling."

Mila responded in her mind, because she couldn't seem to feel her body. *I am willing if there is no other choice. I love our people . . . all people, and will serve if I must. But I love Tal more than life. Have you never had that sort of love in your life? The love that makes you laugh with all the joy of the world?*

Another image flashed, of a young man with wild dark hair and an easy laugh. And then the same man, among the dead . . . taken before she could save him. "I remember . . . love. But I am tired. So very tired. I must think."

Another stab of pain ripped through her mind, so immediate and encompassing that it wiped out everything, including the sensation of Tal's hand on hers. No, she didn't want this. Not like this. Fear and sorrow filled her and she couldn't help but cry, even if no tears would ever roll down her cheeks again.

Falling, falling, down into the darkness, where it was cold and lifeless and empty. But then a spark of warmth and she raced toward it, taking Eva along in her wake. Now there were voices and laughter, surrounding the Tree in Vril. And then Shambala. And Rohm, and Thule. Bright sunlight and flowers blooming. Mila whispered a word and they heard. They all began calling her name, chanting it while touching the rough bark of the Trees.

Not Mila. But *Eva.*

Mila could feel each person the same way she was attached to Tal. It was dizzying, mesmerizing, and so powerful that it made her head feel like it was going to explode. But within the sensation was emotion, and it was stronger than anything else. Love and anger and pain. It grew, faster and stronger, the voices joining into a roar of noise and light and emotion that overwhelmed her. Until—

"Yes." She both heard and spoke the word. "There is much to do, Mila—"

"Mila!"

"Mila, wake up." She blinked. Yes, blinked with eyes that opened. Tal was kneeling above her, his smile radiant. He pulled on her arm to lift her from where she was lying and wrapped warm arms around her. "You're so cold. I thought I lost you."

She nodded and hugged him tight. "You did. Just for a moment." She touched the Tree and it was just bark. "But then she remembered . . . Eva remembered. You reminded her of why she became the Tree. The people haven't forgotten her, nor forsaken her. She'd forgotten they were there. I just had to help her find them again."

"She let you go?" His voice was stunned, filled with disbelief, still afraid it might not be real.

"To save her people." Mila got to her feet unsteadily and wrapped her arms around Tal's neck, giving him a slow kiss. She hoped Eva could still feel the tingles that slowly spread through her as his tongue found hers. She let the Tree taste sweet fire magic and might have imagined it, but thought that Eva might have sighed in bliss. "There's much to do."

She took a deep breath, as the wind began to blow fragrant air toward them. The little pine was green again, sprouting fresh new growth and tiny yellow buds that tickled her nose with pollen. Eva was reborn, fresh and alive with the love of her people. And in the awakening, she'd found new purpose. She planned to heal wounded hearts as well as bodies and Mila knew she could always count on that help as they fought to bring the pandemic Vegre had planned under control. And if in the healing, the Agathians came to forgive the Parask . . . and *themselves*, so much the better.

"C'mon, Tal. Let's go save some people. There are more than I'd thought. It'll take a lot of long nights. 'Cause I work days."

He touched her face and let out a little laugh. "As long as you promise to come home to me at the end of every long night, I don't care. I love you too much to care."

She smiled and kissed his hand. "Every night. I swear on my mark, because I love you, too."

TOR
ROMANCE

Believe that love is magic

P lease join us at the website below
for more information about this
author and other great romance
selections, and to sign up for our
monthly newsletter!

www.tor-forge.com